Six Mile Canyon

Six Mile Canyon

by Kathryn Dionne

ISBN: 978-1-654671-63-1

Cover design by Shondra C. Longino.

10 9 8 7 6 5 4 3 2 1

Dedication

For Savannah

Acknowledgements

I would like to thank all of my beta readers, Jeff Nichols, Sue Alkire, Michele Stull, Mary Beth O'Brien, Abby L. Vandiver, and Eric Praschan. I could not have done this without all of your help.

I'd also like to thank my wonderful husband, Jeff. If it weren't for him, I would not have had the opportunity to stay home and write. His daily sacrifice has allowed me to fulfill a lifelong dream. Every day I watch him leave for work, drive an hour both ways through crazy and dangerous traffic, and spend precious hours away from home so that we can live on our beautiful property.

The best decision I ever made was going to that writer's conference back in 1999 where we met. And the second best decision I ever made was to say yes when he stopped dead in his tracks in front of me, shook his head and asked, "Can I get you a cup of coffee?"

Thank you, Hon, from the bottom of my heart. You are my love and my life. And I appreciate you so very much.

A special thank you goes to Shondra Longino for designing the cover and for her invaluable input. And to my writing partner, Abby L. Vandiver, thank you so much for your honest (and sometimes painful) feedback. I'm a better writer because of you.

Thank you to all of you who have taken the time to read *Six Mile Canyon.* I appreciate the time and the money you've invested in me. I truly hope that I have made your efforts worthwhile.

Prologue

Paris, France, 1789

A crackling blaze coming from the stone fireplace cast a dancing shadow across the gypsy woman's face. Her cascade of dark, wavy hair had been pulled back and secured under a sheer red scarf, exposing a pair of gold, dangling earrings. She paced impatiently in front of a worn wooden table centered in the one-room cottage, as if waiting for someone. And with each outside noise she stopped and stared at the front door.

When the gypsy finally heard a light *tap, tap, tap,* she scurried over to the door and pulled it open, releasing a faint *creak* from the iron hinges.

A young woman wearing a brown woolen cape with a hood pulled down to obscure her face stood at the entry clutching a wicker basket in both hands.

Upon seeing the gypsy, the young woman said in a hushed voice, "Madam Beauton, *je suis-*"

"Shhhh. Not out here." The gypsy grabbed her visitor by the wrist and pulled her through the doorway before she could finish her introductions. She quickly and quietly closed the door and then dropped an iron bar into brackets mounted on the wall, securing them inside.

"Madam Beauton, *je suis Mademoiselle-*"

"Silence!" The gypsy cut her off again, and in French said, "Your name is of no importance to me. Now set the basket over there-" she gestured with her head to the far left edge of the stone hearth and then pointed to the table, "and then take the seat facing the fireplace."

The gypsy appeared to float across the room as her floor-length, dark green dress billowed out behind her. She pulled the chair out from behind the table and slid into it, her back instantly warming up from the fire. "Why have you come?" she wanted to know.

The young woman slid into the seat opposite her and swiped the hood away from her face, letting it pool around the nape of her neck. She seemed taken aback by the question. "Why, for divination, Madam Beauton. I was under the impression you knew that."

"Yes, of course I know that. But what have you come to find out? Are you here to contact a loved one who has departed? Or are you here to seek guidance regarding a romantic interest?" She paused taking in the slightly pale features of the young woman staring back at her. Strands of fine, reddish brown hair seemed to stand on end as if shocked by a jolt of static electricity. In the dim light it was hard to tell what color eyes she had, maybe brown or green. But at the moment they were wide with anticipation.

The young woman remained silent for several seconds.

The gypsy's gaze traveled down to her guest's petite hands folded in prayer fashion atop the table and then back up to her face. "Well?"

The young woman shifted in her chair and said, "Neither. I'm here to find out what is wrong with me. And I was told you could help me."

"I am not a doctor. If you are sick, seek a physician."

The young woman's back straightened, and her eyebrows arched as if surprised. "But Madam Beauton, I don't know for sure that I am sick. I think I might be . . ." she hesitated. "I think I might be possessed." Her words came out elevated and frantic.

The gypsy grabbed a deck of tarot cards sitting in the middle of the table and began shuffling them. "What makes you think this?" She handed the cards to the young woman and said, "Here, shuffle these."

The young woman took the deck from the gypsy and studied the drawings on the front of each card. Hand drawn images of jesters, queens, kings, knights, animals, even the Devil were painted in shades of mustard, crimson, mahogany, and ebony.

As she shuffled the cards she said, "I've been hearing voices in my head. And they tell me things about people and places. Things I shouldn't know." Handing the deck back to the gypsy she added, "I'm worried that I've been touched by the Devil."

The gypsy took the deck and laid down ten cards in the shape of a cross, all face up. She studied the images and symbols, and their placement for several moments. Finally, she said, "When did the voices begin?"

"About a month ago."

The gypsy laid ten more cards down on top of the others. "And how old are you?"

"Seventeen."

Madam Beauton looked up at her through hooded eyes. Now she could see the innocence of age in the young woman's face. She laid out ten more cards, studied them for several more seconds and mused, "Child, you are *not* touched by the Devil." She gathered the cards, restacked them, and then wrapped them in a small swatch of cloth. "No, child, it is not the Devil who's touched you. You have been touched by God." She handed the deck to the bewildered young woman and said, "You are a seer, just like me. Here, take the deck." The young woman hesitated, but the gypsy insisted. "Take it. It belongs to you now."

As the woman slowly reached for the cards the gypsy grabbed hold of her wrist and held it tightly. "Just remember, with this gift comes great responsibility. You were chosen to be the bearer of these visions. You must share them. But be careful, the world does not understand divination, and many have lost their lives for speaking out."

The young woman gasped. "I don't think I want to take them." She tried to pull away, but the gypsy's hand clamped down tighter.

The gypsy's eyes narrowed, and she leaned in. Her voice lowered to a harsh whisper. "If you do not embrace that which God has bestowed upon you, then you will cause your children and your children's children to suffer. You must accept this path that has been chosen for you and for those yet to come." She let go of the woman's wrist, leaned back in her chair and said, "Now go. And take your basket with you."

The young woman scooted back from the table and stood up. "But-"

"Go. *Maintenant.*" The gypsy pushed her chair back, stood up and appeared to float across the room. She lifted the iron bar from the door and opened it, allowing the cold night air to rob the small room of all the warmth that the fire had provided.

The young woman grabbed her basket and stuffed the deck of cards inside next to the apples and figs she had brought as payment. She hurried out the door without uttering a word and scurried down the deserted cobblestone street.

When the girl had vanished in the night, the gypsy closed the door and replaced the iron bar. She strolled over to the dwindling fire, anticipation now absent from her steps, and picked up the fireplace poker. As she prodded the embers she murmured to whatever spirits might be listening, "*Mon Dieu.* She is special, that one. I hope she will, one day, be strong enough to embrace her destiny."

Chapter 1

Carson City, Nevada
May 1, 2008

"Help! Somebody help me." A frantic woman ran through the hospital emergency entrance doors with a young girl draped lifelessly over her arms. A dark red substance dribbled from the child's mouth, staining her pajama top. "Something's wrong with my daughter," she cried out.

A doctor who had been standing by the reception desk ran up to her, took the child out of her arms and placed her on a nearby gurney. "What happened?" he asked as he lifted up each eyelid with his thumb.

The mother couldn't stop crying. "I-I don't know. She just started vomiting blood. I tried to give her Pepto Bismol, but she just threw it up." She sobbed even harder. "And now I can't wake her."

The doctor put a stethoscope to her heart, and then placed two fingers on her neck. "Her pulse is extremely weak." He opened her mouth and smelled her breath. "Hmm. Do you know if she ate anything that she shouldn't have?"

"No. In fact, she hasn't eaten anything for almost two days."

He lifted up her pajama top and examined her belly. Then he pushed up the pant legs of her pajama bottoms. "Her stomach's bloated. So are her legs and ankles." He turned to the nurses tending to the child. "Get a blood panel and start her on dialysis."

"Right away, doctor," said one of them.

When the nurses began to wheel her away, the mother cried out," Where are you taking her?" She tried to catch up to them but the doctor stopped her.

"Ma'am, we're going to take good care of her, but right now we have to clean her blood. We're also going to need to do some additional tests to determine the extent of her illness."

"Oh, God. What's wrong with my daughter?" She threw her hands over her mouth and sobbed uncontrollably.

"It looks like her kidneys are failing. But I won't know what else is going on until I get the test results back."

The woman's knees began to give way, but the doctor grabbed hold of her before she could fall. He helped her over to the waiting room where she collapsed into one of the chairs and cried out, "But she's only six years old. How can her kidneys be failing?"

He sat down in the chair next to her and shook his head. "I don't have an answer for that yet. But based on the vomiting, the swelling, and the ammonia smell on her breath, they're very close to shutting down completely."

"How is that possible?" She swiped at the tears streaming down her cheeks.

The doctor paused momentarily. "Where do you live?"

"In Little Lyon, near Dayton. Why?"

"This is not the first case like this that I've seen from there." He stood up. "I'll let you know what we find, but in the meantime, I'm going to need you to fill out some paperwork giving us permission to admit your daughter, and depending on what the tests say, operate on her if necessary."

"Do whatever you need to do. Please, just save her," she pleaded.

"We'll do everything we can for her." And then he hurried away before she could say anything else.

She sat motionless for several seconds until a receptionist walked up to her, handed her a clipboard and said, "Ma'am, I need you to fill this out please."

Just as she was about to take the clipboard, a man ran through the emergency doors shouting, "Please! I need help."

Another doctor hurried over to the man and said, "What's wrong? Are you hurt?"

"No. It's my wife. She's in a lot of pain. She's got stomach cramps and can't stop throwing up blood."

"Where is she?"

"She's out in the car. Please hurry."

The doctor ordered his team to get a gurney and then they followed the man out of the hospital. A few minutes later they burst through the main entrance wheeling a groaning woman across the lobby then disappeared through a set of double doors marked "Emergency".

The man tried to follow them through the doors but was forced by the doctor to stop. "I'm sorry but you can't go any further. You'll need to wait out in the lobby."

"Will she be okay?" He clutched his wife's purse with worried hands.

"We'll let you know what we find," said the doctor. He hurried to catch up with the gurney, leaving the man dazed and seemingly in shock.

The receptionist hurried over to the man, handed him a clipboard and said, "Please fill these out and get them back to me as soon as you can." She gestured toward the waiting room. "You can have a seat over there, and we'll call you as soon as we hear something."

He shuffled over to where the woman sat, mechanically dropped into the seat adjacent to her, and stared at his clipboard with glassy eyes.

The distraught mother set her clipboard on the seat next to her, pulled a tissue from her purse and dabbed at her eyes. She leaned in slightly and said quietly, "I'm so sorry to bother you, but I couldn't help overhearing. You said your wife was vomiting blood?"

The man looked up at her, his face fraught with worry. "Yes," he said just as quietly.

"I just brought my daughter in here for the same reason."

His face seemed to shift slightly from worry to curiosity. "You did?"

"Yes. She's in dialysis right now. The doctor said that her kidneys are failing." She paused slightly. "May I ask where you live?"

"We live in Dayton. Why?"

Her face fell. "Oh, no reason. I thought maybe you might live in Little Lyon."

"We used to live there. But we moved to Dayton a few weeks ago."

The woman sniffed and then wiped her nose. "When did your wife start getting sick?"

He shook his head. "I don't really know. She doesn't tell me these things because she knows I'll make her go to a doctor. She hates going to them." He seemed to be thinking. "But I do remember her mentioning several times in the last year that her stomach was bothering her. But she always dismissed it saying that it was probably from eating too many desserts." He glanced over at the emergency doors. "I sure hope that's all it is." He looked back over at the woman. "And how about you? When did your daughter's problem start?"

"The vomiting started last night, but it didn't get bloody until this afternoon. She said she had a stomachache and that she wasn't feeling good so I kept her home from school today." She lowered her head and slowly shook it. "I should have brought her in six months ago."

"Why? Was she sick then?"

She pursed her lips, clenching her hand into a fist. "Why didn't I see the signs? The bloated face and tummy, the hair falling out. I just thought it was because her hair had gotten too long. So I cut it. I should have-"

"Wait, her hair was falling out?"

She looked over at him and nodded. "Yes, but it wasn't enough for me to be concerned."

"My wife's hair was falling out, too. She tried to hide it, but I saw it in her brush and in the trashcan. She started washing her hair only once every couple of weeks." He let out a deep sigh. "She didn't think I would notice, but I did."

The two remained silent for several seconds. Then the man smiled politely and said, "Well, I guess I should get these papers filled out."

The woman smiled back. "Yeah, me too."

Before they could complete the paperwork, a doctor dressed in scrubs came out from the emergency room doors and walked toward them. He stopped in front of the pair, pulled off his surgical cap, and scrunched it in his hands. With a slight shake of head he said, "I'm so sorry. We did everything we could for her, but she didn't make it."

Chapter 2

Reno, Nevada
May 1, 2009

One Year Later . . .

The man and woman stood stoically next to a bank of microphones positioned in front of the Reno courthouse. Behind them stood dozens more people, families mostly. Some smiled triumphantly while others cried softly on their loved ones' shoulders.

A reporter yelled out, "Do you feel vindicated?"

The woman leaned into the microphones and said, "That's a tough question. A half a million dollars helps, but it's not going to bring back my daughter." She looked at the man standing next to her. "Nor will it give this man's wife her health back. But at least the state of Nevada had been found guilty of negligence and will be held accountable for the toxic poisoning suffered by the people of Little Lyon."

She gestured to the small crowd standing behind her. "Every one of us is still dealing with major health issues whether personally or with a family member. So, do we feel vindicated?" She shook her head. "No, I don't think so. It's been a year since this situation was first brought to the state's attention, and there are still too many unanswered questions." She let out a deep sigh. "Right now, we're all just trying to get through this ordeal."

"Sir! How is your wife doing?" asked another reporter.

The man stepped forward and said into the microphones, "Thank you for asking. She's doing as well as can be expected. With her immune system being so compromised, she can't seem to fight off infections. And the tumors continue to grow and spread. So we spend most of our time at Carson Tahoe hospital." He glanced apologetically at the woman standing next to him. "But at least I still have my wife." He gestured to the people standing behind them. "Most of these people have lost at least one family member due to the state's negligence in investigating the origins of these poisons. If the mayor and governor would have looked into it when it was first brought to their attention, we might not be in this situation."

"What measures has the state taken to fix the problem?" asked a different reporter.

A man in a suit stepped forward and spoke into the microphones. "I'm the attorney representing the families in this class action lawsuit. The state has agreed to relocate all three hundred and seventy-eight families still living in Little Lyon. They have agreed to pay all expenses, including moving, housing, schooling, and all medical bills, for as long as it takes to find and fix the problem."

"Have they found the source of the poisoning yet?" A young man with straight blond hair and wearing Levis and a brown blazer pushed through the crowd toward the front.

"Not yet," replied the attorney. "Which is why we have also asked for the resignation of the mayor and the governor. We believe that their negligence in taking appropriate measure in a timely manner has exacerbated this terrible problem."

When the young man emerged from the crowd he said, "Marty Dolan, reporter for the Reno Gazette. So what *is* the state doing to solve this problem?"

"Clearly they're not doing enough," said the attorney. "Representatives of the state say they have hired a team of experts to investigate. Right now they are in the process of ruling out where the toxins might have originated. They've also asked local businesses to help by having their own soil, water, and building materials tested."

"And are the businesses complying?" asked Marty.

"So far every company in the Dayton area has agreed to help in this search. They've even had some national companies pitching in."

"Such as?"

"I don't have the list in front of me, but they are companies and individuals who recognize the severity of the situation and have graciously donated their time and resources to help find a solution before it can get any worse."

"Do the experts have any theories as to where the toxins might have come from?"

"No. Not so far. But what they do know is that there seems to be a concentration of it in Little Lyon."

"What are the chances of these toxins getting out and affecting the people of, say, Dayton or Carson City?" Marty stepped closer to the attorney and held up his tape recorder.

"I'm not a doctor or a scientist, but I believe that unless the state takes every measure to find and fix this problem, we could all be in serious trouble."

The crowd of reporters burst into more questions forcing the attorney to hold up his hands. "I'm sorry but that's all the questions I have time for."

"Please. Just one more before you go," yelled Marty. "Do you think this is a natural phenomenon, or do you think it is manmade?"

When the attorney turned back around, the crowd instantly quieted. "Like I said, I'm not a scientist, so I don't know the answer to that. But I can tell you this; if it is determined that someone was responsible for deliberately poisoning all of these people, I will make it my sole mission to catch these monsters and bring them to justice. That, you have my word on!" He started to walk away then stopped and turned back. He leaned into the microphones again, pointed his finger out into the crowd and said, "And I would hope that all of you would make this your mission, as well."

When the attorney left the courthouse steps, Marty pulled his phone from his pocket, punched in some numbers and hit send. The call went directly to voice mail. After the greeting ended he said, "Hey Katie, it's me. Listen, I won't be able to meet you at your folks' house tonight. I have something very important for work I need to do. I'll talk to you soon. I love you. Bye." He hung up and then ran to catch up with the attorney.

Chapter 3

Outside of Carson City, Nevada
May 19, 2009
Midnight

Three Weeks Later . . .

Beneath a partial moon, the sports car plummeted backwards over the side of the mountain and came to rest at the bottom of the ravine. Its headlights faced skyward sending out a flickering beam of light, while smoke billowed out from underneath a crumpled hood. The woman in the driver's seat lay unconscious, her head flopped over to one side with a long gash across her forehead.

Above her, a man got out of his idling pickup truck, shined a flashlight on his front bumper as if to inspect it, then sauntered the few feet over to the edge of the cliff and looked down at the mangled wreck. He pulled his cell phone from his front pants pocket, held it in his hand, and waited.

When the car's headlights dimmed and finally died, he dialed a number and said, "It's done. I'll take care of the rest of it in the morning." He hung up, returned to his vehicle, flipped it around and gunned it, spitting out dust and gravel from his rear tires.

~~~~~~~~~~~~~~~~

At first light, an avalanche of rock and dirt hit the wrecked car's fractured windshield, shattering it. Earth and debris rushed in, filling the front seat of the woman's car as quickly as if it were a torrent of water.

Instantly, her eyes opened, and she gulped for air. Instead of getting oxygen, damp earth packed her mouth, obstructing her airway and making her gag. She coughed repeatedly until the glob of dirt loosened and finally tumbled from her muddy lips. Gasping for breath, she filled her lungs with stale air and screamed out, "Help! Help! Somebody help me!" Over and over she screamed out, but her cries could not escape the confines of her sporty metal coffin.

I'm going to die down here.

She knew that no help would come for her because no one knew she was missing. And in a matter of moments she and her car would be completely buried underneath tons of rock. So even if, at some point, a search party did come looking for her, they would not be able to find any trace of her. That realization caused her to scream out in a desperate panic until her throat grew raw.

If I can just reach the horn.

Rocks and dirt had pinned both arms down to her sides. After several failed attempts to free them, exhaustion forced her to stop fighting and listen. From somewhere far above her she heard a rumbling sound and the revving of massive engines. She recognized that sound.

Bulldozers!

She tried once more to scream for help but the words came out no louder than a crackling whisper.

A moment later more rock and debris tumbled down the mountainside, adding to the mound that nearly engulfed her car.

"Stop," she wheezed. "I'm still in here." But the dirt kept piling up around her until it swallowed her and the car up completely. And then the rumbling stopped.

Dead silence.

She heard nothing, except for the sound of trickling dirt filling up the empty spaces inside her car and the groan of metal protesting underneath the tons of rubble that relentlessly crushed it.

As she stared up at the paper-thin slices of muted daylight filtering through the gaps in the debris, she thought about her mom and dad, and then, her boyfriend, Marty, the person responsible for her being in this position.

If he would have just left things alone.

She squelched a cry.

Her thoughts bounced back to her parents, and she wondered if they were up yet. *Probably not, still too early.* And even when they did wake up, they wouldn't think anything was wrong until tonight when she and Marty didn't show up for dinner. They'd call. And when they couldn't get a hold of either of them, they'd probably stop by her apartment. Once they realized she was missing, they would contact the Carson City and Reno police departments, file a missing persons report, and start the process of looking for her. But by then it would be too late, and she would be nothing but rotting flesh.

That thought caused her to scream out again, "Help me! Somebody help me! I'm trapped!" She continued to scream until her voice grew horse again, and then her words trickled out in a miserable whimper. "Please. Please, somebody help me."

As the day ticked by, she felt herself becoming dehydrated. She could no longer hold her bladder, and she peed in her seat, which made her cry. All that wasted fluid. She screamed out again and again until the final vestige of daylight robbed her of the last bit of warmth and energy.

Exhaustion made her want to sleep. But she knew that if she fell asleep she wouldn't survive another cold Nevada night. Her teeth began to clatter, and she thought, *I have to get my arms free. Otherwise I'll freeze to death.*

She tried to move her torso from side to side, but the rocks and dirt cocooning her held on tight, keeping her immobile. She pushed her body harder against the rocks that pinned her, oblivious to the scrapes and cuts from the jagged boulders and stones. She rocked from side to side and front to back until the debris shifted enough for her to pull her left arm free. She wedged her fingers in between the chunks of rock, dislodging them one at a time, and then tossed them into the small space behind the passenger's seat.

With bloodied fingertips, she dug out more rocks until her right arm pulled free.

She pushed on the horn, but it came out sounding like a deflating balloon. When she leaned on it again, nothing but silence filled the air.

"Help me," she screeched. "Somebody help me!" Tears spilled out of her eyes, leaving tracks down her dirty cheeks. She looked up toward the heavens and cried out, "God, please let someone find me!"

Chapter 4

Scottsbluff, Nebraska
May 19, 2012

Savannah Swift woke up in a coughing fit. She couldn't breathe. Instinctively, she sat up, wrapped her fingers around the neckline of her pajama top and tugged at it, pulling it away from her throat. She sucked in deep, but the air couldn't get past whatever was obstructing her throat.

What little breath she could take in came and went in a raspy wheeze. She felt her lungs burning from the lack of oxygen. So she pounded on her chest with her fist until the invisible plug broke free, allowing her to breathe again. She gulped in air until her lungs were full.

After a few seconds her shaky hands released the shirt, and she laid her head back down on the pillow. "What was that about?" she whispered.

And then she remembered the dream.

A knock on her bedroom door and a muffled voice caused her to sit back up. "Savannah, are you up?"

"Yeah, Mom. I just woke up." Savannah swung her legs out of bed and sat on the edge still reeling from the harsh way she had been pulled from her sleep. She took another deep breath and rubbed her forehead in an attempt to thwart a brewing headache.

"Well, c'mon, sleepyhead. Breakfast is on the table."

"Be there in a minute," said Savannah as she pulled herself up and stepped into yesterday's clothes. She trudged to the bathroom and stared at her reflection in the mirror. Messy auburn hair proved that she spent last night thrashing in her bed. A roadmap of red spider veins dulled her hazel eyes making them look as tired as she felt.

She wet a washcloth with cold water and draped it over her eyes. It felt refreshing and rejuvenated her slightly. After a couple of minutes she wiped the rest of her face with it and then hung it up on the towel rack. She brushed her teeth, ran a quick brush through her hair and then pulled it back into a ponytail. She looked at her reflection again.

Better, but not great.

"C'mon, Savannah. We're waiting." Her mother's voice found its way up from the bottom of the stairs into the bathroom.

"I'm coming," yelled Savannah. She dabbed some lotion on her face and pinched her cheeks bringing a nice flush to them. That seemed to take the attention away from her eyes. Then she hurried down the stairs, following the smell of breakfast into the kitchen.

When she got there, only her mother and her little brother were waiting for her. She pulled out the chair next to her little brother and said as she sat down at the table, "Where's Dad?"

"He'll be down in a minute." Her mother passed the communal plate of bacon to Savannah and said, "You look tired. How'd you sleep?"

Savannah grabbed four strips of bacon then passed the plate to her brother. In return, her brother handed her the plate of scrambled eggs. She scraped a healthy portion onto her plate and said, "Not so good. I had another one of those dreams again last night." She handed the plate of eggs across the table to her mother. "It was so real. Like I was right there."

Savannah was about to take a bite of bacon when her mother scowled and said, "Wait for your father, so that he can bless the food."

Savannah set the bacon down. She wanted to say, 'I thought you were waiting for *me*' but instead said, "This lady in my dream was being buried alive." She thought about the young woman gasping for breath and then thought about her own choking episode.

Hmm, strange.

"She had driven off a cliff and was stuck in her car while bulldozers dropped bucket loads of dirt over the edge. She tried to escape but she couldn't dig herself out. I heard her scream out, 'please let someone find me.' And then I woke up." Savannah started to reach for that same strip of bacon and then stopped.

"Wow, buried alive? Cool," said her brother. He fidgeted in his chair and then picked up a shovelful of eggs with the end of one of his strips of bacon.

"Kyle!" snapped Mrs. Swift. "There is nothing 'cool' about someone being buried alive. And stop playing with your food."

Right then Pastor Swift walked into the kitchen dressed in gray slacks and a light blue, short-sleeved, dress shirt. He poured a cup of coffee and pulled out the fourth chair at the kitchen table. "What's cool? Or not cool depending on whose perspective we're talking about." He scraped the rest of the scrambled eggs onto his plate and snatched the remaining strips of bacon. Then he bowed his head and blessed the food.

After the prayer, Mrs. Swift smiled at her husband. "You look all dressed up for a Saturday. You going to the church?"

Pastor Swift took a bite of eggs, chewed, and said, "Yeah. I've got to finish my sermon for tomorrow, and I left my notes in the church office." He looked at his son and daughter. "So what were you three talking about?"

Savannah gobbled down several forks full of lukewarm eggs, barely chewing them before swallowing. They would have tasted so much better five minutes ago.

"Oh, I was just telling Mom that I had another one of those dreams last night." She bit into the strip of bacon and chewed with vigor.

"Hmmm." Her father rubbed his chin. "Did you watch anything on TV last night after we went to bed?"

Savannah swallowed and tilted her head to the side. "I watched an old episode of the Twilight Zone. Why?"

Her father shook his head and threw her a disappointed look. "Don't you know that stuff is garbage? It's designed to scare you, to put things in your mind that don't need to be there."

"But it wasn't scary."

"Well, clearly it was," her father said. He shook a piece of toast at her oblivious to the crumbs that fell onto the table. "Just because something looks harmless doesn't mean it is. You young people need to be reminded that the Devil is tricky and can find a way into your mind through things like scary movies, or books, or anything that isn't of the Lord." He took a bite of the buttery toast then dropped it on his plate. "No more watching garbage like that, understood?"

Savannah lowered her head and sighed. "Okay, but I really don't think that had anything to do with my dream. I've had them before. So it couldn't be-"

"Vannah, don't."

Pastor Swift's words sounded like the beginning of an argument, so to prevent it, Mrs. Swift looked at her daughter and said, "Vannah, honey, what are your plans today?"

Happy for the diversion, Savannah said, "There's a street fair going on today. Emma, Jade and I were thinking of going." She finished her orange juice, scooted back from the table and took her dishes to the sink. "Then we thought we might go shopping for graduation dresses."

Pastor Swift opened his mouth as if to comment, but before he could say anything Mrs. Swift said, "That sounds like fun. How are you getting there? You want to borrow the car?"

"No, that's okay. Em's picking me up in her car."

Pastor Swift frowned, "Are her parents going?"

"No, Dad. Just the three of us."

"How long has she had her license?"

"As long as I have."

"Any tickets or accidents?"

"Dad . . ."

Mrs. Swift threw her husband a look that spoke volumes. Finally, he said, "Fine, just be home for dinner. And don't get into any trouble."

Savannah put her dirty dishes in the dishwasher and then wrapped her arms around her father's neck. "Thanks, Dad. Love you."

"Love you, too, Vannah." He looked at his son. "And what about you, Kyle. What are your plans?"

Kyle shrugged as he drug his fork through the remaining crumbles of scrambled egg. "Don't know. Maybe I could go with Vannah to the fair."

Savannah looked at her mother. She didn't want her little brother tagging along. That would mean they couldn't talk about things like boys, college, parties, and sex. Especially sex. "Mom . . ."

"Kyle, honey. Let your sister be with her friends. We'll find something else fun to do," said Mrs. Swift.

"But, Mom . . ."

Pastor Swift glanced at his watch. "I've got to go." He slammed back the rest of his coffee, pushed away from the table and stood up. "See you guys tonight," he said as he gave his wife a kiss on the cheek and then ruffled Kyle's hair. He kissed Savannah on the top of her head before heading out of the kitchen and added, "Stay out of trouble."

When Mrs. Swift heard the front door close, she looked at her son and said, "Tell you what. How about if you and I go to see that new movie you wanted to see, you know, the one with all those gory zombie creatures. And we can go for ice cream afterwards." She lowered her voice and threw Savannah a quick wink. "Just don't tell your father."

"Okay, cool." Kyle scooted away from the table with enthusiasm. He jumped up and said, "I'll go get my shoes." And then he scampered up the stairs.

Savannah hugged her mom. "Thanks, Mom. I owe you one." And then she followed her brother up the stairs to take a quick shower and change before her friends showed up.

She had just slipped into a pair of white shorts and a royal blue tank top when she heard a horn honk. She looked out her bedroom window and saw Emma's green Volkswagen Rabbit pull into the driveway. She grabbed her purse, ran down the stairs, and yelled, "See you later, Mom." And then she hurried out the door.

Chapter 5

Savannah opened the back car door, leaned in and grabbed a stack of reusable cloth totes from the seat and tossed them in the way back next to a bag of biodegradable paper cups. She climbed in, fastened her seatbelt and said, "Em, do you really need that many bags? It's starting to look like a recycling bin in here."

From the driver's seat, Emma looked back at her, adjusted her tortoise shell glasses and said, "They're not all for me. I keep them for people like you who still insist on using plastic bags. You want to take a couple?"

"Nah, you keep them for me." Savannah flashed her a dimpled grin.

Emma returned the smile. "One of these days I *will* convert you." She looked at the passenger in the front seat, a petite girl with a waterfall of straight, bluish black hair. "And you, too, Jade."

Jade turned in her seat and smiled at Savannah. "I'm so glad you could go with us today. It'll be fun."

Jade was a beautiful girl. But her most striking feature, and the one that earned her the nickname "Jade," were her dark green eyes. They were the color of the semi-precious stone from the Orient. No one, not even her family, called her by her given name.

"How long can you stay?" said Jade, flicking her long hair back over her shoulder.

"I've got the whole day," said Savannah. "So what do we want to do first? Starbucks and then the fair?"

"Sounds good," said Emma as she pulled out of the driveway.

"Do you guys mind if we take it with us?" said Jade. "I want to get to the fair before all the good stuff is gone."

Before Emma could say anything Savannah smiled, reached in the way back and pulled three biodegradable cups from the stack. She handed them to Jade and said, "See, Em. I'm learning. No Styrofoam." That made Emma grin.

Savannah leaned back in her seat and smiled as they drove through the streets of Scottsbluff. She was so happy to be able to spend the last weekend before graduation with her best friends. Come this fall, all three of them would be going off to different colleges, and their lives would change dramatically.

Less than a half an hour later and with their "green" cups in hand, the girls perused the booths set up along the length of Main Street. Hand thrown pottery, semi-precious jewelry, and fashionable sunglass knockoffs kept them entertained.

Savannah pushed her new sunglasses on top of her head, admired a modern looking turquoise ring and said, "Wow, Scottsbluff is coming up in the world. We didn't have anything close to this at last year's street fair." She tried it on and wiggled her fingers in front of her friends. "What do you think? Should I get it?" Before Emma and Jade could comment, Savannah wrinkled her nose and said, "Nah, I don't like the way it feels."

"You don't like the way if feels? What, is it too big or something?" said Jade.

"No. It fits fine. I just don't like the way *I* feel wearing it." Savannah shrugged and then pulled it off her finger and placed it back in its holder. She smiled at the person tending the booth and gave a nod of thank you.

As they continued to walk languidly through the booths, Savannah said, "Oh, I forgot to tell you guys. I had another one of those dreams last night. But this one was different."

The girls stopped. "What do you mean by different?" said Emma.

Savannah shook her head. "It was really weird. She's in the car like always, but this time the dream was a lot more detailed. I saw her trying to claw her way out of the car, and I could smell the dirt. I even heard her screaming for help." She shuddered. "But the creepiest part about it was that I could actually feel her suffocating. When I woke up, I couldn't breathe. It was like I had something stuck in my throat. I swear, I thought I was going to die!"

"Wow. You were really choking? That must have been scary," said Jade flipping her hair over one shoulder.

Savannah nodded. "It was. I coughed and coughed, but there wasn't anything in my throat that would cause me to choke." She trembled reliving that moment.

"So what do you think it means?" Emma said as she tilted her head to one side forcing her too long bushy bangs to follow.

"Well, my dad says it's because I watched Twilight Zone last night. But I don't think that's it."

Jade tossed her empty cup in the trash and said, "So what do *you* think it means?"

"I have no idea. But it seemed so real. I felt her panicking, and I knew what she was thinking. I even heard her say, 'God, please let someone find me.'" She wrapped her arms around herself and shivered. "It was just so weird."

"Could you see what she looked like?" Emma asked.

Savannah shook her head. "I couldn't see her face. It was like I was seeing things through her eyes. She had torn fingernails, and her hands were all bloody from pulling out the rocks." She glanced down at her own hands as if to inspect them and then looked back up at her friends and sighed. "I know it was just a dream and all, but I haven't been able to stop thinking about that woman."

The three girls remained silent for several seconds until Jade, who had been staring off into the distance, said, "Ooh, I have an idea. I think I know how we can find out what your dream means."

Chapter 6

"Let's go get one of those." Jade pointed to a small white tent with a banner over the entrance that read, 'Psychic Readings'.

Savannah visually followed her friend's finger. When she saw the psychic's tent she balked and said, "No way. My dad would kill me if he knew I did something like that. He says things like that are the Devil's tools. Besides, I don't believe in psychics. I think they're all scam artists."

Jade grabbed her by the wrist and began to pull her toward the tent. "Oh, c'mon, Vannah. It'll be fun."

Savannah yanked her wrist free. "No! I don't want to do it."

"Are you afraid of what you might find out?" said Jade.

"No. I just don't want to be messing with Satan."

Emma put her arm around Savannah's shoulders in a protective manner. "Don't push her, Jade. If she doesn't want to go, she doesn't have to." She looked at Savannah. "Would it bother you if Jade and I got a reading?"

"No, of course not. I just don't want one."

"Fair enough," said Jade.

The three walked over to the psychic's tent. Emma stuck her head in through the slit and said, "Excuse me, we'd like to get a couple of readings."

A pleasant male voice replied, "Sure. It's ten dollars for a fifteen minute reading."

Emma backed away from the tent opening as a young man with a thick mop of curly brown hair and wearing a Stanford T-shirt and khaki shorts walked out through the opening. He smiled at the three girls and said, "Hi, I'm Dominic. Do you all want readings?"

"No," blurted out Savannah. Embarrassed at her outburst, she flushed and said, "I mean, I don't want one, but they do."

Dominic smiled and held open the curtain for them. "This way ladies." He looked at Savannah. "You're welcome to come in and wait if you'd like."

"No, that's okay. I'll just wait out here."

"No, Vannah. Come inside with us." Jade gave her a pout. "It won't hurt to just sit there while we have our readings done. He's got chairs in here. And a fan."

Emma opened the tent door wider so that Savannah could look in. "Come on, Vannah. Just come in and sit. He's not going to bite," she looked over at the young man, "are you, Dominic."

The guy sat down at a card table covered with a light blue tablecloth and laughed light-heartedly. "Not likely, but you never know." He pulled out a deck of tarot cards from their package and began to shuffle them.

Savannah heaved a heavy sigh. She didn't want to ruin their fun just because she had issues with the whole psychic thing. And a fan would be a welcome change from the unseasonably muggy May weather. "Fine. But I'm sitting by the door." She walked through the split in the tent, grabbed one of the chairs and moved it right next to the opening. Her fingers discreetly wrapped around the door flap, and she pulled it open, just in case she needed a quick getaway.

Dominic placed the deck of cards in the middle of the table and said, "So who's going first?"

"I am," said Jade. She pulled the chair out across from him and sat down. "And by the way, I'm Jade. That's Emma. And that's Savannah over there."

Dominic acknowledged them with a nod and then turned his attention back to Jade. "Have you ever had your cards read before?" When Jade shook her head no, Dominic gestured to the cards and said, "Go ahead and shuffle them while I tell you a little bit about what to expect."

Jade flashed Emma an excited smile then took the cards and began to shuffle them as though they were a deck of playing cards. As she arched the stack into a bridge, one card popped out of the deck and landed on the table.

She was just about to pick it up and put it back into the deck when Dominic said, "No. Leave it there. The reading starts the minute you sit down." He turned the card over to reveal a picture of a queen wearing a crown and holding a sword. She stood amongst a garden of fully opened red roses. "I see someone watching over you, a grandmother maybe. Has your grandmother passed on?"

"Yes. She died when I was-"

Dominic stopped her. "I don't want any details because I don't want to be influenced. Just give me a yes or no answer."

Jade nodded. "Yes."

Dominic picked up the card and set it to the side. "She's here with you, you know." His gaze migrated over her left shoulder. "She's standing next to you with her hand on your shoulder. Maybe we'll get a message from her."

Savannah shifted in her seat. She wasn't interested in being involved in a séance. So she stood up and said, "I think I'll wait outside."

Jade turned around and pleaded, "No, Vannah, please don't go. I really want you here. It's important to me."

"You don't need me here. You've got Em to keep you company."

"But what if Grandma has a message for you? She loved you, too, you know. Remember when we were little how she would-"

Dominic stopped her. "Please don't say anymore. I don't want to know anything about your background. I need to keep my mind clear."

Emma picked up her chair and set it next to Savannah's. She grabbed her by the hand and gently pulled her back down. "C'mon. Do it for Jade." When Savannah hesitating, she added, "Tell you what, if you want to leave after it's over, I won't mind having Dominic do my reading alone."

Reluctantly, Savannah sat back down and said, "Okay, but I'm telling you, this makes me very uncomfortable." She glared at Jade. "But I'll do it for you because you two are my best friends. And that's what best friends do."

When Dominic had Jade's full attention again he laid the cards face down in the shape of a pyramid and said, "I'll be doing a general reading, which means that it can be about any subject matter. It'll be about whatever your spirit guides want you to know."

"Spirit guides?"

"Yes. They are the beings or entities assigned to watch over you."

"Oh, yes, of course. Makes sense," said Jade. She tried to sound like she knew what he was talking about, but her wide-eyed expression conveyed she didn't have a clue.

"When I turn the cards over," he said, "I'll tell you what I see and what I hear. I might ask you questions so that I can clarify what it is I'm seeing in my head. Only answer me with a yes or no, nothing more. Do you understand?"

Jade acknowledged with a nod.

Dominic turned over the bottom row of six cards that made up the base of the pyramid. "Jade isn't your real name, is it." It was more of a statement than a question.

"No, it isn't."

He tilted his head and gazed beyond Jade's left shoulder. A moment later he smiled and said to no one in particular, "Yes, I understand." He looked back at Jade. "Your grandmother says you were named after her. I think she said, Janice or Janet."

Jade's eyes widened. "Yes, it's Janice, and I *was* named after her."

Dominic smiled and turned over the next line of five cards. "You plan to attend college in the fall. Go, Huskers!" He chuckled but then frowned slightly. "You might have to postpone it a semester."

Jade furrowed her brow. "Why would I have to do that? I've already paid my tuition for the first semester."

"I'm not sure why. There could be several reasons."

Dominic turned over the next row of four cards and studied them for a moment. He looked up at her. "One thing you have to remember, Jade, is that the future isn't written in stone. It's fluid and can change depending on your decisions and actions." He gestured to the cards. "Readings are based on probabilities and patterns. You might choose to do something way out of character for you that would change the path that you are currently on. And I believe that is the case here. You will be making a decision that will alter your plans for college." He shrugged his shoulders. "I'm sorry, but that's what I see."

He turned the next row of three cards over. "Are you going on a trip?"

"Not that I know of."

"Well, you will be." He turned over the next row of two cards. "Your friends are very important to you. They're like sisters to you, and you would do anything for them."

Jade glanced back over her shoulder at Emma and Savannah. Her eyes softened when she looked at Savannah. "Yes, they are very important to me."

Dominic leaned in a little closer and lowered his voice. "I know you like to be in charge, but sometimes you need to let others take the lead." He turned the last card over at the top of the pyramid, paused for a moment and then said, "Hmmm, this is unexpected."

Jade leaned over the cards. "What? What do you see?"

Dominic's gaze moved from the cards to Jade, to Emma and settled on Savannah. "This one's about her."

The intensity of Dominic's stare caused Savannah to squirm in her seat. She felt like this stranger had, in some ways, just violated her by looking through her clothes and right into her soul. It unnerved her. She wanted to move, to jump up and run out of the tent, but a part of her wanted to hear what this charlatan intended to say about her. What profound knowledge about her past, present, or future was he about to impart on her and her gullible friends? The others might believe in him, but she did not.

"What's wrong, Dominic. What do you see?" Jade's words came out strained and panicky.

Dominic stared at Savannah for several seconds as though he were assessing her. Finally, he smiled and said, "Savannah, I think this deck belongs to you."

Chapter 7

Savannah choked on her saliva. "What? What are you talking about? Those things are not mine. Believe me, they definitely don't belong to me." The last statement carried an indignant tone as the words tumbled out of her mouth.

"But I think they are meant to be yours," Dominic said. "I'd like you to come over here and read my cards for me."

Savannah laughed at the absurdity of his request. Not only did she not believe in psychics, the thought of touching something so blasphemous sent shivers up her spine. There wasn't enough soap in the world that would be able to cleanse her from their devilish residue. She folded her arms across her chest in a protective and defiant manner but said nothing.

Jade wrinkled her brow and stared at Dominic with a look of confusion. "Why would you say those cards belong to Savannah? She wouldn't be caught dead with them. She's the daughter of a Baptist minister."

"And she *would* be dead if her father ever caught her with them, because he'd kill her!" added Emma.

Dominic looked from one girl to the next. "Sometimes a deck will pick out its new owner. And this deck has chosen her." His eyes stayed on Savannah. "You must have some sort of psychic ability, otherwise the spirit guides would not have named you as the new owner. So please come give me a reading."

Savannah let out a high-pitched nervous laugh. "No way. I'm not touching those things. My father told me that any type of divination is Satan's tool. He uses it to open up a doorway to your soul and then he comes in and possesses it." She tightened her crossed arms and shook her head. "No way. I am *not* going to let Satan possess me."

Dominic's stare softened. "I mean no disrespect to your father, but his narrow-mindedness is more from Satan than the ability to read these cards is. I do these readings with the utmost reverence, respect, and love for God."

He began to reshuffle the cards. When he was satisfied, he cut them into three piles, face down. Then he turned over the first card from each stack and laid them on the table above the three piles. He studied the cards for a moment and then said to Savannah, "You've been having reoccurring dreams lately, dreams about death and dying. Is that true?"

"Yes, but-"

He turned over three more cards. "You keep seeing this same woman in your dreams." Without waiting for Savannah to answer, he turned the next three cards over. "Somewhere deep inside you, you know these dreams mean something significant. You don't know what, but you know they are important. You sense it." He turned over three more cards, studied them and then looked up at her. "The dreams are becoming more vivid, more real, more violent."

Savannah's jaw unhinged. How could he have known those details about her? Her arms remained folded across her chest. She crossed her legs protectively and said, "Jade must have told you about the dreams."

Jade objected. "No, Vannah, I swear I never mentioned a word. You've been sitting right there the whole time. You know I didn't say anything. Otherwise you would have heard me say it."

Savannah knew her friend hadn't divulged that information. But the alternative was to accept that this guy really was psychic. No tricks, no smoke and mirrors but a bona fide seer. That went against everything she had been brought up to believe. So what was the truth?

Dominic picked up the cards and restacked them. "Savannah, I think you may have a gift. Please, for your own peace of mind, come over here and read my cards for me."

"I don't have a *gift*, and I don't believe in psychics."

"Then come over here and prove me wrong."

Savannah's voice lowered. "I think you're very good at reading people. I've read about people like you who know how to interpret body language. They know when they've hit on something because their subject's pupils dilate. It has nothing to do with being psychic."

Dominic laughed. "Okay, then prove that I'm a fake."

Savannah was unnerved. She felt angry, frightened, and curious, all at the same time. She uncrossed her body, stood up and took a step toward the table.

No, don't do it, screamed a voice in one ear.

But then a tiny little voice whispered in the other, *Go on, give it a try.* The Devil was already starting to work on her, chiseling at her beliefs and undermining her willpower.

She knew she shouldn't do it. She shouldn't open that doorway and delve into something that she knew nothing about.

Don't do it, they're all Satan's tools.

The words pounded in her head, pressing her to stop before it was too late. But her feet seemed to have a mind of their own, and she walked over to Dominic.

She sat down at the table while Jade and Emma stood behind her staring over her shoulders. "Now what," she said to Dominic.

Dominic offered her a disarming smile. "Lay the cards out however you feel led to do. Then turn them over one at a time and tell me what you see and hear."

Reluctantly, Savannah reached for the deck. Her hand hovered above it momentarily as she thought, *Oh, God, what if I open the door for Satan to come in, and he possesses me?* She remembered the movie "The Exorcist" and pulled her hand away. The thought of spewing green goo made her swallow hard.

Dominic's soothing voice pulled her from that imagery. "It'll be okay, Savannah. I promise."

A momentary sense of peace washed over her, and she grabbed the cards. She laid them out, face down, in the same pyramid shape that she saw him do. And then she paused.

"Go ahead, Savannah," he urged, "turn the bottom row of cards over."

Savannah reached for the first card but hesitated, not sure if she should go any further. If she stopped right now then no damage would be done. But the moment she turned that first card over, all bets were off. Once she opened that doorway, her soul would become exposed to any malevolence Dominic might be trying to introduce to her.

The young man didn't seem evil in his Stanford T-shirt, but the Devil wears many disguises. She looked into Dominic's eyes trying to determine his motives.

Are your intentions good or bad?

Dominic offered her a kind smile and an encouraging nod causing her to agonize even more over what she should do. All of this went against everything she'd been brought up to believe. So why was she willing to risk her soul for the sake of this stranger?

Curiosity.

Don't do it, Savannah. Don't you know curiosity killed the cat? Stop before it's too late. She heard her father's voice screaming at her in her head. She saw him standing at the pulpit holding up the Bible in one hand and pointing at her with the other. *You'll be sorry, Savannah Swift. You'll be sorry when the Devil devours your soul.*

She gasped at the imagery. But in spite of the warning, she turned over the bottom row of cards.

Chapter 8

Savannah stared at the images on the face of the cards and waited. For what, she wasn't sure. And it was the not knowing that made her nervous and sorry she'd given in to her curiosity. She focused on the first picture, that of a young boy carrying a knapsack over his shoulder and whistling.

She reached down and touched the image, and instantly a current of electricity shot through her fingertips, up her arm, and right into her brain. Vivid snapshots flashed through her mind causing her to yank back her hand as though a snake had bitten it. She grabbed the sides of her head and pressed. "Oh God! What's happening to me?"

Dominic leaned forward. "What do you see, Savannah. Tell me." He seemed more curious than worried.

It was as if Savannah were watching a movie with the sound down. It could have been a home movie because the child in her mind looked very much like a younger version of Dominic.

She hesitated and then touched the card again. The scene in her mind began to play out in Technicolor. But this time it came alive with sounds, smells and sensations as though she were right there watching it happen.

She looked somewhat confused at Dominic and said, "D-did you have a tricycle when you were a little kid, maybe a red one?"

This is stupid, she thought. *Every kid had a red tricycle at one time or another.*

"I-I think you might have been around three years old." She waited for him to say something, but he just sat there staring at her.

What am I doing? she thought. *This is ridiculous. I need to stop this right now.*

Instead of stopping, she turned over the next row of cards. In her mind she saw an older boy shove the child hard causing him to fall off of the tricycle.

"W-were you riding it in the street, when some kid, maybe a neighbor, pushed you off of it and took it?" Again Dominic didn't respond. She furrowed her brow and shook her head. "I don't know why, but I keep seeing you being dragged behind the tricycle, like you were holding on to the back of it or something."

She looked up at Dominic and sighed deeply. "Does this make any sense to you?"

He remained silent and indifferent, showing no emotion on his face.

Well, this is just silly, she thought as she turned over the next row of four cards. Again, a current of electricity traveled up her fingertips and spread through her entire body causing it to tingle. She waited for the home movie to resume, but instead she heard a strangely angelic voice whisper in her left ear.

"Pliers. Workbench."

She looked behind her to make sure it wasn't Jade or Emma whispering in her ear.

"What is it, Savannah? What did you hear?" Dominic looked at her with genuine interest.

"I heard a voice." Savannah stuck a finger in her ear and wiggled it around as if a stray glob of wax might have been the culprit.

"What did the voice say?" Dominic wanted to know.

Savannah took her finger out of her ear and opened her mouth to speak, but her apprehension caused her to hesitate. This was all way too strange for her. The voice in her head didn't sound like Satan's, but what other option was there? She looked at the cards again and the voice returned.

"Mother. Garage."

Confused, Savannah looked at him again and said, "When this kid pulled you behind the tricycle," she hesitated, "did you get a rock stuck in your knee?"

Dominic gave her no indication one way or the other.

"And did your mother set you up on the workbench in the garage and pull it out with a pair of pliers?"

Dominic remained neutral.

Even though he offered her no feedback as to whether her reading was right or wrong, she couldn't deny that something strange was truly happening to her. But there was no logical explanation as to where these sights, sounds and sensations were coming from.

She turned over the row of three cards. Her eyes seemed to focus on a man riding a horse and carrying a stick with a green wreath attached to the top of it. Immediately, she thought of marriage. "Are you married?"

This time she didn't expect Dominic to respond and said, "You might not be right now, but I think you will be in the very near future."

She turned over the next row of two cards and saw Dominic and a blonde woman sitting in a restaurant holding hands across the table. She could hear the conversations around them and smell the aroma of freshly baked bread and grilled steak. It was as if she were standing right in the middle of the restaurant.

Behind her she heard a man tell the waiter that his fish tasted funny. Then her mind flashed forward a few hours, and she saw this same man leaning over a toilet vomiting. She shook the image out of her mind and said, "I think you're going to propose in a restaurant. But you should probably stay away from the sea bass."

When she finished the reading she leaned back in her chair, still buzzing from the electrical currents traveling through her body.

What just happened to me?

She couldn't explain the visions, the sounds, or the voices that filled her head. The whole experience seemed so bizarre and foreign, yet something about it felt good and familiar, like being reacquainted with a dear old friend. And when she looked up at Dominic and saw him smiling at her, deep down she knew that his intentions weren't to hurt her but to help her discover something remarkable about herself.

"So, how did I do?"

Dominic laughed. "You were ninety nine percent correct." He reached into his pocket, pulled out a small box, and opened it up to reveal a beautiful solitaire diamond set in white gold. "I had planned on asking my girlfriend to marry me tonight at Morton's Steakhouse. Do you think she'll say yes?"

Savannah grinned. "I'm pretty sure she will."

Her attitude toward Dominic had softened dramatically in the last few minutes. This guy seemed genuine with pure motives. But the threads of her strict upbringing bound her to her beliefs. And one anomaly like what she had just experienced was not enough to sever them.

"So what *didn't* I get right?" she asked. "You said I was ninety nine percent correct. What did I miss?"

"I was two and a half, not three when my older *cousin* took my tricycle." He pointed to the scar on the top of his knee. "And this is where the rock was that my mom pulled out with a pair of pliers."

He gathered the cards up, put them back in their box and held the deck out to her. "I told you this was your deck." When Savannah hesitated he added, "You know, Savannah, whether you want to accept it or not, you are a psychic. You can run from it or you can embrace it. But this gift was given to you for a reason. I believe you were meant to help people with your ability."

Savannah didn't reply.

Dominic stuck his hand out further, urging her to take the box. "I've known a lot of psychics, and believe me, you're up there with the best of them. Just think what you could do if you embraced your talent and practiced. You could do a lot of good things for a lot of people."

Savannah paused for a moment longer then took the cards and dropped them in her purse. "I'll think about it, I promise."

Dominic stood up, walked around the table and placed his hand on her shoulder. "I really hope you do." He reached into his back pocket, retrieved his wallet and pulled out a business card. He handed it to her and said, "Here. Call me if you need to talk, or if you have any questions. I'd be happy to help you."

Emma watched Savannah put the cards in her purse and blurted out, "Hey, what about my reading?"

Dominic said, "Why don't you let Savannah give you one. It will be good practice for her." He handed Emma another one of his cards. "And then I'll give you a reading later down the road, free of charge."

Emma frowned. "Well, I guess that'll be okay." She pointed Dominic's business card at Savannah and said, "You own me a reading."

"We'll see," said Savannah.

Jade handed Dominic a ten-dollar bill for her reading, but he refused it. "It's on the house, today. Just do me a favor, will you? Encourage her to pursue her psychic abilities. She's special. I mean it. She's really got the gift." They both stared at Savannah and then continued talking as if she weren't there.

"I'll do what I can, but she can be very stubborn when she wants to be," said Jade. "She's been known to have a one-track mind."

Savannah planted her hands on her hips in silent objection to Jade's comments.

"That's what I'm counting on," chuckled Dominic.

The girls said good-bye to Dominic and continued to peruse the remaining booths. While they ogled over stretchy summer dresses, wide brim hats, bracelets and bangles, and hot pink, jeweled, cowboy boots, Savannah's mind was elsewhere.

Two hours ago, she didn't believe in psychics. Now, according to Dominic, she was one. How could she accept something in herself that her strict Baptist upbringing considered blasphemous?

The images, the voices, the *knowing* something without really knowing it. She just couldn't explain how she knew those things about that stranger. But know them, she did!

How is that even possible? she wondered.

"So are you going to tell your parents?" Jade admired an amethyst nugget necklace with her hands, rubbing the polished stones between her fingers. She snorted. "Gawd, I can't even imagine what your dad would do to you if he saw you with those cards. He'd string you up alive."

Jade was right. Savannah could never let her dad see that deck of tarot cards. If he found them, he'd march her right down to the church and have the congregation lay hands on her so that they could reclaim her soul before the Devil devoured it.

"I still don't know what I'm going to do with them. Maybe I should just toss them. Or better yet, burn them so no one else will get sucked in by them."

"Is that really what you want to do?" asked Emma.

"I don't know yet." It all seemed so confusing to her.

"Well, if you're going to get rid of them, will you at least do a reading for me before you throw them out? Remember, you owe me one," said Emma.

"I said I don't know what I'm going to do with them yet." Savannah immediately felt bad for being short with her friend. This wasn't her fault that Dominic singled her out. Nor was it her fault that she felt conflicted.

She looked into her friend's pleading eyes and sighed. "Okay, I'll do one more reading, and then I'll decide what to do with the cards."

Chapter 9

Two hours later after the girls made a complete loop around the booths, Jade said, "Well, now what? You want to go to the mall?"

"I'm kind of tired of shopping, and I'm hungry," said Savannah. She looked around at the greasy fair food. "I don't see anything here that looks good. So I'm thinking about heading home. Em, would you mind dropping me off before you guys go shopping?"

"I don't really want to go to the mall either. Why don't we go to my house for a little bite first, and then I'll take you home," Emma suggested.

Savannah didn't need to be a psychic to know that Emma wanted her reading right now and was willing to make them all lunch in order to get it. She looked at Jade. "Are you okay with going over to Em's for lunch?"

"Fine by me."

Fifteen minutes later the three girls walked in through Emma's front door, and Emma yelled out, "Mom, I'm home."

"In the kitchen," came a voice from the back of the house.

"Mmmm, something smells good," said Jade as they walked through the living room.

What smelled good in the living room smelled divine in the kitchen. Dozens of over-sized chocolate chunk cookies covered the kitchen counters. Emma's mother was bent over the opened oven humming an unrecognizable tune. When she turned around she held another tray of freshly baked cookies in her mitted hand.

"Hi, Mrs. Reed," said both girls in unison.

"Hi girls," she said as she set the tray on the counter and then pulled off the oven mitt. "How was the fair?"

"Ah, interesting," said Savannah. The other two snickered quietly.

Emma kissed her mom on the cheek and said, "Why all the cookies? Are we having a bake sale or something?" She grabbed three, handed one each to her friends and then took a big bite of the warm, gooey treat.

"Nope, I just felt like making cookies." Mrs. Reed grabbed the spatula, slipped it under the first cookie and slid it onto the cooling rack. "Did you girls get anything?"

"A few little goodies, nothing special," said Savannah as she wiped the crumbs from the corners of her mouth. She certainly wasn't going to tell Emma's mother what she had hidden in her purse. "But we had a lot of fun."

"That's nice. I'm glad you had a good time," smiled Mrs. Reed, preoccupied with her cookies.

After she placed the last cookie on the rack, Mrs. Reed scooted over to the bowl of dough and began scooping up globs of it and rolling it into large balls. She dropped them on the cookie sheet and said, "You girls hungry? I could whip you up some lunch."

"You don't need to do that, Mom. We can grab something out of the fridge."

"Nonsense. Just give me a minute to finish these, and then I'll make you girls something." She resumed her humming and shoved the full cookie sheet back into the oven.

"Thanks, Mom. We'll be up in my room." And then the three girls tromped up the stairs.

When the girls entered Emma's bedroom, Jade said, "Your mom was in a good mood, making us lunch and all."

"Yeah, I'm not sure what that's all about. But it's a nice change. She's been sort of bitchy to me and Dad lately." She sprawled out on her unmade bed. "So where shall we do it?"

"Do what," asked Jade.

"The reading. Where do you want to do the reading, Vannah?"

Savannah was hoping Emma had forgotten about it. But clearly she hadn't. She looked around the room. Emma's desk was covered in school papers and books. No room there. The bed looked lumpy with bunched up covers and buried pillows. There could have even been a body buried under there for all she knew.

"I don't know, how about the floor?"

"Great idea," said Emma as she slid off the bed and onto the floor. "What do you need? Candles? Incense?"

Savannah sat down next to her and crossed her legs Indian style. "Heck, I don't know." She pulled the deck of cards from her purse and looked at the box. It had seen better days. The corners, sides, and the flaps had been taped up. Without it, the box wouldn't have been a box at all, but a sheet of worn and frayed cardboard.

She pulled the deck of cards out and studied them, too. The corners showed the same frayed wear. The repeating blue and white star pattern on the back of the deck looked faded, like someone had set them in the sun for too long. She started to turn them over to look at the pictures on the front, but something made her stop. Instead, she handed the deck to Emma and said, "Shuffle."

Jade scooted in making a circle. "This is kind of exciting, don't you think, Vannah?"

Savannah just grunted. She was reserving judgment until after the reading. She wanted to see if what happened in the tent was a one-time fluke.

When Emma finished shuffling the deck she set it down in the center of their circle. "Now what?"

Savannah wasn't confident enough to attempt another "general" reading like she had done with Dominic. So she cut the deck into three piles, face down and said, "I think you're supposed to ask a question."

Emma thought for a moment and then said, "What are we having for lunch?"

"Really, Em? That's the question you want me to answer?" Savannah rolled her eyes and let out an exasperated breath.

Emma shrugged her shoulders apologetically.

Savannah flipped over one card from each pile and studied the pictures. When she touched the image of three women, each holding a gold cup, that familiar current of electricity shot through her body and an overwhelming smell of fish filled the room.

Savannah wrinkled her nose and said, "Tuna fish sandwiches." In her mind she saw a clear pitcher of liquid darkening in the afternoon sun. "Ice tea." The rich taste of warmed-up chocolate coated the inside of her mouth, and she added, "And chocolate chip cookies."

Jade scoffed, "I'm no psychic, but even I know that chocolate chip cookies are a good probability."

Savannah arched her eyebrows. "Hey, I'm just telling you what I see."

Before Emma could ask another question, a knock on the door caused Savannah to gather up the cards and discreetly slip them under her thigh.

"Here you go, girls," said Mrs. Reed as she opened the bedroom door. She walked in with a tray of sandwiches, cookies, and a clear pitcher of lemonade with three plastic glasses. She scooted over some of the books on Emma's desk and set the tray down. "Hope you like tuna fish. That's all I had."

"Oh, you brought lemonade. I thought for sure it would have been sun tea," said Emma.

Her mom stopped at the door. "Well, I almost brought you girls tea, but I decided to make a pitcher of lemonade instead. Enjoy." She scowled at Emma's unmade bed. "And bring down the tray of dirty dishes when you're finished. I don't want ants or mice coming in here."

When she closed the door, Emma looked at Savannah and said, "Well, two out of three isn't bad."

Savannah grunted and pulled the deck from underneath her thigh. She had Emma cut the deck, once more, into three piles, face down. "Okay, ask another question."

"What color dress am I wearing to graduation?"

In her mind, Savannah saw Emma dressed in a cute, formfitting, floral dress that zipped up the back, and she heard a specific color being whispered in her left ear. "Those boots we saw at the fair would have gone nice with it. It's pink."

Emma hopped up and went to her closet. She slid open the door and pulled out a fuchsia dress that still had the tags dangling from it. "I picked this up yesterday. I was going to see what you guys thought of it." She shoved it back in her closet and plopped back down. "That was pretty impressive. Okay, let's see what else you can tell me." She thought for a moment and then said, "What are we having for dinner tonight?"

"C'mon, Em, can't you think of something more, I don't know, important or profound to ask?" said Savannah as she flipped three more cards over.

An overwhelming feeling of anguish filled Savannah's heart, making her want to cry. In her mind she saw Emma's mother standing over the bathroom sink crying. Then the picture shifted to an image of Mrs. Reed pouring some gin into her glass of ice tea. She took a sip, scrunched up her face and dumped it down the sink. Then she made a pitcher of lemonade, poured some into her glass and topped it off with a healthy pour of gin. She took a sip, swallowed, and then guzzled the entire drink down. Then she went back into the kitchen and finished making cookies.

Savannah had been right about the ice tea. But it was Mrs. Reed's decision that changed the outcome. She looked up at Emma and in a subdued voice said, "Pizza. You're having pizza for dinner tonight." She gathered up the cards and put them back in the box. "I'm sorry, but I'm really tired. If I decide to throw away the deck, I'll give you another reading before I do, okay?"

Emma must have sensed the change in Savannah's demeanor. She stood up and said, "Sure, no problem. Let's have lunch."

Savannah stood up and said, "I hope you don't mind, but I think I'm just going to go on home."

"Do you want me to drive you?" Emma offered.

"No, that's okay. It's not that far, I'll walk."

Emma walked over to the tray of sandwiches and cookies, and grabbed one of each. "At least take these with you," she said handing them to Savannah. "You sure you don't want a ride?"

Savannah was sure. She needed time to think. Those images of Emma's mother guzzling gin in the middle of the day and sobbing uncontrollably in the bathroom worried her. She always thought of Mrs. Reed as being a happy and stable person. At least that's the picture she always painted. But those images contradicted what Savannah thought to be true.

Should I have told Em? she wondered as she said goodbye to her friends.

Mrs. Reed opened the front door for her. "Come back anytime, Vannah. You know you're always welcome."

Savannah gave her a lingering one-arm hug, thinking that maybe she could use one right about now. "Thanks for the sandwich and cookies, Mrs. Reed."

Twenty minutes later when Savannah walked in her front door, she immediately felt guilty. And knowing what was in her purse made her cheek's flush when her father asked her what they did at the fair.

"Oh, you know, the usual," she said as she hurried past him with only a quick peck on his cheek. "Be back in a minute. I have to go to the bathroom."

That was true, but she needed to find a hiding place for those cards more than she needed to pee.

Once inside her room, she closed the door and glanced around. *Where? Where should I hide these?*

Her mother always put her clean clothes away so she couldn't hide them in a drawer. She thought about hiding them under her mattress, but her mother always changed her sheets. This was one time when she wished that she had been the one doing those mundane chores instead of her mother.

The back of the closet had possibility. But what if her mother decided to clean out her closet? "No, no, not there," she muttered.

She looked at her antique desk. "Bingo." She squatted down by the bottom drawer, pulled it all the way out and placed the deck in the dead space between where the drawer stopped and the back of the desk started. Her mother would never look there. She pushed the drawer closed, stood up and let out a pent-up sigh. She didn't realize she had been holding her breath. Now she felt that her secret was safe, for the time being anyway.

That evening when the Swift family sat down for dinner, Savannah bowed her head and folded her hands when her father blessed the food. And when he asked her what she saw at the street fair, she looked down at her plate and casually replied, "Oh, you know, the usual: jewelry, pottery, greasy food . . . And psychics."

Chapter 10

Pastor Swift's fork slipped through his fingers and clanked loudly when it hit the rim of his plate. He stared at Savannah and said, "Psychics?"

"Yeah, we saw a tent that had a tarot card reader."

Her mother stared at her intently. "You didn't go into the tent did you?"

Savannah immediately regretted telling them about Dominic. And she wasn't even sure why she did. It just came out.

"Well, Jade wanted to buy a reading, so we went in."

"You didn't buy a reading, did you?" Her father's intimidating stare threatened to bore a hole right through her.

"No, I didn't *buy* a reading." She didn't feel the need to tell him that a reading was provided to her free of charge. But she also knew that it was just this side of lying, and that made her feel terrible.

Pastor Swift picked up his fork and scooped up some mashed potatoes. "Well I should hope that you would know better. Those kinds of people are dangerous. They prey on the young and the naive, and then they suck them in with their lies." He shoved the potatoes into his mouth and swallowed. "Things like tarot cards and Ouija boards are tools of the Devil. You need to stay as far away from those kinds of people as possible. They're nothing but evil." He looked at his wife who continued to stare at Savannah. "I can't believe Scottsbluff would allow those kinds of people at the fair. I'm going to have a talk with the city council about that."

"I think you should," said Mrs. Swift without taking her eyes off of Savannah.

Savannah thought about how kind and compassionate Dominic had been to her and her friends. He didn't seem evil at all.

"The guy who did the reading for Jade was really nice, and he seemed genuinely interested in her."

Pastor Swift took a bite of meatloaf and chewed vigorously. "Of course he was interested in her. That's how they get you hooked. They tell you something you want to hear, and then they reel you in to become one of Satan's followers." He scooped up another fork full of mash potatoes and pointed it at Savannah. "It's a surefire way to possession."

Kyle had been playing volcano with his mash potatoes. The once buttery lava that had traveled down micro trenches made by his fork now coagulated in a slick pool around the base. "What does possession mean, Dad?" he asked and then took a bite of potatoes and squished the mash through the gap in his two front teeth.

"It means that the Devil has taken over your body and makes you do bad things like get into fights and steal."

"Fights? Cool," said Kyle and then flashed him a toothy potato grin.

"Kyle!" snapped Mrs. Swift. "Stop saying everything is 'cool.' Possession is certainly not 'cool.' And how many times have I told you to stop playing with your food?" She reached for his plate. "Are you finished?"

When Kyle nodded, she picked up his plate, stacked it on top of hers and walked them over to the sink. Then she came back and picked up Savannah's empty dish. But instead of walking it over to the sink, she lingered at her side with her hand on Savannah's shoulder. "Vannah, please promise me that you won't get involved with something like that."

Something like that? I won't get involved with something 'like' that. I might get involved with 'that', but I'll stay away from things that are 'like' that.

Savannah knew that it might have been semantics, but she looked up at her mom and said, "I promise that I won't get involved with something like that." She felt that knot of deception forming in her stomach again.

Pastor Swift handed his empty plate to his wife and said, "You know, Vannah, you've given me a great idea for next week's sermon, Satan's tools and the effects they have on our children."

Savannah pulled her eyes from her dad and stared out the kitchen window at the diminishing Nebraska sunset. *Why did I open my mouth?* She never should have said anything. She could have just gotten rid of the cards and no one would have ever known. Now, because of her big mouth, the entire congregation was going to hear about it.

~~~~~~~~~~~~~~~~

That evening after she got ready for bed, Savannah grabbed her laptop and hopped on her bed. She typed the word 'psychic' into a Google search and read the definition out loud. "Relating to or denoting faculties or phenomena that are apparently inexplicable by natural laws, especially involving telepathy or clairvoyance."

Well, that certainly described her. *Inexplicable by natural laws.* She couldn't explain the crystal clear voice that whispered in her ear when she turned the cards over. She knew the voices weren't in her head. They were real with a very distinct tone.

She typed in 'telepathy' next. "The supposed communication of thoughts or ideas by means other than the known senses." That described her vision of Dominic as a child riding his tricycle. Something communicated that home movie to her, but what? Was it from God? The Devil? Or was it from some other source?

She typed in the word 'clairvoyant' and read the definition. "A person who claims to have a supernatural ability to perceive events in the future or beyond normal sensory contact." She *knew* without a doubt that Dominic was going to ask his girlfriend to marry him. She *saw* him ask her. She saw him put the ring on her finger. She saw her say "yes". And she saw the man in the restaurant get sick.

Though there was no way to verify that the man in the restaurant came down with food poisoning, the ring in Dominic's pocket proved she was right. Savannah swallowed the lump in her throat and whispered, "Oh no, I'm a psychic!"

A light tap on the door pulled her from her thoughts. "Honey, you decent?"

"Yeah, Mom. Come on in." She closed her computer and slid it under the bed. *Out of sight, out of mind,* she thought. Her mother never questioned what she did on her computer, but given their dinner conversation, she didn't want to encourage that possibility.

Mrs. Swift poked her head through the opened door. "I just wanted to come in and say good night." She walked in and sat on the edge of the bed, patted her daughter's leg and said, "I'm glad you and your friends had a good time at the fair today." She seemed to hesitate. "And I'm glad you've promised to not get involved with all that psychic stuff. The Bible warns about people who use divination to tell the future. But more importantly, it warns us about the ramifications for those who seek out those kinds of people. There's a story in the book of Samuel that talks about what happened to King Saul when he sought out the help of a witch."

Savannah sat up and folded her legs Indian style. "So there really are witches and psychics?"

"Well according to the Bible there are."

Savannah sucked in slightly, pulled her knees up and hugged her legs. "Oh, I didn't know that. So what happened to King Saul?"

"King Saul was going into battle with the Philistines and wanted to know if he was going to win. Instead of praying to God, he disguised his identity and went to see the Witch of En-dor, a medium who practiced divination."

Savannah wasn't sure if this biblical confirmation made her feel better or worse. If the Bible acknowledged the presence of psychics then that meant it must be true. "So what happened?"

"Well, he asked the medium to conjure up the spirit of the prophet Samuel. At first she refused him and said that to do so would bring death upon her because King Saul had decreed that all witches and those that practiced divination were to be banished from the land and killed.

"When he assured her that no harm would come to her, she saw the image of Samuel rise up from the earth, and she cried out, 'Why have you tricked me? You are King Saul.'" Her mother stared into Savannah's wide eyes.

"So she *knew* it was the king in spite of his disguise?" Savannah said.

"Mm hmm. The king asked her to describe the apparition. And from her description he knew that he was in the presence of Samuel's spirit. The spirit spoke to King Saul and said, 'Since you have forsaken God by seeking guidance elsewhere, you and your sons will die in battle.'"

"And did they? Die, I mean?" Savannah wasn't sure she wanted to know. What if she had already set God's wrath in motion by doing those two little readings? She thought about the cards hidden in her desk and knew that her mother might not know they were there, but God sure as heck did.

"Oh, yes. His sons died in battle that following day just as predicted. King Saul was gravely wounded and captured by the Philistines. He was so afraid of being tortured that he ended up killing himself."

Savannah gasped. "He committed suicide?"

"Yes he did. And his sons suffered the consequences of their father's actions." Savannah's mother didn't break eye contact. "The sins of the father . . ." Her words trailed off.

Savannah wanted to cry. She would never forgive herself if something happened to her parents or her friends or even her future children because she caved in to her curiosity.

Silence filled the space between mother and daughter as they stared at each other.

Savannah was tempted to turn away, but to do so would trigger a warning sign to her mother. Her mother knew her habits, her idiosyncrasies, and when she was hiding something.

Finally, her mom smiled, releasing the tension between them and said, "All right then, I'll see you in the morning." She kissed Savannah on the forehead and added, "Sweet dreams."

Sweet dreams? How can I even sleep after you've told me a story like that? God's going to send His wrath down on me and everyone I love, and I'm going to spend eternity in Hell!

Savannah shut off her bedroom light and crawled under the covers. She tried to close her eyes, but they kept popping open. Snippets of the day's events robbed her of any sleep.

Dominic, the readings, the cards, Mrs. Reed crying. They all played over and over in her mind like an endless video loop.

Finally, she laced her fingers together and placed them over her chest. She stared up beyond her ceiling into the heavens and prayed, "God, I'm a good person, you know that. I try to do what's right. I'm helpful, and I go to church. I believe in you, and I trust you to watch over me, my family, and my friends." She took a deep breath. "But I'm so confused. I don't want to be involved with anything that is of the Devil, but I can't explain what happened to me today.

"Dad says these things are of Satan, but yet when I saw Mrs. Reed crying in the bathroom and drinking, my heart broke for her. All I wanted to do was help her. How can that be considered evil?"

She thought about Dominic and wondered if he did ask his girlfriend to marry him tonight. Maybe he hadn't planned on ordering the sea bass. But if he had, then she saved him from getting food poisoning. Surely that was a good thing.

"I just want to do what's right, that's all. Please show me the truth. Amen."

Within moments, Savannah's eyes became heavy. Sleep followed and so did her dreams.

Chapter 11

Near Carson City, Nevada
May 19, 2009
11:00 PM

"Katie, if anything happens to me, promise me you'll take this evidence to the police."

She replayed Marty's last words to her over in her mind as she exited off of Highway 50 and turned left onto the deserted rural road. The Corvette's headlights grazed over the road sign planted on the shoulder, just above the ditch.

Six Mile Canyon Road.

If Katie did have to follow through with that promise, then that meant Marty didn't make it. The thought made her shudder. If, God forbid, he did die, then in order for her to fulfill that promise, she needed to know exactly what evidence Marty had discovered.

She glanced in her rearview mirror and released her breath, relieved that no one had followed her.

The road cut through Little Lyon, now nearly a ghost town. Seeing only a smattering of interior lights, Katie eased her foot off of the gas bringing the engine's rumble down to a purr so as not to wake what few residents remained.

Once she moved past the houses, the road began to curve around the base of the mountains rising up on either side. She pressed her foot down on the gas pedal, releasing the low guttural growl once more, and took the curves with confidence.

A few miles into the canyon and on the right hand side of the road, a ten-foot tall, chain link fence with barbed wire around the top indicated the beginning of private property. Signs hanging every twenty-five feet warned people to "KEEP OUT."

She drove another half a mile and turned right onto a dirt road, stopping in front of a metal gate. Her headlights illuminated a "NO TRESSPASSING" sign posted in the middle of it and another sign underneath it that read, "Comstock Mining Company."

Katie got out of the car and walked up to the gate. It looked like someone had forgotten to lock it. A padlock and chain had been threaded through the fence and left dangling. She pushed the gate all the way open, got back in her car and began to carefully drive up the steep dirt road leading up the mountain.

Once she crested the top, the road flattened out and led her toward a grove of pine trees in the distance. Within minutes, the road sliced through the stand of trees and spit her out into a vast, open, flat area a quarter of a mile wide and littered with heavy equipment. She slowed down and crawled in between the rows of behemoth yellow dump trucks with tires the size of her car and equally mammoth bulldozers with raised buckets full of iron teeth.

As she drove by the machines, her headlights cast moving shadows on them making them seem alive. Intimidated by their monstrous size and the eerie feeling they evoked, she wrapped sweaty hands around the steering wheel and said, "This is ridiculous. Just get a grip, Katie, there's nothing up here."

She pulled up next to a prefab modular building at the far end of the equipment lot and paused. Fifty feet ahead of her was a drop off, leading down into a steep and treacherous ravine. She put the car in reverse, preparing to turn around, when her cell phone rang.

"Hello?"

"Just what do you think you're doing?" came a gruff voice over the phone.

"Who is this?"

"I think you have a pretty good idea who this is."

"How did you get this number?" Katie swallowed the fear creeping up her throat.

"It wasn't hard. You know, you really shouldn't leave your personal information just lying around where anybody can get a hold of it." The caller paused. "Now give it back, and I won't hurt you."

Katie glanced back in the rearview mirror. No lights followed her. "I don't know what you're talking about."

The person on the other end of the line let out a low growl. "Don't play dumb with me. If you don't give it back, you'll end up just like your boyfriend." The caller paused. "He's dead, you know. Didn't make it."

Katie bit back the tears. "You're lying. I'm at the hospital with him right now."

"Oh, so you're in Carson City, huh?" The caller laughed. "What am I, stupid? You think I don't know where you really are? There's no way down from the mine except through me."

Katie sucked in her breath. *He knows I'm up here.*

The caller was right. There was no back road, no alternate exit. The only way back to civilization and safety was by going down the same way she came up. She glanced at a manila envelope on the passenger's seat. Her gaze migrated over to the console where a silver flash drive lay propped up in the cup holder. "I don't have what you're looking for. Marty has it," said Katie as she did a three-point turn, flipping the car around.

"See, now there you go lying again."

"You're the one who's lying. Marty's not dead."

"Oh, he's dead all right. Because I got to him first. And since he didn't have it on him, that must mean he gave it to you. So, I'll ask you one more time. Where is it?"

"I swear to you, I don't have what you're looking for."

The caller let out a *tsk, tsk, tsk.* "Dang almighty, Katie. You should have listened to me when you had the chance."

Suddenly, a pair of headlights flashed on and shined right through the Corvette's windshield, nearly blinding her. She had been so engrossed in the phone call that she had failed to notice the pickup truck creeping up behind her. The truck revved its engine and slowly rolled forward, closing the gap between them.

I'm trapped!

Katie squelched a cry. To her left was the building, to her right, rows of heavy equipment, and behind her that sheer cliff. Her only option was to try to get around him. She revved her engine and turned on her high beams in an attempt to blind the driver of the truck. But they only illuminated the heavy industrial push guard mounted on the front grill, making it impossible to see who was driving.

"One more chance, Katie." The headlights grew larger, now only a few yards away. "Where is it?"

"Please don't hurt me," begged Katie, trying to appeal to the caller. "I'm telling you the truth. I don't have it."

"Do you know where it is?"

"No." Katie's voice began to break. "H-he didn't tell me. I swear."

The truck came to a stop in front of her, and all Katie could hear over the phone was a slow release of the caller's breath. Finally, he said, "Well, if ya don't have it, ya don't have it." And then the driver gunned his truck, ramming it into the front of Katie's car.

Katie screamed when her car lurched backwards. She stomped on the brakes with both feet causing the tires to lock and squeal, but the truck kept forcing the Corvette toward the edge of the cliff. "Stop!" she screeched into the phone.

"Sorry, Katie. But you two should have minded your own business." He grunted and then laughed menacingly into the phone.

The driver of the truck pushed the Corvette backwards until its rear wheels dropped over the edge of the cliff. And then he gave it one more push, sending the car plummeting backwards over the edge.

Katie screamed as the cell phone flew out of her hands. She reached for the steering wheel and gripped it, bracing for impact.

Chapter 12

Savannah's eyes sprang open, and she sat straight up in bed, panting and gasping for air. She grabbed the covers and yanked them to her chest. She tried to wiggle her fingers, but cramps kept them ridged and paralyzed into the shape of claws. It was as if she had been gripping something and holding on for dear life.

She looked behind her, for what, she didn't know. But the thought of eminent danger prompted her to reach over and turn on her bedside lamp. There was nothing there — no Boogey Man, no robber, nothing out of the ordinary. She leaned against the backboard of her bed, put her head in her hands and started to cry. That overwhelming feeling of panic and helplessness made her sob even harder. What had brought this on? Was it the readings? The cards?

And then she remembered the dream.

She swiped at her tears with the back of her hands and whispered, "H-her name is Katie."

For the rest of the night Savannah tossed and thrashed. Images of that woman going over the cliff backwards kept playing over and over in her mind keeping her from falling back to sleep. When daylight broke, she got out of bed, quietly got ready for church, and went down to the kitchen.

An hour later Mrs. Swift shuffled into the kitchen. With a wide yawn, she tightened the belt around her robe and stopped abruptly when she saw Savannah. She sniffed the air and then looked at the cup clutched between Savannah's hands. "You made coffee?" She grabbed a mug from the cupboard and filled it three quarters full. "You're up early."

With shaky hands, Savannah lifted the cup to her lips and took a sip. "Yeah, I didn't sleep very well last night."

"Oh?" Her mother pulled out the chair next to her. "What's wrong?"

"I don't know. I guess I've got a lot on my mind." She didn't want to tell her that she had that dream again because she knew her mother would say that it stemmed from all that talk about psychics. "You know, graduation and all. Going off to college."

"Ah, honey, are you concerned about leaving home?" Her mother tasted the coffee and scrunched her nose. She stood up and walked over to the sink, topped off the cup with hot water and said, "Lincoln is only six hours away. So you can come home on the weekends. Isn't Jade going to U of N, too?"

"Yeah, but she's going to Omaha instead."

"Sweetie, that's only an hour away. I'm sure you two will find a way to see each other."

"Maybe, but you never know. Things can change." Savannah thought about what Dominic had said to Jade during the reading. *'You might have to postpone college for a semester.'*

"Well, I wouldn't worry too much about it." Mrs. Swift smiled at her daughter as she leaned against the sink. "I can't believe you're graduating next week. It seems like yesterday you were in kindergarten. And now here you are getting ready to go off to college." She let out a contented sigh. "I'm so proud of you, and of the remarkable young woman you've become."

Savannah felt guilty and embarrassed. Would her mother still be proud of her if she knew she was delving into that forbidden realm of divination? Somehow she doubted it.

"Have you thought about what you might want for a graduation present?"

"Not really." Savannah took another sip of the strong brew and set the cup down on the table. "I have some ideas, but nothing I'm really crazy about."

Mrs. Swift put one more splash of hot water in her cup and sipped the weakened brew. "Well, think about it, okay? Think about something that you really want." When she heard the *whoosh* of the upstairs toilet she looked at the clock on the wall and said, "Sounds like you're father's up. I guess I better go get ready for church." She started to walk away then looked back at Savannah's shaky hands and said, "Maybe you should switch to decaf. You're too young to have the jitters."

A couple of moments after her mother left the kitchen, Savannah reached down and grabbed the cell phone out of her purse. She scrolled through the contacts and punched the call button. When a sleepy voice said *'hello?'* Savannah whispered, "Jade, I hope I didn't wake you."

Jade cleared the sleep out of her throat. "No, that's okay. What's up?"

"I need to talk with you and Em. Do you think we could meet at the library later this morning?"

"What for?" Jade wanted to know.

"I had another dream last night, and I need to check something out, but I don't want to do it here."

"Sure. You want me to call Em?"

"Yeah, that'd be great, thanks."

"What time do you want to meet?"

"Church ends at eleven, so I could be there by eleven thirty."

"Okay, we'll meet you there." Jade paused. "Vannah, is everything all right?"

Savannah looked toward the doorway just to make sure she was still alone. "I can't talk about it right now." She lowered her voice to a whisper. "But I need to do another reading. I think I know who the girl in my dream is."

"What do you mean you know who she is? You think she's a real person?" said Jade.

"Yeah, I'm beginning to think so. And I'm pretty sure her being down at the bottom of that ravine was no accident."

"What makes you think that?" said Jade.

"I'll explain everything when I see you," she said in a hurried and hushed voice.

They said goodbye and then Savannah went upstairs to her bedroom to retrieve her deck of tarot cards.

~~~~~~~~~~~~~~~~

Like every Sunday, the Swift family arrived at church forty-five minutes early so that Pastor Swift could go over his sermon one final time in the solitude of his office.

Mrs. Swift led Savannah and Kyle to the front pew where they would sit for both services. Kyle slid in first, followed by Mrs. Swift and finally Savannah, who sat next to the aisle.

Savannah disliked sitting in the front row with scores of people staring at her back. She would have preferred to hide in the rear of the church, but her father insisted they sit up front so that his congregation could see what a devoted and well-behaved family should look like.

When the church sanctuary began to fill with worshippers, Mrs. Swift leaned over to Savannah and whispered, "Are you feeling all right? You've been very quiet this morning. You're not still concerned about college, are you?"

Savannah shrugged. "No, not really. I've been a little worried about passing my finals."

That was a bold-faced lie. She felt quite confident that she would nail them with no problem, but she needed an excuse to get away from her family today.

"Would you mind dropping me off at the library after church? I really need to study." She hated lying to her mother. But she figured that as far as lies go, this was a mild one, and hopefully a forgivable one.

Mrs. Swift patted her leg. "Of course. Stay as long as you need to. Just call me when you're ready, and I'll come pick you up."

"Um, actually, Jade and Em are going to meet me there. We're going to study together and then Em will drive me home when we're done." The lie coated her tongue making it feel thick and heavy.

Her mother draped an arm around Savannah's shoulder, gave it a squeeze and said, "I'm so proud of you. I'm very fortunate that you are my daughter."

That made Savannah feel even worse, but she smiled anyway.

At eight thirty sharp, Pastor Swift approached the pulpit. He flashed the congregation an adult version of her little brother's toothy grin. Savannah was grateful that she had inherited her mother's slight features instead of her father's horsey attributes.

Pastor Swift's eyes settled on Savannah momentarily and then bounced back to his congregation. "Good morning everyone and welcome. It's good to see you all here."

The announcements were given, they sang several songs, and then Pastor Swift began his sermon with, "We have a terrible problem here in Scottsbluff. We are losing our children to Satan, and if we don't do something about it right now, their souls will be lost forever."

He looked down at Savannah and gestured toward her. "My daughter, Savannah, informed me there was a psychic reader at the street fair yesterday. Now, I don't need to remind you that our children are very impressionable, and things like that can lead to lying, deceit, promiscuity – all the things that the Bible warns us against."

Oh, dear God!

Savannah wanted to die! He wasn't supposed to do a sermon about that until next week. She felt the eyes of those sitting behind her peeling the skin off of her back and scrutinizing her exposed soul. Why had he brought it up, and why did he have to mention her name?

Savannah, they fear what they don't know.

A crystal clear voice whispered in her left ear causing her to turn around and glance at the person behind her. She looked over at her mother and said, "What did you say?"

Mrs. Swift whispered, "I didn't say anything."

Help her, Savannah. Help Katie.

Savannah barely heard the rest of the service. All she could think about was the woman in the Corvette. Who was this Katie person, and what happened to her? What was she looking for in the middle of the night? And who was the man in the pickup truck?

"Savannah. Here . . ." A whisper pulled her back to the present. A young usher standing in the aisle held out the donation plate, urging her to take it.

"Oh, sorry." She opened her purse intending to pull out her tithes, but when she saw her deck of tarot cards she quickly closed it, handed the plate to her mother and whispered, "Sorry. I spent it all at the fair. I'll give double next week."

Now the lies were flowing like water.

Her mother scowled and dropped an extra ten dollars in the plate for her daughter.

Savannah knew that lying about tithing would surely send her straight to hell. And the thought of having to sit through this sermon a second time caused her to fidget. She set her purse on the floor next to her feet, slumped lower in her seat and thought, *Dear God, let me get through this. And help me find out everything there is to know about this woman named Katie.*

Chapter 13

". . . and may the Lord shine His countenance upon you and grant you peace. Amen."

For the second time that morning, Pastor Swift recited the closing prayer. The moment he finished, Savannah sprang to her feet anxious to exit the church. It felt stifling in there to her, like she couldn't breathe.

A battle between the angelic voice whispering in her ear and the condemning words of her father raged in her mind.

Those things are of the Devil.

They fear what they don't know.

They're Satan's tools.

You have a gift.

They lead to lies and deceit.

They lead to the truth.

So who was right? Savannah felt more confused than ever.

"What did you think of the sermon?" Mrs. Swift asked Savannah as they trotted down the church steps.

Savannah's strides quickened the closer she got to their car. "I don't know. Okay, I guess. But why did he have to single me out, both times, in front of the congregation?"

"Because you brought the situation to his attention, and because you're his daughter. It's up to you to always strive to set a good example for others to follow. And as a preacher's daughter, people are going to scrutinize you and your actions more than most."

"But it was embarrassing." Her words came out curt.

Mrs. Swift grabbed Savannah by the arm, stopping her. She glanced around and lowered her voice, her eyes, narrowing. "You don't know who might have watched you go into that tent yesterday. Your father was just protecting you. Do you understand that?"

Savannah wanted to cry. Of course she understood it. She just didn't like it. She thought about Dominic and how he openly embraced his abilities. Even if she wanted to, she would never be able to share her gift as freely as he did. Her parents would make sure of that. She hadn't decided what she was going to do about the cards yet, but whatever she did, she'd have to do it in secrecy.

By the time Savannah got to Scottsbluff Public Library, Emma and Jade were already waiting by the front door.

"Hey, girl. How was church?" said Jade to Savannah as she trotted up the library steps.

Savannah hugged her friends and said, "Ugh, don't ask. It was brutal. You'll never guess what the sermon was about. Psychics!"

"No-o-o-o," they both echoed as all three walked through the front door and headed straight for the computer room.

"Oh, yeah. And my dad said, in front of the entire congregation, that I was the one who told him about Dominic being at the street fair." She cringed. "I was mortified."

"That's horrible," said Emma. "So what did he say about it?"

Savannah waved her hand like she was shooing away a fly. "Ugh, I don't want to talk about it anymore. We have more important things to do."

When they entered the computer room, Savannah sat down at one of the computers and typed in the words Carson City.

Emma pulled up a chair next to Savannah and said, "Jade said you learned more about the girl from your dreams. Do you really think she's a real person and that someone might have hurt her on purpose?"

"I know it sounds crazy, but yeah, I think she's real. And based on what I saw in my dreams, she went over a cliff somewhere close to Carson City, Nevada." She looked at her friends. "I didn't even know there *was* a Carson City, Nevada."

Jade rolled her eyes as she pulled another chair over. "How could you not know about Carson City? It's the capital of Nevada, for Pete's sake."

"All right, Miss Smarty Pants. Guess I just forgot. It's not like I've ever been there." Savannah pulled up a Google map of Carson City and the surrounding area. "She was driving on some mountain road late at night." Savannah zoomed in on the map until she could see individual roads. When she saw the familiar name, she gasped. "Oh, my God. I can't believe it."

"What? What can't you believe?" Jade moved her chair closer to the screen. "What do you see?"

Savannah saw it plain as day right there on the map. But she just couldn't accept that her dreams had provided such a specific detail.

"Six Mile Canyon Road. That's the road sign I saw in my dream."

Emma sucked in her breath. "Vannah! That's incredible. That's something that you just can't make up. It's such an uncommon name. What else do you remember about the dream?"

Savannah pinched her brow together. "I don't know. I can't remember anything else."

"Think," Jade told her. "Try to recall as many details as you can."

Savannah closed her eyes for a moment trying to conjure up the images of the car, of Katie, and of the mountain roads, but nothing else came to mind. She slowly shook her head. "I can't remember."

"Well, let's think about this for a minute," said Jade. "Zoom back out on the map." When Savannah returned the map to normal size, Jade studied it for a moment. "It looks like this Six Mile Canyon Road is fairly close to Carson City and Reno. Type in both cities, and let's see if there's any information about a missing woman."

Savannah typed in the name, Katie, missing person, Reno, Nevada. The first entry was from the Reno Gazette and dated May 29th, 2009. Savannah clicked on the link. There was a photograph of a young woman who looked to be a few years older than Savannah. She had shoulder length tobacco brown hair that feathered round her face, accentuating her soft, liquid, Bambi eyes. Full and parted lips revealed a white Colgate smile.

Though Savannah had not actually seen what the woman in her dreams looked like, there was something familiar about that picture. "I think this might be her," whispered Savannah. She read the headline out loud. "'Reno Woman Still Missing. Twenty-three year old Kaitlyn 'Katie' McCall has been missing now for over a week. Sources say that neither her family nor her friends have any idea of her whereabouts.

"'Mr. and Mrs. McCall first reported their daughter missing the night of May 20th.

"'When interviewed by the Reno Police Department, the McCalls said that at first they thought their daughter, who had recently moved to Carson City, might have gone somewhere with her boyfriend, twenty-four year old Martin Dolan of Lake Tahoe. But when they contacted Carson Tahoe Hospital the night of the alleged disappearance, they discovered that Mr. Dolan had been admitted the night before with a bullet wound.

"'The McCalls have offered a five thousand dollar reward for any information leading to the safe return of their daughter.

"'If you have any information about Katie McCall's whereabouts, please call the Reno police department.'"

The three girls stared at each other, and Jade said, "Do you know what the date is today?"

"It's the twentieth. Why?" said Savannah.

"Don't you see?" said Jade. "I think there's a reason why you dreamt about her last night, and why it was so vivid this time. It was her anniversary." She looked at Katie's picture. "She went missing three years ago to the day."

They all silently stared at Katie until Emma said, "So now what do we do?"

For the next two hours Savannah and her friends searched on line for anything they could find on Katie McCall, but the information turned out to be limited.

Katie's parents had put up a website not long after their daughter's disappearance. People were encouraged to leave messages and any information about her. Some of the entries were from friends telling the McCalls to "Keep the faith." Some posted premature condolences for their loss, while others posted possible Katie sightings. But none of those posts were ever substantiated.

The last entry by someone other than Katie's parents was dated a year ago, and it looked like the website hadn't been visited since except for repeated weekly posts by her parents saying, "Please help us find our daughter."

Savannah leaned back in her chair and stared into the warm, chocolate brown, doe eyes staring back at her. Now she knew, without a doubt, that Katie McCall was a real person, not just part of some fragmented nightmare cause by watching a scary television show.

As far as Savannah could tell, somehow, though she had no idea how or why, this woman had been reaching out to her, begging for help. She let out a deep sigh knowing that it was time for her to reach back. She looked at her friends and said, "I think I need to do another reading."

Chapter 14

The girls decided that the best place to do the reading would be at Jade's house because they would have the place to themselves.

"My parents drove to Cheyenne this morning to pick up their new Jeep," said Jade. She told them that she suspected the reason for the new vehicle was so that they could give her their old car as a graduation present.

"That'll be great. Then you can chauffer us around instead of me doing it all the time," said Emma as she pulled into Jade's driveway and parked.

The girls got out of the car and walked up to the front door. "So when are they coming back?" Savannah asked as Jade stuck the key in and unlocked the door.

"Not until later tonight. They said they were going to stay up there and do some shopping. So quit worrying. Nobody's going to know about this except for the three of us. This will be our little secret."

"I hope you're right," mumbled Savannah. "The last thing I need is for this to get back to my parents."

"It won't. Now where do you want to do the reading?" said Jade as she stepped into the entryway followed by the two girls.

"I guess it doesn't matter," said Savannah.

Jade stopped at the arched entryway to the living room. "Then how about in here?"

Savannah looked around the room and spotted a rectangular coffee table with a glass top that looked suitable. She pointed to it and said, "I'll do it over there. If you're sure your parents won't come home unexpectedly."

"Vannah, I'm sure. So relax, okay?"

They pulled the coffee table away from the couch and then tossed three oversized pillows on the floor. Savannah sat down on one of the pillows and pulled the deck of cards out of her purse. She took them out of the box and set them face down in the middle of the table while Jade took a seat opposite her.

Emma was about to sit down but then said, "Hold on a minute. I better go to the bathroom first. Don't start without me." And then she trotted down the hall.

When Savannah heard the bathroom door close she leaned over the table toward Jade and whispered, "I didn't tell you what I saw when I did Em's reading yesterday."

Jade leaned in closer and whispered, "What did you see?"

Savannah told her about the vision of Emma's mother crying in the bathroom and about the gin in the lemonade. "I felt bad for Mrs. Reed. I don't know why she was so sad. But I could feel her pain. So that's why I gave her a big hug before I left."

"Did you smell any alcohol on her when you hugged her?"

Savannah shook her head. "No. But maybe she drank after we left. Or it's possible that it's something that will happen in the future. Or maybe she drank it earlier and used mouthwash. I just don't know."

"So are you going to tell Em?"

Savannah shrugged. "I haven't decided yet. I'm torn about what I should do. A part of me feels like I might have seen something that I shouldn't have. And I don't want to upset Em by telling her. What do you think I should do?"

Jade tilted her head to the side and gave her a soft smile. "I don't know, but you'll figure it out."

"Figure what out?" said Emma as she entered the living room and plopped down on the pillow next to Jade.

"Uh, I was telling Jade that I'm still not sure what I should do with the cards, whether I should keep them or get rid of them." Another lie. They were coming out way too frequently and much too easily.

"Oh. Well maybe we can ask the cards what you should do with them."

"I'm not sure it works that way, Em," said Savannah as she stared at the deck.

Part of her was anxious to do another reading. She wanted to see if she could receive any new information about Katie McCall. Maybe the cards would reveal different details, ones that weren't in either her dreams or the newspaper articles. But a part of her felt apprehensive. She knew that the minute her fingers touched those cards, her head would be bombarded with images and voices that she could not control.

Her intentions were to focus the reading on Katie, but what if she uncovered something more about Mrs. Reed? Or saw something bad about Jade, Emma, or her family? Or what if she inadvertently conjured up a demon? She hesitated and said, "Maybe we should say a prayer first."

Jade and Emma glanced sideways at each other.

Savannah knew that neither of them were particularly religious. But since she was doing the reading she felt it was her responsibility to protect them. And this was the only way she knew how.

The two girls shrugged and Jade said, "Sure. I guess that's okay." They all bowed their heads and waited.

Finally, Savannah raised her head and said, "I don't know what to pray." She'd heard hundreds of different prayers in the seventeen years of going to church. But none of them seemed appropriate for this occasion.

"Well, make something up," said Emma.

"Yeah, Vannah. I don't think it really matters what you say. Just 'Dear Lord, blah, blah, blah, amen,' and you're done."

Savannah took a deep breath and let it out. "Okay, I'll give it a whirl." She still wasn't sure what to say, but she bowed her head again and prayed, "Dear Lord, open my eyes so that I may see beyond this realm of possibility and know the truth in all things. And protect us from any evil entity that may try to come through the veil and harm us. May only good come out of these readings. Amen."

Jade raised her head and her eyebrows. "Well, that was . . . interesting. Very new agey."

Savannah grabbed the cards and said, "We'll see if it works. So who wants the first reading?"

It was determined that Emma would go first. She shuffled the cards and cut them into three piles face down. Savannah still didn't feel confident enough to do a general reading, so she decided that they would go straight to the question and answer portion.

Emma asked her first question. "Is Katie McCall alive or dead?"

Savannah turned over three cards, one from each pile. The first image was of a skeleton dressed in a black robe and holding a sickle. Beyond the sickle, a white rose bloomed. Savannah studied the card and then touched it with her fingertip. She anticipated the electrical current. So when it shot up her arm and into her brain, she wasn't frightened.

Instead, she waited for the images to come into focus and solidify. She saw flashes of the Corvette going backwards down a steep ravine and coming to rest at the bottom of a cliff. She saw the man get out of a white pickup truck, walk to the edge of the cliff and look down. Then she saw an early morning crew of men put on their hard hats, climb aboard grungy yellow bulldozers and start them. The last thing she saw was Katie's car being swallowed up in an avalanche of tumbling rocks and boulders as the bulldozers dumped bucketsful over the edge.

Savannah slowly shook her head and said, "I don't think she's alive."

My body's gone, but my spirit is still here.

Savannah gasped when she heard the voice whispering in her ear. It sounded different than the angelic voices she'd heard before, and she knew whom the voice belonged to. "K-Katie just spoke to me."

"Are you sure it was her?" Jade asked.

Savannah nodded. "Yeah. I don't know how I know. But I *know* it was her voice in my head."

"Who killed you, Katie?" said Emma.

Savannah turned three more cards over. When she saw the card with the head of a black goat and a pentagram in between its spiraled horns, she knew this card represented something evil. "Someone very bad and very powerful killed her."

"Katie, is your body somewhere along Six Mile Canyon Road?" asked Emma.

Savannah turned over three more cards. Her eyes focused on an image of a mountain range. An arched trellis draped in multi colored flowers stood in front of it reminding Savannah of the entrance to a national park.

"I think she's somewhere in the mountains off of that road."

Jade pulled out her smart phone. A moment later she said, "There's a mountain range that runs along Six Mile Canyon called, Flowery Mountain." She stared at the arch of flowers on the card. "Well, that's pretty coincidental. Don't you think?"

Emma asked, "Katie, what else can you tell us?"

Savannah turned over three more cards. Her eyes focused on an image of a woman in a boat. "I feel like she's trying to tell me something about a lake."

Jade buried her head in her phone again and a moment later said, "Lake Tahoe is less than forty five miles from there. And it kind of looks like that card. It's surrounded by lots of trees." She looked up. "And didn't that article in the Reno Gazette say that her boyfriend was from Lake Tahoe?"

"Yeah, it did," said Emma. She looked back down at the cards. "Katie, is there anything else you want us to know?"

Savannah turned over three more cards, now comfortable with the currents of electricity traveling through her body. She focused on the image of a man dressed in armor holding a jewel-encrusted saber in front of his face. When she heard Katie's voice whispering in her ear, she said, "We're supposed to look out for a man with a sword."

"What the heck does that mean?" said Jade.

Emma scrunched up her nose. "A man with a sword? Like a knight or something?"

Savannah stared at the image and slowly shook her head. "I have no freakin' clue."

Chapter 15

When Emma's reading was over, Savannah grabbed the cards and slid the deck toward Jade. "Your turn."

Jade picked up the cards, shuffled them, and then cut them into three piles. "Do you see anything more about Katie?"

Savannah turned three cards over. She stared at the images, but nothing seemed to pop out. She touched the first one, but no electricity traveled through her fingers. She looked at Jade and said, "I'm sorry, but I'm not getting anything."

"That's okay. Maybe you can just do a reading about me instead, you know, tell me something new about me."

"But Jade, I've known you for so long that there isn't anything I don't already know about you. So that wouldn't work."

"Then what do you what to do?" said Jade.

"I don't know." She paused. "But I know I need more practice." She looked at her friends. "I mean, we don't know if this new information about Katie is even true." She looked down at the cards. "Somehow, we have to find a way to prove that what I'm seeing is real."

The girls grew quiet until Emma said, "Sounds to me like you need to do a reading for someone you don't know."

Jade nodded. "I think that's a good idea. Look Vannah, it's pretty clear that you really are psychic. But you can't test or develop your skills on us. You know us too well. What you need is to do a reading for a stranger and see how that goes."

"Ah guys, I don't think I'm ready for that yet."

"Well, maybe you are. Maybe that's why you aren't able to see anything else, because the cards want you to try them out on someone new," said Emma.

Savannah blew out her breath. "I don't know . . ."

Bzzzz! Bzzzz! Bzzzz!

Jade grabbed her phone off of the coffee table and looked at the number. "Oh, shoot. I forgot about her."

"Forgot about who?" said Savannah.

"Carrie, my lab partner. She called me last night and asked if she could come by sometime today and pick up my biology notes. I told her it wouldn't be a problem. Are you guys okay if she comes over?"

When both Savannah and Emma said they were fine with it, Jade answered her phone. "Hi Carrie. How are you? No I didn't forget about it. When did you want to come over?" She glanced at Savannah. "Perfect. I'll see you in about fifteen minutes. Oh and Carrie, I have a little surprise for you when you get here." She ended the call and stared at Savannah. "Coincidence? I think not."

Savannah had agreed to do a reading for someone she didn't know. But she hadn't expected it to be quite so soon. How should she approach Jade's friend? She didn't want to go up to her and say, "Hey Carrie, I'm a psychic. You want a reading?" What if it upset her, or what if Carrie laughed at her? She sighed and thought, *I guess I'll wait for the cards to lead me.*

When the doorbell rang, Jade jumped up and answered it. She returned with a chunkier female version of Harry Potter. Carrie's bangs hung over the rim of her round glasses making them look more like half-moons rather than circles. An oversized, black and green, Bob Marley T-shirt hid the beginnings of a potbelly and hung down to her mid thighs, covering the upper portion of her black leggings.

"Hey guys, this is Carrie. Carrie, these are my friends, Savannah and Emma."

"Hi," she said with a half wave. She turned to Jade. "Sorry, I didn't know you had company."

"Oh, that's okay. We were just sitting around. Have a seat," she said gesturing to the couch.

Carrie plopped down and eyed the strange looking deck of cards. "What are those?"

"Those are Savannah's tarot cards. She does readings for people," said Jade.

Carrie's eyes widened. "Really?"

Emma chimed in. "Yeah, she's psychic, you know."

Carrie looked at Savannah. "So you do psychic readings?"

"Uh, yeah, sort of." She caught Carrie's hopeful expression and said, "Would you, uh, like me to give you a reading?"

"Really? You would do that for me? Right now?"

Savannah smiled and handed her the cards. "Sure. Go ahead and shuffle these. Just to let you know, though, I'm not very good at this yet because I'm still getting used to the cards. But I'll tell you what I see and what I hear."

"Don't let her fool you," said Emma. "She might not be used to the cards yet, but she's a natural at it, the real deal. You'll see."

Savannah flashed Emma a look.

After Carrie had shuffled the cards, Savannah took them and laid them out in the same pyramid shape. Maybe now would be a good time to try a general reading. She turned over the bottom row of cards, and just like before, vivid images flooded her mind. "Do you have an older brother?"

"I have two. They're both in college."

Savannah turned the second row over and said, "Did one of them get a new car? A red one?"

Carrie shook her head. "No, not that I know of."

"Are you sure? I think it's the oldest brother, the one with the girlfriend."

"Neither one of them has a girlfriend."

"Are you sure?" Savannah scrunched her face.

"Pretty sure."

Savannah could tell that Carrie wasn't too impressed so far. *So much for being ninety nine percent correct,* she thought.

She turned the next row of cards over and saw the same young man driving a brand new car with his girlfriend in the passenger's seat. "I don't know why, but I keep seeing this same guy in a red car," She looked at Carrie. "I'm sorry. Like I said, I'm not very good at this yet."

"It's okay. But now I'm curious about the guy in the red car."

Savannah laughed. "I know, me too." She turned over the next row of cards and gasped.

"What do you see?" asked Carrie.

An image of the guy in the red car popped into her head. "It's late at night. This guy and his girlfriend are driving the red car. She's asleep in the seat next to him. He knows he should have waited until morning to drive, but he was anxious to get wherever they were going.

"Pretty soon he nods off and drifts to the other side of the road. As they round a curve a car comes barreling around the bend and hits them head on killing both the guy and his girlfriend."

"Wow," said Carrie. "Sure hope you can figure out who the guy is and warn him before it's too late."

"Yeah, so do I." Savannah stared at the next row of cards, not really wanting to turn them over.

They were silent for a moment and then Carrie said, "Can I ask a question?"

"Sure."

"Can you tell me where I lost my earring?"

Savannah turned the next row of cards over and stared at the images for a moment. "Were they your mother's?"

Carrie nodded. "Yeah, and I'm going to be in deep you-know-what if I don't find it."

Savannah turned the final card over, and an image popped into her head. "I see a silver dangly earring with an amethyst tear drop at the end of it."

"That's it!" squealed Carrie. "That's the earring I lost. Do you know where it is?"

"I see it underneath the bushes outside of the school between the south side of the building and the sidewalk that goes to the running track."

Carrie jumped up off the couch. "I walked by there on Friday. I've got to go see if it's still there." She thanked Savannah and said to Jade, "I'll get the notes from you later." And then she ran out the door.

While Jade and Emma jabbered about inconsequential subjects, Savannah couldn't stop thinking about the guy in the red car.

What is it with me and dead people in cars?

Chapter 16

When Savannah got home, she immediately ran up to her room, hid the cards and then hurried into the kitchen to help her mother with dinner.

"So how was the library? Did you get a lot of studying done?" Her mother handed her the vegetables to make the salad and then turned up the heat on the oven to ensure a nice crust on the roast.

"Yeah, we went over all of the subjects that we thought might be on our finals. And then we quizzed each other." The lies tumbled easily out of her mouth as she peeled the cucumber, cut it into small chunks and tossed it into the salad bowl. "And then we stopped over at Jade's house for a little bit." She felt the need to throw something in there that wasn't a complete lie.

"Oh, that's nice. Were her parents there?"

"No. They went to Cheyenne to get a new Jeep. Jade thinks they're going to give her their old car for a graduation present."

"Speaking of graduation presents, did you decide what you wanted?"

"Sorry, Mom. I really don't know yet what I want."

"Well, you better come up with something. Time's running out."

Savannah finished making the salad and put it on the table. She grabbed four plates from the cupboard, along with silverware and cloth napkins from the drawer. But before she could set the table her phone rang. She grabbed it out of her back pocket, looked at the picture, pressed the green button and said, "Hey Jade, what's up?"

"You're not going to believe this," Jade said over the phone.

"Believe what?"

"Well, I just got a call from Carrie. And guess who was waiting for her when she got home."

"I don't know, who?"

"Her brother, with his new *girlfriend*. And guess what they were driving."

Savannah sucked in her breath. "Please don't tell me it was a new red car."

"Yep! It was the girlfriend's new car. And to top it off, apparently they'd spent the weekend at her parents' place in Alliance and decided to stop by and visit his family for a few hours before driving back to the university at Fort Collins . . . tonight."

Savannah's heart sank. So it *was* Carrie's brother she saw die in the car wreck. She glanced toward the kitchen to make sure her mother wasn't listening, and then she lowered her voice just in case she was. "Well, maybe what I saw isn't written in stone yet. Remember the lemonade? We were going to have ice tea with our lunch until Mrs. Reed changed his mind. Maybe Carrie's brother will change his mind and not drive back at night."

"Well, here's the kicker," said Jade. "Carrie got so freaked out when she saw the girlfriend and the new red car that she told her family that her brother and his girlfriend were going to die in a car wreck if they drove back tonight. She said that Savanna Swift, the psychic, told her so! She showed them the lost earring, said it was right where you said it would be. And then she started screaming, 'She knows things. You're gonna die! You're gonna die!'"

Savannah dropped the napkins and watched them float to the floor as if in slow motion. So many images flashed through her mind—her father yelling and shaking the deck of cards at her, and then praying over her lost soul; her mother crying because of the embarrassment and the condemning accusations she would soon face; the kids at school afraid to be near her for fear of finding out their fate.

She felt her knees wobble.

"This is my worst nightmare, Jade. I should never have let you talk me into doing a reading for someone I didn't know. Now look what happened. If my parents find out, I'm dead." Her lips started to quiver. "I'm so dead."

She hung up and shoved the phone back into her pocket, picked up the napkins off of the floor and refolded them. She swiped at the tears pooling and thought, *maybe they won't find out.*

The dinner conversation might as well have been spoken in Greek. She saw their lips moving, but she couldn't comprehend the words coming out of their mouths. Her mind was trapped in a whirlwind of *whatifs. What if Dad finds out? What if I really did save their lives? What if I'm delving into something I shouldn't?*

She really didn't know anything about the cards or what the images on them were supposed to mean. All she knew was that she saw things when she turned the cards over. She had more questions than answers. But there was one person who might be able to help her.

Dominic.

After dinner, Savannah helped her mother clean the kitchen, then excused herself and said that she was going up to her room to study.

Her father looked up from the TV and said, "You know, Vannah, there's such a thing as too much studying. Why don't you give your mind a break and come watch the news with me?"

If only she could give her mind a break. But watching TV with her dad sure wasn't going to do it.

"No, that's okay. I think I'll just study a little bit and then turn in early. I've got my first final in the morning."

"Honey, are you feeling okay? You look a little peeked," said her mother as she sat down on the couch holding a cup of tea.

Get it together, Vannah.

She flashed them a beatific smile and said, "I'm fine. I'm just a little tired, that's all."

She kissed her parents goodnight and climbed up the stairs feeling their gaze boring into her back every step of the way.

Once in her room, she closed and locked the door. She rarely locked it, because there was no need to. She had nothing to hide. But things had changed dramatically in the last twenty-four hours. And tonight it was imperative that she secured her privacy.

She grabbed her wallet from her purse and pulled out Dominic's card from behind her driver's license. She stared at it for a moment. *Dominic DeCarlo, Psychic.* He seemed to have nothing to hide either. Had he always embraced his gift? Or did he have to hide it at one time, too? She dialed the number and waited, hoping he would pick up.

A second later a voice said, "Hello?"

"Uh, hello. May I speak with Dominic?"

"Speaking."

"Dominic, hi. Uh, this is Savannah Swift. I met you yesterday at the street-"

"Hey, Savannah, how are you? I was just thinking about you."

"You were?"

"I sure was. I was sitting here with my girlfriend, Leslie, talking about you. Oh, and by the way, she said 'yes' last night. So I guess she's my fiancé, instead of my girlfriend."

"That's wonderful, Dominic. I'm happy for you."

"So what's going on? Did you do a reading for your friend?"

"Well, that's kind of why I'm calling. I'm really confused."

She began to tell him all that had happened since receiving the deck of tarot cards. She talked about the things she saw, heard, and felt when she touched them. She relayed the details they'd discovered about Katie, and then she told him about her premonition of Carrie's brother and his girlfriend dying in that head on collision.

"Wow, Savannah. When you decide to do something, you really jump in with both feet, don't you? So what can I do to help you?"

"Can you help me understand what's happening to me? I mean, why is this happening all of a sudden?"

"Chances are it isn't all of a sudden. You've most likely been psychic all your life, but you were never able to put a name to it. The cards were just the catalyst to make you aware of your abilities. Can you think of a time when your psychic abilities might have helped you avoid an accident? Or maybe you knew something was going to happen before it did?"

Savannah tried to think of something significant but nothing specific came to mind. "Sometimes someone's name will pop into my head and a minute later I get a phone call from them. That happens to me a lot."

"Anything else you can think of? Maybe when you were little?"

At first Savannah's mind was blank. But then she said, "Wait a minute. Come to think of it, I do remember something that happened a few years ago. My mom used to go power walking with a group of ladies at the same time very day. And she always parked in the same place. This particular day she was just getting ready to walk out the door when I got this overwhelming feeling that I didn't want her to go.

"I told her that I wanted her to stay home so that we could talk. She said she was running late, that she'd be back in a couple of hours and we could talk then.

"Now that I look back at it I remember feeling terrified about her going. I started getting really bad stomach cramps, and I doubled over. She helped me onto the couch, got me a heating pad and a glass of water. The feeling only lasted about ten minutes, and then it was gone, just like that. I felt fine, so she left."

"What happened?"

"When she arrived, there were police cars and an ambulance blocking where she normally parked, so she parked elsewhere. One of her friends said to her, 'You were sure lucky today.' Apparently, a drunk speeding down the street lost control of his car and T-boned the driver's side of the car that was parked right next to where Mom would have been. It completely totaled the parked car. And it happened at exactly the same time that she would have been sitting in the car, with her legs out the driver's door, putting on her walking shoes."

She paused for a moment. "The thought never occurred to me until this moment, but I think I might have saved my mom's life."

"That's incredible, Savannah. You were able to manifest a physical illness in order to stop your mom from leaving. You changed the outcome. That's a powerful ability. But it doesn't surprise me. When a psychic has a vision that is meant to be shared, the higher self will find a way to get the message out, even if it means manifesting an illness."

"Do you think that's the same case for my dreams about Katie?" She shifted on her bed.

"Absolutely. Your psychic visions showed up in your dreams where they couldn't be stifled."

"But I just don't understand why it's happening to me."

"Because you're a real, honest to God, psychic. And you were born that way for a reason." He paused for a moment and then said, "Do you know if anyone else in your family is psychic? Maybe your mother, possibly a grandmother?"

"Not that I know of."

"Well regardless, you certainly have the gift."

Savannah groaned. "This is terrible." She remained quiet for a moment, thinking about her options. "What if I don't want to pursue this? Could I decide to just forget the whole thing, you know, pretend like none of this ever happened?"

"Savannah . . ."

"I mean, if I don't do anything about it then no one will know, and I can just go on about my business. No harm no foul."

Dominic let out a deep sigh. "Savannah, I'm sorry, but it doesn't work that way. Your ability is a gift from God for the benefit of others. You have to understand that being a psychic is all about service. You do it to give others insight so that they can make better choices for a better life."

She groaned into the phone.

"Regardless how much you try to fight it, or hide it, your true nature *will* come out, one way or the other."

Savannah paused in thought and then said, "You're saying that all this stuff that is happening to me is a gift from God?"

"Absolutely! And it's meant to be shared for the greater good. You were put on this earth to help people."

Savannah never thought of it that way. Maybe this psychic stuff wasn't of the Devil like she'd been told. If it truly was a gift from God, then she should share it openly. But would she ever be able to convince her parents of that?

Not in a million years.

When Savannah didn't respond, Dominic said, "You need to start thinking of yourself as a spiritual advisor. We go to doctors when we need physical healing. We go to psychiatrists when we need emotional healing. We go to church when we need spiritual healing. Just like talking with a pastor or a doctor, this is another way of seeking help."

Savannah Swift, Spiritual Advisor. She liked the sound of that.

"You've given me a lot to think about, Dominic. I appreciate your time and insight."

"Keep in touch and let me know what you've decided to do."

"I will."

After she hung up, she lay down on her bed and stared up at the ceiling hoping that the hand of God would scribble the answers up there.

While she waited, she thought about everything that Dominic had told her and everything that her parents had said on the subject. Then she thought about the cards and the readings. From what she could see, nothing about her readings had been malicious or deceitful. In fact, all she wanted to do was help these people: Mrs. Reed, Carrie, her brother and his girlfriend.

Her intentions toward all of them had been pure. And if her visions really did prevent two deaths, what could she do on a larger scale?

Savannah's mind began to race with the possibilities. And then Katie came to mind. What if she could find her body? Then the girl's parents could finally find closure. She couldn't imagine how much turmoil they must still be going through, not knowing if their daughter was alive or dead.

If she could help end their misery by bringing Katie's body home to them, then they could give her a proper burial, and hopefully move forward with their lives. To her, that would be a gift from God, not the Devil.

Savannah had a lot more thinking to do. But there was one thing for certain; she finally knew exactly what she wanted for a graduation present.

Chapter 17

The halls of Scottsbluff High School buzzed with excitement and anticipation. Today marked the first day of Finals Week, the most dreaded week of the year. But the allure of an exciting summer vacation awaited, just beyond those last scholastic hurdles.

For Savannah, her friends, and the rest of the graduating class, this week meant the final gateway before adulthood. It meant that come this Saturday they would earn their freedom and the right to choose their own destiny.

And that is exactly what Savannah intended to do.

While she waited by her locker for Jade and Emma, Savannah glanced over her history notes one last time before her final. A feeling as if someone was watching her caused her to look up.

"Witch," said a girl under her breath as she walked by and scowled.

Not sure she heard what she thought she heard, Savannah said, "What did you say?"

The only response Savannah received from the girl was a condemning glare followed by a turned up nose.

Behind the strange girl, two other girls stared at Savannah as they walked by her. They cupped their hands to their mouths shielding the whispers that transferred between them.

A boy that Savannah had seen around school but didn't know personally walked by, flashed her a snarky smile, and said, "Hey Savannah, where's your crystal ball?"

Savannah's jaw unhinged. How could people have found out already? If she knew that Carrie was such a gigantic blabbermouth she never would have consented to the reading.

How many others know?

The stares and whispers coming from more of the students walking by answered her question—a lot of them.

But what if it wasn't Carrie who told? She pulled her phone from her pocket and texted Jade.

- So mad at you right now.

- Why?

- They all know.

- Huh???

- Just meet me in the girl's locker room and bring Em.

- Can't. Got my econ final in a few minutes.

- NOW!!! Or I swear to God I'm going to kill you! I may still do it anyway.

- WTF??

- Two minutes. Be there!

Savannah shoved her phone in her pocket, slammed her locker, and with her head down, she hurried to the girl's locker room where she waited and fumed.

A few minutes later Jade walked in with Emma in tow. She raised her hands and said, "Geez, Vannah, what's with the cryptic, and may I add, hostile message?"

Savannah peeked around the gym lockers to make sure they were alone. "They know. They all know."

"Who knows what?" said Jade. "What are you talking about?"

Savannah planted her hands on her hips. "Did you tell anyone about the reading?"

"No, of course not. Why?"

Savannah's stare migrated over to Emma who seemed quiet and more subdued than normal.

"Don't look at me. I didn't say a word to anyone," said Emma

Savannah threw her hands up in the air. "Well, somebody sure did. Because the whole school knows about it." She told them about what happened in the hall and then added, "This really sucks. What if my parents find out?"

"So what do you want us to do about it?" said Jade.

"Well, for starters you can tell your friend, Carrie, to shut her pie hole and quit blabbering about it to everyone. That was meant to be something private between her and us."

"Okay, I'll talk to her as soon as I see her. But that's not going to stop the people who she's told from telling others. And I can't do anything about that."

"I know," growled Savannah through clenched teeth. "But it makes me so mad. This is exactly what I *didn't* want happening. I can't even walk around here without somebody making some kind of snide remark." She let out a deep sigh. "I was thinking about something last night that I wanted to run by you guys. And now, in light of what's happening around the school, this might be the ideal time to do it."

"Do what?" said Jade.

"My mom has been after me to come up with a graduation present. So I was thinking about driving to Carson City, Nevada to look for Katie's body. But before I ask my parents, I wanted to check with you guys first. What do you think? Would you girls be up for a road trip?"

Jade's eyes brightened and she said, "Absolutely! Count me in. So when were you thinking of leaving and how long would we be gone?"

"I was thinking we'd leave Saturday afternoon right after graduation. Maybe be gone for ten days, two weeks. I thought we could tell our parents that we wanted to drive to San Francisco, then take the coast all the way down to LA and San Diego." She told them about her conversation with Dominic and added, "I think it's important to go look for Katie. But I don't want to go by myself. And since you two know just as much about her as I do, you could help me look for her."

"I-I don't think I can go," said Emma almost in tears.

Savannah put her hand on Emma's shoulder and said, "What's wrong?"

Emma couldn't hold in the tears anymore and cried out, "My parents are getting a divorce."

"What?" Savannah hugged her and said, "I'm so sorry to hear that. Why?"

"I don't know *why*. They didn't say *why*. They just said that after a lot of *discussion* they've decided that it's in everyone's best interest that they split up." And then she sobbed in her hands. "They've been married for twenty years. Why would they get divorced now?"

Jade sucked in her breath and said in a hushed tone, "Vannah, maybe that's why you saw Em's mom crying and drinking."

Emma lifted her head, sniffled, and looked at Jade. "What? What are you talking about?"

Before Savannah could open her mouth to speak, Jade blurted out, "When we were at your house, Vannah had a vision of your mom drinking gin in the bathroom and crying."

Emma looked at Savannah. "Is that true?" When Savannah nodded, she said, "Why didn't you tell me? How could you keep something like that from me?"

"Because I didn't know what it meant." She took a step closer to Emma. "Here I was doing a reading for you, answering your question about what we were going to have for lunch, and then all of a sudden I'm standing in the bathroom watching your mom cry while leaning on the sink." She shrugged, her hands out, palms up. "What was I supposed to say?"

"D-did you know they were getting a divorce?" Her lower lip started quivering.

"No, Em. Of course I didn't know." She put a comforting hand on Emma's shoulder. "All I knew was that she was very sad. And that's probably why she was drinking in the middle of the afternoon."

Emma nudged Savannah's hand off of her shoulder and sat down on one of the benches separating the rows of lockers. "I don't think I can take this. Divorce, college, finals . . ." She pulled her phone from her pocket and looked down at the time. "I've got to go. My math final is already starting. And if I don't pass it then I won't be going to college." She stood up and shuffled to the door leading out to the gym, her shoulders bent with defeat.

"Em, please think about going with us. Maybe this road trip is exactly what you need to take your mind off of things," said Savannah.

"I'll think about it," said Emma as she walked out the door without looking back.

When the door closed behind Emma, Savannah turned to Jade and said, " I love you, but sometimes I wish you would just shut the heck up!" And then she hurried out of the locker room.

~~~~~~~~~~~~~~~~

After she finished her history final, Savannah slinked out of the classroom, hurried out of the main doors and ran around to the back of the school. She sat underneath a large cottonwood tree and leaned back against its massive trunk. She figured this would be a safe place to hide out until her next class, away from all of the jeers and stares.

Savannah had never been very popular, probably because she was a preacher's kid. Having this rumor circulating around the school was sure to bring her notoriety, just not the kind she wanted.

Witch!

She thought about what that girl had said. She wasn't a witch. She was a psychic. Though she didn't know much about either, she knew that both labels carried a negative connotation. And however erroneous people's perceptions might be, she was certain she wouldn't be the one to change their minds.

She let out a groan. "This is so bad."

She thought about her parents and knew there was real possibility they would find out. If they did, what would she tell them? Would she lie to cover her own behind, or would she stand up to them and embrace her psychic title?

She pictured her father's wrath. *You're grounded until you're thirty, young lady!*

She thought about her mother's reaction. *How could you shame us like that?*

Savannah dropped her head in her hands and muttered, "What am I going to do?"

"Excuse me, Savannah? Savannah Swift?"

The voice caused Savannah to look up. A slight girl, probably a sophomore based on the books she carried, stood in front of her. Her long blonde hair had been pleated into one single braid that draped over her left shoulder. Four strands of beads accented with pink and purple feathers dangled from the end of the braid. When she moved her head, the beads clattered together.

"Yes?" said Savannah.

"Uh, hi. I'm a friend of Carrie's."

Savannah pushed herself up, gathered her books and said, "I gotta go."

"Wait. I was hoping you could help me." She hesitated. "My dog is missing. We don't know if she ran away or if somebody took her. And I was hoping that maybe you could help me find her."

"I'm sorry, but I don't know what you want me to do for you," Savannah said as she started to walk away.

The girl grabbed her arm, stopping her. "Please, Savannah, could you do a reading for me, like you did for Carrie?"

Savannah pulled her arm free. "I don't know what you're talking about."

"Please," the girl pleaded. "She's been missing now for over a week. She could be hurt somewhere or maybe someone took her and is keeping her tied up so that she can't get home. Her name's Greta."

As soon as the girl said the dog's name, an image of a gray and white dog with long fur and a pink collar came to mind. Savannah tried to block out the picture, but the dog seemed to be barking at her from behind a chain link fence, as if to say, "I'm here. I'm here."

Savannah looked at the girl and said, "Is she an Australian Shepherd?"

"Yes! Do you know where she is?"

Savannah saw the dog behind the fence and an arm with a tattoo on it tossing some chunks of meat to the dog. "A guy with a cobra tattooed on his forearm has her penned up. But she's okay." She closed her eyes and turned her head from side to side as though she were looking around. "It's like a junk yard or something because there are wrecked cars all over the place, and they're stacked on top of each other."

The girl gasped. "I know where that is. It's the wrecking yard at the other end of town." She hugged Savannah. "Thank you so much for your help. You're amazing!" And then she hurried off, presumably, to reclaim her dog.

The rest of the day Savannah kept her head down and focused solely on her finals instead of the stares coming from the students and some of the faculty. And when she went to her computer class and sat down at her normal station, instead of reacting of the words "Savannah Swift is a Devil worshiper" typed on her computer screen, she quickly erased it, ignored the sniggers coming from the back of the room, and got busy with her computer finals.

She couldn't wait for this day to be over!

Chapter 18

That afternoon when she got home, Savannah found her mother sitting at the kitchen table holding a mug of coffee with both hands. She didn't even look up when Savannah walked in. Instead, she gestured with her head to the chair across from her and said, "Take a seat."

When Savannah sat down her mother took a sip of coffee but still didn't look at her. Several moments of silence passed between them. Finally, Mrs. Swift set the cup down and for the first time since Savannah walked through the door, she looked at her.

"I had a very interesting phone call this afternoon from a Mrs. Renfro. She said that you did some kind of psychic reading for her daughter, Carrie. Is that true?"

I'm so screwed!

Her mother's intense stare caused Savannah's mouth to go dry, so she said nothing. She should have just said "no" right off the bat. But the words wouldn't come out.

"You tell me right now, Savannah Anne Swift. And don't you *dare* lie to me. Are you or are you not involved with that stuff?"

Savannah remained quiet not quite sure what to say.

"Answer me, right now. Or so help me I'll-"

"Yes," Savannah blurted out. "I am, but it's not like what you think. It's-"

"Don't tell me what I think," her mother snapped. "You promised me you would not get involved with that psychic stuff. You lied to me."

"Well, technically, that's not what I said. I promised that I wouldn't get involved with stuff *like* that. Like Ouija boards or crystal balls. And I haven't. I've only done tarot card readings for a couple of people."

Mrs. Swift slammed her fist on the table, spilling some of her coffee and making Savannah jump. "Stop mincing words, Savannah. You knew what I meant, and you did it anyway."

"But Mom, if you would only try to understand that there's nothing wrong with it. I think by giving Carrie that reading I might have actually saved her brother's life."

Her mother let out an exasperated breath. "Savannah, you have no idea what you're delving into. It might seem harmless on the surface, but believe me, it's far from it."

"How can saving someone's life be considered harmful? I don't understand."

"First off, you are speculating that you saved his life. You have no concrete evidence or proof of that."

Savannah stared at her mom. "You're right. I don't have proof. All I have is faith."

"Don't you dare associate faith with that garbage." Her mother glared at her. "Faith comes from God-"

"And so do these abilities," challenged Savannah. She locked eyes with her Mom. "Why are you so convinced that all psychics are evil and that their motives are to hurt or deceive others?"

Her mother didn't answer.

"Mom, if you want me to understand all of this, then explain it to me. Help me understand why you are so against it."

Her mother stared down at the splotches of coffee on the table but remained quiet.

"Mom, you want me to stop this, but you won't give me a good reason why. Just give me one reason why you-"

Her mother cut her off. "Because I know someone who got involved with it, and it ruined their relationship with their family." She looked up at Savannah. "And I just don't want the same thing happening to you. It's a painful and lonely existence for my, uh, friend. And it's a blemish on her family."

Both remained quiet for several moments—Mrs. Swift looking at her coffee cup, while Savannah stared at the spilt splotches.

Finally, Mrs. Swift reached out her hand urging her daughter to take it. Her voice softened, and she said, "Sweetheart, you're almost an adult. And once you leave home I won't be able to stop you from doing whatever you want to do.

"But what I can do is try to make you understand the damaging consequences your choices can have on others. Your intentions may be honorable, but you know what they say about good intentions; the road to hell is paved with them."

Savannah stared at her mother. Worry and concern in her mother's eyes made them grow darker and her face appear craggy and more wrinkled. Even her hair looked frizzier than normal as though she'd been running worried hands through it. She looked old right at the moment, much older than a forty-five year old should look.

Savannah hated herself for forcing her mother to have this conversation with her. Maybe she should just concede, promise to never do it again, and ask her mother for forgiveness.

But she just couldn't make herself drop the subject.

"So what happened to your friend?" Savannah asked.

Mrs. Swift shrugged. "I don't know. I haven't talked to her in a long time."

Savannah didn't know what to think or what to do. Now that her mother had found out about her she was pretty sure her parents would not let her go on a road trip. She hesitated and then said, "Are you going to tell Dad?"

"That depends."

"On?"

"On whether or not you promise to never do another tarot card reading ever again."

Savannah stared at her mom. This was an impossible situation. She didn't want to lie to her, but she also didn't want to give up doing readings, especially if it gave her a greater connection to God.

She felt a strange draw to those cards, almost a protective attitude toward them. But then a thought struck her. Based on this afternoon, she realized that her psychic abilities were becoming stronger. She was able to see things without the use of the cards. Maybe she could give the cards back to Dominic and try doing readings without them.

"If I promise to not do anymore tarot card readings, then I want something in return," said Savannah.

"Savannah, this is not a negotiation."

"Well, Mom, you want something from me, and I want something from you."

Her mom's brows furrowed. "What do you want?"

"I want to go on a road trip to California with Jade and Em as my graduation present."

Mrs. Swift's eyebrows arched into half-moons. "A road trip?"

"Yes, to California. I will get rid of the cards if you agree to let me go on this trip. We'd be gone no more than two weeks. And we'd check in every day so that you knew we were safe."

"I don't know about that, Savannah. Two weeks? That's a long time to be on the road. When were you thinking of leaving?"

"Saturday afternoon, right after graduation."

"This Saturday? That's only a few days from now. And you'd be gone over Memorial Day." Mrs. Swift tightened her lips and slowly shook her head. "I don't know . . ."

"I'm not asking for a car or even money. All I really want for graduation is to be able to go on this road trip." She paused. "Please, Mom?"

Mrs. Swift stared at her daughter. She seemed to be thinking. But before she could say anything else, the phone rang. She stood up, walked to the counter, picked up the phone and said, "Hello."

For several moments she didn't say anything except, "Uh-huh. Uh-huh. I see." Throughout the one-sided conversation Mrs. Swift kept glancing at Savannah. Finally, she said to the person on the phone, "I'll ask her, and then I'll let you know."

Mrs. Swift hung up the phone, folded her arms across her chest as she leaned against the counter and stared at Savannah without saying anything.

Uh oh, more bad news?

Finally, Mrs. Swift said, "That was your Aunt Helen. She wanted to know if you would be interested in coming out to Salt Lake City to visit her before you started college."

"Wow, you haven't spoken to her in a long time. It's strange that she called you now."

Her mother continued staring at her. "Yes. Strange. Isn't it."

Chapter 19

That evening after much cajoling, negotiating, compromising, and even a little bit of praying, Pastor Swift finally said "yes" to the road trip. But it didn't come without a price.

"No boys. No bars. No drinking. No partying. And no picking up hitchhikers, understood? You will check in with us every night, and you will let us know where you are staying once you leave your Aunt Helen's place. Ten days, not two weeks. Agreed?" He stared at his daughter from across the kitchen table.

"Agreed. Thanks, Dad." Savannah jumped up and hugged her father then moved over to her mother. "Thanks, Mom."

Her mother leaned in to the hug and whispered in her ear, "I'm trusting you to keep your promise to me."

Savannah offered her mother a discreet nod and said, "I've got to go call the girls and give them the good news." Then she scampered up the stairs.

Once inside her room, she closed the door, plopped on the bed, and called Jade. When her friend answered she said, "You're not going to believe what happened to me when I got home." She told

Jade how her mother confronted her and then said, "But the good news is, we're going on a road trip."

"Maybe not. My parents said they're selling our old car on Craig's List. So I can't drive." She paused. "I can't believe they didn't give it to me for a graduation present. I was so sure they would!"

Savannah groaned. "That means Em *has* to go. Otherwise we can't go."

"What about your parents' car?" said Jade without much enthusiasm.

"I told them Em was driving. I'm pushing the envelope as it is. So I can't go back and ask them for the car, too." Savannah sighed. "Listen, I'll call Em, see if I can convince her to go, and then I'll call you right back." She hung up and immediately dialed Emma.

"Hey, Vannah." Emma sounded tired when she answered the phone.

"Hey, Em. I wanted to let you know that we got permission to go on the trip. Have you thought anymore about it?"

Emma sighed dramatically into the phone. "Yeah, I've thought about it."

"And?"

"And I talked to my folks about it . . ."

"And?"

"And they thought . . ." She paused.

"And they thought what?"

"They thought that it would be good for me to get away with you two." Her voice suddenly became animated with excitement. "So, I guess we're going on a road trip." And then she laughed. "Fooled you, didn't I?"

"Oh Em, I could kiss you right now." Savannah made smacking noises into the phone and said, "I can't believe it. We're actually going to go look for Katie's body." She said good-bye and then called Jade back to give her the good news.

With the trip now a reality, Savannah had a hard time sleeping. Thoughts like, *We need maps, first aid kit, maybe try to find out more about Katie's boyfriend*, kept her mind buzzing. But soon her eyes closed, and her thoughts faded into nothingness as sleep conquered her mind and her body.

And the dreams followed . . .

~~~~~~~~~~~~~~~~~

May 19, 2009
10:00 PM

Katie pulled into Carson Tahoe emergency entrance, slammed the car in park and raced into the front doors. "Help! Somebody help me!" she screamed out. "A man's been shot."

That got the attention of a doctor standing near the admittance desk. "Where is he?"

"He's in my car. Hurry, he's in real bad shape."

"Get a gurney," he said to one of the nurses, and then he followed Katie out the door to the idling car. He opened the passenger's side, glanced at Marty's bloody stomach wound and placed two fingers on his neck. "His pulse is weak. We need to get him into surgery right away."

"Is he going to make it?" Katie allowed the tears to fall.

Medical personnel were already loading him onto a gurney. "We won't know until we can get in there and assess the damage," said the doctor.

Katie ran alongside the gurney as they wheeled Marty through the front doors. "Hang on, Marty."

Marty's head flopped to the side and his eyes caught hers. He reached trembling fingers toward her and said in a raspy voice, "R-remember what you p-promised."

Katie latched onto his hand and nodded through her tears. "You just stay strong."

"Miss . . ." A nurse gently touched her shoulder bringing her to a stop. "They're going to need you to fill out some paperwork at the admittance desk. Please come with me."

Katie's gaze stayed focused on the gurney carrying her dying boyfriend until it disappeared behind the double doors of the trauma unit. Then she swiped away her tears, looked at the nurse and said, "I need to go get my purse and move the car. I'll be back in a minute."

She walked out the automated glass doors and stopped. Marty's Corvette was still idling near the entrance. Her eyes scanned the parking area to see if the man who shot Marty had followed them. She didn't see him, but that didn't mean he wasn't hiding somewhere, watching her. She hurried to the car, got behind the wheel and pulled into a spot right near the entrance designated for handicapped. She figured she would rather park up front and pay a fine, than park in some dark corner of the vast parking lot and pay with her life.

She glanced down at the manila envelope on the floor, quickly snatched it up, grabbed the silver flash drive from the cup holder and put it in her pocket, and then she hurried back into the hospital to the admittance desk.

"Are you with the young man who was just brought in?" When Katie nodded, the receptionist behind the desk handed her a clipboard with some hospital forms and said, "Are you his wife?"

"No, his fiancé."

"Fill these out the best you can. And when you're done, bring them back to me."

Katie clutched the clipboard to her chest and said, "Can you tell me if he's okay?"

The receptionist shook her head. "I'm sorry. I don't have that information. But I'm sure the doctor will come talk to you just as soon as he knows something."

Katie walked over to one of the lobby chairs and began to fill out the paperwork. But her attention was disrupted every time someone came through the doors. Her eyes migrated over to an armed security guard standing next to the entrance, and she released some of her angst. If the man who shot Marty had followed them there, surely he wouldn't come after her in a crowded emergency waiting room. Would he?

She stuck her hand in her left pants pocket, pulled out the flash drive and thought, *If whatever is on here is that damaging, then maybe he would.*

She shoved the flash drive back into her pocket and began to fill out the forms. When she was finished, she walked back over to the desk and handed the paperwork to the receptionist. "Excuse me, but do you know where I might find a computer?"

The receptionist pointed down a wide corridor and said, "There's a small business center right across from the cafeteria that has a couple of computers you can use."

"Thank you." Katie started to walk away and then turned back around. "If you find out anything about Marty Dolan, will you let me know?"

The receptionist handed her a sticky notepad and said, "Here, write down your name and cell phone number, and we'll call you just as soon as we know something."

Katie jotted her information down and left it on the counter. Then, with envelope in hand, she hurried down the hall in search of a computer. She needed to find out what was so important on that flash drive that it was worth killing over.

She walked into the business center and looked around. This looked like the place for people to kill time while waiting for news about loved ones. Most of the visitors seemed to be using their own laptops. Near the back of the room she spotted an empty computer and was just about to walk over to it when a young kid, probably junior high school age, hurried past her, sat down, and immediately started pulling up different websites.

She walked up to him and looked over his shoulder at his Facebook page. "You going to be on that very long?"

He shrugged indifferent shoulders and said, "I dunno. Maybe."

Katie sighed and looked over at the only other computer. A guy in a tweed sports jacket occupied it, his fingers dancing over the keyboard with intent. By the amount of paperwork scattered around his area of the desk, it looked like he might be there awhile.

So she decided to walk across the hall to the cafeteria. Thinking that it was probably going to be a long night of waiting, some strong hospital coffee might help give her the boost and the stamina that she needed.

The cafeteria was just as crowded as the business center, but luckily it had more capacity. Spotting an empty table near a window that overlooked the parking lot, she grabbed a cup of coffee from the self-serve, paid the clerk and hurried over to the table before she lost out on it, too.

Cupping her hands around her eyes, she looked out the window at the lit parking lot. From her vantage point she could see Marty's Corvette, and it looked undisturbed, no ticket on the windshield or stranger loitering around it.

She slowly sipped her coffee forcing herself to calm down. And when she finally started to relax, she grabbed the manila envelope and opened it. "Okay, let's get a better look at this, see what he found so compelling." She pulled an eight by ten photograph out and studied the images. She tilted her head to the side and said, "Hm. Marty's right. That *is* odd."

Right then her cell phone rang, and she answered it. "Hello?"

"Hello. May I speak with Katie McCall?"

"Speaking."

"Miss McCall, this is the hospital receptionist. The doctor who operated on your friend is here and would like to speak with you."

"Thank you. I'll be there in a minute." She hung up, slipped the photo back in the envelope, and hurried to the front desk, praying that the doctor had some good news.

When she got there, the doctor's face held no hint of his news. He handed a clipboard to a nurse who was standing next to him and turned to Katie. "Luckily, we were able to remove the bullet and clean out the wound."

"Will he be okay?" she asked hopefully.

"It's too soon to tell. But he's stable at the moment."

"Can I go see him?"

The doctor shook his head. "No. Right now he's in ICU and heavily sedated."

"When can I see him?"

"It depends on how he does tonight. The first twenty-four hours are the most critical. So we're going to keep him in intensive care where we can monitor him more closely." He placed a comforting hand on her shoulder. "The best thing you can do for him now is to take care of yourself. Why don't you go home, get some rest, and we'll call you if there is any change in his condition."

"Thank you," said Katie.

She started to walk away then turned and opened her mouth to say something.

As if anticipating what she was going to say, the doctor said, "Don't worry, this is the very best place for him to be."

Once outside, Katie walked to her car and looked around the parking lot. Only a few vehicles remained, none of which she recognized. She slid in behind the wheel of Marty's Corvette, tossed the envelope on the seat, pulled the flash drive from her pocket and dropped it in the cup holder. She put the key in the ignition, but instead of starting the car she just sat there.

There's nothing I can do for Marty here, but I don't want to go home and be alone.

She glanced over at the envelope, thought about the picture and what she had seen on it, and knew what had to be done.

"I need to go up to the mine. Tonight."

Chapter 20

Savannah's eyes sprang open, and she cried out, "No, Katie. Don't go up there. You'll die!" She catapulted out of bed and began pacing the floor. A feeling of helplessness overwhelmed her. In her mind she knew this Katie person was long gone, but in her dreams she was still alive. And that made Savannah want to protect her. She knew she couldn't reverse something that had happened three years ago and bring Katie back from the dead. The only thing she could do now was to try to find out everything she could about what happened to this woman the night she went missing.

She grabbed her computer and pulled up a blank word document. "Katie, if I'm going to help you, then you're going to need to help me remember the details so that I can piece it all together." She began to write down everything she remembered about all of the dreams: Katie being buried alive, her being pushed over a cliff by a man in a white pickup truck, a photograph, a flash drive, Marty getting shot in the stomach.

She looked up from the computer screen and gazed at the ceiling as if, by her stare alone, she could conjure up the rest of the information. She rubbed her chin and whispered, "What was the name of that company?"

An image of Katie driving by the chain link fence with *NO TRESSPASSING* signs posted on it flashed into her mind. She saw Katie pull off onto a dirt road and walk up to a metal gate. And through Katie's eyes she saw another sign underneath it that read, *PRIVATE PROPERTY . . .*

"The Comstock Mining Company!" she exclaimed.

She pulled up a Google page and typed in Comstock Mining Company. Excitement caused her stomach to flip when the first site that came up was their official website.

"It's a real company," she said excitedly.

As she read through it, she discovered that the Comstock Mining Company was based in Dayton, Nevada, only a few miles from Carson City. And the entrances to the majority of their mines were located on, of all places . . .

Six Mile Canyon Road.

She continued to read through the website. And when she got to the bottom of the page she noticed an italicized byline that said, *A Division of the Geneva Corporation.*

She clicked on the name, and it took her to the company's official website. She read through the home page and discovered that they were a multi-billion dollar holding company based out of New York and a major shareholder in thousands of companies across the country. They seemed to be involved in all kinds of companies including printing to plastic manufacturing to . . .

Silver mines in Nevada!

She clicked on the "About Us" icon on the left hand side of the page. It took her to the list of Executive Officers. The first photo was of a middle-aged man dressed in what looked to be a very expensive gray suit and tie that matched the color of his hair and made his pale blue eyes stand out.

She read his bio out loud. "'Harrison Taylor is president and CEO of the Geneva Corporation, one of the largest holding companies in North America.

"'After graduating from Boston University with a PhD in finance, Mr. Taylor joined the company as an entry-level sales executive. Because of his savvy business sense and keen negotiating skills, Taylor was offered a position as Senior Director. He quickly rose to the top of the organization to become the president and CEO.'"

She leaned back on her headboard and thought about everything she had just read. There seemed to be too many connections to be coincidental.

If Savannah had doubts about her abilities before, this new information put all of those doubts to rest. Details that she couldn't have possibly conjured up in her mind proved to be real.

Wait 'til I tell the girls.

She looked over at her bedroom clock. It was only three thirty in the morning, too early to get up. But she was too excited to fall back asleep. Her mind raced with everything she had learned about Katie McCall and about the Comstock Mining Company.

Suddenly, it was as if ten-pound weights had been attached to her eyelids. She just couldn't keep them open anymore, and she fell deep asleep, still clutching onto her computer.

~~~~~~~~~~~~~~~~~

South Lake Tahoe
May 19, 2009
9:00 PM

Katie impatiently drummed her fingers on the tabletop as she stared out the large picture window of the Gun Barrel Tavern, watching for Marty's Corvette. She glanced at her watch. It was already quarter after nine and the restaurant had become loud with obnoxious partiers.

"Where are you?" she muttered under her breath. She scooted the menus to the side, picked up her water glass, took a sip, and set it back down. The finger cadence resumed as she continued to stare out the window at the nearly full parking lot across the street.

After another five minutes, and still no Marty, she pulled her phone from her purse, ready to dial his number when he burst in through the doors carrying a manila envelope down by his side. His eyes darted around the rustic dining room as if searching for her.

"Finally," muttered Katie as she held up her hand and waved him over.

When he spotted her, he hurried over, slid in across from her, and dropped the envelope on the seat beside him.

"Sorry I'm late," he said out of breath. He looked at the full glass of water in front of him then lifted his hand and summoned over a waiter. "A bottle of Sierra Nevada Pale Ale, please," he said as soon as the waiter arrived. He glanced at Katie's water glass and added, "Make that two." The waiter nodded and hurried off.

"I'm just glad you made it." Katie handed him a menu and said, "So what was so important that you needed to meet me all the way out here tonight? Couldn't it have waited until tomorrow morning?"

"No, it couldn't." He dropped the menu back on the table without even looking at it.

"Well, you could have at least picked somewhere quieter and closer to my place." She looked around the packed restaurant. "You know I don't like it here. It's always so crowded." She picked up her glass, tipped it back and took a long drink.

"It needed to be a crowded place." He glanced out the window as a car drove by then slumped a little lower in his seat.

"Marty, what's going on?" She set the glass back on the table and stared at him with suspicious eyes. "Why are you acting so weird?"

Before Marty could respond, the waiter set a bottle of beer in front of each of them. "Here you go. You guys ready to order?"

"We're not eating," said Marty abruptly to the waiter.

Katie shrugged her shoulders, offered the young man an apologetic smile and handed him the menus.

"No problem," said the waiter. "Let me know if you need anything else."

After he walked away Katie said, "So what's going on? Did you have a bad day at the newspaper or something?"

Marty scooted his water glass to the side then picked up his beer, took a swig, and set it back down on the table. "Work was fine."

"Did you have a fight with your grandparents?"

Marty shook his head then glanced out the window again when another random car driving by grabbed his attention.

Katie eyed him with concern. "Are you sick or something?"

Marty hesitated. "Not that I know of."

"Well, something's wrong. What is it?"

Marty took another swig of beer, lowered his voice and said, "It's about the story I'm working on."

"Which one?"

"You know which one I'm talking about."

Katie leaned forward and whispered, "Marty, I told you not to pursue that one anymore. You need to just let it go."

"I can't."

"Why not?"

"Because the public needs to know what I've uncovered. They-"

"What you *think* you've uncovered," said Katie, interrupting him. "You don't have any evidence to back it up."

Marty grabbed the envelope off the seat and slid it across the table to her. "I do now."

Katie looked at the envelope. "What's this?"

"Proof of what I've been telling you all along."

She eyed him then opened up the envelope and pulled out a photograph. After studying the darkened and grainy image for several seconds, she scrunched her brow and said, "Where was this taken?"

"Up at the mine near Flowery Peak."

"When did you take it?"

"The night before last."

"So is that where you were when I tried to get a hold of you?" she asked.

He nodded. "I couldn't get to my phone in time."

She glanced at the photo again and then stared at Marty with quizzical eyes. "What would possess you to go up there?"

"It was the only way to get the proof I needed."

She slid the picture back to him and shook her head. "This doesn't prove anything. It's just a picture of a bunch of heavy equipment."

"It's not the heavy equipment I was shooting. It was this." He pointed to a delivery truck parked in the middle of the equipment with several men congregated near the opened back end.

"Well, it doesn't matter what you were intending to shoot. It still doesn't prove anything."

Marty reached into his pocket, pulled something out and held it in his closed palm. "Not by itself, no. But it does with this." He slid a silver flash drive across the table to her. "I just picked this up from a friend at the university, which is why I was late." He leaned in even closer. "And trust me, the stuff that's on there will prove everything I've been saying."

Katie stared at the flash drive for a second then looked back up at him. "So what do you want me to do with it?"

"I want you to look at it so that you will finally believe me. And then I want you to hide it somewhere safe. Just in case."

Katie scoffed. "C'mon, Marty, you're being ridiculous and paranoid. You've been watching too many crime shows on TV."

Marty stared intently at her. "This isn't a joke, Katie. It's real." He glanced once more out the window. "This is much bigger than

I originally thought." His eyes darted around the room. "And now I think my life might be in danger because of it."

Katie scoffed, "Oh c'mon, Marty . . ." But when she saw real terror in his eyes her face dropped and she said, "You're serious."

"Dead serious." He lowered his voice further, his eyes darting around the room. "You need to promise me that if anything happens to me, you'll take that flash drive and the photograph to the police."

"Marty, you're starting to scare me," she said in a hushed whisper.

"You should be scared. We should all be scared." He pushed the flash drive closer to her.

When she reached for it, Marty latched onto her wrist. She tried to pull away but he held on tight. "Marty, stop it. You're hurting me."

"Promise me. Promise me that you'll do it."

"I promise. Now let go."

Marty released his grip. "When you look at it, you'll see that everything I've been trying to tell you is true."

A pair of headlights caused him to look out the window toward the brightly lit parking lot across the street. His face went ashen and he said, "We've got to go."

Katie looked out the window in time to see a man exiting a white pickup truck and begin walking toward the restaurant. She looked back at Marty, his eyes still tracking the stranger, and said, "Do you know that man?"

He shoved the photograph back into the envelope, grabbed the flash drive, dropped a twenty-dollar bill on the table and said, "Let's go." He led her out the side entrance used for takeout then peeked around the front corner of the building.

When the man entered the restaurant, Marty grabbed Katie by the wrist and yanked her behind him as he ran across the street to his waiting Corvette at the far end of the parking lot.

"Marty, stop it." Katie halted abruptly near the passenger's side and said, "I'm not moving another inch until you tell me who that man is."

Marty turned around and faced her. "Katie, just get in the car. Please, you have to trust-"

A loud *Pop! Pop! Pop!* instantly silenced him, and he dropped to the ground.

"Marty!" screamed Katie when she saw the red gush of blood coming from his gut. She looked behind her and saw the same man from the restaurant hurrying across the street toward them, his gun now discreetly down at his side. "Marty, get up." But he didn't move. She grabbed him underneath the armpits and yanked him to a sitting position, causing him to groan.

At least he was still alive.

She grabbed the keys and the flash drive that had tumbled out of his hands, unlocked and opened the passenger's door then snatched up the envelope off of the ground and tossed it onto the floor.

With the strength of Samson, Katie hoisted Marty to his feet, pushed him into the passenger's seat, slammed the door and ran around to the driver's side. She slid behind the wheel, dropped the flash drive into the cup holder and then slipped the key into the ignition. She cranked the car to life and rammed her foot down on the gas pedal sending the car fishtailing out of the parking lot and down the street. In her rearview mirror, she saw the man change directions and run back to his pickup truck.

"I've got to get you to a hospital, Marty. I'm taking you to Barton. It's only a couple of miles from here."

Marty groaned but didn't move. His body lay slumped over with his head propped up by the window.

Seconds later, a pair of bright lights coming up behind her fast flashed in her rearview mirror. An instant later she screamed when the pickup truck rammed into the back of the Corvette causing it to lurch forward. She rammed her foot all the way to the floorboard forcing the car to go faster. They pulled away from the truck. But in doing so, she inadvertently zoomed past the exit to the hospital.

"Marty, I'm going to have to take you to Carson City instead. Just hang on." She downshifted and pushed the car faster around the mountainous curves.

"Hang on, Marty. We're almost there," she said looking over at him. The dashboard lights cast a ghostly hue over his face. She clicked on the overhead light to get a better look at the slick, black, saucer sized, splatter of blood that oozed across his stomach.

"It'll be okay, Marty. They'll get the bullet out, stitch you up, and you'll be good as new." He responded with a painful sounding groan that contradicted her words. "Stay with me, Marty. Don't fall asleep." Her voice cracked as she bit back her tears.

When she looked at him again, his eyes had glazed over. She shook his shoulder to rouse him. "Marty, talk to me. Who was that man, and why did he shoot you in front of a restaurant full of people?" When he didn't respond, she gripped the steering wheel and rammed her foot all the way down on the gas pedal.

As she raced toward the lights of Carson City in the distance, she cried out, "Dear God, Marty. What on Earth have you gotten us into?"

Chapter 21

A light tap on Savannah's bedroom door caused her to wake. "Hey, you up yet?" came her mom's muffled voice.

Still clutching her computer, she looked over at the clock. Only moments ago it was three thirty. Now it was quarter to eight. "Oh, crap," she said under her breath and then yelled out, "Yeah, I'm up, but I'm not quite ready yet."

"Well, hurry up. Breakfast is on the table. And the bus will be here any minute."

"Be right down," said Savannah. She closed the links, saved the document, and threw on a strappy cornflower blue sundress, foregoing a shower. Three minutes later she had a piece of buttered toast in hand and was out the door, running to catch the waiting bus. Fueled with excitement about what she had uncovered last night caused her to sprint the last few yards.

Later that morning as she stood by her locker going over her biology notes, she ignored the stares coming from those walking by. Even the rude comments and whispers fell on deaf ears today.

She had more important things to do than to pay attention to petty gossip and childish behavior.

She had a mystery to solve.

When Jade and Emma walked up, Savannah tossed her notes into her locker and said, "Follow me. I need to show you guys something. I had more dreams about Katie last night, and she showed me more new details."

She led them into the empty computer room and slid into the seat in front of her usual computer. As she relayed the dreams to them she pulled up a map of Carson City and the surrounding area and said, "From what I can figure, Marty got shot somewhere near South Lake Tahoe."

"How do you know they were in Lake Tahoe?" asked Jade.

"Because I saw them in a restaurant called, The Gun Barrel Tavern. I checked it out, and there is one in South Lake Tahoe at the Heavenly Ski resort. Also, Katie said that she was going to have to take Marty to Carson City hospital." She pointed to a string of roads that fingered out from highway 50 near the bottom part of Lake Tahoe.

"Are you talking about her boyfriend, Martin?" said Jade.

Savannah nodded. "Yeah, but she called him *Marty*." She pulled up the Geneva website. "I wanted to show you guys this."

Emma looked at the title and said, "What is the Geneva Corporation?"

"It's a huge multi-billion dollar holding company that has subsidiaries all over the country, including Nevada." She clicked on the long list of subsidiaries, scrolled down until she came to The Comstock Mining Company and clicked on it, which redirected her to their website. "The Geneva Corporation has their hands in pretty much every kind of product and manufacturing company you can think of, including gold and silver mines."

"Gold mines? Like the gold rush of the 1800's? Those kinds of gold mines?" Emma said.

"Uh-huh. And this company called Comstock Mining owns dozens of these mines around the Carson City and Virginia City area. And guess where the majority of these mines are located? You guessed it, on Six Mile Canyon Road." She pointed to Flowery Peak mountain range and added. "I'm pretty sure that Katie's body is buried somewhere right around there."

"So how are we going to find her?" asked Emma.

Savannah closed down all of the sites and shut the computer off. She leaned back in her chair and said, "I think the only way is to go up to each one of the mines until we find the one that matches the one in my dreams."

Emma groaned. "But they have so many of them. Can't you do a reading before we go, maybe narrow it down a little?"

Savannah sighed. "I told Jade, but I didn't tell you what happened between my mom and I last night." After Savannah relayed the story, she added, "So I decided to give the cards back to Dominic."

"Well, maybe he could do a reading for you," said Emma.

Savannah grinned exposing a straight line of white teeth. "I was kind of thinking the same thing. I thought maybe I could call him and see if he had time to do a reading for me this afternoon. You girls want to come with me?"

When the girls nodded, Savannah said, "Great. Em, maybe Dominic would have time to do a reading for you, too, see if he has any insights into what's going on with your parents."

Emma stood up from the chair and smiled, "No, I'm good. I'm coming to terms with things. It's funny, but both my parents are being extra nice to me. They even gave me a thousand dollars for our trip. Maybe the divorce won't be such a bad thing after all."

Murmurs from just outside the classroom door told the girls that the next class was about to start, and that it was time for them to leave while they still could.

As they swam through the sea of students pouring in, Savannah said to her friends through the heads bobbing by, "Let's meet at Em's car after school. And I'll call Dominic to set up a time for the you-know-what." She didn't want to say the word out loud, just in case some of those bobbing ears were listening.

The rest of the day zoomed by for Savannah. Her biology finals turned out to be a breeze, leaving her with an extra thirty minutes before she was supposed to meet Emma and Jade. She decided to go wait under the same big cottonwood tree, maybe grab a quick nap.

As she walked toward the front double doors, she saw Carrie standing by the drinking fountain taking a drink.

"Hey, Carrie," said Savannah.

Carrie's head popped up and immediately a look of embarrassment washed over her face. "Oh. Hi, Savannah. H-how are you?"

"I'm good. How's your brother?"

Carrie wiped her mouth with the back of her hand and said, "He's fine." She paused for a moment, then walked up to Savannah and lowered her voice. "I'm really sorry about what happened. I didn't mean to get you into any trouble. It just sort of came out."

"It's okay, Carrie."

Carrie's mouth twisted into a crooked grimace, and she shook her head. "I couldn't believe my mom called your mom. I had no idea she'd do that."

"Yeah, that was a surprise to me, too." She paused, and when Carrie didn't say anything else she said, "Well, guess I'll see you around. You have a nice summer."

Savannah turned to walk away, but before she could get out the door Carrie said, "Hey, Savannah, I was wondering. Would you . . ."

Savannah turned around. "What?"

"Oh, never mind. See you later."

Savannah smiled and then hurried out the door. She knew that Carrie wanted another reading. But shortly she wouldn't have any cards to do a reading with. Maybe it was for the best. Look how much havoc they had caused already.

Yes, but look at how much good they've done, she thought.

Once outside, Savannah hurried to the large cottonwood tree at the far end of the campus lawn and plopped down underneath it. She leaned up against the trunk, pulled out her phone and called Dominic.

When he answered she said, "Dominic? Hi, it's Savannah."

"Hey, Savannah. What's up?"

"Well, I was wondering, if you aren't too busy this afternoon, would you mind doing a reading for me?"

"Sure. I'm actually free for a couple of hours. But you'd have to come to my house. Are you okay with that?" He paused for a moment and then offered, "Leslie will be here." It was as if he sensed her hesitation.

"That would be great. Do you mind if I bring Jade and Emma with me?"

"No, of course not." He gave her his address and said, "I'll see you girls around two thirty."

Not long after Savannah hung up, she got a text from Jade.

- *Where r you?*

- *Under the C tree.*

- *We r at E's car. Hurry up.*

- *On my way.*

She dropped the phone in her purse and stood up just as two boys came walking toward her. They seemed to be headed in the direction of the baseball diamond.

"Look, there's Savannah, the teenage witch," said the burly one, nudging the other guy who looked like a softer, plumper version of him. "Better not go near her otherwise you'll get warts."

"Yeah, I heard if she touches you your hair will fall out," said the plumper guy, and then he cackled.

Savannah tried to ignore them, but they stopped in front of her.

"Where's your broom, witch?" said Plump Boy.

"I'm not a witch," said Savannah as she turned to leave.

"Hey, witch, don't walk away from me when I'm talking to you." Plump Boy reached out his doughy paw and latched on to her arm.

As soon as he touched her, an image of an older man, roughly the same age as Savannah's father, popped into her head. The man stood over Plump Boy with a leather belt in his right hand and screamed, *"Get up. And quit your damn crying. I ain't gonna baby your fat ass like your mother does."*

In the image, Plump Boy remained on the ground in the fetal position with his hands and arms covering his face. Savannah flinched when she heard the *crack* of the belt across Plump Boy's back and the agonizing cry that followed. She stared at him with saucer eyes and then yanked her arm out of his grip.

"Hey, c'mon ye two. I dunna have all day," yelled someone standing near the gate to the baseball diamond.

Savannah looked over at a young man leaning against the fence. He had a large athletic bag slung over his shoulder with a couple of bats hanging out one end. He wore a blue baseball cap with a fringe of red hair peeking out from underneath it. She couldn't really see his facial features, but by his broad shoulders and by the way he was able to grab her two antagonists' attention, he must have been older than them, maybe a student teacher.

"Be right there, Brady," yelled Burly Kid. He looked over his shoulder back at Savannah and laughed, "See ya later, witch." And then the two boys trotted over to the baseball diamond.

What just happened?

Logically she should have been upset about their taunting her. But that's not where her thoughts settled. All she could think about was seeing that poor boy being beaten by-

The word *"stepfather"* entered her mind.

Even though this kid had been mean to her, she felt sorry for him. It was clear to her that he learned how to be a bully from his stepfather, and that saddened her. She wondered if the beatings might still be happening to that boy. She could probably find out just by focusing on him. But a part of her didn't really want to know the truth because then she would be compelled to do something about it.

How could I have possibly known all that?

She didn't know how she was able to see into that boy's past just by touching him. But there was one thing that was crystal clear . . .

Savannah's psychic powers were evolving.

Chapter 22

Fifteen minutes later the girls entered into the parking lot of Dominic's apartment complex and parked. Located in an older section of town, these grounds showed their age. The area wasn't fancy, but it looked tidy with various flowerbeds skirting the base of each building.

"I think his apartment is in that building over there," said Savannah, pointing to a long, red brick, building shaded by a large red leaf maple tree.

When they found the right address, Savannah knocked on the door. A moment later, Dominic answered it wearing sweats pants that had been whacked off into shorts just above his knees.

When he saw Savannah, he smiled broadly and said, "Hey guys, come on in. Did you have any problems finding the place?"

"Hi Dominic. No, not at all," said Savannah as the girls entered his apartment and stood in the small tiled foyer.

Dominic gestured to the living room. "Go ahead and grab a seat on the couch. Leslie will be out in a minute."

The girls huddled together on a dark green leather sofa with their hands in their laps, looking somewhat uncomfortable. They had only seen this guy the one time. So they really didn't know for sure if he was legit. For all they knew, he could have been some kind of psychopath or a rapist, using the pretext of being a psychic to lure young girls into his lair.

"Be out shortly," came a singsong voice from down the hall.

When a petite blonde entered the living room, she looked at the girls, smiled showing a dimple on her right cheek, and said with a slight twang to her voice, "Sorry I'm late, y'all. Hi, I'm Leslie, Dominic's fiancé." She put the accent on the last syllable.

The girls immediately relaxed.

Savannah recognized Leslie as the woman in her vision seated across from Dominic in the restaurant. She returned the smile, stood up, extended her hand and said, "Nice to meet you, Leslie. I'm Savannah Swift."

When Leslie took her hand, Savannah couldn't help but notice the sparkling diamond on her finger, and the way it winked every time she moved her hand. She gestured to her friends. "This is Jade and Emma."

Leslie nodded to the girls. "It's a pleasure to meet y'all. Would you girls like something to drink? I just made a pitcher of sweet tea."

Savannah answered for all of them. "Yes, thank you."

Leslie smiled at Dominic. "Baby, would you like one, too?"

Dominic blushed slightly. "Sure, thanks." He looked at Savannah. "So, shall we get started?"

"Okay, but before we do, I have something for you." She reached into her purse, pulled out the deck of tarot cards and handed them to Dominic. "I'm sorry, but I need to give these back to you."

Dominic looked surprised. "Don't you want to keep them?"

"Actually, I do. But I promised my mom that I would return them to you. You can't believe how much trouble these things have caused me."

"Sorry to hear that," he said as he took the cards. "I certainly didn't mean to cause you any problems by giving them to you."

"Oh, I know that."

Emma piped up. "But they've also done some amazing things for her. I think her abilities have evolved *because* of the cards." She looked at Savannah. "Go on, Vannah, tell him what you told us driving down here."

Savannah explained to Dominic what happened under the cottonwood tree less than an hour ago. "I don't know how, but I *knew* that this poor kid had been beaten by his stepfather. It was as if I were standing right there watching it happen.

"And when he hit that kid, I literally felt the sting of the belt across my back. I wanted to reach out and help him, but I couldn't. It was the most horrible feeling, not being able to stop his stepdad from hitting him."

Dominic leaned back in a matching green leather club chair. "That doesn't surprise me about you. You're what's known as an empath."

"What's an empath?" said Savannah.

Leslie walked back into the living room carrying a tray of five glasses filled with amber colored tea and an orange slice stuck on the rim of each glass. "An empath is someone who has a highly developed sensitivity to the emotions and emotional states of others," she said as she set the tray on the coffee table and gestured. "Please, help yourselves." She sat down in an identical club chair across from Dominic and said, "All empaths are psychic, but not all psychics are empaths."

Dominic grabbed one of the glasses and took a sip. "She's right. I'm a psychic, but I don't consider myself an empath. When I do a reading for someone, I'm able to see what has happened to them. But I can't feel what they feel. And I don't have that overwhelming urge to step in and save them. But with you, Savannah, it sounds like you are compelled to help. Is that correct?"

"Absolutely! I feel like I have no control over my actions. It's as if some other force is driving me. Their problems become my problems." She took a sip of her tea. It tasted overly sweet to her, like it came out of a can. But she took another sip in spite of it because she didn't want to appear rude.

"It's the same thing with this person named Katie who I've been dreaming about. I feel *compelled* to help her. That's why we're heading out to Carson City on Saturday after the graduation, to see if we can find her."

"Wow, that's a big step for someone just starting out on their psychic journey," said Dominic.

"I know it is." Savannah set the tea down on a coaster and folded her hands across her lap. "You know, I thought that once I stopped doing the readings this ability of mine would go away. But it hasn't. In fact, it seems like it's getting stronger." She looked at him with troubled eyes. "How is it that I'm able to see things without the use of the cards?"

"Remember what we talked about over the phone. Your abilities are going to come through whether you want them to or not." Dominic took a sip of tea, set the glass on the coffee table and said, "So what would you like me to do for you?"

"Since I promised my mom that I wouldn't do any more tarot readings, I was hoping that you could do one for me to see if you can get any more insight into Katie and a company called the Comstock Mining Company. I think that they-"

Dominic held up his hand. "Stop. Don't tell me anything else. I don't want to be influenced by what you say."

He took Savannah's tarot cards out of the deck and handed them to her. "Here, shuffle these." While she shuffled them he looked at the other two girls and said, "So what are your thoughts on psychics."

Emma spoke first. She pushed her glasses up the bridge of her nose and said, "Well, before all of this happened, I didn't really believe in them. But I didn't disbelieve either. I just didn't know that much about them because I didn't know anyone who was one."

She looked over at Savannah. "But watching Vannah through all of this, I've come to realize there are so many things in this world we can't explain. And just because we can't explain them doesn't mean they don't exist."

"And what about you, Jade?" Dominic looked at her. "What are your thoughts?"

She flicked her hair to one side, folded her arms across her chest and said, "Based on what I've seen, I think that Vannah probably does have psychic abilities, and that she could become very good at it . . . someday. But right now, she's just learning about her gifts, and I'm worried that if we pursue this Katie person's disappearance we might be getting into something that we shouldn't be." She paused, glanced at Savannah then looked back at Dominic. "I'll be honest, I'm concerned that we could be getting in way over our heads."

"That's a valid concern," said Dominic. He took the cards from Savannah and laid them out in the shape of a pyramid, face down. He turned over the bottom row of cards, studied them for a moment and then said, "It looks like you have good reason to feel that way, Jade."

He pointed to the first card, that of a boy carrying a knapsack over his shoulder and whistling. "You all are looking at this trip as a fun adventure, and you think that you've got all the details of your trip lined up. But there's a warning here—you need to be very careful because you don't have all the information. And it's those missing details that can hurt you."

He touched a card that had a black horse and a white horse on it. "I'm also seeing that you need to be mindful of a black vehicle and a white vehicle."

Savannah stifled a gasp. She hadn't mention the white pickup truck from her dreams to anyone and wondered if that might be the one he was referring to.

Dominic turned over the next row of five cards, studied the images for a moment and then said, "Emma, this row of cards is about you. You cannot fix what is going on with your parents. This is something that has been brewing for a long time. There will be yelling, crying, fighting, and hurt feelings. But in the end all will be resolved."

Emma fought back the tears. "Do you think they'll end up getting divorced or will they stay together?"

Dominic turned over the next row of four cards.

Emma recognized the card with the mountains and the flower covered arch. As she looked at it closer she furrowed her brow. "That's strange. I remember that card from when Savannah did a reading. But I never noticed that castle on top of the mountain before."

Dominic smiled. "That's normal. Our eyes focus on the part of the image that pertains to the question." He pointed to the arch on the card and said, "Those blooming flowers represent a harmonious home. So I can't say whether or not your parents will follow through with the divorce, but I can say that at some point your home will feel peaceful and complete, and it will be filled with love again."

He turned over the next row of three cards and tapped the first one with his finger. It was of an angelic woman suspended in the center of a wreath adorned with various animal heads. "Savannah, you have a lot of spirit guides watching over you. Did you know that?"

"I'm sorry, but I don't know what a spirit guide is."

"It's an entity, spirit or angel that watches over you and helps you through difficult times. We all have a multitude of them around us at any given time. But certain ones step forward to help us when we are about to embark on something significant."

This made Savannah feel uncomfortable. "Do you see something bad happening to us?"

Dominic turned over the next row of two cards. "Not necessarily. But you must be careful not to go into a situation blindly just because you are anxious." He looked up at Savannah and said, "You must always be aware of your surroundings and trust your instincts and intuition. That is what will keep you safe."

He turned over the final card, and Savannah gasped when she saw the Devil card. She wasn't sure what it meant, but she knew it couldn't be good.

Chapter 23

Savannah remained quiet in the back seat as they drove away from Dominic's place. She thought about everything that he had told her. *You're an empath. Trust your instincts and intuition. You don't have all the information.*

She thought about the Devil card and wondered if maybe Jade was right. What if they were about to get in over their heads?

Emma looked in the rearview mirror. "You doing okay back there? You're pretty quiet."

"Yeah, I'm fine. I've just got a lot to think about."

"I've got something that will take your mind off of things." Emma flashed her a cryptic smile.

"Yeah? What?"

"Did you hear about that party on Friday night at Dawn Seavers' house? Everyone's going."

"Yeah, I heard something about a big party."

Dawn Seavers, head cheerleader and daughter of Congressman Seavers, wasn't exactly high on Savannah's list of close friends. She knew her, but the two of them hadn't spoken more than two words to each other in the entire four years of high school. And with all the gossip floating around about her, Savannah wasn't interested in thrusting herself into the middle of a bunch of staring, name calling bullies.

"I don't think I'm going to go."

Jade turned around in her seat. "Ah, c'mon, Vannah. You have to go. We're the three Musketeers, one for all and all for one."

"Yeah," said Emma, looking at her in the rearview mirror. "Besides, we're going with you to Carson City, so . . ."

Savannah raised her hands in surrender. "Okay. You win. I'll go. But if anyone there makes even the slightest comment about me being a witch, I'm leaving. Deal?"

"Deal," said both Emma and Jade in unison.

~~~~~~~~~~~~~~~~~

For the next three days, Savannah stayed busy with the last of her finals and preparing for her trip. Preparations included much more than packing a suitcase. It meant finding out as much as she could about the Comstock Mining Company before they left for Carson City.

She figured the best and most private place to conduct her search would be the library, but she would need help, so she called Jade. While she waited for her to answer, Savannah stuck her head out her bedroom door, peered up and down the hallway, and then quietly shut it so that her end of the conversation would stay private.

"Hey, Vannah."

Savannah plopped down on her bed and said, "Hey, Jade. You busy?"

"Not really, why? What's up?"

Savannah lowered her voice. "Do you think your parents would let you borrow their new Jeep?"

"Oh man, I don't know. My dad's gotten pretty attached to it, acting like some teenage boy, driving around with the top down and the music blaring. What do you need it for?"

"I need to go to the library."

"The library? Why?"

"Remember when Dominic said we needed to have all of the facts so we don't rush in blindly? Well, I thought that we could do a little research before we leave tomorrow. You wanna help?"

"Sure. Hang on a sec. I'll ask and see what he says. Hey Dad," she yelled.

Savannah heard her muffled voice over the phone but could not hear her dad's reply.

A few seconds later Jade said, "Well, I'll be. He said okay. So I'll see you in twenty."

"Thanks, Jade. You're a good friend."

"I know." Her smile came through the phone.

Twenty-five minutes later when Jade pulled into the driveway in a brand new sporty, black, four-door Jeep Wrangler with oversized tires and chrome rims, Savannah yelled out to her mother, "Be back in a few hours. Love you."

From somewhere at the other end of the house, Savannah heard a distant and muffled, "Okay. Love you, too. Bye."

Savannah walked out the front door, stopped, and stared at the sexy looking metal beast in her driveway. Jade had taken the soft top down, exposing the saddle colored leather interior and a black roll bar. She slid into the front seat and exclaimed, "Wow! Nice ride!"

"I know, right? Plus it's a blast to drive." As she pulled out of the driveway, Jade said, "So what exactly are we going to be looking for?"

"Information," said Savannah.

They called Emma on the way, and by the time they got there, she was already standing by the library entrance waiting for them.

As soon as they trotted up the steps, she opened the door for them and said, "Let's hurry up and get this done. Remember, we've got that party tonight." She looked at Jade as she walked by. "Nice ride, by the way."

"I know, right?" smiled Jade.

"Shame it's not a hybrid."

The three walked down the hall toward the computer room near the back of the building. Normally, this section of the library was filled with students studying, doing homework, or preparing for tests. But luckily, being that today was the last day of finals for the rest of Scottsbluff High School, the computer room was empty.

Once the girls picked a computer and settled in, Savannah pulled up a blank Google page and said, "I thought we could start by searching all of the newspaper archives for the Reno, Lake Tahoe and Carson City for the last few years. We're looking for anything that might pertain to the Comstock Mining Company."

With all three focused on their tasks, it didn't take them long to find something.

Emma pulled up a website called NevadaAppeal.com. She clicked on the archives and scrolled down until she saw "New acquisitions for The Comstock Mining Company" highlighted in blue.

She clicked on the article, skimmed it for a few seconds and then said, "Listen to this, guys. This article is from June 2007." She read an excerpt out loud. "'The Comstock Mining Company, located in Dayton, Nevada, has just purchased four more 'dry mines' in the Flowery Peak area near Virginia City.

"'When asked what the company intends to do with the land, a spokesperson for the Comstock Mining Company said that the purchases were made on behalf of Mr. Harrison Taylor, the CEO of their holding company, the Geneva Corporation. Any plans will remain private until Taylor decides to makes the details public.'"

"What are dry mines?" said Jade.

Emma shrugged her shoulders. "I don't know. Let me see what I can find out." She continued to skim the article.

In the meantime, Jade pulled up a site on her computer and said, "Here's an article from the Huffington Post, dated about a year ago." She began to read it out loud. "'Comstock Mining Company is at it again. They have just purchased another five dry mines near Virginia City, making them the largest owners of depleted mines in the state of Nevada.

"'Private landowners in the area have been jumping on the bandwagon for years now, hoping to get their share of the Comstock pie before their golden goose flies away.

"'Even though Comstock is paying them only a fraction of what the land originally went for back when the mines were viable, it's still more than the land's current value.

"'Said one farmer, 'Since there ain't no more gold or silver in them there hills, I guess pennies on the dollar is better than no pennies at all.'

"'When asked if the landowner knew what the new owners intend to do with the mines, he replied, 'Don't know. Don't care. I got my check so it's none of my business anymore.'"

Jade scanned the article for a few seconds then continued reading out loud. "'In addition to the dry mines, Comstock owns the majority of the hard rock mines in the area, as well as-'"

"What are hard rock mines? Aren't all rocks hard?" said Savannah interrupting her.

Jade looked up from the computer screen. "I'm not sure. I was thinking the same thing."

Emma piped up. "This is from the Comstock website. It says, 'There are two types of mines: underground shafts, also call hard rock mines, and open pits. Underground hard rock mining refers to various underground mining techniques used to excavate hard minerals such as gold, silver or iron. Whereas, open-pit mines are used when deposits of minerals are found near the surface.

"'Both types of mining still exist in the area, however, most of the mining today is done in open pits and is still Comstock's main source of revenue.'"

Savannah's mind flashed on the dream of Katie being buried alive. She saw front-end loaders getting buckets full of dirt and rocks from large piles then dumping them over the edge and wondered if it might have come from one of their open-pits.

Jade said, "Here's an article about the Comstock Mining Company in the Lake Tahoe Daily Tribune. It also mentions the purchases of several 'dry' gold and silver mines. But none of the articles state why either." She looked up from her computer. "What do you think they want with them?"

"I have no idea," said Savannah.

"Maybe they're planning a new housing development," said Emma.

"It's possible," said Savannah. She paused in thought then looked from one friend to the other. "I don't know what, but something's going on out there. I can feel it in my bones."

Jade looked at her. "Maybe it's Katie's bones you're feeling it in."

Chapter 24

That evening while getting ready for the party, Savannah couldn't stop her mind from whirling with all of the information they dug up that afternoon. Dry mines, open pits, hard rock — she didn't understand any of it. She sensed they were pieces of a puzzle, but she just didn't know how to make any of them fit together.

After she pinned her hair into a soft up-do, she slipped on a short, strappy, red dress, and looked at her reflection full on in the mirror. Then she turned to the side, sucked in her stomach and pushed out her chest. "Not bad, if I do say so myself." She tugged on the hem, hoping that the length would pass her father's inspection.

While she sat on the bed pulling on a pair of sleek, black, three-inch heels, she thought, *I know who can help me piece this thing together. Dominic.*

She pulled her cell phone from her computer bag and dialed his number.

After two rings, Dominic said, "Hello?"

"Hi, Dominic. It's Savannah."

"Hi, Savannah. How are you?"

"I'm good. Do you have a minute?"

"Not really. I'm on my way out the door. Could we talk tomorrow?"

Savannah sighed. "I suppose so. But I have my graduation ceremony at ten o'clock tomorrow morning and then we leave for our trip right afterwards."

"Can you call me first thing in the morning?"

Savannah tried to keep the disappointment out of her voice. "Sure. Thanks, Dominic. I'll talk to you tomorrow."

She ended the call and tossed the phone in her small black clutch. At the moment she felt alone and frustrated. The only person who could offer her any helpful insight was Dominic, and he had something more important to do.

What could be more important than this?

She let out a deep sigh as she grabbed her purse off of the bed and headed for the stairs. *I guess I'm just going to have to learn how to figure this out on my own.*

When she got to the bottom of the stairs, Mrs. Swift was waiting for her with her camera dangling from her wrist like a charm bracelet. She clasped her hands together and said, "Vannah, you look fantastic! Turn around."

Savannah flashed her a wide grin and pirouetted for her, forgetting momentarily that she was depressed. "You like it?"

Her father walked in from the kitchen, stood next to his wife and arched his eyebrows. "A little short don't you think?"

Mrs. Swift nudged him in the ribs. "Honey, it's what all the kids are wearing. Just tell her she looks nice."

Pastor Swift kissed Savannah on the forehead and murmured, "You look beautiful, honey."

Savannah didn't need to be psychic to know that he was having a hard time seeing her all grown up. She hugged him and said, "Thanks, Dad."

Right then, the doorbell rang, breaking up their father/daughter embrace. "The girls are here," she said to him as she gently pulled away and opened the door.

"Wow! Look at you, girl," said Jade as she and Emma walked through the door. "Great color on you."

"Thanks! You guys clean up nice, too."

Emma had on a pair of black Levis with black sequins stitched up the outer seams, a tight silver tank top that accentuated her chest, and her hair had been blown straight, giving her a rock star look. Instead of wearing her glasses, she had put in a pair of colored contact lenses, giving her eyes a deep turquoise hue.

Jade wore a tight, knee length, emerald green, Japanese style dress with a slit up the left side. Her hair had been pinned up with a pair of black, enamel chopsticks, exposing a pair of gold, dangling earrings.

"Stay right there, you two," said Mrs. Swift. "Vannah, go stand next to them. I want to get your picture." She pulled her camera off her wrist and aimed it at the girls. When the trio posed she zoomed in and clicked a few shots. "I can't believe how great you girls look." She clicked a few more shots.

"Okay, enough pictures. We've got to go." Savannah gave her mother a kiss on the cheek and then walked over to her father, hugged him again and said, "We'll be home before midnight."

Her dad hugged her back and said, "Remember, no drinking. And if there are any drugs there I want you to leave immediately."

Savannah rolled her eyes as she pulled away, but not in a disrespectful way. It was more of an "I'm-smart-enough-to-know-better" kind of eye roll.

"Dad, it's at the congressman's house. I really doubt that he would allow any drugs there."

"Well, you just never know." He pulled his eyes into an intimidating glare.

When Savannah stared into her father's stern eyes, she heard a softer version of his voice waft into her left ear. *I'm not ready for my little girl to leave home.*

Her eyes softened, and she wrapped her arms around her father's neck and whispered in his ear, "I love you, Dad."

And then the three girls hurried out the front door.

By the time they got to the Seavers' mansion, the place was jammed with partiers coming and going. Valets in red vests ran from car to car, opened up doors to let the passengers out, and then shuffled the vehicles off to some unknown destination.

As soon as the valet opened up Savannah's door, the sound of pounding base coming from inside the house hit her chest with full force.

"Good evening. Welcome to the Seavers' residence." A twenty-something hunk held out his hand for Savannah to take. Not feeling quite stable on her heels, she welcomed the extra support. He then opened the back door and extended his hand to Jade. As she gracefully climbed out, the guy's eyes migrated down to the bare skin of her left thigh. "Welcome to the Severs' residence."

"Thank you," said Jade in a flirty fashion to the hunk. By the way she fluttered her eyes at him, she must have noticed him checking her out.

On the other side of the car, Emma's usher had helped her out and was already in the driver's seat waiting for his partner to close the passenger door so that he could move the car.

The valet shut the car door, flashed Jade a charming grin and said, "Have a nice time, ladies."

As the three walked up the grand steps to the marble pillars flanking the front double doors, Savannah said, "I wasn't really looking forward to this. But now that I'm here, I can't wait to get in there and dance."

"See, I told you it'd be fun," said Emma as they walked past a coat check girl standing by the front door.

When the three girls entered the house, they stopped abruptly in the foyer and gawked, unprepared for the majesty that greeted their eyes. The place looked like a palace with white marble floors and rows of crystal chandeliers dripping from the three story ceilings. To the right, a wide curved staircase seemed to lead all the way up to heaven. Life size paintings of people, probably ancestors, dressed in period attire lined the stair case wall leading up to the second and third story.

Live potted trees interspersed with elegant marble statues of half-naked women holding vases lined the walls in front of them leading into the expansive living room.

Beyond the living room's everyday décor, Dawn's parents spared no expense in transforming this part of the mansion into the ultimate party palace. Mirrored balls suspended from the ceiling spun slowly casting rainbow reflections on the walls and floors. A music video of Bruno Mars' "Up Town Funk" lit up the back wall. And atop four different stages, dancers bumped and gyrated to the music.

"Welcome, Ladies. Would you care for some punch?" A white-gloved waiter dressed in a black suit with a red bowtie and holding a tray of crystal goblets stood just inside the entrance to the living room. He handed a glass to each of the girls and then gestured toward the activity. "On behalf of Congressman Seavers and his family, welcome and please enjoy the party."

Mesmerized by all of the stimuli, the girls slowly walked in a few feet and then stopped so they could take it all in before being sucked up by the crowd.

When Savannah saw the different hors d'oeuvre stations filled with chilled lobster, crab cakes, mac and cheese cups, mini sliders, an array of salads, endless potato chips, and towers of cupcakes, she said, "I've died and gone to heaven."

"Well, hello there, ladies," came a male voice from behind them.

The girls turned and smiled.

"Dominic! Leslie!" said Savannah. She immediately felt better knowing that he hadn't just brushed her off earlier.

Dominic took hold of Leslie's hand and said, "C'mon you guys, let's join the party."

While Dominic led Leslie to the dance floor, the three girls trolled the different food stations salivating over all of the delicious looking platters of bite-sized delights. Jade and Emma stopped at the tower of cupcakes.

"I'll meet you guys over there," said Savannah eyeing the salad table.

She strolled over to the table, picked up a mac and cheese cup and was about to take a bite when she felt the presence of someone standing behind her. She turned around and stared up into a pair of the deepest blue eyes she had ever seen.

Chapter 25

Oh. My. Goodness!

Who was this amazing hunk standing in front of her? It took Savannah a moment for recognition to set in, but then her mind flashed on the guy in the blue baseball cap leaning up against the baseball fence. Now she could see waves of thick, russet colored hair. And boy, did they make his blue eyes pop.

"Hi." The guy flashed her a sheepish grin then grabbed a plate and put two mac cups on it.

"Hi," she said trying not to stare. She grabbed a plate and set the mac and cheese cup on it along with a few carrots and some celery sticks.

"Nice party, dunna ye think?"

"Um, yeah. It's nice." She felt her palms starting to sweat.

He seemed to hesitate for a moment then stuck out his hand and said, "I'm Brady. Brady McTavish. What's yer name?"

"McTavish. Is that Irish?"

"No, Scottish."

Now she noticed just a hint of a Scottish brogue that clung to the back end of each word. "Nice to meet you, Brady. I'm Savannah Swift," she said as she discretely wiped the sweat from her hand then shook his.

Instantly, a feeling of warmth flooded Savannah's body. Images of Brady filled her mind. Snapshots of him as a baby, a toddler, an older child, a teenager, and finally, images of him as a young man bombarded her mind. And in all of them he was smiling and happy. And that made her smile.

"What?" he said.

"What, what?"

"What are ye smiling about?"

Savannah began to blush. "Nothing. I'm just happy to be here, that's all."

"Aye, me too."

Savannah nibbled on one of the baby carrots. She wanted to gobble down the mac and cheese but she didn't want to look like a pig in front of this Scottish god. "So, Mr. McTavish, what brings you to Scottsbluff?"

"I'm here on an internship program at Regional West."

"Really? Are you studying to be a doctor?"

"No. And dunna ye dare laugh. I'm studying te be a nurse."

Savannah arched her eyebrows. "A nurse?" *You can take my temperature anytime.* The thought made her blush.

"An A.R.E.A nurse te be exact." He must have noticed the puzzled look on Savannah's face and added, "It's an acronym for Advancing Rural Emergency Acute Care."

"Wow. That's a mouthful." She paused, discreetly taking in the sharp angles of his slightly bristled jaw line. "So what made you decide to become a nurse?"

Brady took a bite of mac and cheese. "My father."

Savannah took the tiniest bite of hers. "Oh, was your father a nurse?"

Brady shook his head. "No. He worked in a gold mine back in Scotland."

Savannah's eye lit up. Remembering their research from earlier she said, "A gold mine? What type of hard rock mining were they doing? Open pit or shaft?"

He seemed surprised and said, "Well, ye do know yer mines, don't ye, lass." He took another bite of his mac and cheese. "It was an underground mine, and the shafts went deep into the mountains outside our little village of Tyndrum. Gold was discovered there back in 1994. But the price of gold had dropped so much that it was not profitable te mine it, so they closed it down."

"I didn't realize that Scotland had gold mines."

"Aye, a lot of them." He munched on a potato chip. "This particular one remained abandoned up until a few years ago. Not long after they reopened it, my father, along with three other miners, died when one of the shafts collapsed."

"Oh, my gosh, I'm so sorry. That must have been awful." She felt the urge to reach out a comforting hand to him but resisted.

"Aye. The truly awful part is that they could have survived had our town had the medical resources needed te save them. But Tyndrum was out in the middle of nowhere, and by the time help finally arrived from Stirling, they were already dead."

Savannah gasped. "Oh, that's so tragic."

"Aye. It was. That's why I'm studying te be a rural nurse, so that I can help others in similar situations." Silence fell between them for several seconds until Brady said, "But enough about me. Let's talk about ye."

"There's really not much to talk about. I'm not that interesting." She nibbled on another carrot.

"Somehow I doubt that," he said, a smile tugging at the corners of his mouth.

Savannah was reluctant at first, but something about him made her feel comfortable. Maybe it was his kind eyes, or that impossibly sexy accent. Whatever spell he seemed to have over her caused her to open her mouth and allow her entire life to spill out. She told him about her family and that her father was a pastor.

She talked about her two best friends and their plans for college, and she even told him about their trip to Carson City, omitting the reasons why.

When she couldn't think of anything else to say she stopped and said, "That's pretty much it, my life in a nutshell. I told you I wasn't very interesting."

"Hmm," was his only comment. After a few seconds of silence between them, Brady leaned in a little closer and said, "Can I ask ye a question?"

"Sure."

He seemed to hesitate for a moment and then said, "I couldn't help but overhear what those two daft dobbers said te ye the other day."

Savannah scrunched her eyebrows not at all sure what he was talking about. "Huh?"

"Ye know, that yer a-" He lowered his voice and said, "-a witch."

Savannah leaned back slightly. "Oh, that."

"Is it true?" His eyes seemed wide with curiosity.

Savannah stared at him for a moment and then laughed. "No, of course it isn't true."

"Whew." Brady's face seemed to relax.

"But I am a psychic."

Brady's facial features froze for the briefest moment. Then his eyes grew wide and he said, "So it's true, then, that ye predicted that girl's brother would die in a car crash?"

Savannah nodded. "Uh-hmm."

For a moment neither of them spoke. Then Savannah said, "Does that bother you?"

"No, but it does make me a little nervous."

Savannah tilted her head to one side. "Why would it make you nervous?"

Brady shrugged. "I dunna know. Maybe because I'm afraid ye might see something like that happening te me." He paused and stared into her eyes. "*Do* ye see anything like that in my future?"

"I don't know. Give me your hand."

As soon as she held his hand images of Brady in his late twenties flashed into her mind again. He wore the same beaming smile. But this time she noticed that he was wearing a black tux jacket.

The image zoomed out further and she saw that he was dressed in a red and black plaid kilt with an elegantly stitched, black leather, sporran tied loosely around the front of his waist. He was standing on a beautiful lawn with his back to a white arch decorated with white roses and pink star lilies. An aisle separated two sections of white folding chairs, and all of them filled with people dressed in similar tartan attire.

Savannah smiled but kept the image of his impending wedding a secret. She let go of his hand and said, "I wouldn't worry about that if I were you. I think you're going to be around for a long time."

"That's good te know." Brady wiped imaginary sweat off of his brow and smiled.

Right then Emma and Jade walked up out of breath. "I haven't danced that much in forever," said Emma.

"At least the guy you were dancing with knew how to dance. Mine just stood there bobbing like a zombie." Jade looked from Savannah to Brady then back to Savannah. "Aren't you going to introduce us to your friend?"

Brady stuck out his hand. "Hi I'm Brady McTavish. Ye must be Jade and Emma. Nice te meet ye. And might I say ye lasses look lovely tonight."

The two girls giggled and gushed but said nothing intelligible. Both were seemingly tongue-tied, which birthed a slight smile on Savannah's face.

For several seconds the four of them stood there in awkward silence until Brady said, "So I understand ye lasses are leaving for a road trip te Nevada tomorrow."

Jade flashed Savannah a look as if to say, *I thought it was supposed to be a secret* and then said, "Yeah, we're going to visit

Vannah's aunt in Salt Lake City first, and afterwards drive down the California Coast."

"That sounds like fun." He turned to Savannah. "So how long will ye be gone?"

Savannah smiled up at him. "Ten days."

You are so cute, she thought as she set her plate of barely touched food back on the table and brushed away a strand of hair that had come loose.

He returned the smile, not taking his eyes off of her or the movement of her hand. "Well, when ye get back maybe we could go see a movie or something."

Savannah blushed again. "That would be nice. I'd like that."

"Good. It'll be a date, then."

Acting as if they were the only ones in the room, the two of them continued to stare and smile at each other, until Dominic walked up and said, "Hey Savannah, can I talk to you for a second?"

Savannah reluctantly pulled her gaze away from Brady and looked at Dominic. "Sure." She looked back at Brady and said, "You mind hanging here with Jade and Emma for a minute? This won't take long."

Brady winked at the two girls causing them to blush. "I'm sure the three of us can find plenty of things te talk about until ye get back. Dunna ye think, ladies?" That made Jade and Emma giggle.

Savannah followed Dominic toward the entrance and said, "So, what's up?"

"I'm sorry I wasn't able to talk to you earlier when you called. I could sense that you had something important on your mind. We can talk now if you want."

Savannah glanced over and caught Brady staring at her. Her friends were chatting with him, grinning and giggling like a couple of idiots. When she smiled at him and he smiled back she knew that her questions could wait.

Without breaking eye contact with Brady, she said to Dominic, "Nah, it's okay. It wasn't that important."

Chapter 26

The next morning, Savannah woke with a grin on her face. She had several dreams during the night. But for the first time in a long time they weren't about being buried alive.

They were about Brady.

Savannah stretched up her arms and smiled, remembering those dreamy blue eyes of his and how they sparkled every time he looked at her.

She let out a lingering sigh and leisurely looked over at the clock on her nightstand. "Oh crap!" she shouted. It was already eight thirty. Her graduation ceremony started in an hour and a half.

She shot out of bed, flung open her bedroom door and almost collided with her mother.

"Mom, why didn't you wake me? I've got to shower, get ready, make sure my gown is pressed, and I haven't even packed for my trip yet," she said as she ran into the bathroom and closed the door.

"Sorry, honey. I wanted to give you a few extra minutes to sleep." Mrs. Swift pulled Savannah's red graduation gown with matching cap from the closet and said into the bathroom door, "You just get yourself ready. I'll take care of your gown and get you some breakfast. Do you want eggs?"

"No," came the muffled response over the sound of the running shower. "Just a piece of toast and some OJ."

Fifteen minutes later, Savannah pulled a light green, floral, summer dress from her closet and carefully slipped it over her freshly blow-dried hair, so as not to mess it up or smear her makeup. She zipped up the side of the dress and slipped on a pair of cream colored, open toed, pumps. She pulled her soft-sided suitcase from the back of the closet and began filling it with pants, shorts, tops, shoes, socks, and underwear. Then she plucked a hot pink bikini from her drawer and threw it in the suitcase, just in case.

She scampered down the stairs, dumped her suitcase by the front door and then hurried into the kitchen where both her parents were sitting at the table finishing their breakfast.

Her mother pointed to her toast and said, "Eat before it gets cold." Then she gave a slight glance to Mr. Swift that didn't go unnoticed by Savannah.

"Thanks for ironing my robe, Mom. I saw it hanging by the front door."

"You're welcome," said Mrs. Swift. She took a sip of coffee and threw another cryptic look at Mr. Swift.

"Ah, honey . . ." Mr. Swift pulled a white envelope from his shirt pocket and slid it across the table to Savannah. "This is from your mother and I. It's a little something for your trip."

Savanna ripped open the envelope and pulled out a congratulations card. When she opened it, a Visa card fell into her lap.

She looked from one parent to the other. "What's this?"

Her mother set the cup down and said, "It's a prepaid Visa Card for your trip, you know, gas, hotels, meals . . ."

"And a little extra, just in case of an emergency," added her dad.

Savannah looked at the Visa card then up at her parents. "How much extra?"

"We put a thousand dollars on there for you," said Mr. Swift.

Savannah's eyes ballooned. "A thousand dollars?" She knew they couldn't afford that amount of money. "But Mom, Dad, that's way too much."

She started to hand the card back to them but her father pushed it back toward her and said, "We want you to have it. And what you don't use for your trip you can put toward your college."

"Besides, we know that California is pretty expensive, and we don't want you to have to skip Disneyland just because you ran out of money," said her mother.

Savannah choked back the tears. It wasn't because of their generosity that she wanted to cry. It was because of the lies that she had told them about where she was really going. She started to open her mouth to confess but then thought better of it. If they knew the real reason, they'd never let her go.

"Thank you so much. I love you guys." She tucked the Visa back into the card, got up and hugged both of her parents. "I promise I'll use it wisely."

A horn honking in the driveway caused her mother to swipe away her tears. "The girls are here. You better go. We'll see you at the graduation."

Savannah grabbed her robe, purse and suitcase and hurried out to greet her friends.

"Unlock the back, and I'll throw my suitcase in," Savannah said to Emma as she walked around to the back of the car. When she pulled open the hatchback, Savannah's eye widened. Crammed in the back were portable shovels, Coleman lanterns, a box of flashlights and batteries, solar blankets, six plastic gallon jugs of water, a sleeping bag, and a cooler.

"You realize that Carson City isn't the Wild West, don't you?" said Savannah. "They do have modern conveniences like motels and grocery stores."

Emma laughed. "I know. I just want to be prepared."

"Prepared for what," laughed Savannah, "the end of the world?" She wedged her suitcase in the mix, slammed the hatch and hopped into the back seat.

When they got to the high school parking lot Brady was standing next to the main double doors holding a bouquet of pink and orange Gerber daisies with yellow mums, all tied together with a hot pink ribbon. He seemed to be intently watching all of the cars enter the parking lot.

"Awwww," said Jade and Emma in unison.

"Did you tell him to meet you here?" asked Jade.

Savannah peered in between the seats through the windshield. "No, not at all," she said trying to hold back her excitement.

"Well, it looks like somebody might have a date to their own graduation," teased Emma as she parked the car and shut it off.

"But what does he expect you to do with those flowers? Take them with you? He knows we're leaving on a road trip right after graduation," said Jade.

"It's a sweet gesture, assuming those flowers are for me," said Savannah stepping out of the car. She tugged at her hemline and smoothed out the wrinkles.

"Oh, they're for you," said Emma when Brady smiled broadly the moment he saw Savannah and began walking toward them.

When Brady got to the car he held out the flowers and said, "Hey, Savannah, these are for ye. Now, I know that ye'll be leaving right after the ceremony, but I still wanted ye te have them."

Savannah blushed when she took the flowers. She glanced at the small card pitchforked into the middle of the flowers. It read:

Congratulations on your graduation, Savannah.

Brady.

And underneath his name he had written his cell phone number.

"They're beautiful. Thank you, Brady. That was very nice of you." She handed the flowers back to him and said, "Would you mind holding on to them for me until after the ceremony? You know, in case I don't graduate." Before he could take them, she plucked the card from its holder and dropped it in her purse, just in case she needed it.

Chapter 27

After the graduation ceremony, Savannah, Emma and Jade changed into their travel clothes and waded through the crowd of happy graduates and their families, stopping periodically to give and receive hugs. They had told their families that they would meet up with them on the high school lawn where punch and sheet cake were being served by the Home Ec class.

Savannah spotted her family first. They had already made it through the refreshment line and were chatting with Jade's parents.

She looked at her watch and said to her friends, "It's already noon. Let's only stay for a few minutes. I'm anxious to get on the road."

The two girls agreed with her. Salt Lake City was over five hundred miles away. Even if they left this minute, they wouldn't arrive at Savannah's aunt's place until after eight o'clock.

Savannah waved her hand in the air and shouted, "Mom! Dad!"

Mr. Swift waved back, tossed his empty paper plate into a nearby trashcan and began walking toward them.

"Congratulations, girls. Do you want some cake?" said Mr. Swift as soon as he reached them.

Savannah spoke for the three of them. "Sorry, Dad. But we need to get on the road."

"Nonsense. You have time to spend a few minutes with your families. Now follow me."

Mr. Swift led the girls back to where the rest of the family stood. And when they got there, Emma's folks had joined the group, although they weren't standing next to each other.

"Congratulations, honey," said Mrs. Reed as she enveloped Emma in a big hug. Then she hugged Jade and Savannah. "I'm so proud of you girls."

When Mrs. Reed released her and pulled away, Savannah noticed that her eyes were red. The makeup she wore did little to camouflage the puffiness. "Thank you, Mrs. Reed. It's hard to believe we finally graduated."

More hugs were exchanged and accolades given until Brady walked up carrying the same bunch of flowers.

Savannah beamed when she saw him and said, "Brady! Hi."

"Now it's official," he said handing her the flowers again.

She took them from him and said, "Everyone, this is Brady. Brady, these are my parents, and my little brother, Kyle. Brady is interning at Regional Medical."

Brady shook their hands. "It's a pleasure te meet ye, Mr. and Mrs. Swift. And ye, too, Kyle."

Kyle shoved the last bit of cake in his mouth, smiled and squeezed it through the gap in his front teeth. An abrupt smack on the back of his head caused him to shut his mouth. When he looked behind him into his mother's laser eyes, he swallowed the cake and mumbled, "Nice to meetcha."

Savannah flashed her little brother a nearly identical laser stare then continued with the rest of the introductions.

"Do I detect a bit of an accent?" asked Mr. Swift.

Before Brady could answer, Dominic walked up and said, "Congratulations, you guys. You did it." He gave Savannah a hug and whispered into her ear. "I need to talk to you."

Savannah pulled away and looked from Dominic to her parents. Their raised eyebrows indicated that they were interested in finding out who the stranger was that was hugging their daughter.

"Uh, Mom, Dad. This is Dominic DeCarlo. Dominic, these are my folks."

"Nice to meet you," he said.

Mrs. Swift tilted her head to one side. "Are you also a senior?"

"No, ma'am."

"I didn't think so. You look too old to be in high school."

Savannah knew her mother was fishing for information and said, "Dominic is a student counselor." It wasn't a complete lie. She *was* a student, and he *had* counseled her.

"A counselor? Oh, that's nice."

Mrs. Swift opened her mouth to say something else but Jade cut her off. "Mrs. Swift. That is such a pretty dress you're wearing. Where did you get it?"

"Yes, Mrs. Swift, it's such a nice color on you. Did you get it at the outlet mall?" said Emma.

While Mrs. Swift continued to be ambushed by the two girls, Savannah grabbed Dominic by the arm and discretely snuck away.

"What's up?" said Savannah once they were safely behind her favorite cottonwood tree.

Dominic's face seemed fraught with worry. "Savannah, I think you should reconsider going on this trip."

"What? Why?"

Dominic lowered his voice a little. "I did a reading for Leslie last night, and your name came up."

"Well, that's not that surprising, is it? I mean, you said that general readings are general because anything can come up, right?"

"Yes, I did. But this was more than just some little tidbit about you. It was a warning."

Savannah sucked in her breath. "A warning? About what?"

"About this trip and your safety. About the people you are delving into. About the circumstances surrounding the death of this woman." Dominic put a hand on her shoulder and looked into her eyes. "Savannah, I'm really concerned about the three of you going out there alone. It's not safe. So for your sake and the sake of your friends, please reconsider."

Savannah saw the terror in his eyes. She knew this was something serious and not to be taken lightly.

"Did the cards give you any indication as to what trouble we might potentially get into?"

Dominic shook his head. "No. And every time I asked for clarification, all I got was an image of David fighting Goliath."

"Well, that's not all bad. David won." She tried to sound reassuring. But it didn't seem to help. Dominic's brow still remained creased with worry. She grasped Dominic's hands. "We'll be really careful. I promise."

"I know you will think you're being careful, but if this truly is an unsolved murder and you start poking around into something you shouldn't, the same thing could happen to you."

"That's not going to happen."

"Savannah, you don't know that. You guys will be out there on your own with no protection." He let out a sigh. "If you really feel the need to take a road trip, please consider going to California instead of Carson City."

She released Dominic's hands and shook her head. "Dominic, this goes way beyond going on some road trip. I know I'm being led to find Katie McCall. She's been trying to contact me for a very long time. And now that I'm aware of it, I can't abandon her. She needs me. You, of all people, should understand this."

Dominic pinched the bridge of his nose as if frustrated. "Savannah, I do understand it, but I also know that you are a brand new baby when it comes to being psychic. And babies by nature are innocent and completely trusting. They don't know when they are in the midst of danger. They only survive because someone else is watching over them." He paused. "Please, I'm begging you, reconsider."

"I'll think about." Savannah glanced back at the group and noticed that her mother was looking intently in her direction. "We should get back."

They started to walk when Dominic snapped his finger and said, "Oh, I almost forgot. There was one other thing. I kept seeing a man with a sword." He shook his head as if anticipating her next question. "I'm sorry, but I don't know what it means."

Savannah sucked in her breath remembering her own reading and whispered, "Look out for the man with the sword."

Chapter 28

When the two returned to the group, Savannah pasted on a smile and said to Jade and Emma, "We should probably be on our way. We don't want to get to Aunt Helen's place too late." She ruffled her brother's hair then turned to her parents and hugged them. "I love you, guys. Oh, and Mom, will you take these flowers home and put them in water?"

Her mother nodded with tight lips as she took the bouquet and clutched it to her chest. "Call as soon as you get there, okay."

"I will." She could tell her mother was fighting back the tears.

Savannah's eyes migrated over to Brady and lingered on him for a few seconds longer than they probably should have. She didn't want to be obvious, but she wanted to memorize his features. Now that she had met him, ten days seemed like a very long time.

"And thank you again for the flowers, Brady. That was so nice of you."

Brady returned the smile, but his face held the look of a sad puppy.

Finally, her gaze fell on Dominic. She didn't say anything to him because she didn't want her mom to interrogate him after she left. But in that split second, his eyes reiterated the warning. *Be careful.*

In response, Savannah flashed him the barest hint of a nod.

Just as the girls were about to leave, two other girls walked by talking loudly. Savannah recognized the two senior cheerleaders and knew they meant trouble.

"Hey, have you seen that stupid show on TV?" The blonde said it loud enough to grab all the parents' attention.

"Which one?" the brunette responded equally as loud.

"*Witch* one is right. It's the one about that pathetic girl who thinks she's a witch." They slowed their steps and then paused right next to Savannah's parents.

"Oh, you mean *Savannah*, the Teenage Witch?"

"Yeah, that one," said the blonde. "It's so nauseating, don't you think?"

"It's disgusting." The brunette smacked on a wad of gum. "I mean, anyone who goes around telling people they have special powers has got to be delusional."

"And pretty full of herself, too," added the blonde.

They threw Savannah a smug look and then continued walking toward the refreshment tables.

Savannah's jaw dropped and she momentarily locked eyes with her mom. She could see the pride that filled them only moments ago had been replaced with anger and disappointment. She avoided looking at her dad because she knew he was staring at her, too. In fact, they were all staring at her.

Before her mom could say anything, Savannah shook her head as if dismissing their conversation and yelled out to them, "It's *Sabrina,* the Teenage Witch." She looked back at the group and plastered on a big smile. "Guess we better hit the road. C'mon guys."

The three girls hurried across the lawn toward Emma's car, not giving Savannah's parents a chance to respond.

"OMG!" said Jade when they reached the car. "I can't believe those girls did that."

Savannah crawled into the back seat, leaned her head back and let out a deep breath. "I can't either. I thought for sure my parents were going to cancel the trip and ground me for life."

Emma stuck the key in the ignition and cranked the engine to life. "Hopefully, your parents bought it."

Savannah reflected on her mother's look. "I think my dad might have bought it, but I'm not so sure about my mom. She's had a major reaction to this whole psychic thing. And I don't know why. I mean, I understand her being upset, worried even. But her reactions have been off the charts."

"Well, you don't have to worry about it for ten days," said Emma looking in the rearview mirror at Savannah. "I'm sure that by the time we get home it will all have been forgotten." She pulled out of the parking lot and turned left toward Highway 71. "By the way, what did Dominic want?"

Dominic! How could I have forgotten?

Savannah debated whether or not to tell them about the warning. What if after hearing what he had to say, Jade and Emma decided it was just too risky to go snooping around Carson City?

She paused for a moment and then said, "Oh nothing much. He just wanted to wish us luck. But he did say that he did a reading last night, and he also saw a man with a sword."

Jade turned half way around in her seat and stared at Savannah. "This is really happening, isn't it? We're really driving half way across the country to hunt for a missing girl." An air of excitement filled her words.

"Yep, it really is happening." Savannah's voice carried none of the enthusiasm that her friend's did.

Yesterday Savannah was excited about this trip, anxious to put her newly discovered gifts to the test and possibly find this woman who had been missing for three years. But after talking with Dominic, her confidence was beginning to wane.

He was right about her being a baby. Her psychic abilities were still in their infancy. How could she assume she'd be able to run when she barely just learned how to crawl? And what if she really was putting them all in danger just because she had something to prove?

She stared into her friend's beautiful green eyes and thought about Dominic's original reading when he said that Jade was not going to be attending college in September. What if her friend ended up getting hurt on this trip, or worse? She didn't think she would be able to live with that guilt.

Maybe I should call this whole thing off before it's too late.

Savannah considered it, but then how would she explain the abrupt change of plans to her parents? She really wasn't prepared to be in the hot seat while they dug into her motives. Nor was she ready to answer questions concerning the comments those girls made about her.

As the town receded behind them, Savannah leaned back in her seat and stared out the window at the farmland quilted in varying shades of green.

Savannah liked Scottsbluff. It was a good place to be from. But like any teenager, she dreamed of escaping the comfort and confines of her family and friends and leaving this quaint Nebraska town behind. She dreamed of seeing what opportunities the rest of the world might have to offer. And now, in light of her newly discovered abilities and in spite of Dominic's warning, she felt even more compelled to immerse herself in as many of those adventures as possible.

She was ready to start living her dreams.

While Emma and Jade jabbered excitedly about what the next ten days might bring, Savannah shifted her gaze out the windshield at the long straight road ahead of them and thought, *I pray all of my dreams don't turn into one great big nightmare.*

Chapter 29

For the next eight hours, the girls took turns driving, navigating, and buying coffee. By the time Savannah pulled into her aunt's driveway it was already after nine o'clock. Tired and hungry, the girls drug themselves out of the car, grabbed their luggage and trudged up the sidewalk to the lit front porch.

Before they could ring the doorbell, Savannah's aunt opened the door. Dressed in a floor length, multi-colored, tie-dyed shift, with her thin auburn hair pulled back into a small ponytail, she reminded Savannah of an aging but classy hippie.

"Savannah! I'm so glad you made it. Come in. Come in." She flashed her a warmer version of her mother's smile making Savannah immediately feel welcome.

Savannah hadn't seen her aunt since she was a baby and was concerned that there might be some awkward moments. But that all vanished when her aunt enveloped her in a lingering embrace.

"Thank you for letting us stay with you, Aunt Helen." Savannah released her and introduced her friends.

"Lovely to meet you both," Aunt Helen said closing the door. "Are you girls hungry? I have some homemade spaghetti sauce simmering on the stove. And the pasta won't take but a few minutes to cook."

All three girls nodded vigorously.

"Good," said Aunt Helen. She grabbed the suitcase out of Savannah's hand and started down the hallway. "Let's get you three settled in first. I've got Emma and Jade in the spare room, and Savannah, I hope you don't mind, but I've put you in the den on the hide-a-bed."

"Thanks, Aunt Helen. That will be just fine."

Aunt Helen dropped Savannah's suitcase in the den on the way to the spare bedroom. She turned on the bedroom light and said, "I hope you two don't mind sharing a bed."

"Of course not, Mrs., uh . . ." Jade paused.

Savannah realized she had never told them her aunt's last name. "Alliette. Her last name is Alliette."

Jade smiled. "This will be just fine, Mrs. Alliette."

Aunt Helen waved her hand in the air as though she were brushing away the formalities. "It's Ms. but please, just call me Helen."

"Alliette. Is that French?" asked Emma.

"*Oui,*" Helen said with a nod.

"Vannah, you never told us you were part French," said Emma.

"I didn't? I thought you knew. Alliette was my mother's maiden name."

Aunt Helen led them out of the hallway and into the kitchen. "Savannah's great, great, great, great grandparents came over from Paris in the late seventeen hundreds when they were very young. I believe she was barely twenty, and he, not much older."

"I didn't know that about my relatives." Savannah pulled out one of the kitchen chairs that hugged the circular wooden table and sat down.

Aunt Helen walked over to the stove and turned the burner on high, quickly bringing the already hot water to a boil. She grabbed a handful of spaghetti sticks, broke them in half and dropped them in.

"It's true. In fact, your great, great, great, great grandmother was pregnant at the time and gave birth here in America." She looked at her niece's head. "You're like me. You have the Alliette trademark hair, thin and flyaway."

Savannah instinctively ran her hands over her reddish brown hair. Now she knew whom to blame for the curse of her limp locks.

When the pasta was ready, Aunt Helen said, "Okay girls, grab a plate and dig in." She put napkins and silverware on the table, along with a shaker of Parmesan cheese. Then she poured four glasses of ice tea.

During dinner, they chatted about graduation, colleges, boys, and plans for the future. The conversation flowed as easily as the ice tea.

But when yawns surpassed the laughter, Aunt Helen said, "It's getting late. You girls go ahead and get ready for bed. I'll clean this up."

With no resistance, the three girls headed to their rooms.

A few minutes later, Savannah came back into the kitchen dressed in her "When-pigs-fly" pink pajamas. She grabbed the dishtowel draped over the oven door handle and started drying the dishes.

Aunt Helen smiled at her. "Honey, you don't need to do that. I usually just let them dry overnight."

"It's okay. I don't mind. Besides, I wasn't sleepy enough to go to bed."

Aunt Helen dried her hands on the towel and said, "Well, I'm glad you decided to stay up. You want a cup of tea?"

Savannah nodded.

"You get comfy in the living room, and I'll bring it in when it's ready."

Savannah shuffled into the living room, curled up on the left side of the couch, and covered herself with the brown and green crocheted afghan draped over the arm. She glanced around the room at all of the tchotchkes and collectables displayed on bookshelves and end tables. It seemed to be an eclectic combination of antique trinkets and new age paraphernalia, which immediately added more depth and dimension to her aunt's personality.

Ancient apothecary jars sat next to clear quartz crystal balls. Native American ceremonial pots overflowed with large amethyst clusters. And antique Venetian glass vases held bundles of dried sage instead of flowers. Each item seemed to have a story to tell about the past.

And Savannah wanted to know about all of them.

When Aunt Helen walked into the living room carrying a wooden tray with a floral English tea service, Savannah said, "Wow, Aunt Helen, you sure have a lot of cool things."

Aunt Helen poured them each a cup of tea, handed one to Savannah and glanced around the room.

"I'm glad you like them. I've spent many years collecting them. And each piece is special to me." She pointed to the largest of the crystal balls. "That one is my favorite. An old gypsy woman gave it to me before she passed away. She said it once belonged to a Druid priestess who could tell the future with it."

That surprised Savannah. "You believe in things like that?"

Aunt Helen gazed at her niece. "Yes, I do. Don't you?"

"Well, I'm beginning to believe there are many things out there that we can't explain."

Aunt Helen took a sip of tea. "You sound as if you've experienced some kind of unexplainable phenomenon. Have you?"

Savannah hesitated. She wasn't sure whether or not she should tell her aunt about her newly discovered psychic abilities. What if her aunt ended up reacting like her mother did, condemning and chastising her? Then she would have two family members mad at her.

"Well . . ." Savannah stopped.

The rest of the words didn't seem to want to come out. How could she tell her aunt, whom she barely knew, this intimate detail about herself? She thought about how the kids at school taunted her, making her feel like a freak. She didn't want her aunt seeing her with similar eyes.

Aunt Helen's face softened. "You can tell me. I won't react like your mother. I promise." She set the cup of tea down on the glass table. "Your mother and I are very different from each other. She's never been open to the unexplainable. And I suspect she hasn't changed much in the last fifteen years."

Savannah let out a sigh. "No, she sure hasn't. Sometimes it's hard to talk to her because she doesn't want to listen to anything that might contradict with church teachings."

Aunt Helen nodded. "I know what you mean. She was that way when we were kids. It really put a wedge in our relationship."

Savannah set her cup on the coffee table and looked at her aunt. "So what *did* happen between you two, if you don't mind me asking?"

"We had a fundamental disagreement about something. And neither one of us was willing to concede."

"Has it really been fifteen years since the two of you have spoken?"

Aunt Helen nodded. "Up until a couple of days ago."

"So why did you decide to call her now, out of the blue, and invite me to come see you? It seems a little odd to me."

Aunt Helen draped a hand over Savannah's. "My dear, I called because you needed me."

"But I don't understand," said Savannah.

Aunt Helen stood up and walked over to one of the bookshelves that actually held books, thumbed through them then pulled one of them out. She walked back and gently placed it on the coffee table right next to Savannah.

When Savannah saw the title she sucked in her breath. *How to Develop Your Psychic Abilities*. With round eyes she looked at her aunt and said, "You believe in psychics?"

"Oh, very much so. Don't you?"

"I'm not sure. Sometime I do believe that people can have psychic abilities. But then other times I think that maybe it's just coincidence."

Aunt Helen threw Savannah a mischievous look. She picked up her teacup, took a sip and said, "Well, you should believe in psychic abilities, because they run in our family."

Chapter 30

Psychic abilities run in our family.

When Savannah heard those words, it was as if her aunt had just given her a spiritual enema. She started talking, and she couldn't stop. She told her aunt everything. She told her about the dreams, about Katie and Marty, about the Comstock Mining Company, about meeting Dominic and him giving her the tarot cards. She even told her about Dominic's warning.

"Now you know why we are going to Carson City. I have to find Katie McCall. She needs my help. You understand that, don't you?"

Aunt Helen pulled her own afghan around her shoulders to fight off the chill that had begun to dominate the room sometime within the last hour.

"Yes, of course I understand, but I'm concerned that you didn't bring your tarot cards with you. It's times like this when you need them the most. They can give you insight and information that your dreams won't. And they can provide important details that you might, otherwise, overlook." She smiled at her niece. "Just because you're psychic doesn't mean you have all of the answers in that sweet little noggin of yours. Sometimes you need help."

Savannah sighed. "I'm realizing that now. I thought the stronger my abilities got the clearer things would become and information would just be, I don't know, handed to me."

"What do you mean? Like plucked out of thin air? I'm sorry, sweetheart, but it doesn't work that way," Aunt Helen said kindly. "No psychic knows everything. We're not meant to. Only God knows everything. We're only given certain bits of information, and then we have to follow the clues and figure the rest out on our own, just like any other human being." She took a sip of tea and held the cup in her hands as if to warm them. "So why didn't you bring your cards with you?"

Savannah pulled her legs in closer and tucked her feet under the afghan. "I couldn't. I had to give them back to Dominic because I promised Mom I wouldn't use them anymore."

Aunt Helen tightened up her lips and shook her head. "Your mother's ignorance still irritates me. She has no idea how much danger she could potentially be putting you girls in just because she refuses to believe. I'm so tired of her narrow-minded vision." She huffed, set the cup back on the table and threw the blanket off of her. "Well, I'm not going to let that happen to you." She stood up, walked over to one of the bookcases and grabbed a small wooden box from the top shelf.

Somehow, Savannah had missed it.

When her aunt sat back down on the couch Savannah said, "That looks old."

"It is. This belonged to your great, great, great, great grandmother Sabine. It was one of the few possessions she brought with her to America." She opened up the box and pulled out something rectangular wrapped in a worn piece of russet colored fabric. She carefully unfolded the edges to reveal an ancient looking deck of tarot cards tied together with a purple ribbon.

As she untied the bow she said, "My mother—your grandmother—gave these to me when I was eighteen. They should have gone to your mother because she's the oldest, but she refused to use her gifts and-"

"Whoa, whoa, whoa. Hold on a minute. Are you saying my mom has psychic abilities?" Savannah's eyes had widened.

Aunt Helen nodded. "Yes. But she refused to use them because she thought they came from the Devil."

Savannah leaned back on the couch. "Oh my gosh. It all makes sense now. No wonder she seemed so hypersensitive about the whole subject." She paused then looked at her aunt. "What about my dad? Does he know?"

Aunt Helen shook her head. "Oh no. He has no idea. When your mom first met him he had just started seminary school. They started dating, fell in love and decided to get married."

She set the box down on the coffee table and gently placed the cards in her lap. "Your mom and I got into a huge fight right before the wedding. I told her that she needed to tell your dad about her psychic abilities before they got married. He had a right to know, and if she didn't tell him I would."

"So what happened?"

"She threatened to never see me again if I ever mentioned it. She said that since she had renounced her psychic abilities it was no longer an issue."

"Did she really believe these abilities came from the Devil?"

Aunt Helen slowly shook her head. "No, I don't believe so. I think she just used that as an excuse because she was too ashamed of the real reason she gave them up."

Savannah tilted her head. "The real reason?"

Aunt Helen took a deep breath and let it out as if debating whether or not to continue. Finally, she said, "It was because of a boy. And I warned her about this. But she wouldn't listen." She paused. "Your mother was not the most popular person in school, and that bothered her a great deal. So she decided she was going to use her psychic abilities to help her get the captain of the football team to notice her. She figured if they were dating then she would become popular.

"I told her that what she was doing was wrong and that our gifts weren't meant to be use to manipulate people. I warned her that if she continued, the universe would make her pay."

Savannah fidgeted. She wasn't quite comfortable hearing these details about her mother, but maybe by hearing them she would be able to understand her a little better. "So what happened?"

"Oh, at first, nothing but great things. Through tarot readings she was able to find out details about him, like what his favorite foods were, his favorite hobbies, and his favorite music—all of those little details that make a person sit up and take notice. And she used them to her advantage.

"Well, he fell for her, and I mean hard." Aunt Helen's eyes drifted to the side as though she were gazing into the past. "He told her that he had never met anyone who knew him right off the bat the way she did and that it was clear to him that they were meant to be together forever. They started dating and even planned on getting married once they graduated high school."

Savannah's eyes widened. "I didn't know that."

"Oh yes, it was like a match made in heaven. And they truly loved each other."

"So what happened?" Savannah asked leaning in.

Aunt Helen's eyes held a hint of sadness in them as she looked at Savannah. "Your mother had a journal where she kept detailed notes on all of her readings. One day, she accidentally left her journal in the boy's car, and he read it. He was so devastated that he drove to her house with the journal and confronted her."

"What did she do?" said Savannah in a hushed tone.

"At first she denied it. But it was all right there in the journal—dates and everything. So she finally admitted to him that she used her psychic abilities to get him to fall in love with her." She shook her head. "He was so distraught leaving her house that he wasn't paying attention and drove right through a red light. A semi-truck coming from the other direction T-boned the driver's side of his car, killing him instantly."

Savannah threw a hand over her mouth. "Oh no! That's horrible. Poor Mom."

Aunt Helen nodded. "Your mom was so guilt-ridden that she renounced her abilities right then and there, shoved them as deep down inside of her as she could. She said that this would have never happened if her abilities had come from God. So the only other option was that they came from the Devil." She stared intently into her niece's eyes. "Your mother abused her gifts, and she suffered the consequences."

Savannah gulped. *Why do I feel like this is a warning?*

Chapter 31

The two of them sat motionless for several moments, seemingly lost in their own thoughts. Savannah had not known any of this about her mother. And now that she did, she couldn't help but look at her through different eyes. Now she understood why her mother had reacted the way she did—because she wanted to spare her daughter the same kind of heartache.

But just because she messed up doesn't mean I will. Does it?

Aunt Helen reached over, picked up the teapot and filled both of their cups. She smiled gently and said, "Do you have any other questions?"

Tons of them!

Savannah took a sip and said, "So back to Dad. You never said anything to him about Mom's abilities?"

Aunt Helen shook her head. "Not a word."

"If you didn't tell him, then why haven't you and Mom spoken for so long?"

Aunt Helen tilted her head to one side and sighed. "Because of you."

"Me? Why me?"

"Remember I told you these gifts run in the family? Your mom knew that you would, most likely, also be born with the same abilities and would, one day, start asking questions about them. I suspect that the reason she so vehemently and publicly denounced everything having to do with the supernatural was because she was hoping that if you did end up being a psychic, you would reject it just like she did."

Savannah scrunched her brow. "But I still don't understand what that has to do with you not coming to visit all these years."

"The reason your mom didn't want me around you is because she knew I would never allow that to happen. I would make sure that you knew the truth about your gifts. It's your birthright."

Savannah shook her head. "I just can't believe it."

"Well, believe it because it's true, all of it. And because your mom refused to use her psychic abilities, these cards reverted to me."

Aunt Helen handed the deck to Savannah and said, "When Sabine was seventeen she went to see a gypsy because she started hearing voices in her head and thought that maybe she'd been touched by the Devil.

"When the gypsy was finished with the reading, she told her that her gift came from God and that she was to use her abilities to help others. Then the gypsy gave her those very cards. And they have been in our family ever since."

She looked at Savannah with glistening eyes. "Now, my dear, they belong to you."

Savannah reverently held the cards and studied them. Images similar to those on the deck that Dominic had given her had been hand painted on the front side in rich shades of red, saffron, ochre and black. The colors had somehow retained their vibrancy, making the deck look like it could have been painted last week.

"They're absolutely beautiful," said Savannah in a hushed tone. "How old are they?"

"I don't know for sure. But I suspect they are at least three hundred years old, maybe older."

Savannah carefully turned the top card over and looked at the backside. It contained a simple line drawing of a crescent moon and a star. "Do these symbols mean anything?"

Aunt Helen reached over and took the next card from the deck. She seemed to study it briefly and then said, "Oh yes. They're very significant, and powerful. They represent the shifting from darkness to light. These markings have been used for thousands of years to represent the goddess and her ability to bring forth new life, or in this case, new insight."

She looked at Savannah. "There is great responsibility that comes with being the caretaker of these cards."

"Caretaker?"

"Yes, since one can never really own them, we are charged with ensuring their safety and making sure they stay intact. We manage them for a short while and then we pass them on to the next owner, just as I am doing to you. Now it is your turn to care for them and protect them. And one day, when the time is right, you will pass them on to your daughter, that is, assuming that you agree to take on the responsibility of the cards."

"And what happens if I don't?"

Aunt Helen's gaze turned dark. "Then your children, and your children's children will suffer."

"That sounds a little dramatic," mumbled Savannah.

"Savannah, you were born with a special gift. You have the ability to see beyond the veil. And you have barely scratched the surface. There is so much more to your abilities and so much you can do with the knowledge you will begin to receive. Sharing your visions and insights with others will help them make better choices. You want that for people, don't you?"

Savannah said nothing but continued to stare at the images of the crescent moon and the star.

"When you find Katie McCall, you will be giving her parents a great gift. Just think of all the other families out there like the

McCalls who are also looking for answers. You could provide those for them, too."

"But Aunt Helen, I'm just not that confident yet. Half the stuff I've gotten in the readings hasn't even been proven yet."

"Trust me, it will be. And every time a detail from your readings is confirmed, your confidence will grow."

"But what about my parents? You know how much they disapprove."

"You're almost eighteen. Your parents can't dictate how you live your life anymore. That is up to you. And you have to be the one who decides what path your life will take, not your parents."

Savannah remained quiet, deep in thought. This was a pivotal moment for her. She could ignore her psychic calling and just go on with her normal and mundane life. Or she could embrace this path by spiritually coming out to her parents and to the world.

Based on the reaction she received from the students at school, if she did decide to come out, would she be able to handle any ridicule she might receive from the rest of her town? And what about the heartache and disappointment she would surely cause her parents with this news? How would her dad be able to explain it to his congregation? And what about her mother? She would be so upset that she would probably disown her just like she disowned her own sister.

This was an important decision for Savannah, one that required careful consideration. And once made, the decision could never be reversed.

What should I do?

After several minutes, Savannah handed the deck back to her aunt.

Aunt Helen's face fell. "You're not taking them?"

Savannah smile. "Oh, I'm taking them. I just wanted you to put *my* cards back in the box so that they didn't get dirty. They're my responsibility now!"

Chapter 32

The next morning after breakfast and with their luggage already stuffed in the back of the car, the four of them stood in the driveway exchanging hugs and saying good-bye to each other.

"Thank you so much for everything, Mrs., uh, I mean, Aunt Helen," said Emma.

"Yes, Aunt Helen. Thank you," said Jade. "I'm sorry that we ended up crashing and leaving you with that mess in the kitchen. I really wanted to stay up and talked with you some more, but I was just so tired. I think I fell asleep before my head hit the pillow."

Aunt Helen smiled at Jade. "Heaven's, don't give it another thought. Savannah and I managed it. Besides, it gave us a chance to get to know each other a little better." She threw Savannah a subtle wink. "You girls sure you got everything? You didn't leave anything behind, did you?"

Savannah patted her purse. "No, Aunt Helen, we got it *all*." She threw her arms around her aunt and whispered in her ear. "Thank you so much for *everything*. I love you."

Aunt Helen whispered back, "I love you, too, dear. Be careful and keep me posted."

"I will. I promise."

By the time they released each other, Jade had already climbed into the back seat and Emma behind the wheel, leaving the front seat for Savannah.

As they pulled out of the driveway, Savannah rolled down her window, blew Aunt Helen a kiss and waved good-bye. When the gestures were returned, Savannah heard her aunt's voice in her head. *Be careful, sweet girl. And trust your instincts.*

Savannah gave her a subtle nod and watched her until they turned the corner. When she could no longer see her aunt, Savannah discretely wiped a tear from her cheek and turned back around in her seat.

"Your aunt is really nice," said Jade.

Emma agreed. "Yeah. I would have liked to spend more time with her, but it was like I had been drugged. Just like Jade, I couldn't keep my eyes open either."

Savannah wondered if maybe her ancient ancestors had something to do with that, giving her the opportunity to talk with her aunt. If her friends had decided to stay up, or if she hadn't gone back into the kitchen, she would have never known about her family secret.

She thought about everything her aunt had told her regarding her mother and the special item tucked safely away in her purse. She thought about all of the things that had happened to her as of late: the dreams, the visions, the instant ability to read tarot cards. Now it all made sense. She knew exactly why these things were happening to her—because she was a true psychic.

"It's okay," said Savannah. "I enjoyed helping her. Then we went into the living room and had the most interesting conversation."

"So what did you talk about?" asked Emma as they continued on Interstate 80 toward Elko, Nevada.

Savannah reached for her purse down on the floorboard, pulled out the box with the cards and began telling them about her family history.

When she was finished Jade said, "Wow! I can't believe that about your mom. And I can't believe your dad doesn't know."

Savannah turned in her seat and looked back at her friend. "And we can't be the ones to tell him. It has to come from Mom."

"Are you going to confront her?" asked Emma.

"I don't know yet. A lot is going to depend on what happens on this trip. We'll just have to wait and see how it all plays out."

"So what *is* our plan of attack," said Jade.

"Well, I was thinking that before we just go out looking for Katie, we should probably see if we can find her parents and talk to them," said Savannah. "They might have more information for us."

"Hopefully, they still live in the area," said Jade. She shook her head. "I can't even imagine how awful it's been for them not knowing if Katie is alive or dead."

"They have to still be there," said Emma. "I know if it were me, and my daughter had disappeared, I wouldn't be going anywhere. I'd stay put just in case she came home."

"Yeah, that's what I was thinking," said Savannah. "Once we get to Reno, we'll find a phonebook and see if they're listed."

"Do they even make phonebooks anymore?" said Jade.

"I'm sure a gas station will have one," said Emma. She looked over at Savannah. "If we are able to find them what are you going to say to them? Are you going to tell them that you're a psychic?"

Savannah shrugged. "I'm not sure. I don't want to scare them away."

"Maybe you could say you're a reporter and you're doing a story on her," said Emma as she pulled into a mini mart next to a gas pump. "Anyone want coffee? I'm getting some hot chocolate."

Jade reached in the way back, pulled three cups from the stack and handed them to Emma. "Lots of cream, no sugar. But only if it's the real stuff. None of that powdered crap."

Savannah reached into her purse and pulled out her prepaid visa card. She handed it to Emma and said, "Use this to fill the car. I'll pump. Oh, and tea for me if they have it."

Savannah had filled the tank and was already sitting in the driver's seat when Emma returned with the drinks. With one hand, she opened the door, handed them over the seat to Jade and then scooted in.

"What took you so long," said Savannah. "Did you have to go to the bathroom?"

Emma had a mysterious smile on her face. "Nope. I was on the phone."

"With who?" said Jade.

Emma flashed them a Cheshire cat grin. "With Mrs. McCall. Turns out, the Elko Mini Mart had a Reno phonebook." She pulled a piece of paper from her pocket and handed it to Savannah. "Here's their address and phone number. She wants us to come by as soon as we get into town."

Savannah looked at the information on the partial page ripped from the phonebook. "What did you tell them?"

"I said you were a friend of Katie's and that you might have some information about her disappearance."

Savannah groaned. "Em, you didn't."

"I did."

"But why'd you say that? Once they see me they'll know that I'm not old enough to be her friend. Geez, I would have only been fourteen when she went missing."

'Well, I figured at least that would get us in the door. Then it's up to you to keep us there."

Savannah groaned again as she pulled out of the parking lot and got back onto the freeway. She hadn't planned on seeing them quite so soon. She wanted to have at least a day to prepare her story. Now she only had a few hours to decide if she was going to feed them a line or tell them the truth.

Oh, Katie, I sure hope your parents don't end up calling the cops on us. That would be a real bummer!

Chapter 33

By the time the girls got to Reno, the sun had already begun to set over the purple Sierra Nevada Mountains. Sweeping brushstrokes of gold, lavender, and hot pink stained the evening sky, creating a living painting for the trio.

But Savannah was too nervous to enjoy it.

She exited McCarran Street and turned off onto Laurel Park Way. The McCalls lived in what looked to be one of Reno's older subdivisions. Dated houses stood partially obscured by large pines and poplars.

"Keep an eye out for their house," said Savannah as she drummed her index finger on the steering wheel. She still hadn't decided what she was going to say to Katie's parents. She had run all of the scenarios through her mind but none of them, not even the truth, sounded plausible. She could feel the butterflies doing a war dance in her stomach, making her nauseous.

"I think this is it," said Emma pointing to a Wedgewood blue with white trim split-level house on her right hand side.

Savannah pulled up in front of it and idled next to the curb. She stared at the front door and said, "I don't think I can do this."

Emma placed a hand on her shoulder. "Yes you can. Remember, you're here to help them."

"But I still don't know what I'm going to tell them."

Jade leaned forward toward the front seat and looked at her. "I think you should just tell them the truth."

"But what if they don't believe me? Or what if I end up causing them more pain?" She chewed on her bottom lip as she looked at her friends. "I'm not ready for this."

Emma leaned over and turned off the car. She gently removed the keys and said, "Yes you are. You're just scared because you're facing your first real test. But remember what Dominic told you. He said all you need to do is trust your intuition and you'll be fine." She opened up her door. "C'mon, they're waiting for us."

The girls walked up the sidewalk to the front door, with Emma in the lead. "Just be yourself," she said as she rang the doorbell. "And stop worrying. Nothing bad is going to happen."

When the door opened an older couple, maybe in their fifties, stood in the entry way. Mr. McCall, a tall thin man with gold wire rim glasses stood behind a much shorter and heavier woman with a hopeful look on her face. His right hand was draped over her right shoulder while hers gripped the doorknob.

"Mr. and Mrs. McCall. My name's Emma Reed. I spoke with you on the phone a few hours ago."

"Of course, please come in," said Mrs. McCall stepping aside. As the girls entered and stood in the foyer, she looked up at her husband. "Harland, please show them to the living room while I get us some refreshments." She looked at the girls. "Is tea okay?"

The girls nodded and Emma said, "That would be nice. Thank you."

Once inside the living room, Harland motioned to the couch. "Please have a seat." He sat down in a dark blue, tweed La-Z-Boy across from them, crossed one leg over the other and looked at

Emma. "My wife, Trudy, made some fresh cinnamon rolls right after she hung up with you."

"They smell wonderful," said Savannah, sniffing the air.

Mr. McCall turned his attention to Savannah. "And you are?"

"My name is Savannah Swift. And this is Jade Willows."

He looked from girl to girl. "So which one of you knew my daughter?"

Before they could answer, Mrs. McCall entered the living room carrying a tray with a teapot, five cups, and a plate of those warm cinnamon rolls. She set the tray on the coffee table and began pouring the tea. As she handed one to Emma she said, "I must tell you, you're not what I was expecting. You're all so much younger than Katie." This caused the girls to glance nervously from one to another. "Emma, you said that your friend might know something about Katie's disappearance. So which one of you knew Katie?"

Savannah opened her mouth to answer, but before she could say anything Jade blurted out, "I am. Well, actually, it was my oldest sister. She's the one who knew her."

Mrs. McCall handed Jade a cup. "Really? What's your sister's name?"

Savannah glanced at Jade. *What are you doing? You don't have a sister,* she thought.

"Um, Amber. Her name is Amber."

"Hmm," said Mrs. McCall. She took a sip and then set the cup down on the saucer. "I don't recall Katie ever mentioning an Amber Willows. How did they know each other?"

"Well . . ." Jade paused for a moment as if to think. "They worked together."

"Oh really? Your sister also worked for Comstock?"

Savannah sucked in her breath. *Oh, my gosh. Katie worked for Comstock Mining Company!* "How long had Katie worked for them?"

Mrs. McCall looked over at her husband. "I think she had been a secretary with them for about two years before she, uh, went missing. Right, Harland?"

Mr. McCall nodded. "Sounds about right." He looked at Emma. "So you said over the phone that you might have some information about Katie's disappearance?"

Savannah asked, "Did Katie work in the Dayton office?"

"Mostly," said Mrs. McCall. "Sometimes they had her doing the daily reports up at the mines."

"So she would have to go up there?" said Savannah.

"Yes, from time to time."

"And what about her boyfriend, Marty. Did he also work for them?" asked Savannah.

"No, Marty was a reporter for the Reno Gazette," said Mrs. McCall.

"I understand he got shot the night Katie disappeared. Did he survive?" Savannah took a bite of the warm pastry. "This is delicious, Mrs. McCall."

Mr. McCall uncrossed his leg and leaned forward in his chair. "Wait a minute. How do you know that she went missing the night Marty got shot? She was at the hospital with him. People saw her. She talked to the doctors and then she went home. We assumed she went missing sometime the next day or the day after."

Savannah shook her head. "I don't think she went home that night. I think she went up to one of the mines and something happened to her."

Mrs. McCall threw her hand over her mouth and gasped. Tears began to well in her eyes and she said, "What on Earth would make you say something like that?"

Savannah took a deep breath. The time had come for her to tell them the truth. "Because I saw her."

"You saw her? When? Where?" Mrs. McCall's voice elevated. "Where's my daughter?"

Savannah looked at both of them. "I believe she went missing somewhere up near Flowery Peak."

Mr. McCall's eyes narrowed. "And you know this how?"

Here it goes.

"Because I'm a psychic."

There it was, out in the open. She finally slapped that label on herself. Hopefully, they would have an open mind and listen to what she had to say.

Mr. McCall jumped up. He pointed at the front door and said, "Get out of my house."

"But-"

"Now! Get out of here before I call the police and have you arrested."

Mrs. McCall's head dropped into her hands and she began to sob.

Savannah's eyes pooled with tears. "I'm so sorry. I didn't mean to upset you."

"Out. Now!" yelled Mr. McCall.

The three girls catapulted off of the couch, apologizing as they backed their way out of the living room. Mrs. McCall stayed slumped over in the other recliner sobbing in her hands, while Mr. McCall followed them to the door, opened it, and stood by it as they scurried down the sidewalk. He shook his fist at them and yelled, "If I ever see you again, I will call the police!" Then he slammed the door.

The girls quickly piled into the car with Emma behind the wheel. As she started it, put it in gear and pulled away from the curb, she said, "Well, that didn't go very well."

"No kidding," said Savannah. She glanced out the passenger's window and saw Mr. McCall scowling at them through the part in the living room curtains.

"Well, now what?" said Jade from the back seat. "Are we going to head to Carson City to find a hotel?"

Savannah, trying to shake off the horrible incident at the McCalls, leaned back in her seat and mumbled, "Yeah, I guess so. There's no point hanging around here."

Right then Emma's phone rang.

"Hello?" Emma was quiet for a few seconds and then handed her phone over to Savannah. "It's for you."

"Who is it?" asked Savannah as she took the phone.

Emma looked at her. "It's Mrs. McCall."

Chapter 34

The girls were nearly finished with their Paninis and drinks when Mrs. McCall walked into the Starbucks.

She glanced around the store, and when she saw them sitting at a table in the corner, she quickly shuffled over to them.

Placing her hand on the empty chair, Mrs. McCall said, "May I sit down?"

The girls nodded and Savannah said, "Of course, Mrs. McCall. I'm glad you wanted to meet with us." She paused while Katie's mom took a seat. "I wanted to apologize again. I'm really sorry for-"

"Please, I'm the one who should apologize. Harland can be pretty gruff sometimes, but it's only because he feels so out of control. And he hates it when I cry."

"I didn't mean to upset you, Mrs. McCall." Savannah lowered her eyes.

"Call me Trudy." She slipped off her jacket and draped it over the chair. "You didn't upset me. I cried because I was really hoping and praying for some kind of viable lead to my daughter's disappearance." She tilted her head to Savannah. "No offense."

"I know it's hard to believe, but I'm telling you the truth. I saw your daughter. That's why we're here."

"But where did you see her?"

Savannah paused briefly. "I saw her in my dreams." She quickly held up her hands, palms out. "Now just hear me out before you say anything."

She began to relay everything that had happened to her in the last couple of weeks: the dreams, the visions, the voices in her head, the tarot cards. She omitted the part of seeing Katie being buried alive. She thought that it would just be too much for the woman to bear.

When Savannah was finished Mrs. McCall said, "Well, that's quite a tale. It's hard not to be skeptical, but at this point I'm open to just about anything." She shook her head. "Three long years of searching, and the police still haven't been able to find her. In fact, there hasn't been one good lead since she disappeared. So, as bizarre as it all sounds, I'm willing to take a chance with you." She leaned forward and folded her hands on the table. "So what do you need from me?"

The three girls visibly relaxed and Jade said, "Mrs.- I mean, Trudy, can I get you something to drink? It looks like we might be here awhile."

Several minutes later Jade returned with their drinks and set them on the table. "Did I miss anything?"

"No. We waited for you," said Emma.

Once Jade took a seat Savannah looked at Mrs. McCall and said, "You had mentioned that Katie worked for the Comstock Mining Company."

"Yes, that's right."

"Did she ever mention why they were buying up all of the dry mines in the area?"

Mrs. McCall shook her head. "No she didn't. But they've been doing it through their parent company for years. Why do you want to know? Is it important?"

"I'm not really sure," said Savannah.

Follow the clues and figure the rest out. Aunt Helen's words lingered in the back of Savannah's mind.

Mrs. McCall seemed to be thinking. Then, after a few moments she said, "It could have something to do with EarthFirst."

Jade scrunched her brow. "What's EarthFirst?"

"It's a non-profit organization started by the head of the Geneva Corporation," said Mrs. McCall.

"Wait a minute. I remember that name. It was on the bottom of the Comstock website," said Savannah.

Emma's eye lit up. "Oh, I've heard of EarthFirst. They're really into land conservation, aren't they?"

Mrs. McCall shrugged. "I don't know for sure. I think their focus is more on biodiversity. But honestly, I don't know that much about them other that what I've read in the newspapers."

Savannah took a sip of her tea. "What does biodiversity mean?"

Jade pulled out her smart phone and Googled EarthFirst. "It says here that Harrison Taylor started the organization in January of 2007 with the help of wealthy contributors to help manage and maintain biodiversity hotspots.

"Their goal is to create plant and animal diversity in areas where migration is almost nonexistent."

She skimmed the rest of the website. "According to this, they work throughout the United States, but their main effort is the Sierra Nevada Mountain Range near Carson City."

"Hmmm," said Emma. "Sounds to me like they're buying up the mines in order to preserve the land."

"Could be," said Savannah.

They all remained quiet for several moments until Savannah looked over at Mrs. McCall and said, "Trudy. You never answered my question back at your house about Marty. Did he survive the gun shot?"

Mrs. McCall slowly shook her head. "No, I'm afraid he didn't. He died in the middle of the night. From what I understand he was resting fine in ICU but when the nurse came in to do her 3am rounds, she found him dead."

Savannah felt deeply saddened by that news. She was hoping that the person in her dreams had lied to Katie. "Do you know if Marty had any friends at the university here?"

"Oh, I'm sure he did. Both he and Katie graduated from there. They were both popular, and college sweethearts. In fact, they were engaged. They were going to get married in Lake Tahoe at the top of Heavenly Ski Resort." Mrs. McCall pulled a Kleenex from her purse, dabbed at her eyes and then dropped the Kleenex in her lap. "They had planned on starting a family right away."

Savannah remembered Katie telling the hospital receptionist in her dream that she was Marty's fiancé. "So you approved of their relationship?"

"Oh yes, he was a terrific young man with a great career ahead of him."

"So, did the police ever find out who shot him?"

Mrs. McCall slowly shook her head. "No, I'm afraid not."

"Then it's an unsolved murder."

"Murder?" Mrs. McCall's eyes grew wide, and she said in a hushed tone, "You think he was murdered?"

Savannah took a sip of tea and nodded. "I think that whoever shot Marty did it on purpose and then came into the hospital that night to finish him off." She paused briefly. "And I'm pretty sure that the same person who killed Marty is responsible for Katie's disappearance."

Mrs. McCall's face turned serious, and she looked down at her coffee cup. She remained quiet for a moment and then said, "Savannah, I need to ask you something, and I want you to be perfectly honest with me." She paused. "Do you think Katie is still alive? Somewhere?" Her knuckles turned white as she gripped the cup.

Savannah took a deep breath, let it out and slowly shook her head. "I'm so sorry, Mrs. McCall."

"But why would anyone want to hurt them?" Tears spilled down Mrs. McCall's cheeks. "They were two, normal, happy kids who would have never hurt anyone." She picked up the Kleenex from her lap and swiped at the tears. "So why did this happen to them? It just doesn't make any sense."

When Savannah looked into the woman's distraught eyes, she realized it wasn't going to be enough just to find her daughter's body.

I'm going to have to bring her answers.

Savannah leaned forward and lowered her voice. "I believe that Marty was working on a story that had to do with something he discovered up at one of the Comstock mines. In my dreams he handed Katie a flash drive and said that he had just come from speaking with a friend at the university. He told Katie there was some important evidence on it to prove his theories and that if anything happened to him she was to take it to the police." Savannah gently placed her hand over Mrs. McCall's forearm. "I need to find this person from the university. Do know who he might have meant?"

Mrs. McCall shook her head. "I'm sorry but I didn't know any of his friends." She paused as if thinking. "But I think I can put you in touch with someone who might."

"Who?" said Savannah.

"Marty's grandparents. If anyone would know about his friends it would be them." She pulled her cell phone from her purse; scrolled through the contacts, and when she found the right one she pressed send.

A moment later, an elderly sounding voice said, "Hello-o-o-o?"

Mrs. McCall put her on speaker. "Hello, Mrs. Dolan? This is Trudy McCall. How are you?"

"Trudy? What a pleasant surprise. How are you and Harland doing?" Her voice seemed to crackle.

"We're fine. Thank you for asking." She paused. "Mrs. Dolan, there's someone I'd like you to talk to."

"Oh-h-h-h? What about?"

"About Marty."

They all heard Mrs. Dolan suck in her breath.

"I have a young lady with me that may have some answers for you. Would you be willing to talk with her tomorrow?"

There was a moment of pause. "Wel-l-l-l . . ." Her word seemed to draw on forever. "I suppose that would be oka-y-y-y. But Pa's leaving real early in the morning to go fishing. He'll probably be gone 'til suppertime."

Mrs. McCall put her hand over the phone and whispered to Savannah. "Do you need Mr. Dolan there?"

Remembering how Mr. McCall reacted to the news, she shook her head vigorously and whispered, "No. I'm sure I can get what I need from her."

Mrs. McCall took her hand away from the phone. "How about ten o'clock tomorrow morning? Will that work for you?"

"Wel-l-l-l, I suppose so-o-o-o."

Mrs. McCall took her off speaker. "Great. I'll give her your address. Oh, and by the way, her name is Savannah. Savannah Swift. And whatever she tells you, no matter how crazy it sounds, just listen to her, okay?"

After she hung up, Mrs. McCall wrote the information on a Starbucks napkin and handed it to Savannah. "I hope she can help you find the answers you're looking for."

"So do I," whispered Savannah as she took the napkin and stuffed it in her purse. "So do I."

Chapter 35

Jade and Emma said their good-byes to Mrs. McCall and climbed into the Rabbit while Savannah stayed behind a moment.

"Thank you for giving me another chance," said Savannah, giving the woman a hug. Instantly, a wrenching feeling of sorrow overwhelmed her heart, one like she had never known before. And she knew that even though Mrs. McCall seemed to be handling Katie's disappearance outwardly, inside, the woman was still being tortured by grief and guilt.

Knowing that this poor woman had been living with this unbearable burden day and night for three years caused Savannah to hug her even tighter.

"I promise you, I will do everything in my power to find Katie and bring her home." Savannah could feel the gesture being returned and sensed that by hugging her, Mrs. McCall felt like she was, in some way, embracing her daughter's spirit.

"Thank you." Mrs. McCall smiled kindly at her. "And thank you for coming all the way out here to find my daughter. Now I know how difficult it must have been for you to put yourself out there to be scrutinized and possibly ridiculed. You are one brave young woman." She took hold of Savannah's hand. "Just be safe out there."

Savannah nodded. "I will. I'll call you if I find out anything." She gave Mrs. McCall's hand a quick squeeze then hurried over to the car and slid into the passenger's seat.

As the girls drove away, Savannah watched Mrs. McCall walk to her car. Her shoulders seemed to have lifted, making them look more squared than when she had entered the Starbucks. Maybe they had been inflated with hope.

If so, then please don't let me be the one who deflates them, she prayed.

With very little traffic, it only took the girls thirty minutes to drive to Carson City. They spotted a Motel 6 right off of Highway 50, pulled into the lit parking lot and parked right up front near the main entrance.

Though plain and somewhat utilitarian looking, the tan brick building was tidy and free of litter. Bright spotlights strategically placed on the edge of the roof and pointing down at the sidewalk made it look like it was the middle of the day instead of eight thirty at night.

An inviting row of square, terracotta planters filled with pink and white geraniums lined both sides of the walkway up to the lobby entrance. It was a welcome invitation since fatigue had already begun to set in.

As soon as they entered the lobby, an older woman with bright red hair, clearly from a bottle, and wearing a pair of horned rimmed glasses that were attached to a purple beaded lanyard hanging around her neck looked up and smiled at them.

"Evening, ladies. Welcome to Motel 6. May I help you?" Her voice came out sounding surprisingly deep and gravelly as though she'd been smoking two packs of cigarettes a day since she was eight.

"Hello," said Savannah. "We'd like a room, please." Based on the empty parking lot, she didn't figure there'd be any problem.

"Well, lemme see what I've got." She adjusted her glasses, pecked at the computer keys and then stared at the screen in front of her. A few seconds later she said, "I have a nice room on the ground floor with two queen beds. Would that work for you?"

"How much is it?" asked Savannah.

"Fifty six dollars a night, not including tax. Unless you're students, then you get a ten percent discount." She looked over the top of her glasses at Savannah. "You girls students?"

"Well, sort of," said Jade. "We just graduated high school but we don't start college until the fall."

The woman looked at her over the rim of her glasses and snorted. "Now ain't you a pretty thing." She typed on the keyboard and said, "Ah, what the heck, I'm gonna give y'all the discount anyway, cuz I like ya."

"Thank you," said the three girls in unison.

While Savannah filled out the registration card, Emma picked up a paperback book off of the edge of the counter and began thumbing through the pages.

"A local yokel wrote that about the Comstock Lode," said the receptionist as she handed Savannah two room keys. "Your room is around the left side near the back of the building. You should be able to park right in front of it."

"What's the Comstock Lode," said Emma putting the book back on the counter.

"Only the first and largest discovery of silver in the United States. Nevada attained statehood because of it." She threw Emma her now trademark over-the-glasses look.

"Wow, I didn't know that," Emma said pushing her glasses up the bridge of her nose.

The receptionist smiled then leaned in toward Emma as though she were about to divulge some juicy gossip. "Yep, in 1859 two brothers by the name of Grosh claimed to have found a gold deposit on their property. But before they could file a claim, they both died in bizarre accidents."

"So what happened to their gold?" said Emma.

"Both bodies weren't even cold yet when a prospector by the name of Henry Comstock said that the Grosh brothers had been infringing on his property and that the land rightly belonged to him. So he took possession of it and spent the next few years looking for their gold deposit."

"Did he ever find it?"

"Nope. Oh, he found little bits here and there, but nothing significant like what the Grosh boys had claimed. Comstock figured those two had just been blowing smoke up everyone's behind, probably to get attention. So he ended up selling the parcel to some poor sucker. Thought he'd really pulled the wool over this guy's eyes.

"Then one day the new owner discovered a bluish clay on the land, and he realized it was silver, not gold, underfoot."

The receptionist stepped out from behind the tan Formica counter. She wore a tight black and white striped dress that stretched over her wide hips and round stomach making her look like a pregnant zebra.

She leaned back against the front of the counter, crossed her arms and rested them on her belly as she continued her story. "Well, news spread quickly about the unprecedented amount of silver mined from Henry Comstock's old property and-"

"How much did they find?" said Emma, interrupting her.

"Final tally was worth over three hundred million dollars! Can you imagine that kind of money back in the 1800's?"

Emma's eye grew wide. "Not even! That's a lot of cash."

"Yep, it surly is. Anyhoo, Virginia City boomed and soon became the most important city between Chicago and the Pacific. It attracted royalty from Europe, politicians, and even some big time movie stars. But mostly it attracted prospectors—thousands of them. They came in by the droves. And everyone was making money hand-over-fist. Everyone that is, except for Ol' Pancake Comstock."

"Pancake?"

"That's what people 'round these parts called him back then because he was too lazy to make bread. He was always looking for the easy way to make a buck. But this time it backfired on him."

"Wow," said Jade jumping into the conversation, "that must have made Mr. Comstock pretty upset."

The old woman nodded. "Sure did. When old man Comstock heard about the discovery, he had a royal fit and tried to get the land back. Said the new owner had swindled him."

"Did he? Swindle him, I mean?" asked Jade.

"Nope. The sale was done fair and square. Comstock soon became the town laughingstock and the butt of every mining joke imaginable. After a while, his poor wife just couldn't take the embarrassment anymore, and left him. I think she ended up going back to Utah. But don't quote me on that."

"What happened to Mr. Comstock after his wife left him?" said Emma, pushing her glasses up the bridge of her nose.

"Comstock was so distraught over the whole ordeal that he ended up shooting himself right in the head." The old woman paused and gazed out the window as though she were looking into the past. "Poor bastard could have been the richest man in the world if he would have just been a little more persistent. But instead, he ended up dying a penniless pauper." She looked down at the floor and shook her head. "It was the biggest blunder in these parts. And to this day, there ain't been another one, screw up I mean, to even compare."

Everyone stood reverent for a moment until Jade said, "So, are they still finding silver in the mines?"

That pulled the old woman back to the present. "Some, but nothing as significant as back then. I believe most of the mines around Virginia City are closed down now."

"Doesn't the Comstock Mining Company have some near Six Mile Canyon that are still operational?" said Emma.

"Yes. I believe they do, close to Flowery Peak," said the woman. "But even those aren't producing much anymore."

Jade chimed in. "That's good to know that they're still open. We were hoping to visit some of the mines while we are here. Do you know who we would talk to at Comstock to set up a tour?" She pulled out a small note pad and pen from her purse, ready to jot down any information.

"I don't think they give tours." The woman scrunched her face and rubbed her chin. "In fact, I'm pretty sure they don't even allow anyone up there. The mines are completely fenced off with large Private Property signs posted everywhere. And around here, people don't take too kindly to trespassers."

The woman walked back around the counter, reached under it, pulled out a small yellow telephone book and handed it to Jade. "But I'm sure you can call their office in the morning to find out." She looked over at Emma who had picked up the book again. "So you wanna get that book, even though I've already told you the whole story?"

Emma smiled at her. "I'm sure there are still a few surprises in here." She pulled out a ten-dollar bill from her wallet and handed it to the woman who promptly tucked the money into the top part of her bra.

The girls thanked the receptionist, exited the motel, and walked down the sidewalk to Emma's car.

"Why don't you two go ahead. I'll walk," said Savannah handing Jade one of the room keys. "I need to give my parents and my aunt a call, let them know we made it here okay."

"Yeah, we should probably call ours, too," said Emma.

As soon as Emma and Jade drove away, Savannah pulled her phone out of her purse and punched in the number. When she heard the familiar voice on the other end say 'hello', she smiled and said, "Hey, Brady. It's Savannah."

Chapter 36

The next morning all three girls were up and dressed by eight o'clock. Even Jade, who was not a morning person, was already out the door before Savannah could tie her tennis shoes.

"Let's get a move on, ladies. We've got a lot to do today," Jade said to them as she started to walk down the sidewalk toward the motel lobby.

"So, today's the day we start looking for Katie," said Emma as she grabbed her backpack and headed out the door. "You excited?"

Savannah closed and locked the motel door behind them. "Yeah, excited. But if I'm being honest, I'm a little nervous, too."

"Hurry up, you two," yelled Jade.

"Coming," said Savannah in a chipper voice.

As the two girls trotted to catch up with Jade, Emma looked at Savannah, who had a huge smile plastered on her face, and said, "You're sure in a good mood this morning. What's up?"

Savannah tried to keep the memories of last night's phone call with Brady from showing on her face. "Nothing's up. I just feel good, that's all." When they caught up with Jade, she raised her arms up and stretched, her eyes sparkling. "What a beautiful day. Don't you think?"

Jade narrowed her eyes at her. "All right, spill it."

"Spill what?" Savannah pursed her lips to keep from smiling, but it blossomed anyway.

"Why you're so darn happy this morning," said Jade.

"No reason."

Both Emma and Jade stopped mid stride and looked at her.

Savannah knew they would not give up until they pulled it out of her so she said, "Okay, fine. If you must know, I talked to Brady last night."

"Well that explains the shit-eating grin on your face." Jade flicked her hair over her shoulder. "So what did Mr. Sexy Highlander have to say?"

Savannah's face started to flush. "Oh, nothing much except that he misses me, and he can't wait until I get back. Said he's got a special place picked out for our first date." She released a deep sigh. "His voice is so sexy, especially when he rolls his Rs." She had a dreamy faraway look in her eyes for a moment then shook her head and said, "But enough about my love life. Let's talk about the plan for today. I was thinking that after we talk to Mrs. Dolan, depending on what she tells us, we should take a drive up Six Mile Canyon and scout the area."

"Good morning, ladies."

The motel receptionist had been bent over the terracotta pots watering the geraniums with a silver watering can. But as soon as she saw them she set the can down and straightened up.

Today's outfit was a pair of stretchy, red leotards with a black and white, sleeveless, polka dotted top that hit mid-thigh. Swollen feet had been wedged into a pair of black, pointy toed heels. Her brassy hair had been pulled up into a messy topknot, exposing a pair of large, black plastic, hoop earrings.

She swiped at a line of sweat on her brow and said, "Phew, it's gonna be a hot one. So what do you girls have planned today?"

"We were thinking of maybe taking a hike somewhere. Do you know if there are any hiking trails off of Six Mile Canyon?" said Savannah.

"I don't do much hiking cuz of my gout and all, but I have a hiker's guide for sale inside if you want to take a look at it."

Emma's eyes brightened and she smiled at the woman. "That'd be great."

As they followed the receptionist inside Jade said, "You don't, by any chance, know of a good place to eat around here, do you?"

"Sure do. Grandma Hattie's just across the parking lot. They have the best corned beef hash in all of Nevada. Just tell them Ol' Dolly from the motel sent you, and they'll give you extra biscuits." She walked behind the counter, pulled a booklet from a rack on the wall and handed it to Emma. "Sorry, it has a few smudges on the cover and it's a couple of years old, but I don't think much has changed up there since this was published. You should be fine as long as you stay on the trails. Just be sure to drink plenty of water so that you don't get dehydrated. And pack extra, just in case. It's a desert out there, ya know."

"How much do I owe you?" asked Emma.

Dolly waved her hand as though she were swatting at a gnat. "Ah, just take it. Looks like someone might have dog-eared a couple of the pages. So I wouldn't have been able to sell it anyway."

Emma thanked her and tucked it in her backpack next to the other book. The girls said good-bye and headed over to the restaurant.

Grandma Hattie's looked like it could have, at one time, been someone's home. Turquoise clapboard siding covered the entire two-story building. The windowpanes looked like they had recently been repainted a vibrant white to match the white railing that lined the wrap-around porch. Wooden rocking chairs added charm and a place for the overflow to sit.

They climbed the steps to the porch, and as soon as they opened the door to the restaurant, the aroma of freshly baked pies hit them. They walked in, stood at the entrance and looked around. The place was packed, mostly with loud men in Levis, flannel shirts, and work boots. This looked like the place where the locals came to get breakfast before work.

"Welcome to Grandma Hattie's." An elderly waitress, who could have been Grandma Hattie herself, stopped midstride. Dressed in a pink shift with a white apron and holding a coffee pot, she gestured with her head, "Go ahead and sit anywhere."

Savannah led them to a booth underneath one of the big picture windows facing the motel. She slid in first with Jade scooting in next to her. Emma dropped her backpack on the opposite seat and then plopped down next to it. She pulled out the hiking book and began thumbing through it.

"Good morning, ladies. Would you like some coffee?" The same waitress who met them at the door stood in front of them smiling. On their nod, she filled their cups and then handed them each a menu. "Here you go. I'll give you girls a few minutes to look it over."

"That's okay. I think we know what we want. Dolly, from the motel, told us to come here. She said you had the best hash in town," said Savannah.

"Sure do, and that's a fact."

"Then we'd like three of them, please."

The waitress picked up the menus and said, "Comes with two eggs sunny side up and a side of biscuits. Is that okay?"

The girls nodded vigorously.

When the waitress was gone, Emma returned to the book again and said, "There's an entire section on Flowery Peak. It says that there are several hiking trails in the area around Six Mile Canyon, but there are only a few that are open to the public right now. Here's a list of all of the trails."

She turned the book around so both Jade and Savannah could see it and pointed to a small, orange triangle icon that appeared right after several of the trail names. "The ones that have these small triangle markers are ones that have been closed due to avalanches. Apparently, some of the mining companies were blasting in that area, and it caused a lot of rockslides, making the area too dangerous for hikers. So they've closed those trails down."

She shut the book and set it on the edge of the table. "Even if the trail is closed, we can still drive up there and take a look around, don't you think?" She pulled out the Comstock Lode book from her pack and began to peruse it.

"Here ya go, ladies. Grandma Hattie's famous corned beef hash and a few extra biscuits on account of Ol' Dolly sending ya over." The waitress set a plate of food in front of each girl.

Emma set the book on top of the hiking book to make room for the gigantic plate of food. "Wow, looks amazing."

Jade looked down at her plate. "There's enough food on there to feed our entire football team."

Eying the books, the waitress said, "You girls on vacation?"

"Yes," said Savannah and then took a big bite of the hash. "Oh man, this is so good."

The waitress seemed pleased. "So where ya'll from?"

"Scottsbluff, Nebraska," said Emma in between mouthfuls.

"What brings you all the way out here?"

Savannah smiled. "We just wanted to check out the area. Maybe do a little hiking near Flowery Peak."

The waitress frowned slightly. "There aren't many good trails up there anymore. Nobody maintains them because of all of the avalanches. If you really want to hit some nice trails you should hike around Lake Tahoe. It's so much prettier there, and safer than Flowery Peak."

She pointed to the Comstock Lode book. "You know, Benjamin Burke, the guy who wrote that, is pretty famous around here. And I just saw in the newspaper that he's going to be in the mall tonight doing a book signing for his new book. You should check it out. Maybe he'll sign this copy for you."

"What's the new book about? Do you know?" asked Emma.

"I haven't read it yet, so I don't know for sure. But if I remember correctly, the paper mentioned it having something to do with the legends of the Comstock Lode."

"Thank you for letting us know. We'll be sure to check it out," said Savannah trying to be polite. It didn't sound the least bit interesting to her, but by the way Emma gazed up at the waitress, completely engrossed in what she was saying, they would probably have to make the time.

The girls gobbled down every bit of hash and were finishing the final bites of breakfast when Savannah looked at her phone and said, "Oh crap, it's already quarter after nine. We've got to get going." She waved her hand at their waitress, and when she showed up she already had their bill in hand.

Emma took the check and said to her friends, "My treat."

"Great. Thanks," said Savannah. I'm going to hit the ladies room, and I'll meet you out front."

"I need to go, too," said Jade.

Both girls scooted out of the booth and hurried to the bathroom while Emma finished her biscuit, then gathered up her books and put them back in her backpack. She downed the last bit of her coffee and then pulled some money from her wallet and slid it underneath her coffee cup, along with the bill. She stood up, leaned over to grab her backpack but something caught her attention. She stopped and stared out the window toward the motel.

"What the heck . . ." she murmured.

A few seconds later, Savannah tapped her on the shoulder and said, "C'mon, Em. What are you doing? We've gotta go."

As they walked out of the restaurant and started down the steps, Jade said, "What were you looking at back there, Em?"

"Wait here a second," said Emma as she trotted to the edge of the building. She looked around the motel parking lot and then up and down the main road. A few seconds later, she walked back, crinkled her brow and said, "I don't know, but I'm pretty sure I just saw some guy in a black car checking out our car."

Chapter 37

"Em, I'm not saying you didn't see a black car. But c'mon, why would anyone want to mess around with your car?" said Jade from the passenger's seat.

"I don't know why." Emma sat in the back seat clutching her backpack. "But I know what I saw. And I saw a guy in one of those old cars that have an open back end like a truck bed. I don't remember what they're called."

"You mean an El Camino?" said Jade.

"Yeah, one of those. Anyway, the guy pulled up next to my car, got out, looked in the driver's window and then walked around to the back end." She turned in her seat and glanced out the rear window at Carson City in the distance. "I'm not making it up."

"Nobody said you were, Em," said Savannah as she drove along Highway 50 toward Lake Tahoe. "Maybe the guy mistook your car for someone else's. For all we know he might be staying at the motel." She glanced in the rearview mirror at her friend. "I wouldn't worry about it if I were you."

Emma's face showed concerned. "But don't you remember the reading? It said to be mindful of a white vehicle and a black one." She looked out the back window again. "What if the car I saw was the one that the reading was talking about?"

Jade turned in her seat and looked at Emma. "It wasn't, okay? Whatever you think you saw had nothing to do with us. But if it will make you feel better, we can tell Dolly about it when we get back to the motel this evening. Okay?"

"Okay . . ." Emma settled back in her seat and muttered under her breath, "But I *know* what I saw."

As soon as they crested the mountain, the scenery changed from barren to lush. Off the right hand side of the road a massive body of sapphire blue water peeked through groves of dark green pines. Mini mansions, log cabins that looked like ski lodges, and exquisite resorts lining the water's edge made the area look like a destination designated exclusively for the rich and famous.

After a few miles, Savannah slowed down and turned right onto Skyland Drive. The road wound through a cluster of mini estates tucked in between the pines and then dead-ended right past a long driveway on the right. The name on the mailbox confirmed that this was where the Dolans lived, so she pulled in.

The driveway opened up to a parking area in front of a beautiful, ranch style, log cabin right on the shores of Lake Tahoe. Large picture windows that looked out over the lake offered, what must have been, breathtaking views. Steps leading up to a wraparound porch sprinkled with clusters of redwood tables and Adirondack chairs gave the place a bed and breakfast feel to it.

Savannah parked the car, and the girls got out. They began walking toward the steps, but before they could get to the porch, an elderly woman with gray hair pulled back into a tight bun and wearing a yellow floral shift opened the door.

She stepped out onto the porch and said, "You must be the lady Trudy was telling me about." She smiled slightly at them, but she seemed somewhat nervous. She held her hands balled up near her abdomen, kneading them.

Savannah flashed her a disarming smile as she climbed the stairs. "Hello, Mrs. Dolan. I'm Savannah Swift and these are my friends, Emma Reed and Jade Willows." She stood next to her and held out her hand. "Thank you for seeing us."

Mrs. Dolan grasped it loosely. "Well-l-l-l, I don't rightly know what I can do for you, but Trudy said I should listen to what you have to say. So I will." She held open the front door. "Please come in."

She led them into a large living room with open beamed ceilings that must have been twenty-five feet tall and a massive stone fireplace that took up the entire back wall. She gestured to a mission style leather couch that faced the picture window and said, "Please have a seat while I fetch us something to drink." She looked at them. "Is coffee okay or would you prefer something else?"

"Oh, you don't need to do that, Mrs. Dolan," said Savannah. "We actually just finished breakfast and-"

"But if you've already made some," said Jade, "I'd love a cup."

"I've always got a pot brewing. Mr. Dolan loves it day or night. Drinks it like it was water."

She vanished into the hall and a few minutes later came back with a wooden tray filled with four brown ceramic mugs, a coffee pot and creamer, and a plate of Oreos. "Sorry, but Mr. Dolan ate the last of the pecan pie before he left this morning." She set the tray on the oak coffee table, poured the coffee and handed a cup to Savannah.

"So what information did you have about my grandson?" She poured the rest of the coffee, handed a cup to each of the girls and then sat down on a matching leather chair across from them.

Savannah took a sip then set the cup on a coaster. "Well, I'm still trying to figure it all out, and I was hoping you could help me by maybe answering a few questions."

"I will if I can."

"Do you know if Marty had any friends at the university?"

Mrs. Dolan seemed to be thinking. "I didn't really know many of his friends, but I think he knew people there, because of his work."

"He worked for the Reno Gazette, right?" said Savannah.

"That's right. Got a job as a reporter right after he graduated college."

"I understand that he was working on a story the night he, uh, died."

Mrs. Dolan lowered her head. "I'm sorry, I don't know of any story that he was working on. But it wouldn't surprise me. He was always researching one thing or another. He was so . . ." She seemed to be fighting back the tears.

"I'm sorry," said Savannah, "I didn't mean to upset you."

Mrs. Dolan sniffed a little. "It's all right, dear. It's just so hard not knowing what really happened to him. It just makes no sense that someone would shoot him. He was a good boy." She looked up at Savannah. "But at least I know where his body is because we buried him. But poor Trudy and Harland, they're still looking for answers." She stared out the window and slowly shook her head. "I can only imagine how painful it must still be for them."

Savannah wanted to tell her everything to help ease the old woman's mind, but instead she said, "Did Marty spend a lot of time here with you and Mr. Dolan?"

"Yes, of course he did. He grew up here."

"Oh? I didn't know that," said Savannah.

Mrs. Dolan seemed to anticipate her next question. "His parents—my son and daughter-in-law—died in a car accident when he was eight years old. So we raised him."

"I'm so sorry," said Savannah.

Mrs. Dolan nodded as if accepting her condolences. "Marty moved out when he went to college. But when Mr. Dolan got diagnosed with Parkinson's, it became too difficult for me to take care of both my husband and this place. So Marty moved back in to help. I suppose I could have managed by myself, but Marty wouldn't think of it." She wiped away a tear as it slid down her cheek. "He was such a fine young man, always helping people. He didn't deserve to die that way."

They both grew quiet for several moments until a thought struck Savannah, and she said, "Marty had a bedroom here, right?"

Mrs. Dolan nodded. "Yes, just down the hall. Why?"

"Do you mind if I take a look in it?"

"I guess not. But what do you hope to find in there?"

Savannah shrugged. "Answers."

Chapter 38

Mrs. Dolan lightly closed the door to Marty's bedroom, leaving Savannah alone in there with his belongings—what there were of them. The room looked sparse and more like a guestroom than someone's bedroom. A bed, a dresser, and a nightstand with a lamp on it made up the room's ensemble. A few freestanding, framed pictures set here and there gave the room the only personal touch.

Savannah picked up one of the pictures off of the dresser and stared at it. A young man with straight, sandy blond hair and jovial blue eyes, most likely Marty, stood in between the Dolan's near a boat dock. They looked happy. A wide smile trailed across the young man's face. He looked to be in his early twenties.

She glanced out the bedroom window and noticed the Dolan's boat dock. It was the same one as in the picture, and she couldn't help but wonder if maybe Katie was the one taking the photo. She also wondered how long after this picture was taken that both Marty and Katie were murdered.

She set it back down, walked over to the nightstand and pulled open the drawer. A paperback book rested on top of two spiral notebooks. And to the right side were three ballpoint pens. She pulled the drawer open a little further and saw a gallon-size Ziploc plastic bag. She pulled it out and stared at the contents: a cell phone, a wallet, some change, and a business card. She sat down on the bed and opened the bag.

A light *knock, knock, knock* on the door caused her to look up.

"Savannah, it's Mrs. Dolan. May I come in?"

Savannah closed the plastic bag and set it next to her. "Yes, come in." She stood up and smoothed out the wrinkles on the bedspread, not sure how Mrs. Dolan would react to her sitting on her grandson's bed.

"I was wondering if you found what you were looking for?" Mrs. Dolan stepped into the room, her hands, once more, balled up near her abdomen.

"I hope you don't mind, but I found this in the drawer." Savannah held up the plastic bag. "Did these belong to Marty?"

"Yes, those were the contents of his pockets the night he died."

"Did you, by any chance, check the messages on his phone?"

Mrs. Dolan shook her head. "I'm sorry, but I don't know how to work those newfangled things."

"Do you mind if I take a look at it?"

Mrs. Dolan shook her head. "No, of course not."

Savannah pulled out the iPhone and pressed the button, but the screen remained dark. "The battery's dead. Do you know where Marty kept his charger?"

Mrs. Dolan shook her head again. "No, I surely don't." She paused for a second as if thinking and then said, "Wait here a minute." She hurried out of the bedroom and returned a couple of minutes later holding a white cord. "Is this what you're looking for? Marty always kept this plugged in in one of the bathroom sockets." She handed it to Savannah. "After he passed away, I just shoved it in one of the drawers."

Savannah took the charger, plugged it into the wall and attached the phone to it. She waited a few seconds until the Apple icon showed up on screen. Then she swiped the unlock button but was immediately stopped at the passcode keypad. "You wouldn't happen to know his password, would you?"

Mrs. Dolan shook her head again and began kneading her hands. "I'm sorry, I don't. Do you have to have it?"

"Unfortunately, yes. I can't get into his phone without it. It would be a four digit number." She looked around the room and locked on to the picture of Marty next to his grandparents. "What's Marty's birthday?"

"July tenth, nineteen eighty five, why?"

Savannah entered 0710 but the phone remained locked. She looked over at the other pictures lining the dresser and stopped on a close up picture of the woman from her dreams. "How about Katie. Do you know her birthday?"

Mrs. Dolan pinched her chin. "Well-l-l-l, let me see. I know it's in April sometime. Toward the end, I believe."

Savannah punched in the code 0420. When that didn't work, she tried 0421, then 0422. And on 0423, the phone opened up to a picture of Katie sitting on the dock with a coquettish grin on her face and a bottle of wine tucked between her legs. Lake Tahoe glistened in the background.

"I got in." She touched the phone icon. The voicemail icon showed that there were five unheard messages. She started to push the button but then stopped and looked at Mrs. Dolan. Worry lines crinkled the woman's brow even further. "Would you mind if I took the phone with me? I promise to bring it back to you." She pulled out the business card, looked at it and said, "And this, too, if it's okay."

"No, of course I don't mind. Please, take them. You can keep the card. I don't need it. But I would like the phone back when you are done." Mrs. Dolan paused for a moment, looking as if she wanted to say something else.

Savannah's intuition told her what it was. "I know that Mrs. McCall told you that I might have some answers for you about what happened to your grandson. But I need to do a little more research before I can give you any. Would it be all right if I came back in a couple of days?" She slipped the card in her back pocket and put the Ziploc bag with the wallet and change back in the nightstand drawer. "I'll give you the phone back then if you're okay with that."

Mrs. Dolan's faced seemed to relax slightly. "Yes, dear. That would be fine."

Savannah was just about to close the drawer when her eyes caught sight of the spiral notebooks again.

Take them, Katie's voice whispered in her ear.

She pulled them out and held them up. "May I take these, too?" When the woman nodded, Savannah closed the drawer and pulled the charger from the wall.

Mrs. Dolan led her out of the bedroom and back to the living room where Jade and Emma were still sitting on the couch munching on the last of the Oreos.

When they saw her, Jade said, "Did you find anything?"

Savannah gathered her purse and stuffed the phone and charger in it and tucked the notebooks under her left arm. "I think I might have found a lead for his friend at the university." She pulled the card from her back pocket and read the name. "Dr. Sebastian Wells, Professor of Biochemistry and Molecular biology, University of Nevada." She turned the card over and looked at it. Scribbled across the back was a date and time.

"Hmm, 5/19 - 7pm," said Savannah.

She flashed back to her dream, remembering that Marty had told Katie that he had just come back from seeing a friend at the university. She looked at Mrs. Dolan. "I think this is the person Marty went to see, the night he got shot." Her gaze migrated over to her friends. She held the card up and said, "We need to talk to this guy. I believe he may know what Marty was working on."

Chapter 39

The girls waved good-bye to Mrs. Dolan as Savanna drove them out of the driveway. She turned left onto Skyland Drive and wound back around through the mini mansions until she got to Highway 50, and then she turned right toward South Lake Tahoe.

"Where are you going? I thought we were heading up to Six Mile Canyon," said Jade from the back seat.

"I figured that as long as we were this close, I wanted to find The Gun Barrel Tavern. I think it's only a few miles from here."

Emma looked over at Savannah. "Why? Are you hungry?"

"No, I just wanted to see if the place looks the same as what I saw in my dreams. Plus, I wanted to walk around the area."

"Well then, as long as we're stopping we might as well have lunch there," said Jade. "I wouldn't mind getting a big burger and a double order of fries. Or maybe some onion rings."

Savannah glanced at her in the rearview mirror. "It's not fair, you know."

"What's not fair?" said Jade.

"That you can eat like a horse and not look like one."

Jade just smiled.

A few minutes later they entered the outskirts of South Lake Tahoe. High-rise casinos with flashing neon signs advertising all-you-can-eat buffets and mega jackpots lined Highway 50. But once they passed the casinos, the buildings turned rustic, more reminiscent of a mountain ski village. Red cedar lodges with dark green shingles seemed to be the town's theme.

"Jade, will you look up the address for me?"

"Sure." She pulled out her phone and Googled the restaurant. "It's on Heavenly Village Way, not even a block off the main drag. Make a left at the next light."

It wasn't too difficult for Savannah to find the restaurant. As soon as she saw the building, she recognized it from her dreams. She pulled into the parking lot across the street, drove to the far end where she had seen Marty's Corvette and pulled into one of the spots. She got out and began walking around the immediate area while searching the ground.

"What are you looking for?" asked Emma as she got out of the car and stood next to her.

Savannah looked back across the road toward the restaurant. "I'm not really sure."

Jade walked up and stood on the other side of her. "You didn't really expect to find anything, did you? It's been three years. I'm pretty sure that if there were any evidence, it would be long gone by now."

"I know," she said, still looking at the restaurant. "But standing here, right where they were that night makes me feel, I don't know, closer to them somehow." She squatted down and placed her hand on the ground. A sharp pain right below the rib cage caused her to groan and lose her balance.

"What's wrong?" said Emma. A concerned look washed over her face as she reached down and helped Savannah to her feet.

"I don't know, but it felt like someone stabbed me in the stomach." She reached under her shirt and swiped a hand across her abdomen. She pulled it back out, half expecting to see blood, but it came out clean.

"It's probably just hunger pangs," said Jade. She started to walk across the parking lot toward the restaurant. "C'mon. Let's go get something to eat. I'm starving."

Emma looked over at Savannah. "You sure you're okay? You look a little pale."

"Jade's probably right. I'll be fine once I eat something," she said. But in her gut she knew that this was the exact spot where Marty got shot. She quickly reached back into the car, grabbed the two spiral notebooks, and then she and Emma hurried to catch up with Jade.

When the three entered the restaurant, Savannah looked around the room. It didn't look exactly like her vision, but close enough for her to know which booth Marty and Katie had been sitting in that night. She glanced at the sign that read 'seat yourself' and said, "Follow me."

She stopped in front of the middle booth underneath the large picture window facing the parking lot and scooted in first with Jade sliding in next to her.

Emma sat across from them, watched as Savannah dropped the two notebooks on the table and said, "So what's in there?"

"I don't know. I haven't looked yet." Savannah grabbed the top one and opened it up to the first page. She scrunched her nose. "It looks like nothing but a bunch of chicken scratch. I can barely read his writing." The words looked like they had been shaken up in a scrabble cup and poured out onto the page. Some were diagonal across the page. Some had dashes and numbers next to them, while others were just one-word sentences. She thumbed through the rest of the notebook, finding nothing but the same.

She picked up the second notebook. It looked nearly identical to the first one with similar random words that had been underlined. But this one had crude drawings that could have been Marty's attempt at a graph of some sort.

Though most of it was unreadable, there was one word in all of that mess that she did understand — *Comstock*.

She flipped to the last page and noticed a phone number scribbled on the inside back cover with the initials, *SW* and *cell* written above it. She pulled the card from her back pocket and looked at it. The only number on it did not match the one in the notebook. It seemed to be the line to the university because there was an extension number attached to the end of it.

"Welcome to the Gun Barrel. Can I start you off with something to drink?" A young girl, not much older than them with long blonde hair pulled back into a ponytail, handed them a menu.

"How are your burgers," asked Jade.

"Awesome," said the waitress with a huge grin. "My favorite is the buffalo burger."

Jade handed her the menu. "That sounds good. Can I get onion rings with that?"

"Sure can." She looked at the other two girls. "And how about you two? I can come back later if you need more time."

"No, that's okay," said Savannah. "I'll have that, too."

"Make that three," said Emma. "And three iced teas."

After the waitress left, Savannah pulled her phone from her purse and said, "I'm pretty sure that this cell number belongs to Dr. Wells." She punched the number into her phone and waited with anticipation for the call to connect.

A couple of seconds later a voice on the other end said, "Hello?"

"Hello. May I speak with Dr. Sebastian Wells?"

"Speaking. May I ask who's calling?"

"My name is Savannah Swift. I got your name and number from Mrs. Dolan." When he didn't respond, she said, "Marty Dolan's grandmother?"

"Ah, yes. How may I help you?" His voice sounded friendly over the line.

"I understand you talked to Marty the day he died."

"Who did you say this was?" His voice began to take on a more business-like tone.

"My name is Savannah Swift, and I am trying to help Mr. and Mrs. Dolan get some answers about their grandson."

"Are you with the police?"

"No."

"Are you a reporter?"

"Uh, no."

"Then, in what capacity are you helping the Dolans?"

"I'm, um, an investigator."

"With what company?"

"I don't work for any company. I'm doing this on my own. And I just wanted to ask you a few questions."

Dr. Sebastian paused briefly. "You should probably just call the police, but thank you for calling."

"Wait. Don't hang up." Savannah took in a breath. "I know you met with Marty at 7:00 the night he died and that you gave him a flash drive. I need to know what was on it."

Dr. Wells didn't say anything.

"Please Dr. Wells, it's very important."

"What makes you say that?"

Savannah let out her breath. At least he wasn't hanging up yet. "Because I think someone shot him in order to get whatever information was on that flash drive. And I'm assuming that since he got it from you, then you know what was on there." The line went silence for several seconds. "Please, Dr. Wells, we need your help. Don't you want to know what really happened to him? Who shot him, and why?"

Dr. Wells remained quiet for several long seconds. Finally he said, "Where are you?"

"We're at the Gun Barrel Tavern in South Lake Tahoe."

"We?"

"Yes, I'm with two of my friends. Why?"

Dr. Wells seemed to let out a long breath. "Do you know where Job's Peak Ranch is?"

"No, sir. What is Job's Peak Ranch?"

"It's where I live."

.

Chapter 40

Dr. Wells gave them his address, and thirty-five minutes later, after slamming down their burgers, they pulled up next to a brick security booth in front of Job's Peak Ranch subdivision.

As soon as Savannah unrolled her window, a man dressed in a security uniform and carrying a clipboard walked over, leaned down and said, "May I help you?"

"Yes, we're here to see Dr. Sebastian Wells."

"Your name?"

"Savannah Swift."

He skimmed his clipboard. "License and registration, please." When Savannah handed him the documents he walked around to the front of the car, glanced at the license plate and jotted something, presumably the numbers, down on his clipboard. He walked back around to the driver's window and said, "Wait here a minute, please." Then he walked back into the security booth, printed out a small rectangle piece of paper and then handed it to her through the window. "Keep this on the dashboard." He stepped back into the booth, pushed a button, and massive metal gates slowly began to swing open.

Savannah pulled the car forward, and once they cleared the gate, she slowly accelerated. As the road began to wind its way toward the base of Job's Peak she said, "Keep an eye out for Five Creek Road."

A few seconds later Emma pointed to a road sign on her right hand side and said, "There it is."

This seemed to be no ordinary subdivision. And the houses in this area were like nothing the girls had ever seen before. Even the mini mansions near South Lake Tahoe seemed small in comparison. These homes looked like log cabins on steroids. Massive wood and stone structures the size of hotels peeked out between groves of pine trees. With no fences to indicate property lines, it was hard to tell where one estate ended and another one began.

And when they pulled into Dr. Wells' circular driveway, they discovered that his place was no exception. They stopped in front of two massive log pillars that looked like they came from giant Redwood trees. Holding up a sixty-foot long portico, these columns, three on each side, led up to the entryway. A pinwheel chandelier made of intertwined elk horns hung from heavy, wrought iron chains over a set of carved wooden doors that had to be at least twenty feet tall.

As Savannah rang the doorbell, Jade murmured, "This place is insane. It looks like a freakin' ski lodge."

"No kidding," said Emma touching one of the varnished pillars and craning her neck as her eyes traveled to the top of it. "It's humongous. I didn't think a university professor made that kind of money."

Right then they heard the click of a lock, and one of the front doors began to open. A slight, spindly man, who wasn't much taller than Savannah, with thinning grey hair and silver wire rimmed glassed smiled at them. He wore a pair of belted Levi's and a blue plaid shirt that was neatly tucked in.

"Professor Wells?" said Savannah.

"Yes." He opened the door wider and gestured, "Please come in."

"Thank you for seeing us," said Savannah as the trio stepped into the foyer. She immediately stopped causing Emma to bump into her. This place made the Seavers' place look like a shack. An expansive stone entryway led into an open great room. On the far right hand wall, a stone fireplace climbed thirty feet up to the ceiling with an opening so large that all three of them could stand upright in it.

To the far left stood a rustic but elegantly varnished wooden table that could seat twelve. Above it hung a smaller version of the elk horn chandelier. And centered in the great room were two distinct sitting areas, both with matching plush leather chairs and a leather couch. One area faced the stone fireplace while the other faced the back wall, which was made up entirely of glass doors. No doubt it was to take advantage of the magnificent view of the snowcapped Job's Peak.

"Oh, my gosh, Professor Wells. This is an amazing place." Savannah tried to take it all in, but there was just too much to look at.

"Thank you. My wife and I designed and built it. Took us nearly ten years to finish it." Dr. Wells led them to the couch facing Job's Peak and gestured, "Please have a seat. May I offer you something to drink?"

Right then a female version of Dr. Wells dressed in gray slacks and a tailored red blouse entered the great room carrying a tray of coffee cups and a carafe. She set it on the glass and wrought iron coffee table, wiped her hands on the apron tied around her waist and said, "I'm Wilhelmina, Sebastian's wife. But everyone calls me Willie." She brushed back a strand of silver white hair that had come loose from the bun on the top of her head.

Savannah smiled at her. The woman's warmth and casual manner instantly put Savannah at ease. "It's nice to meet you,

Mrs.- I mean, Willie. I'm Savannah Swift and these are my friends, Jade Willows and Emma Reed. Your home is beautiful."

Willie looked around and gestured with a graceful hand. "This ole' shack? Well, thank you. We like it." She poured her husband a cup of coffee and handed it to him. "Doc, honey, why don't you pour some for the girls while I get the strudel out of the oven."

Dr. Wells smiled up at his wife. "So that's what smells so good." His eyes followed her as she strolled out of the great room, presumably toward the kitchen. When she was gone, he looked back at the girls. His light-hearted manner had turned serious. He lowered his voice and said, "I'll tell you everything I know about what happened that night, but my wife doesn't know about any of this, and I want to keep it that way, understand? I don't want her worrying."

The girls' mouths flapped open at the change in Dr. Wells' demeanor. It caused a shiver to run down Savannah's spine. "O-of course, Dr. Wells. We understand."

Dr. Wells looked back over his left shoulder toward the kitchen somewhere past the great room, and then he leaned into the girls and said, "A few days before Marty died, he brought me a soil sample and a water sample and asked if I would test them for him."

"Test them? For what?" asked Savannah.

"He didn't say. All he said was that he was working on a big story and that he needed the results ASAP."

Dr. Wells took a sip of coffee then glanced back over his shoulder again. "I told him I was leaving that afternoon for a few days to do a lecture in New York, but that I would have my assistant run the tests." He set the cup back down on the table. "On the evening that I was due back in town I had a message on my voice mail from Marty saying that he needed the results that night, and that time was of the essence.

"I called him back as soon as I landed in Chicago, told him my flight wasn't do in to Reno until six thirty that night but that I could meet him at the university by seven.

"Unfortunately, my flight was delayed by several hours, so I called my assistant and asked him to meet Marty. But he had a birthday party to go to in Lake Tahoe that night, so he downloaded the results onto a flash drive and left them at the reception desk for Marty." He glanced once more over his shoulder.

"So what was on the flash drive?" asked Savannah.

Dr. Wells shook his head. "I don't know. My assistant didn't tell me. But he must have discovered something important because that night, the same night that Marty was shot, my assistant was killed."

The girls gasped and Savannah said, "Oh, my gosh! What happened?"

Dr. Wells glanced back over his shoulder and then back at the girls. "It was a car accident. They found his car down near the edge of the lake. The police said it looked like he had been speeding and miscalculated a curve.

"Apparently, he'd been going so fast that when he hit the brakes, it left a fifty-foot skid mark. His car flew over the edge of an embankment and rolled several times, crushing it so badly that firefighters had to use the Jaws of Life to cut him out of there. But by the time they got to him, he was already dead."

From somewhere in the house, presumably the kitchen, Willie yelled out, "Sorry it's taking so long. I had to let the strudel cool for a couple of minutes before I could slice it up. Be there in just a second."

Dr. Wells stared at the girls for a brief moment. His voice lowered again. "My assistant's death was no accident."

"How do you know that?" said Savannah.

"Because he knew those roads like the back of his hand. There is no way he misjudged that curve." His eyes darted from one girl to the next. "I think someone deliberately forced him off the road."

Savannah immediately thought of Katie being pushed over the cliff and said, "Did you find any copies of the test results when you got back to the university?"

Dr. Wells shook his head. "Nothing. His computer had been wiped clean." He let out a breath. "Whoever murdered my assistant went to great lengths to keep whatever was on that flash drive from getting out."

Willie walked in to the great room carrying a platter of five small saucers of sliced apple strudel drizzled with a butter cream frosting. She set it on the table and said, "Please, dig in while it's still warm."

Dr. Wells' light-hearted manner returned, and he smiled sweetly at his wife. "I'm sorry, honey, but our guests just told me they have to be going." And then he stood up, signifying that this was the end of their visit. He ushered the trio to the door, opened it and flashed Savanna a look of concern. He shook her hand, leaned into her and whispered into her ear so that his wife could not hear, "If I were you, I would go home and forget this whole thing."

Savannah looked into his eyes, slowly shook her head and whispered, "I can't do that, Dr. Wells. I can't really explain it to you, but I need to find the answers that I came looking for. And I can't leave until I do."

Worry washed over his face, and he gave her hand a gentle squeeze. "Then be careful. Whoever those people are, they're very dangerous."

Chapter 41

The girls remained quiet while Savannah drove them out of Job's Peak Ranch and turned left onto Highway 395. It wasn't until they were near the outskirts of Carson City that Jade finally said from the passenger's seat, "Well, that was tragic."

"I know, right?" said Emma. "I can't believe someone deliberately killed Dr. Wells' assistant."

"Yeah, I can't believe that either. But that wasn't what I was referring to."

Savannah looked over at Jade. "Then what were you talking about?"

"The strudel. It smelled so good! It was tragic that we didn't get to eat it."

Savannah's eyebrows arched. "You're kidding, right?" She paused. "Right?"

"Of course I'm kidding. Geez, I'm not that heartless." Jade paused briefly then smiled. "But you gotta admit. It did smell really good."

"So what's our next step?" said Emma.

Savannah glanced in the rearview mirror at her. "Well, I think we should still drive up Six Mile Canyon like we had planned, maybe see if we can find some of the mines and check them out."

"But it's Monday. What if people are up there working?"

"You forgot it's Memorial Day. I doubt that they will be open."

Jade pulled the sun visor down and checked herself in the mirror. She fluffed her bangs and pressed her lips together. Satisfied, she flipped it back up and said, "Well, if they're not open, then how are we supposed to get in there?"

Savannah shrugged her shoulders. "I don't know yet. We'll figure it out when we get there." She accelerated to just a few miles over the speed limit and followed Highway 50 out of town toward Dayton.

Twenty minutes later, they turned left on to Six Mile Canyon Road. Instantly, Savannah had a sense of *déjà vu*. The small ghost town on her right looked just like the one in her dreams. As she passed by the rows of cookie cutter houses, she thought about Katie driving this same road the night she died.

"Hey, There's Little Lyon," said Emma. "I remember that town being in the news a few years back. It's where everyone was getting sick."

Jade looked at her and scrunched her brow. "You remember that? I sure don't."

"That's because you never watch the news," said Emma. "Mom's been making me watch it since I was little. She said that being informed is much more important than being popular." She flashed Jade a look and then said with a smiled, "Looks fade, but brains last forever."

Ignoring the playful dig, Jade said, "Did they ever figure out what caused it?"

Emma shook her head. "No, I don't think they ever did."

While Jade and Emma discussed the fate of Little Lyon, Savannah's mind flashed on Marty sitting in the Gun Barrel

Tavern and how rattled he seemed when he got to the restaurant. Something must have frightened him prior to getting there.

Savannah sucked in her breath. *Marty had to have looked at the flash drive sometime between the time he picked it up at the university and before he met up with Katie.* But his grandmother never mentioned that he was there the night he died.

"I need to call Mrs. Dolan." She handed her phone to Jade. "Will you find her number in there and call it?"

"Sure," said Jade as she scrolled through the recently dialed numbers. A few seconds later she punched the call button and handed the phone back to Savannah.

Savannah put the phone on speaker, and when Mrs. Dolan answered, Savannah said, "Hi, Mrs. Dolan. This is Savannah Swift. I hope I'm not disturbing you."

"No, of course not, dear. What can I do for you?"

"I was wondering . . . On the night Marty was shot, do you remember if he stopped by your place before going to meet Katie?"

"Yes, he did," she said immediately. "But it was brief. He ran up to his bedroom and then a few minutes later ran back down. He was out the door before I could stop him. Didn't even say good-bye." She sniffed. "If only I could have said good-bye to him and told him that I loved him." She went quiet for a moment and then said, "Why do you want to know?"

"When I was there I forgot to look for his computer. Do you know where he might have kept it?"

"Well, he usually kept it on his desk. But after he died, I put it in a box and stuck it in our closet. I don't know why I put it there. I guess it made me feel like a part of him was still here with us."

"Could you do me a really big favor?"

"I think so. What do you need?"

"Mrs. Dolan, could you get Marty's computer and take it over to Dr. Wells' place. He doesn't live too far from you."

"Yes, I could do that if you think it's important."

"I do, Mrs. Dolan, very important." She gave her his address and said, "Just tell him that he might be able to find some answers on there." She was about to hang up and then added, "Oh, and tell him the password is probably 0423, Katie's birthday."

"I will."

"Thank you, Mrs. Dolan. I'll give Dr. Wells a call and let him know you are on your way." After she hung up, she made a quick call to Dr. Wells and gave him the information so that he could intercept Mrs. Dolan at their door before his wife had the chance.

When Savannah was finished Emma said, "Do you really think that Marty might have copied whatever was on the flash drive onto his computer?"

"It's possible. And if he did, then maybe Dr. Wells can access it and tell us what the results said."

"That's some smart thinking," said Emma glancing out the back window at the road behind them. "Hopefully he'll-" She stopped mid-sentence and sucked in her breath.

"Hopefully he'll what?" said Jade looking back at her.

"Did you see that?" Emma was completely turned around in the seat and staring out the back window.

"See what?" said Savannah glancing at her friend through the rearview mirror.

"That car behind us. I swear I just saw the same black car that I saw from Grandma Hattie's restaurant. It's following us."

Jade turned around and peered out the back window. "I don't see anything."

Emma gasped again. "There it is. Did you see it?"

Jade sighed. "No, I didn't see anything." She turned back around in her seat as they followed a curve in the road.

Savannah glanced in the rearview mirror at the road behind them. "Em, you must be seeing things. There's no car following us. And besides, even if there is a black car back there, there's no way that it could be the same one from the motel. It's impossible."

"I swear it was the same one," said Emma with conviction in her voice.

"C'mon, Em, let's be a little realistic," said Jade. "There are a gazillion black cars out there-"

"But not very many black El Caminos," Emma shot back.

"You're just being paranoid," said Jade. "So relax, okay?"

"I know what I saw." Emma turned back around and sunk a little lower in the seat. "Just once, I wish you guys would believe me."

When Savannah saw the beginnings of a ten-foot tall, chain link fence with barbed wire crowning the top on the right hand side of the road, she eased off the gas.

"Why are you slowing down?" asked Emma.

Savannah flashed back to her dreams. "Because this place looks familiar to me. I think this is one of the Comstock Mines."

NO TRESSPASSING PRIVATE PROPERTY signs hanging every fifty feet made it very clear that uninvited visitors were not welcome.

She rolled up to a dirt road and stopped. "I'm pretty sure this is where Katie turned in."

"Wow," said Jade looking out the side window. "The place looks like a prison yard." She looked over at Savannah. "Why build such a big-ass fence for a mine that doesn't produce much silver anymore?"

"Good question," said Savannah as she turned right onto a dirt road leading up to a metal gate and stopped in front of it. "Look. It's unlocked." A thick chain with a padlock dangling on the end had been threaded just through the chain link fence.

Emma leaned forward in her seat and peered out the windshield at the gate that was slightly ajar. "That must mean someone's up there."

"What do you think? Should we go in?" Savannah looked up and down the fence line and then surveyed the gravel road that snaked up the hill and disappeared over the summit. Not seeing anyone or spotting any vehicles she glanced at her friends. "Well?"

"Heck yeah," said Jade.

Emma groaned. "Maybe we shouldn't. We could get in trouble." She leaned up further in between the front seats and stared out the windshield at the narrow, rutty road that seemed to go right up into the clouds. Her fingers gripped the tops of both seats. "I don't know, guys. It looks awfully steep. I don't even think my car will make it up there."

Jade opened her door, seemingly ignoring Emma's concern. "I'll get the gate." She got out, closed her door and walked up to it.

While Jade was opening the gate, Savannah looked back at Emma and said, "Don't worry. We'll be fine. If it gets too dangerous, I'll just turn around."

"Turn around? Where? There's no place to turn around once you start up that road." Emma stared at the dangerously steep slope that even a mountain goat would have a tough time traversing. "And what if we run into someone? What will we tell them?"

"If someone stops us, I'll just say we're lost and that we're looking for the Flowery Peak hiking trail, okay?" Savannah caught Emma glancing out the side window, probably searching for that black car that had not yet materialized. "Em, it'll be okay. Nobody's going to think twice about three lost college girls out for a day hike. We'll go up there, look around and then come right back down. Easy peasy."

"I sure hope so," mumbled Emma. She leaned back in her seat and glanced once more out the side window. "I gotta bad feeling about this."

When the gate was fully opened, Savannah pulled through and then waited as Jade closed it behind them, trotted back to the car and climbed in.

"Well, here goes nothing," said Savannah slowly pushing down on the gas pedal. The Rabbit gradually began to climb the steep incline. With both hands gripping the steering wheel, she carefully maneuvered the vehicle around large rocks and potholes, goosing the little car on the steeper parts to keep the momentum.

So far so good, thought Savannah.

The last hundred yards looked much more treacherous. The road seemed to go straight up into the air and then vanish. Savannah pushed down further on the gas pedal causing the car's engine to strain.

"Hang on," she said. "I'm going for it." She goosed the car causing loose gravel to shoot out from the back tires.

Jade gripped the dashboard. "Holy crap! This is steeper than it looks."

"Vannah, stop! I don't think we're going to make," cried Emma bracing her arms against the back of Jade's seat.

Savannah let off slightly on the gas, and the engine began to sputter.

"Don't stop," screamed Jade, "otherwise we'll start sliding backwards. Just go! Go!"

"Oh God, we're going to roll over," shrieked Emma.

"No we're not!" Savannah gripped the wheel firmly, leaned forward in her seat, and stomped on the gas pedal sending the Rabbit shooting up the remaining part of the road. All three girls screamed as the car flew over the top and became airborne.

When they hit the ground, Savannah slammed on the brakes causing the Rabbit to skid to a stop sideways. She rested her forehead on the steering wheel and let out her breath, not realizing she must have been holding it.

"Well, that was a real butt clencher," Savannah said once her heart slowed down to a normal cadence.

All three girls broke into nervous laughter. And Jade said, "I actually think I might have peed a little."

That caused the girls to laugh harder until Emma spotted a white truck coming toward them. "Uh oh. I think we're busted."

When the truck got closer, it slowed down. "Let me do the talking," said Savannah. She straightened the car up, put it in park and rolled down her window just as the truck came to a stop beside them.

The driver, a man wearing a black baseball cap with a Comstock logo on the front of it and a pair of dark sunglasses, had a cigarette dangled from his lips. He put the truck in park, rolled down his window, and hung his elbow out the opening. He took a puff, exhaled the smoke, and held the cigarette between his fingers as he adjusted his glasses without removing them.

"This is private property, and y'all are trespassin'." He took one more hit and blew the smoke out his nostrils.

Savannah flashed him an innocent smile. "We were looking for the hiking trail to Flowery Peak. Isn't this it?"

"No, young lady, it ain't." He jacked his thumb behind him. "It's further up Six Mile Canyon about a mile. You go over a bridge that crosses a big ravine and it's off to the right."

"Oh, Geez. Sorry about that."

She started to put the car in gear when the man opened his door, stepped down and rambled over to the Rabbit. He dropped his cigarette butt, ground it into the dirt with the toe of his boot and then placed his hand on the roof of their car. He leaned down and peered into the opened window at each of the girls. Wet pit stains had turned his light gray T-shirt dark under the arms.

Savannah immediately felt apprehensive. She leaned away from the window as far as her seatbelt would allow. "Like I said, we're very sorry. We'll just turn around and go find the hiking trail."

The man kept his left hand planted on the roof of the car. He removed his sunglasses with his right hand and stared at Savannah. "I can't let you do that."

Emma's jaw unhinged. She leaned forward and looked up at him with wide eyes. "But, sir, we didn't mean to trespass, honest."

The guy pulled his lips into a tight grin. And for a split second Savannah thought she saw the Devil in his eyes. He let out a short laugh causing the corners of his mouth to relax slightly and said, "I can't let you do that because that trail is closed due to avalanches. The area is just not safe for you ladies. You'd be much better off hiking near Lake Tahoe." He looked directly at Savannah. "You know where that is, don't you?"

"O-oh sure, we know where it is," said Savannah. "We'll do that instead."

The man straightened up, tapped on the roof of their car with the palm of his hand and said, "You do that now. Sure would hate for something bad to happen to you girls." He put his sunglasses back on, adjusted the oval, silver belt buckle holding up his Levi's, and then sauntered back over to his truck. He hopped in, waited until Savannah turned the Rabbit around, and then he took off in front of them down the hill.

"Oh, my God," said Emma. "I thought for sure he was going to kill us."

Jade shook her head and snorted. "Good lord, Em. You're so paranoid. You think everyone's out to get us."

"Well, you have to admit he was a little creepy."

"A little? No, he was a *lot* creepy. And skinny. He reminded me of Ichabod Crane." They both started laughing.

Emma took in a breath. "And did you see that belt buckle? It was the size of-"

"Guys," said Savannah gripping the steering wheel, "I need to concentrate. This part is really steep and rocky."

"Sorry," they both said in unison.

The girls remained quiet as Savannah took her time maneuvering the rocks and ruts back down the hill. And by the time they got to the entrance, the man had already exited his vehicle and was standing by the opened gate, waiting for them.

As Savannah slowly drove through it, she threw a quick wave at the man. His head followed them but he didn't wave back. Maybe he hadn't seen the gesture. His lips remained in a straight rigid line, his facial features stiff and unyielding. But a second later he drew his lips up into a slight smile and waved back.

Savannah waited briefly before turning onto Six Mile Canyon. She looked right, knowing that Flowery Peak trail was just a short ways up that way. The man said it was across a big ravine and on the other side. Could that be Katie's ravine? If the trail took them near enough to the mine it's possible that she would be able to scan the cliffs from the opposite side of the ravine and spot something that looked familiar to her.

She looked left. Only delays and unanswered questions lay that way.

Which way should I go?

When she looked in her side mirror, she saw that the man had already closed and locked the gate and was idling right behind them. His stone features had returned. Another lit cigarette dangled from his lips, and his right index finger tapped the steering wheel as if impatient.

Reluctantly, she put on her left blinker and pulled out onto the road with the truck following closely behind her. As she accelerated she said, "We'll come back here tomorrow and try to find the hiking trail."

Emma turned around and glanced out the back window. "Probably a good idea. It doesn't look like he's going to let us out of his sight. She swiveled back around. "So I was thinking . . . Would you guys be up for going to that book signing tonight?"

"What book signing?" said Jade.

"You know, the one at the mall. The waitress at Grandma Hattie's told us about it." She reached down toward the floorboard, unzipped the top of her backpack and pulled out the Comstock Lode book. "Benjamin Burke. I wouldn't mind picking up his new book, maybe have him sign this one."

Savannah smiled at her in the rearview mirror. "Sure, we could do that, right Jade?" She flashed Jade a sideways glance.

"Sure. It'll be fun." Jade smiled, but her tone contradicted her words.

When they rounded a curve, Savannah noticed a vehicle farther up parked on the right hand side of the road. So she slowed down. As she got closer she realized that it was a black older model car with the back end of a truck.

The El Camino!

As she passed it, the man seated behind the wheel glanced at them and then quickly looked away. But it was long enough for Savannah to see his features: a military-type buzz cut, clean shaven, strong jaw line with close set, beady looking eyes. She glanced in the rearview mirror at Emma who was also staring out the window at the black car and clutching her book to her chest.

As soon as they passed him, he slowly pulled back onto the road, right behind the man in the white pickup truck.

Chapter 42

"So, do you still think I'm crazy?" Emma's arms were crossed over her chest and her chin jutted out. 'There's no way that guy was just some random stranger that had pulled off the road and happened to be driving the exact same type of car as the one I saw at the motel." She glanced back at the white pickup truck a few cars behind them. "It's the same one. I know it!"

"Is it still back there?" said Jade without turning around in her seat.

Emma tried to spot it but the traffic on Highway 50 heading back toward Carson City was beginning to get thick, obstructing her view. "I can't see it. But our friend in the truck is still back there." She paused. "Oh wait, it looks like he's turning off on one of the exits for Dayton."

"Thank God!" said Savannah loosening her grip on the steering wheel. "He's probably heading back to Comstock's office."

"We could turn around and go back up there. Now that he's not following us," said Jade.

"No!" said Emma. "I've had enough drama for today."

Jade looked over at Savannah. "How about you? What do you want to do?"

Savannah tilted her head, giving her an apologetic glance. "Sorry, but I'm with Em on this one. Let's just go back to the motel, maybe grab something to eat at Grandma Hattie's and rest a little before we head on over to the mall." She pulled her phone from the cup holder and looked at the time. "It's already after three. And I could use a nap before we get ready to go out."

"Well, now that you mention it, all the excitement did make me a little hungry." Jade wiggled her eyebrows. "Maybe they're still serving that great hash."

Savannah shook her head and chuckled. "You kill me. I swear to God you have tape worms."

Now that they were beginning to know their way around Carson City, it didn't take them very long to get back to the motel. Savannah turned into the parking lot and pulled up right in front of their room. She shut off the car and grabbed her phone. "You guys go ahead and go on in. I'm going to make a couple of phone calls first.

"One of those calls wouldn't be to a Scottish hunk named Brady, would it?" said Jade batting her long black eyelashes at Savannah.

"Aye, yer such a fine lass," mimicked Emma as she opened her door. "I just want to rub haggis all over yer body and lick it off."

"Eww!" Savannah flung a hand at them. "Go on. Get out of here." She tried to look serious, but she couldn't suppress the giggles that were bubbling up. She watched them until they entered the room, then she dialed Brady's number.

Almost immediately he said, "I was hoping ye would call today. How are ye?"

Savannah felt her cheeks beginning to burn. "I'm good. Great, actually. And you?"

"Well, I wouldn't go so far as te say I'm great, but I'm doing good." He paused. "I'd be doing much better if ye were here." He paused again. "I miss ye."

Savannah smiled into the phone. "Miss me? I haven't been gone that long."

"Aye, ye have. Two very long days."

"But I talked to you last night."

"Aye, and as lovely as it is hearing yer voice, it's not the same as seeing ye." He groaned. "I don't think I'm going te be able te last another eight days."

Savannah giggled. "They'll go by quick."

"I sure do hope so. Because this is truly torture." He paused and cleared his throat. "But seriously, are ye okay?"

Savannah sighed. "Yes, we're fine. But we did have a bit of a scare today." She told him about the guy in the white pickup truck and their meeting with Dr. Wells.

Brady sucked in his breath. "Vannah, please be careful. I'm worried that ye might be getting into something bigger than ye anticipated. If that guy's assistant really was murdered then ye should not be getting involved."

"I'll be fine."

"Ye don't know that."

She thought about telling him about the man in the black car. But she knew that it would only fuel his concern, so she kept it to herself.

"Tonight we're going to the mall to a book signing. Em's discovered a local author and wants to get his autograph."

"Well, that sounds fun—and safe. I'm glad yer doing something other than spending all of yer time searching for a dead person."

"Her name's Katie. Katie McCall." She could feel herself getting defensive. "And I met with her parents yesterday."

Brady seemed to sense a change in her demeanor. "I'm sorry. I dinna mean te upset ye."

Savannah ran her finger around the steering wheel. "No, you didn't upset me. I'm just frustrated. I guess I thought that I would come up here and just, I don't know, be led right to her. But that's not happening. I still don't have any answers. In fact, I have more questions now than when I started."

Brady's voice softened. 'Ye'll figure it out. I have no doubt about it. I may not know ye very well, but one thing I do know about ye is that ye don't give up easily."

That made Savannah smile.

They talked about things that were happening in Scottsbluff for a few more minutes and were just about to hang up when Brady said, "I almost forgot te tell ye. The big news around here is that the owner of the junkyard at the edge of town was just charged with animal theft. Apparently, a girl from the high school went over there and found her dog penned up in his yard, along with several other stolen dogs."

The girl with the feathers in her hair flashed into Savannah's mind making her smile again. At least that was one happy ending. "Listen, Brady, I better go. I still need to call my parents."

"Okay. Will ye be calling tomorrow?"

Savannah heard the anticipation in his voice. "I'll try. But I'm not sure what time. What's a good time?"

"Any time's a good time as long as it's yer voice I'll be listening te."

They said good-bye but before she could dial her parents' number, her phone rang.

"Hello?" said Savannah.

"Vannah, it's your Aunt Helen. I was calling to make sure that you were okay."

"Hi Aunt Helen. I'm fine."

"You're sure?"

She thought about telling her about the incident up at the mine, but since nothing happened to them there was no point in making her worry. "Yes, why?"

Aunt Helen seemed to hesitate. "Oh, nothing. You were just on my mind, that's all."

Savannah felt like there was something that her aunt wasn't telling her. She didn't push her, though. Instead she told her about their plans for the evening.

"Well, I won't keep you, then. You girls have a good time."

"We will, Aunt Helen. And thank you for calling. It's nice to be able to talk to you."

"You know you can call me anytime—day or night—no matter what. I'll always be here for you."

That made Savannah feel warm inside. Knowing that they shared this psychic ability made her feel closer to her than to her own mother. "Thanks, Aunt Helen. I appreciate that." She said good-bye, hung up and then called her parents before the phone could ring again. She made the conversation brief.

"So how's California?" asked Mrs. Swift. "Are you having a good time?"

"Yes, we're having a really great time."

Is it as pretty as they say? Have you seen the ocean yet?" Excitement caused her mother's voice to sound breathy.

"Well, there's been a change of plans."

"What sort of change?" Her mother's tone shifted.

"We decided to spend a few days in Carson City before heading out to California."

"Carson City? Why there?" Her mother sounded surprised.

"Well, as it turns out, it's kind of a cool place. Lots of historical sites like Virginia City." She told her some of the facts that she could remember from the book. "For some reason Em has become interested in learning more about the Comstock Lode. She picked up a book written by a local author and come to find out, he's doing a book signing tonight. So we're going to go to that."

"Well, that sounds like a lot of fun. So when will you leave for California?"

Savannah swallowed. She really didn't want to lie to her mother, especially now knowing that she, too, was psychic. Would she sense it? Or had she suppressed her gift for so long that she wouldn't recognize a psychic inkling if it hovered in front of her face. "Maybe tomorrow. We really haven't decided yet, but I'll call you and let you know for sure."

"Okay, honey. You girls have a wonderful time. And stay out of trouble."

Oh, Mom. Too late!

Chapter 43

Savannah grabbed the two notebooks that she had tucked between the console and her seat and exited the car. As she shut and locked the door she heard over her shoulder, "Did you girls have a good day?"

She turned around. "Oh, hello Dolly." The motel receptionist was sweeping the sidewalk with a straw broom. She still had on the same polka dot outfit but the bun on top of her head had, somehow, slipped over to the side making her look like she'd been caught in a big wind storm. "We had a nice day. How about you?"

She stopped sweeping and leaned on the broom. "Well, I'm still walkin' and breathin' so I guess I had a good day, too."

Savannah laughed. "I can't argue with that."

"So what do you girls have planned for the rest of the day?" She propped the broom up against the side of the motel and pulled a water bottle from the waistband of her stretch pants.

"We were going to go to that book signing tonight for that local author. I can't remember his name right now . . ."

"Benjamin Burke." Dolly took a drink then wiped her mouth with the back of her hand.

"That's right."

"Well, if you get a chance to talk to him, tell him ol' Dolly says, *Hey*." She took another sip then tucked the bottle back in her waistband. "But only if his wife ain't there. She don't like me much on account of he had the hots for me awhile back." She blew back a strand of hair from her face, tilted her head and grinned like a schoolgirl.

Savannah's eyebrows arched. "Um, okay. I will if I can." She started to walk away but stopped. "Oh, I almost forgot. My friend, Emma, thought she saw some guy in a black El Camino walking around her car this morning while we were having breakfast at Grandma Hattie's. Just thought you should know."

Dolly's smile faded and she looked around the parking lot. "Don't you worry none. I'll keep an eye out. This here's a safe place, and I aim to keep it that way. But if you do happen to see him again, try to get his license plate number, and I'll have my friends at the sheriff's department look into it."

Savannah smiled. "You sure do know a lot of people around here."

"Well, I should. I was born and raised right here in Carson City." She grabbed the broom and started sweeping again. "It's always good to have an ex-boyfriend with a badge." She snorted. "As long as you're still on good terms, that is."

That made Savannah chuckle. "Well, I better go. We'll talk to you later. Happy sweeping."

When she got to the room both Emma and Jade had stripped off their jeans and were already asleep on their beds. Seeing them all curled up made her feel tired and drained. No doubt it had been a stressful day. And without the adrenaline keeping her focused, her body and mind were beginning to shut down. She yawned as she quietly closed the door, slipped her shoes off and gently slid onto the bed next to Jade.

Within moments she fell into a deep sleep.

~~~~~~~~~~~~~~~~~~~

Six Mile Canyon Road
May 17, 2009
11:00 PM

Marty eased the Corvette off of the road and turned his lights off so as not to warn the driver of the delivery truck in front of him that he was being followed. Marty had been tailing the vehicle since it left the Comstock Mining Company warehouse in Dayton.

When the truck turned right onto a dirt road and stopped in front of a metal gate, Marty cut his engine and headlights. He grabbed a pair of binoculars off of the seat next to him and focused on the man standing in the truck's high beams, fiddling with the gate's padlock.

Once the gate was unlocked, the man swung it open then waved his hand in the air. Immediately, the truck rolled forward, indicating that there was another person in the vehicle. The man closed the gate behind the truck then hopped into the passenger's seat.

"What is so damn important that it has to be delivered this late at night?" murmured Marty as he watched the truck slowly maneuver the dirt road snaking up the steep slope.

This was the third truck in as many nights to travel this route. And Marty had tailed all of them. But this was as far as he'd gotten. He'd been too apprehensive to follow them any further. Between the ten-foot chain link fence lined with barbed wire and the heavy-duty metal gate, it was pretty clear that these people didn't want any visitors. And in these parts, people who got caught trespassing on private property usually ended up in jail—or worse.

When the truck disappeared over the crest, Marty started his car, turned on just his parking lights, and slowly drove along the fence line. He turned right onto the dirt road and stopped in front of the gate.

Luckily, it was unlocked.

He got out of his car, pushed opened the gate, and then drove through, leaving it open behind him. As he stared up at the steep grade in front of him he prayed that his car could handle the ruts and rocks. Last thing he needed was to get high centered on a boulder. He shut off his parking lights and began the steep and treacherous climb.

With no moonlight, Marty had trouble navigating the potholes and cursed each time his car bottomed out. But he didn't have a choice. Whatever was going on up there, the fact that they were doing it at night told him that they wanted it kept a secret. And if they spotted his headlights, chances were pretty good they would shoot first and ask questions later. He also knew how easy it was for someone to vanish in these hills without so much as a trace.

Once he crested the top, the road straightened out and Marty was able to speed up. He followed it to the edge of a band of pine trees and then pulled off the road and idled. He had never been up here before, but Katie had—many times. She told him about the heavy equipment and the prefab office building that lay in a clearing just beyond those trees.

He flipped the car around, just in case he needed a quick getaway, grabbed his phone and a small flashlight from the seat next to him and tucked them both in his jacket pocket. Quietly he opened the door, stepped out into the cool, black night and gently closed it with a soft *click*. Then he sprinted toward the tree line.

Thick underbrush made it nearly impossible for Marty to maneuver through the dense forest. And without light he had a hard time determining which direction he was going.

"Dammit," he cursed when he tripped over a low stump, nearly losing his footing. Frustrated, he pulled the flashlight from his pocket and turned it on.

In the deep blackness, his light sliced into the night like a laser, so he quickly shut it off. The key to his success and his safety was being able to stay invisible. He would just have to take it more slowly and hope that whatever those guys were doing up there, they would still be doing it by the time he got there.

He wasn't sure how long he had been trekking through the trees. Maybe ten to fifteen minutes. But when he saw a dim light coming from somewhere in front of him, he knew that he was near the edge of the forest.

Rows of parked bulldozers and dump trucks confirmed it.

He slowed his pace, careful not to snap any twigs underfoot, and when he reached the final row of trees he stopped and hid behind the trunk of a massive pine tree.

Thank God, thought Marty. He let out a quiet breath when he saw the delivery truck parked in the middle of the lot with light coming from the opened backend. He pulled the phone from his pocket, made sure the flash was off, and then began shooting pictures. With not much light, the photos were useless. They showed nothing but black blur.

I've got to get closer.

Marty hunched down and quietly stepped over the final fringe of brush. Once in the clearing, he silently sprinted for cover behind one of the yellow bulldozers. Now he was only thirty feet from the delivery truck and the men standing behind it. Not only could he get better pictures, but he could also hear their conversations. He took a few more shots and then switched his phone to video.

After a few minutes Marty smiled and thought, *I've got you now. Won't be able to weasel your way out of this one.* He finished videotaping, dropped the phone in his pocket and turned to start back into the trees.

Brriinngg! Brriinngg! Brriinngg!

Marty's phone went off in his pocket. *Dammit! I forgot to put it on vibrate!* He fumbled for the phone but by the time he was able to shut it off, the damage was already done.

They knew he was there.

The men working around the back of the truck stopped what they were doing and turn toward Marty's direction.

"Who's there," yelled a man who must have been the one in charge. "Whoever you are, you're trespassing on private property. Now show yourself." He shined his flashlight in the area around the bulldozer.

Marty flatten himself against the machine and froze.

"I'm not gonna ask twice. Now c'mon out." The man waited for a few more seconds then nodded his head in Marty's direction and said to the men standing next to him, "Go find whoever is there and bring them to me."

When Marty saw four men trotting in his direction, he bolted across the open area toward the trees, disregarding the noise he made. Stealth no longer mattered. The only thing that did matter was that he got back to his car before they could catch him.

"There he is," yelled one of the men coming toward him. "He's heading into the trees."

"Grab him. Don't let him get away," yelled the one in charge.

With their flashlights trained on Marty, the men broke into a run.

Did they see my face?

Marty didn't think so, but there was no way to know for sure. He sprinted through the trees, jumping over brush and swatting at saplings, oblivious to the cuts and scrapes across his face and arms. Adrenaline pumped through his veins as he raced toward his waiting car. He glanced back over his shoulder at the lasers of light searching for him. They were closing in on him so he pumped his legs as hard and as fast as they would go.

If they catch me now, I'm a dead man.

Chapter 44

Savannah sprang from the bed and yelled, "Oh my God! It's on his phone." Her outburst caused both Emma and Jade to jump up.

"Holy crap! What's wrong? Is the motel on fire?" said Emma bumping into the nightstand as she catapulted out of the bed.

Jade was nearly out the door before she realized that she was standing in the doorway with just her top and underwear. She quickly grabbed her jeans that were draped over a chair by the window and slipped them on. "What the heck, Vannah? You trying to give us heart attacks?"

"I'm sorry, guys. I didn't mean to scare you," she said digging through her purse. She fished out Marty's phone and held it up. "But it's all on here."

"What's on there?" said Jade closing the door and falling into the chair. She yawned deeply and rested her head on the small, round table underneath the window.

Emma pulled out the chair across from Jade, plopped down and began rubbing her knee where it had clipped the edge of the nightstand. "Ouch! That's gonna leave a mark. Probably a bruise, too."

Jade sat up. "Well at least you didn't give the boys at Grandma Hattie's a show like I did. I can't believe-"

"Guys, will you shut up and listen to me?" Excitedly, Savannah held up Marty's phone again. "Whatever Marty saw up there at the mine is on here." She pulled up the camera icon on his phone and clicked on it. "I saw him in my dreams taking pictures. Whatever photograph he showed Katie that night at the Gun Barrel is on here."

Savannah pulled out the third chair and sat down. The girls leaned in as she put the phone in the middle of the table and began scrolling through the photos.

Emma scrunched her nose and tilted her head sideways in an attempt to get a better look. "What are they pictures of? It's too dark to tell."

Jade tilted her head, too. "Looks like a big blur to me."

Savannah stopped on an image that wasn't as dark and grainy as the others. A boxy, Comstock delivery truck with its back doors open and light shining out from the back end, sat parked in the middle of the equipment arena.

A line of what looked like fifty-gallon drums stood upright on the ground behind it. It was unclear whether the barrels had been removed from the back end of the truck or whether they were being loaded onto it. The photo captured a forklift that looked like it might be preparing to pick up one of the barrels.

The last image was a video. She clicked on the arrow and the scene came alive. Though shaky, she could see several men standing at the back end of the truck helping to line up the drums, but she could not make out any specific features. By the grunts and groans, the barrels must have been heavy.

The camera focused in on the forklift as it lifted one of the barrels up off of the ground. But before the drum was completely secure on the metal forks, the forklift lurched forward causing the drum to topple to the ground and land on its side. Shouts followed, and several of the men scurried to help.

"Dang almighty, Darrel. Watch what you're doing, will ya?" The man speaking trotted toward the toppled drum and said, "Is it damaged?"

The man from the back of the delivery truck had already jumped down and was squatted next to the barrel with his flashlight trained on it. "Yep. Seal's busted, and it's leaking all over the ground." He looked up at the man standing over him. "What do you want us to do?"

"For God's sake, you moron. What do you think I want you to do? Clean it up!" He looked around and then barked, "C'mon guys, help him get this thing back upright." The man pulled off his baseball cap and swiped a hand across his head. "Dang it. Now I'm gonna have to tell the boss man. He ain't gonna be too happy about it neither."

The driver of the forklift jumped down and helped bring the drum upright. He ran his fingers around the lip then rubbed the contents between his thumb and fingers. "It's leaking real bad. Sorry 'bout that, Lou."

"Well don't touch it, you idiot. Go on, now. Go wash that stuff off your hands before it eats the skin away." Then he yelled out to the group, "C'mon, let's get a move on. We gotta take care of this shit before daylight."

Three guys were wrestling the drum back onto the forklift when the video stopped abruptly.

"What were they doing with those barrels?" ask Emma.

"Yeah, and what did that guy mean by 'take care of'?" added Jade

Savannah shook her head. "I don't know. Hopefully Dr. Wells will be able to access Marty's computer and maybe find some answers."

Emma pulled her phone from her pocket and looked at the time. "Hey guy's we better get a move on if we want to grab a bite before heading off to the book signing." She looked out the window at the restaurant parking lot across from them. "Looks like Grandma Hattie's is pretty busy. What do you say we find a different place to eat? I'm sure there are lots of places around here that are just as good."

The girls agreed that there wasn't much they could do right now anyway, so they spruced up a bit and then headed out the door in search of a different restaurant.

As they pulled out of the motel parking lot and turned right, so did the black El Camino three cars behind them.

Chapter 45

The book signing turned out to be at the Barnes and Noble right next to the mall. The line was already out the door and beginning to wrap around the side of the building by the time the girls got there.

"Wow! He must be pretty famous for all of these people to show up," said Emma excitedly clutching her book to her chest as they joined the end of the line.

"Either that or there isn't a heck of a lot else to do around here," mumbled Jade. She glanced at the mall with a longing look in her eyes. "How late do we have to stay?"

"Until it's over," said Emma jutting out her chin in defiance. "I saw on line that he's going to read from his new book and then he's going to do a signing and have pictures taken. I can't wait to have my picture taken with him." She squealed when the line started to move. "Oh, isn't this exciting?"

"About as exciting as a root canal," mumbled Jade.

Savannah elbowed her in the ribs then smiled at Emma. "It's very exciting, Em. I'm glad it worked out that we could be here for this. So are you going to buy his new book?"

"Well, yeah, of course I am. And I've got some questions to ask him, too. It's not often you get to talk to an author who's a historical expert."

"So what are you going to ask him?" said Savannah.

Jade glanced at the author's picture on the back cover and arched her eyebrows. "Not bad looking for an older guy. So what are you going to ask him, if he's married?"

Emma scowled at her and wrinkled her nose. "Eew, no! He's old enough to be my father—and yours, too, I might add. No. I'm going to ask him if he knows why the Comstock Mining Company is buying up all of the dry mines."

Savannah sucked in her breath and grabbed Emma by the arm. "No!" she said in a hushed voice. "You can't ask him that. It might draw too much attention."

"Well, I won't word it quite like that. I'll say something like; in your opinion, what would be the value in buying up mines that no longer produce?"

"What makes you think he would know that?" said Jade. She flicked her hair back over her shoulder and smiled at a blond guy dressed in a black leather jacket, tight Levi's and cowboy boots as he walked by. His jaw dropped open, and he stared at her until he bumped into the person who had stopped in front of him, nearly knocking them both to the ground. Jade giggled and turned to her friends. "Boys. They're the same no matter where you go. So like I was saying-"

"I'm sure Mr. Burke will know the answer to that," said Emma sounding somewhat defensive. "He's an expert in that field."

By the time they entered the store, there was standing room only along the back wall. Emma stood on her tiptoes, bobbing from side to side. "Darn it, I can't see anything. She looked around the room then pointed. "There's an open spot along the side wall near the front. I'll bet if we squeezed together all three of us could fit. You guys want to go up there?"

Savannah looked at the packed area, not seeing room for one let alone three. "Why don't you go ahead and go. We'll wait here."

"Ok. I'll meet you right back here when it's done." Emma began worming her way through the crowd, using her shoulders and arms to forcibly nudge people out of her path. "Excuse me. Pardon me," she said loudly. And if they didn't willingly respond to her request, she bulldozed her way through, ignoring the complaints and objections that followed.

When she finally wiggled into the tiny sliver of space no more than ten feet from the author's table, Jade mused, "Wow. That girl was on a mission." She leaned back against the wall and crossed her arms over her chest. "A human tank with attitude."

Savannah chuckled then waved when Emma turned around and grinned wildly at them. "No kidding. I didn't know she had that in her."

A few minutes later a slight woman dressed in a navy blue pants suit and a chic bob of gray hair stood in front of the author's table causing the murmurs coming from the audience to immediately subside.

"Good evening, ladies and gentlemen. Thank you all so much for being here. This is a special treat for us." She held a hardback book in one hand and did a 'Vannah White Wheel of Fortune' gesture with the other. "We are so fortunate to have this gentleman here with us tonight to do a reading from his latest book, 'Legends of the Lode', and to answer any questions you might have for him." She glanced at the author sitting behind the table next to her, batted her eyes at him, and then grinned broadly at the audience. "And might I add, who is a legend in his own right. Ladies and gentlemen, please give a warm welcome to our incredible guest, Mr. Benjamin Burke." She began to clap feverishly causing the audience to respond with equal enthusiasm.

When the applause died down, Mr. Burke stood up. Tall and weathered, but in a handsome Marlboro Man kind of way, he surveyed the crowd, and then said in a deep baritone voice, "Thank you so much for that incredible welcome. I didn't realize we had so many history buffs in the audience. Hopefully, I will be able to impart some new and different knowledge about the history of this fine state and the area in which we all call home." He grabbed a hardback book with paper tabs sticking out of the top and flipped to the first one. "I would like to read a few excerpts for you, if that's all right."

The audience erupted into applause again.

When the room was silent he began with, "Legends of the Lode, Chapter 4. 'If you've lived or spent any time around the Carson City/Virginia City area then you have, no doubt, heard of the miners who put Nevada on the proverbial map. Men like Peter O'Riley and Patrick McLaughlin, who were the first to actively mine and hit pay dirt right off of Six Mile Canyon, started the silver rush. They found what Ol' Henry 'Pancake' Comstock could not.

"'But it was James 'Old Virginny' Finney, John 'Big French' Bishop, Aleck Henderson, and Jack Yount who kept the rush going and helped Virginia City to become a boomtown.

"'While these men were legendary because of their discovery, rediscovery, and mining of the Lode, they are not the legends of which I speak. The legends I am referring to brought order where there was chaos. They offered solace to those broken in body and spirit. They imparted wisdom when necessary, and wit when it was needed. They were revered by some and loathed by others.

"'Worldly and generous, these legends helped make Virginia City the most influential, political and social hub of the American West. They became exalted in the eyes of many a man. And yet, their names have gathered no ink in the history books.

"'So who were these legendary figures of the Comstock Lode, despised by some yet revered by others?'" He paused dramatically and looked around the anticipatory audience. "'They were the madams of Virginia City.'"

A gasp fell across the room.

Mr. Burke turned to the next tabbed area of the book, pulled a clicker from his pocket and pushed the button. Immediately, a vintage, sepia-toned photograph of a woman in a low cut bar gown filled the screen behind him. Her hair was done up on top of her head with an ostrich feather sticking out of the top. She sat perched on a bar stool with one leg crossed over the other, showing off a thigh high garter belt that peeked out from beneath a slit running up her left leg.

He pushed the clicker again and another similarly dressed woman filled the screen.

He glanced back briefly at the picture behind him and then continued reading from his book. "'While most believe that the title, 'Queen of the Comstock', referred to Virginia City because of how quickly it rose to become the center of the West. In actuality, the title belonged to the *women* who kept the town thriving, that is, the madam and her ladies of easy virtue.'"

Picture after picture of different madams and her 'girls' shown on the screen behind him.

"'These women were the ones who entertained, kept secrets, and fostered relationships. They maintained diplomacy and decorum. They were the voice of reason. They instilled manners and taught etiquette to the miners. And they did so expertly with their womanly wile. And through it all, the men had no idea they were being directed, herded, and manipulated.'" He flipped to the next tabbed section in the book.

"'Ah yes, the madam and her purveyors of pleasure. So what ultimately caused their demise in Virginia City?'" He clicked on another photograph. A tight-lipped man dressed in a vintage jacket stood next to a woman dressed in a long skirt with a long sleeved blouse that closed tightly around her wrists and neck. Her left hand was looped through the man's arm revealing a gold wedding band. "'The wife.'"

That caused the audience to burst into laughter.

He looked up at the audience and said, "Shall I keep going?"

"Yes!" came a thunderous response.

"'It was the gradual influx of quote *respectable* women that caused the madam to fall from her pedestal. Or shall I say—to be yanked from it.

"'As Virginia City's notoriety grew, women from around the country and the world ventured out West in search of a rich husband. And as it turned out, it wasn't just the madams and her ladies of the evening who knew how to manipulate. It was the wives, as well.'" He looked out into the audience. Women and men glanced at each other. "I can see things haven't changed much since then." That brought a mixture of chuckles and groans.

He flipped to the next tabbed section. "'With the influx of women to the area, a new situation arose.'" He brought up a picture of women holding babies. "'Children. And lots of them. This is not to say that there weren't children prior to the flood of nuptials. There were. But they were illegitimate.

"'The public women, or 'Prairie Doves' as they were sometimes referred to, who ended up pregnant did not ask nor expected marriage. It was simply a risk of the job, and if it happened to them, they dealt with the consequences silently and on their own.

"'The men gained families but remained single. They continued to socialize with these calico queens, and for a long time all was copasetic.

"'The problem came when these new wives began getting pregnant and creating families of their own with these miners. The wives manipulated their husbands into shunning their preexisting children.'" An image of a madam standing with her arms draped protectively over a young boy and girl filled the screen.

He closed the book and set it back down on the table. "Questions?"

Someone yelled out, "So what happened to the kids?"

He laughed. "Guess you'll have to read the book to find out." He looked out into the audience again. "Any other questions?"

Emma raised her hand, waved it wildly and yelled out, "I have a question."

Chapter 46

Emma had not stopped talking since they left the book signing. Clutching the new book tightly to her chest, she said from the back seat, "That was so much fun! And did I tell you what he wrote in my book?" Enthusiasm burst from each word causing her voice to raise an octave.

"Yes, Em, you did," mumbled Savannah and Jade in unison. Savannah tried to stifle a yawn with a fist over her mouth.

"About a dozen times," said Jade from the driver's seat. She pulled into the motel parking lot and parked right in front of their room.

"Well, I thought what he wrote was special. 'Emma, Hope to see you again real soon. All the best . . .'" Emma let out a deep sigh. "And did I tell you how he signed his name? Not Mr. Burke or Benjamin Burke, but BB. Like we were old friends or something."

"Not to stick a pin in your balloon," said Jade, "but that's probably how he signed all of them. Now can we bring it down a decibel? I've got a raging headache from all of that clapping and screaming. My goodness, you would have thought that we were at a rock concert." She pulled the keys out of the ignition, handed them back to Emma and then opened the door, illuminating them all.

Emma latched onto the keys and said, "Well, he may have signed all the books that way, but I'll bet you a plate of Grandma Hattie's hash that he didn't give his phone number to all of them."

"Whaaat?" Savannah turned around in her seat, the sleepiness now replaced with curiosity. "He gave you his number? You never told us that."

Emma threw her a sly wink. "There are a lot of things I don't tell you, believe it or not."

"Okay, give," said Jade grabbing her purse and getting out of the car. "Why did he give it to you?"

Emma climbed out of the back and stood next to Savannah, still clutching onto her book with one hand and the straps of her backpack with the other. "I told him that we were doing a research paper on the history of the Comstock Lode and that if it was okay with him we would like to use his name as a reference. So he gave me his number and said that if we needed any additional information, he would be happy to help if he could."

Savannah unlocked the door to their room and tossed her jacket on the back of one of the chairs. "But why would you tell him that?" She walked over to the far bed closest to the wall, slipped her shoes off and fell back onto it. That small burst of energy she got in the car had already dissipated.

"I don't know why I told him that. It just sort of popped out." Emma dropped her backpack by the door, plopped on the other bed and began thumbing through the book. "But it can't hurt having his number. Right? I mean, he is an expert, and he did say to call him if we had any questions. Maybe he can help us."

"Help us what? Find a dead girl?" Jade fell back onto the bed next to Savannah, grabbed the two remaining pillows and stacked them. She leaned back against them and said, "Well, at least you didn't invite him to go with us tomorrow. Speaking of which, are we still planning on hiking up the canyon?"

Savannah scooted up and leaned back against her pillows. "Yeah, I thought we would get up early, see if we can find the Flowery Peak trail."

"How early?" Jade glanced over her right shoulder at Savannah.

"Early! We need to get up there before it gets too hot and before it gets busy with traffic to the mine. I was thinking that we should be at the trail head no later than six."

"Six? In the morning?" Jade arched her eyebrows. "Are you serious? That's way too early for me. How about eight."

Savannah narrowed her eyes.

"Okay, then seven."

Savannah crossed her arms over her chest defiantly. "No. Six."

Jade looked over at Emma who seemed focused on the pages of her new book as she thumbed through them, stopping periodically to read bits. "Em, help me out here."

 Without looking up, Emma murmured, "Six is fine."

"Geez, thanks, Em."

Seemingly not listening to the conversation and with her head still buried in the book, Emma said, "Hey guys, listen to this. This chapter is about the prostitutes who got pregnant." She began to read. "'Prior to the twentieth century it was illegal for illegitimate children to inherit property. But unlike the rest of the country, this was not an issue for these children of Virginia City. Money flowed like whisky from the wealthy miners to the prostitutes, offering great care and financial support to their offspring, thus eliminating the need for inheritance.

"'The issue arose when marriage forced fathers to start neglecting these children. Because of the illicit activities with the prostitutes, the wives considered their husbands' offspring to be an affront to morality. Threats of divorce caused the miners to reluctantly turn their backs completely on the prostitutes and their children.

"'Soon, the financial wells dried up for the madams and her ladies. Most of the women, now mothers, who succumbed to the hardship chose to leave the area rather than stay and become a burden to those men who had, at one time, offered them financial aid. '"

Emma stared at the old photograph of a woman with her arms draped around two children. It was the same picture that Mr. Burke had projected on the screen at the reading. "That's terrible. Look at these poor kids." She handed the book over to Jade. "They're so sad. You can see it in their eyes."

Jade took the book from Emma and glanced at the picture. "It must have been a pretty hard life back then. I sure don't envy them."

Savannah leaned in over Jade's shoulder and said, "Can you imagine being tossed around like that and being abandoned by your father?" She took the book from Jade and stared at the picture. Her eyes gravitated toward the young boy. Though it was a black and white photograph she could tell that his eyes were light, probably blue. And they seemed to stare right through her.

She quickly closed the book and handed it back to Jade. "We better get some sleep. Five o'clock is going to come awfully early."

While the girls got ready for bed Savannah couldn't help but think about Virginia City during the time of the silver rush. While it made lots of millionaires, it also made lots of orphans. And she couldn't help but wonder what had become of them.

As she drifted off to sleep, the last thing she saw in her mind's eye was a pair of troubled blue eyes staring back at her.

Chapter 47

Virginia City
June 05, 1869

"Would you like to hold him?" The woman, a young beauty with waves of fire red hair pulled to the side and tied with a green ribbon, held out an infant wrapped in a soft woolen blanket. The movement caused him to squirm. He tried to lift his arms but they were pinned tightly in his swaddle, making him cry. "Shhh. No need for all that fuss," she cooed gently.

When the child had quieted down some, she looked back up at a much older looking man standing in front of her, held the bundle out a little farther and said, "Go on, take him. He's your son."

The man hesitated.

"He won't break if that's what you're worried about." She stepped closer to the man, swaying slightly to help ease the baby's fidgeting.

The man removed his brown, weathered hat, combed his bunched up bangs to the side with the palm of his hand and wiped away a trickle of nervous sweat before it could slip into his eyes. "Dang, Isabel, I ain't so sure about that. He's so . . ." The man paused as if searching for the right word. "So frail. Like a kitten or something."

This made the young woman chuckle. "Believe you me, he ain't so frail. Your boy is a strappin' lad. Eight pounds three ounces he was when he was born. Probably weighs a lot more now on account of all that milk he's gettin'. And birthin' him? Lordy, it was like pushin' a watermelon through a keyhole."

The man winced slightly. "So whatcha be callin' him?" He flashed her a hopeful look that made the wrinkles around his eyes diminish.

"His name is Harry. Hank for short." She smiled down at the child when she said his name.

The man's face fell slightly for the briefest moment. Then he put his hat back on his head and held open his arms. When the woman placed the child in them, he cradled the infant's head in the crook of his arm, looked down at him and said in a hushed tone, "Hey, little buck. I'm yer pa, and I'm real proud to meetcha."

They stood outside and to the left of the saloon doors, both admiring the child as he gurgled up at them. They seemed to be oblivious to the stares and murmured comments that filtered from the mouths of those who passed by them.

Nothing seemed to distract them from this intimate family moment.

The woman pulled a lace hanky from her milk-swollen bosom and dabbed at the drool seeping from the infant's mouth. She tucked it back in her brassiere and said, "He has your eyes, you know. Blue as the Nevada sky."

"Wish he had my name, too," the man murmured.

She glanced up at him with sad eyes and sighed. "I know. I do, too. But it's real close to your name." She touched his shoulder. "Only you and I will know what Hank really stands for."

"It's not the same."

She smiled slightly. "I know. But it will have to do."

She stepped to the side, and for the first time the man noticed a fabric satchel pushed up against the building. His eyes bounced from the bag, to the woman, to the baby, and then back to the woman. His head tipped to the side, his eyes pleading. He opened his mouth but the only word that came out was, "No."

She mirrored him and pulled her lips into a slight smile that tried to convey hope but failed. "I have to. I have no other choice. You know that."

"But how will you survive? Where will you go?"

"I don't rightly know yet. But wherever we end up, we'll be fine. You've paid me well, these past couple of years. And I've saved up quite a little nest egg — enough for Hank and me to have a fresh start."

He looked, once more, down at the child. "But if you leave, I won't get to see this little doggie grow up." He paused for a moment as if in thought. Then he took her hand with his free hand, looked into her eyes and said, "I don't want my son being called a bastard for the rest of his life. Let me give him my name."

She let out a deep sigh. "You can't. You're already married. Besides, even if you weren't I would never ask you to settle down with the likes of me. It would ruin your good name."

He laughed. "Haven't you heard? It was already ruined long before I met you. Besides, I don't love that ol' battleaxe I'm hitched to. I love you."

"Oh, come on, now. She's not that old."

"Older than you. And nowhere nears as pretty. She's nothing but a dragged out, money grubbing, high falutin' old hag that-"

"Hobble your lips, old man!" A shrill voice came from behind them. And when they turned around they saw a short stodgy woman dressed in a long black skirt and a white, button up, long-sleeved shirt barreling up the wooden walkway toward them. With balled up fists, her arms pumped back and forth at her sides making her look like a squatty locomotive. The loose bun on top of her head bounced in rhythm with her angry strides.

When she got close enough to the couple she shook her finger at the man and shouted, "If you don't stop cavorting with that painted up whore, I swear to the good Lord above I will divorce you, take all of your money and leave you high and dry. You will end up with nothing except your bad name and your bastard child. Do you hear me, Henry Comstock?"

~~~~~~~~~~~~~~~~~

Savannah woke and sat up in bed. She glanced over her left shoulder at Jade who seemed to be sleeping peacefully, as was Emma in the other bed. She checked the clock on the nightstand between the two beds. It was only three o'clock in the morning—too early to get up, but too late for her to fall back asleep. Even if she wanted to sleep, her mind was reeling from the dream.

Two weeks earlier she would have blamed the dream on the chapter Emma read to them. But now, knowing that she had these abilities, she knew that this dream meant something.

But what?

Snippets of it floated through her mind. She thought about the beautiful woman that couldn't have been more than twenty, and her child of only a couple of weeks. She was being forced to abandon her town and her profession, albeit a questionable one, because of changing societal rules.

She thought about Henry Comstock. Both Dolly and Mr. Burke seemed to portray him as a braggart, a swindler, and somewhat of a sleazy character. But in her dreams he seemed kind, compassionate, and an honorable man who wanted to do right by his child. So which version of this man was correct?

Does it matter?

Savannah stared out the sheer curtains at the lit parking lot trying to figure out what the point of the dream was. How could this new bit of information possibly help find Katie?

Frustrated, she lay her head back down on the pillow, turned over on her right side and stared at a rectangle of muted light on the wall. The lights from the parking lot shining through the thin curtains caused wavy lines to form.

"Maybe it has nothing to do with Katie," she murmured quietly.

Within minutes weariness crept back in, and her eyes began to flutter shut. A shadowy movement on the wall caused her to open her eyes. But like lead weights atop a feather, her eyelids became too heavy to stay open. In the split second that her eyes closed, the shadow seemed to transform into a figure with two arms rising up and cupping the wall, as if peering through a window. Then just as quickly, it disappeared.

She thought briefly about getting up to investigate, but she was just too tired to move.

Chapter 48

When the phone alarm went off, Jade growled, and swiped at it, sending it clanking to the floor. "Nooo," she groaned, "it's too early." She sandwiched her head in between the two pillows and pulled the covers up over her shoulders. "You guys go ahead. I'm staying right here," came her muffled voice.

Savannah yanked the blanket back and said, "Get up, Sleeping Beauty. We've got lots to do today."

"Go away." Jade pulled the blanket back up to her neck.

"Up. Now." Savannah grabbed the blanket and pulled it all the way off the bed, exposing Jade's Hello Kitty pajama shorts and top. "C'mon. It's already quarter after five." She walked around to the other side of the bed, picked the phone up off of the floor and set it back on the nightstand. Jade still hadn't move, so she yanked the pillow off of her friend's head and said, "I'll buy you a latte on the way out. Now, *andele, andele! Pronto!*"

Emma was already out of bed and on her way to the shower.

Savannah threw yesterday's jeans at her and said, "We don't have time for that. You're going to get dirty and sweaty anyway, so just get dressed and let's go." She looked back down at Jade and clapped her hands together. "Chop, chop. Let's get a move on."

"Geez, Vannah, chill out. I'm up." Reluctantly, Jade pulled herself out of bed, slipped on her jeans and grumbled, "It better be the biggest latte they make—*and* a scone. That's all I gotta say."

Within fifteen minutes all three girls were dressed, teeth and hair brushed and were on their way out the door. Savannah said to Emma, "Bring your book, the new one with the phone number in it."

"Why?"

"I'll explain on the way."

"Okay, no problem." Emma grabbed the book off of the small table, shoved it in her backpack, and hurried out the door.

While Emma unlocked the car and got in the driver's seat, Savannah locked up their motel room. As she turned around, she noticed something on the sidewalk. Right beneath their window was a small pile of crushed cigarette butts.

She paused momentarily and stared at it, causing a chill to run all the way up her back. Were they there last night when they got to the room? Would she have even noticed if they were? She glanced around the parking lot and then back down at the cigarette butts. She was beginning to think that Emma's paranoia was legitimate.

"Well, c'mon, Vannah. Let's get a move on. Chop, chop," mimicked Jade. She climbed into the back seat, grabbed Emma's backpack and used it as a pillow. "Wake me up when we get there."

Savannah climbed into the passenger's seat and said, "Something weird's going on."

"What do you mean *weird*?" Emma pulled out of the parking lot, turned right and headed toward the closest Starbucks.

Savannah furrowed her brow. "I'm not sure yet, but something is definitely going on." She told them about her dream but decided not to say anything about the cigarette butts for now. It could be nothing, and she didn't want to worry them unnecessarily.

When Savannah was finished Emma looked over at her and said, "What do you think it means? Why dream about Henry Comstock and some prostitute?"

Savannah shrugged her shoulders. "I don't know. But maybe your author friend might have some insight into it. I'm sure he uncovered a lot of information that he didn't use in the book. Who knows, maybe he found something on a prostitute named Isabel." She looked over at Emma. "Would you be willing to call him and ask him?"

"Sure!" Emma's enthusiasm made Savannah smile. Over her shoulder, Emma said, "Jade, will you grab my phone and the book out of the back pack? His number is right underneath the autograph."

Jade rummaged around in the pack until she found the phone, opened the book, and then type the number into the phone. She was about to press send but stopped. "Guys, you can't call him right now. It isn't even six o'clock yet."

The two giggled from the front seat and Emma said, "Oh my gosh, I was so excited I forgot what time it was." She looked over at Savannah. "I'll call him while we're hiking."

With a brief stop at Starbucks, and no traffic, the girls made it to Six Mile Canyon by five forty five. As they drove past the entrance to the mine Savannah said, "The gate's still locked. Looks like we got here before them. Keep an eye out for the road to the trail. Remember, the guy in the pickup truck said it was about a mile up the road, just past the ravine and on the right hand side. Hopefully, once we go over the bridge we'll see a sign."

Though weathered, the wooden signpost was still there. Emma turned onto the dirt road. But a few yards in, a fallen log across it forced her to stop. "Now what do we do?" she said.

"We're going to have to try to move it," said Savannah getting out of the car.

Emma put the car in park and both she and Jade got out and stood next to Savannah.

"Do you see the size of this thing? How are we supposed to move it?" said Jade with her hands planted on her hips.

"Maybe we can lift it and move it far enough to drive around it," said Savannah.

All three girls got on one end, and on Savannah's count they tried to lift it. But it wouldn't budge.

After the third try, Jade said, "This is pointless. It's too heavy. So now what do we do?"

Savannah looked over the right edge of the road. It had already started to slope dangerously down toward the ravine, making it too steep for them to drive around the log. She visually followed the dirt road as it zigzagged up the steep hill and disappeared over the crest. "Looks like we're going to have to walk to the trailhead."

Jade groaned. "Well, how far is it?"

"I don't know," said Savannah. "It could be several miles. So we should probably get started."

"Wait. I have an idea," said Emma. She walked around to the back of the Rabbit, opened the hatch and began rummaging around. A few minutes later she emerged holding a rope. "Maybe this'll do the trick." She walked to the front of her car, squatted down and tied one end of the rope to the frame and then gave the other end to Jade. "See if you can tie this around the log, and then I'll try to pull it with the car." She got in behind the wheel, rolled down her window and stuck her head out. "Let me know when you're ready."

Savannah and Jade wedged the rope under one end of the log and tied it with a slipknot. They stood up and Jade yelled, "Go ahead and try it."

Emma nodded and started the car. She put it in reverse, slowly pressed down on the gas pedal and then turned in her seat to watch where she was going. When the rope went taught, the Rabbit began to stall, so she gave it more gas, causing the car to strain. But little by little, the log began to move.

"Keep going, Em, you almost have it," yelled Savannah as she and Jade got behind the log and pushed.

When the log was far enough out of the way so that the Rabbit could pass, Savannah yelled, "Okay, that's good." She turned to Jade. "Go untie it from the car. I'll get this."

Once the rope was untied, Jade wound it up, tossed it in the backseat and crawled in next to it. "Great thinking, Em." She patted her shoulder and added, "I'll never harass you again about all the junk you keep in your car."

"I think you owe *Jessica* an apology," said Savannah.

Emma chuckled. "So do I."

Jade sighed dramatically. "Oh all right." She stroked the seat next to her and said, "I'm sorry, Jessica. I'll never call you a 'packrabbit' again. I promise."

Emma patted the dash. "She forgives you."

The climb up the mountain was certainly not intended for a compact car. With each bump, the Rabbit bottomed out, scraping the undercarriage and causing Emma to wince.

"I hope we get there soon. I don't think Jessica can take much more of this. Too bad we couldn't have taken your Jeep, Jade."

Jade released a deep sigh. "I told you, it's not my jeep. Wish it were, but it's not." She shook her head and muttered, "Still can't believe they didn't give me their old car." She braced herself against the back of Savannah's seat as the Rabbit bumped and bounced up the rough dirt road.

"Jade, start looking for anything that might seem out of place," said Savannah peering out her window"

While Jade looked out her window she said, "So Vannah, have you thought about what you're going to do if we do happen to find Katie? You know, if you do find her, people will start asking questions. Are you prepared to answer them?"

Savannah gripped the dash when the car hit a rock and bounced. "That's a hard question to answer. Of course, I would contact Katie's parents first, then the police."

"The police will surely ask questions like, 'How did you know to look there?' and 'What were we doing up there in the first place?'" said Jade.

"All we have to do is say that we were hiking and we just happened to stumble across her. That's all," said Savannah.

"Just happened to stumble across her? Vannah, how many policemen and search and rescue teams do you think have been out here looking for her? These are people who know the area. Do you really think they would believe that three girls from out of town just happened to stumble upon a missing girl?" Jade leaned back in her seat. "If we find her, maybe you'd be better off calling in an anonymous tip after we're gone. Let someone else come out here and dig her up."

Savannah shook her head. "She contacted me, Jade, not her parents, not the police, but me. She wanted me to find her. I made a commitment to Katie. So, regardless of what happens to me, I'm going to see this thing through to the bitter end. I hope you can understand that."

"I do, Vannah. Really I do, but-"

"We're here, guys," interrupted Emma. She rolled up to the trailhead sign and parked.

The girls got out of the car, grabbed their canteens and hats out of the back and applied sunscreen to their exposed skin. Before closing the hatch, Emma grabbed a pair of binoculars and hung them around her neck.

Once the girls were geared up, the three looked at each other and Savannah said, "Okay, ladies, let's go find Katie."

Chapter 49

The trail, which followed the ridgeline, started out gently making the girls wonder why it had been closed in the first place.

"Remember," said Savannah, "we're looking for anything that might seem out of the ordinary." She pointed across the canyon. "If she went over the cliff somewhere along that ridge and ended up at the bottom, we just might be able to spot something from this side."

Forty-five minutes in, they found themselves climbing over and around unstable rocks and boulders. Now it was clear why the trail had been closed—because it was treacherous. The path had virtually become non-existent, buried somewhere underneath tons of fallen rock. One misstep could send them tumbling down the mountainside to the canyon far below.

The three continued to inch their way forward, struggling over slippery boulders the size of cars until Emma finally cried out, "Vannah, stop. It's getting too hard and too dangerous." With her face beet red, she gasped for air and leaned against a large boulder that looked as if a simple sneeze would send it tumbling down the cliff. "We're not hiking anymore. We're rock climbing." She tried to suck in more air but couldn't seem to catch her breath. "I think . . . We should turn around . . . Head back."

Savannah felt it in her gut that Katie was somewhere in these mountains. And with each step forward that feeling grew, but so did the real threat of danger.

"But I *feel* like we're almost there," said Savannah as she unclipped her canteen from her belt and took several deep swigs. Even though it was barely eight o'clock, the sun had already begun to heat up the ground and the rocks around them. She wiped the sweat from her brow and clipped the canteen back onto her belt. "Katie's close. I just *know* it."

"Are you sure about that? Because this is getting pretty hairy, even for me," said Jade. She craned her neck over the edge but quickly retracted and pushed her back against the same boulder as Emma. "It's an awfully long way down there. One wrong step and we'd splatter like bugs on a windshield."

Savannah tugged on the neck of her T-shirt and wiped away a new trail of sweat trickling down her temple. "I'm pretty sure it's just a little bit further. We can't turn around now, not when we're so close." She didn't really know for sure if Katie was anywhere near them, but if they turned around now she would always wonder, *would we have found Katie if we'd only gone just a little bit further?*

"Fifteen more minutes. That's all I'm asking for. And if we haven't found her by then we'll turn around and go back." When neither of the girls responded, Savannah said, "Ten minutes, then. Please? And we'll turn back no matter what. I promise."

Jade and Emma looked at each other. "What do you think, Em. You want to keep going?"

"Well . . ." Emma's breathing slowed and her color was beginning to return to normal.

"Please, Em," pleaded Savannah. "We can't give up now."

"I don't know, Vannah. Let me think about it for a minute while I call Mr. Burke. You still want me to call him, don't you?"

Savannah nodded emphatically. So Emma pulled her phone from her pocket, checked for a signal and then pushed the send button.

A couple of rings later, a gravelly voice said, "Hello?"

Emma put the phone on speaker and said, "Good morning, Mr. Burke. This is Emma Reed. I met you at the book signing last night. I hope I didn't wake you."

Mr. Burke cleared his throat. "No, no. I'm awake. Who did you say this was?"

"Emma. Emma Reed? I met you last night at your book signing. I'm the one who is doing a report on the Comstock Lode. You gave me your number and said I could call you if I had any questions."

"Oh, yeah. I remember you now. You're the one who asked me if I was married." He cleared his throat again. "So what can I help you with?"

"Well, I was wondering if while researching your book, you came across any information about a prostitute named Isabel."

"Isabel what?"

"I don't have a last name. But it's possible that she might have had Henry Comstock's illegitimate son."

"A son?" The sleep in Mr. Burke's voice immediately cleared. "Do you have any documentation to prove this?"

"Uh, no, sir. That's why I'm calling. I was hoping maybe you might have run across something that could substantiate it."

"No, I sure didn't. Believe me, if I had it would have ended up in my book." He paused for a moment and then said, "Where did you get this information?"

Emma glanced at Savannah who mouthed the words, "Aunt Helen."

"My friend got the information from her aunt who lives in Salt Lake City," said Emma

"Hmm. That's very interesting. It's well documented that Mrs. Comstock was from Salt Lake City and that she did leave Henry. That might have been the reason why. If so, then it's also possible that she moved back to Salt Lake City. Your friend's aunt just might be on to something." He grew quiet again for a few seconds as if thinking. "Now you've piqued my interest. Let me do some checking on this and I'll get back with you. This number that you're calling from, is it your cell phone?"

"Yes, it is."

"Do you have any other information that might help me find out more about this woman?"

Emma looked over at Savannah who was pointing to her hair. "Oh, um, we think she might have had red hair and was pretty young, maybe nineteen or twenty years old."

"That's good. Anything else?"

Emma looked at Savannah again as she mouthed the infant's name. "We think the child's name was Harry."

"This is very exciting, Ms. Reed. If I can substantiate any of this, we might be able to find actual living heirs of Henry Comstock." Enthusiasm caused his voice to elevate slightly.

"How do you even begin proving something like this? It could take months, years even."

"I have a few tricks up my sleeve that should help expedite the process. I'll let you know if I find out anything."

"Thank you, Mr. Burke."

He laughed. "No, thank you, Ms. Reed."

When she hung up, Emma looked at Savannah and said, "Okay, I think I can handle another fifteen minutes of climbing."

Savannah threw her arms around her friend's neck and said, "Oh Em, I could kiss you right now." Then she planted a loud smack on her cheek.

"All right, ladies, let's get a move on," said Jade. "This ain't a picnic."

Emma reached into her pack and pulled out three granola bars. "Well, it could be. Here." She handed them each one.

"Good idea, Em," said Savannah. "I am a little hungry."

The three girls found a relatively flat place to sit and eat their breakfast bars. They talked about the dream, the phone call to Mr. Burke and what new information might surface because of it.

After a ten-minute break and with a renewed boost of energy, the girls were ready to attack Flowery Peak trail again—at least for the next fifteen minutes, anyway.

But Savannah hoped that her friends wouldn't hold her to that promise.

The boulders in this part of the trail didn't seem as treacherous. Maybe it was because they were getting used to the terrain. They had gone about another half of a mile in and stopped at a lookout point that gave them a one eighty view up and down the canyon and of the ridgeline across the ravine.

Savannah stood close to the edge and said, "Hey, Em, let me see those binoculars for a second."

"Do you see something?" Emma pulled them from around her neck and handed them to Savannah.

Savannah noticed a light-colored stripe running down the mountain on the ridge opposite them that seemed to fan out at the bottom. She put the lenses up to her eyes and followed the stripe all the way up to the ridge where it seemed to originate. "See all those rocks over there right below that flat area? It kind of looks like there might have been an avalanche there at one time." She handed the binoculars back to Emma. "That looks like it could be close to the Comstock mine. That line of trees look sort of familiar." She surveyed the area and added, "I'd like to find a way to get over there."

Emma looked through the binoculars and then handed them to Jade. "You could be right. How far do you think it is?"

"I'd say maybe a quarter of a mile further up. But we'd have to get across the ravine," said Savannah.

Emma peered over to edge and down the canyon. "How are we supposed to get down there? It looks pretty steep."

"Very carefully," said Jade, looking through the binoculars. She scanned the ridgeline but stopped suddenly. "What's that?"

"What's what?" said Savannah.

Jade handed the binoculars to Savannah and said, "Over there, across the ridge near that rockslide. I thought I saw something shiny in the trees."

Savannah looked through the binoculars at where Jade was pointing. "I don't see anything."

The light that Jade said she saw had vanished. But just as quickly as it went, it came back again, flickering like a mirror glinting off sunlight.

"There!" said Jade. "Do you see it?"

Savannah caught sight of the shiny glare, but only for a moment before it vanished again. Her stomach clenched. She handed the binoculars back to Emma and said with urgency in her voice, "C'mon. Let's go."

Before they could resume, Savannah's phone rang. She pulled it from her pocket, pushed the button and said, "Hello?"

"Hello? Savannah?"

"Yes, this is she."

"Savannah, this is Dr. Wells. I hope I'm not calling too early."

Savannah put the phone on speaker. "Oh, good morning, Dr. Wells. No, it's not too early. How are you? Were you able to get into Marty's computer?"

"Yes, as a matter of fact I was. That's why I'm calling."

"Did you find out anything?"

"I did." He seemed to hesitate. "And what I found was, shall we say, very disturbing."

"What did you find?"

"I'd rather not say over the phone. Can you come to my house, say, in an hour?"

"I'm sorry, Dr. Wells, but we're hiking on Flowery Peak trail, out near the mine."

"You're there now?" He sounded alarmed.

"Yeah, we've been hiking for over an hour."

Dr. Wells sucked in his breath and said, "You girls need to get out of there right now!"

Chapter 50

"No, Vannah, absolutely not. You heard what Dr. Wells said. We need to get out of here right now!" said Emma.

"But he didn't tell us why. Maybe it's nothing for us to be worried about. I think we should just keep going," argued Savannah.

Emma's bottom lip started to quiver, and she crossed her arms over her chest. "I'm not going any further."

"Please, Em. We have to. Otherwise-"

"No, we don't," interrupted Jade. "For once I'm on Em's side." She walked over, stood next to Emma and crossed her arms over her chest, as well. "We need to get the heck out of here now. And it's going to take us awhile to get back to the car."

"You guys, please-"

"No," said Jade emphatically. "We're going. But if you want to stay and maybe kill yourself in the process, you go right ahead. But Em and I are going back to the car."

Savannah glanced back over her shoulder at the discolored stripe of rock, her eyes traveling down the entire length of the cliff. "But you guys, I really think-"

Savannah! Help me!

Savannah's head snapped back around, and she stared at her friends. "I-I really think-"

Savannah! Please! I need your help! I can't breathe.

Savannah grabbed her chest and began to wheeze. She clutched at her collar, yanking it away from her throat.

"Vannah, are you okay?" Emma dropped her arms, hurried over to Savannah and put a hand on her shoulder. "What's wrong?"

Savannah, still clutching her chest, struggled to speak. "I. Can't. Breathe."

Jade raced to her other side and grabbed her arm. "Vannah, you need to sit down. Here, let me help you."

Savannah shook her head and pulled free from Jade. "No. S-she's here." She sucked in hard, gulping for air. "K-katie is here. She needs me." Her words came out in a raspy whisper.

Within a few seconds her breathing returned to normal. She turned back around and stared at the fan shaped rock formation. "Katie's down there. I *know* it." And this time, she really did know it.

Jade pulled her phone from her back pocket. "I'm calling 911."

"No! You can't." Savannah grabbed the phone out of her hand then let out a deep breath. "Look, I understand if you two want to go back to the car, but I have to keep going." Her brows creased with concern. "Katie just spoke to me. I heard her voice."

Without breaking eye contact with her friends, Savannah pointed a forceful finger back at the avalanche area on the other side of the canyon and said, "She's down there. And I'm going to go find her with or without you guys." She handed the phone back to Jade, took one more swig from her canteen and then began climbing the next boulder.

"Wait," said Emma. "I'm coming with you." She took a step forward but Jade latched onto her arm.

"I thought you wanted to go back to the car?" Jade pulled her lips into a tight, thin line.

Emma turned and tilted her head to the side. Her face had lost all its anger and fear. "I did, but I don't anymore." She looked over at Savannah then back at Jade. "For whatever reason, Katie chose her. Maybe it was so that Vannah could embrace who she really is. If that's the case then she needs to do this. She needs to go find Katie. And as her best friends, we need to support her."

Jade threw her hands up in the air. "But what about what Dr. Wells said? He said we needed to leave now."

Emma's stance turned rigid. "Since when have you ever been compliant?"

"Since when have *you* ever been defiant?"

The two locked eyes with each until Jade finally shook her head and said, "Okay, you win. Sometimes, you really surprise me, Em." She looked over at Savannah and yelled out, "Hang on. We're coming with you."

Savannah smiled back at them with a look on her face that said *I knew you would.*

~~~~~~~~~~~~~~~~~

Their climb down into the canyon took much longer than they had anticipated. Boulders piled on top of each other forced the girls to choose their footing carefully. They wedged through, climbed over and slid down so many rocks, that their hands were starting to blister.

Savannah tried to keep her mind off of the return trip. Getting back to the car would be exhausting and strenuous. She could only hope that the excitement and adrenaline of finding Katie's body would be the fuel they needed to make that journey back up the mountain.

Periodically, she glanced across the canyon and up to the other ridgeline to see if she could spot that flickering light. She never saw it again. Maybe it was just sunlight reflecting off of a car. It sounded like a logical explanation, but something in her gut told her differently.

By the time they reached the canyon floor, it was nearing ten o'clock. Exhausted and running low on water, Savannah tried to sound hopeful. "We're so close. I think that avalanche area is just around that next bend."

"It better be," mumbled Jade.

From their vantage point, they couldn't see the light colored stripe of rock anymore. It had disappeared behind another hill in front of them. But on Savannah's encouragement, the girls continued to trudge along the dry sandy riverbed for another twenty minutes, nursing what little water they had left.

Little by little their energy and their canteens were becoming depleted.

"Hey, guys. Look at that." Emma pointed to a small stream of water seeping down from a crevice in the mountain. She uncapped her canteen, bent down and held it underneath the drops trickling off of the rocks.

"Em, don't," said Savannah pushing her canteen away from the trickle.

"But I don't have any more water," she replied licking her lips.

Savannah handed her her canteen. "Then have some of mine."

Emma shook it. "You don't have much either."

"Then just take a little."

Jade shook her canteen, as well. "I'm running low, too." She wiped the sweat trickling down the side of her face then looked down at the water seeping from the rocks. "We may have no choice *but* to drink it." She leaned down and took a sniff. "Smells a little funky."

Emma sniffed then wrinkled her nose. "Yeah, it sure does. But how bad can it be coming right out of the mountain?"

"C'mon, let's just keep going. We're so close," said Savannah. "We'll figure out what to do once we find her." They set off again with Savannah in the lead, then Jade, followed by Emma.

A few minutes later Jade said to Savannah, "So do you really think she's buried under all that rock?"

"I think so," replied Savannah over her shoulder. "I really believe that's where we're going to find her."

"But don't you think that after all these years, someone would have spotted the car by now? I'm sure this trail got a lot of use before it was closed." She glanced back at Emma. "Hey, Em. Do you know when this trail was closed?"

"No, the book didn't say. But if Comstock Mining was trying to cover up Katie's disappearance, then maybe they were responsible for all of the other rockslides. Maybe they caused the avalanches on purpose to keep people from coming down here to look for her."

"You might be right," said Savannah. "If so, then they're probably the ones who put the log across the entrance."

"If that's the case," said Jade, "let's pray that they're not actively watching it."

When they rounded the next bend, Savannah stopped. There in front of them was the beginning of the landslide. Boulders and rubble spilled from the top of the ridge all the way down, blocking the trail. Savannah looked up at the spot where it originated. That part of the ridge had no trees on it. She couldn't be one hundred percent sure, but chances were pretty good that this was where Katie was pushed backwards off of the cliff.

Savannah trotted over to the pile and started removing the smaller rocks from around the edge. "C'mon, help me," she said tossing the rocks to the side. But with each rock she removed another one tumbled down into its place.

"Let's climb up it a bit and see if we can dig down," said Jade.

The three girls carefully started to climb the mammoth pile of rubble.

"There must be a million tons of rock here," said Emma scanning the entire avalanche area. "Where do we even begin?"

"Let me see if I can *sense* anything," said Savannah. She stopped, picked up a small stone and held it in her hand. After a few seconds she shook her head, dropped it and moved to the left several dozen feet. She picked up another rock, and this time a shock immediately went from the palm of her hand right to her brain. "I think we should start here."

Savannah dropped the small rock and picked up a much heavier one with both hands, groaning as she heaved it a short distance. It caught momentum and rolled the rest of the way down, coming to rest at the base of the pile.

Jade and Emma scampered over to her, and together, they pushed a much larger rock down the slope, but the struggle quickly drained them.

"We'll be here for days at this rate," said Jade wiping sweat from her brow leaving a dirty streak above her right eye.

"We don't have days," said Savannah tossing rock after rock. "So keep going."

Both Jade and Emma bent down, grabbed more rocks and tossed them onto the growing pile below them.

After a while, the three got into a rhythmic groove, each bending down, picking up rocks, and tossing them. And soon a hole began to form in the middle of the rockslide.

By now, the sun was high overhead, and all three were drenched in sweat. Savannah stopped briefly to take a sip of water. It wasn't enough to satiate, just enough to dampen her parched mouth. As weary as they all were, rest would have to wait.

"Savannah, look. I think I found something." Emma was down on her hands and knees digging through the rubble. She began to wipe away the sandy dirt off of a flat surface. Savannah and Jade dropped to their knees and helped her. Soon, they pulled free a chunk of what looked like fibrous plastic.

Savannah looked at it and scrunched her brow. When the realization of what it might be hit her, she said, "This looks like fiberglass." She started to pull more rocks from the pile, digging frantically until her nails began to break and bleed. When she found another piece of fiberglass, she said excitedly, "That's got to be part of her Corvette. C'mon, keep digging. We're so close."

With their heads down and their attention focused on finding more of Katie's car, the three continued to dig.

Chunk after chunk of fiberglass began to surface. And soon, the girls started finding shards of glass. Like an assembly line, rocks and debris went one way, while potential car parts when another.

Then Jade pulled out a shred of cloth wedged in between two rocks, and handed it to Savannah. "Do you think this belonged to her?" she asked.

Savannah took the fabric, held it in her hand and closed her eyes. Instantly, images of Katie came to mind. And with each flash of imagery, her body jolted from the currents of electricity that surged through her. She recognized the faded and stained blue cotton blouse from her dreams. Katie had been wearing it when she took Marty to the hospital the night he got shot. And as she looked closer, she saw what could have been splotches of Marty's blood. "Yes! It's hers. She's down here."

That spurred the girls to dig even faster. "We're coming, Katie," said Emma. "Just hold on."

"Dang almighty," came a voice from above them. "I told you it wasn't safe for you girls to be hiking up here."

The three stopped digging and looked up.

There, standing on a ledge about fifty feet above them was the guy from the white pickup truck with a set of binoculars hanging around his neck and his hands planted on his hips. "You should have gone hiking at Lake Tahoe like I suggested."

Dang almighty . . . Dang almighty. Savannah scrunched her brow. *Where have I heard that phrase before?*

Flashes of the video from Marty's phone popped into her mind. *Dang almighty, Darrel, watch what you're doing.* Her mind jumped to Katie's phone call right before she went over the cliff.

Dang almighty, Katie, you should have listened to me when you had the chance.

Once she connected the pieces, the confusion on her face morphed into revelation and Savannah exclaimed, "Oh my God! He's the one who pushed Katie off of the cliff."

The man's jaw stiffened momentarily. He glanced at the pile of debris for several seconds then shook his head slowly and said, "Well, shoot." He reached around behind him, pulled a pistol from his backside and pointed it directly at them. He cocked it and said, "You should have listened to me when you had the chance."

Chapter 51

Oh God! We're going to end up just like Katie, thought Savannah.

The man looked down at the trio, rubbed the stubble on his chin, and then spit on the ground. "Dang almighty, I didn't want to have to hurt you girls, but now I ain't got no choice. You stuck your noses where they didn't belong." He started to climb down the rocks while keeping his gun trained on them. "Why are you here, anyway?"

Frozen on their hands and knees, the girls were too frightened to speak.

"I said, why-are-you-here?" The gangly man seemed to be as sure-footed as a mountain goat as he picked his way down the unstable rubble. His eyes left them briefly, but his gun never did.

"Because I had a dream," said Savannah in a frightened and hushed voice.

"Speak up. What'd you say?" The man's voice held no mercy.

Savannah pushed herself up onto trembling legs. She brushed off the palms of her hands on her pants, swiped at the tears that had dribbled down to her chin, and repeated in a little bit louder voice, "I-I said I had a dream."

"You and Martin Luther King," he laughed jumping from rock to rock toward them. "So tell me about this dream of yours."

Through the side of her mouth Savannah whispered, "Get up. You're going to make a run for it." She yelled back to the man, "I dreamt about her."

Emma discreetly looked around. "Where? There's no place to hide."

Savannah whispered, "There're some bushes down at the bottom of the ravine."

Emma glanced at the clump of brush some thirty yards away then looked up at her with wide eyes and whispered, "Are you crazy? He'll kill us before we can get there."

"He's going to kill us anyway," whispered Jade. "At least this way we might have a chance." She looked up at Savannah and gave her a slight nod. Then she and Emma stood up and began to back up ever so slightly.

The man stopped momentarily and stared at Savannah. "I didn't hear ya. What'd you say?"

"I-I said I dreamt about Katie being buried here underneath all of this rock. I dreamt it was an accident."

"I coulda swore I heard you say that I pushed her."

"I-I was wrong. She accidentally drove off of the cliff right above you and landed down here."

"Is that so, now? You psychic or something?" He laughed again.

Savannah whispered out the side of her mouth, "When I say three, you run as fast as you can."

"But what about you?" whispered Emma.

"Don't worry about me. Just do it," whispered Savannah.

"I asked you a question," the man yelled down at her. "You psychic?"

Savannah whispered, "One, two . . ."

Coming from somewhere below them, a deep voice yelled out, "Don't move another step or I'll shoot."

The girls spun around, looked down and saw a gruff looking man with short-cropped hair come out from behind a boulder. He pointed his gun up toward them and said, "One more step and I'll shoot."

Savannah's mind flashed back to the man in the black El Camino on the side of the road. Immediately, she knew he was the one who had been following them, the same one who Emma saw snooping around her car.

"Oh, God," cried Emma. "We're surrounded. What are we going to do?"

The girls looked back up the mountain. Now the first gunman was only thirty yards away from them. He stopped, aimed his gun down at them and pulled back the trigger.

Suddenly, gunfire erupted forcing the girls to fall flat against the rubble and cover their heads. They began to scream, and Jade flung her body over both Emma and Savannah as bullets ricocheted off of the rocks right next to them. "Stay down," she cried over the deafening crack of ignited gunpowder.

When they heard a loud groan coming from above them, they looked up in time to see Pickup Truck man collapse. A blossom of red oozed out near his right shoulder. He let go of his gun, sending it bouncing off of the rocks and tumbling down toward the girls.

From behind them, they heard footfall. They looked down and saw the second gunman running toward the rock pile.

Jade cried out, "He's coming. Run!"

They jumped up, and like rabbits, they bolted down the opposite side of the pile of rubble. But Jade's foot got caught in between two rocks snapping her to a halt. She screeched from the excruciating pain. "Oh God, my leg!" The white jagged tip of a broken tibia pierced through the skin causing her to collapse.

Savannah and Emma each grabbed Jade under the armpits, stopping her before she could fall to the ground. "C'mon, Jade," cried Savannah, "he's coming. We have to go."

But the movement caused Jade to cry out in agony.

"Wait! Stop!" yelled the gruff man now only a few yards from the pile of rubble.

Emma started to cry. She dropped Jade's arm and collapsed onto the rock pile. "He's going to kill us, and no one will ever be able to find us. We're going to end up just like Katie."

Savannah struggled trying to hold all of Jade's weight, and they, too, collapsed onto the rock pile. Soon, all three girls sat huddled together crying.

This is it, thought Savannah. *We're going to die. And our parent's will never know what happened to us.* She wiped her nose with the back of her hand. *We should never have come here. This is all my fault.*

Savannah and Emma scooted in closer, sandwiching Jade in between them. They latched on tighter to one another and sobbed. All they could do was watch as this second shooter began to climb up the rock pile toward them.

At twenty feet away he stopped, pointed his gun up toward them and yell, "Stop right there, or I'll shoot." Before they could say anything, he shot off three rounds.

From behind them they heard a groan, a loud clatter and the sound of rocks tumbling. The girls turned around and looked up just in time to see Pickup Truck man collapse a mere ten feet away from them. The massive spillage of blood pooling out around him told the girls that unlike the first shot, this one was fatal.

When they looked behind them, the second shooter was already upon them, his gun still pointed in their direction.

But instead of shooting them, he holstered his gun, hurried past them and squatted down next to the body. He placed two fingers on the man's neck, presumably to check for a pulse.

Satisfied, he stood up, turned back around and said, "Are you girls okay? Did he hurt you?" He slid the few feet back down to them and squatted next to Jade. "Here, let me take a look at that." He examined the compound fracture then shook his head. "This is going to hurt. You two hold on to her shoulders and keep her still." He pushed up his long sleeves, grabbed hold of her ankle and yanked hard until the bone popped back under the skin.

Jade screeched from the jolt, and her eyes rolled back into her head.

"You killed her!" cried Emma, pulling Jade's limp body into her lap.

The stranger felt Jade's forehead and her pulse. "She's not dead, just passed out." He stripped a daypack from his back, set it aside and slipped off his shirt, exposing a black T-shirt underneath it. He gently wrapped it around her leg and ankle and secured it with a knot.

Savannah stared at the man's bare arm and gasped. Tattooed on his right forearm was an image of an anchor and a sword. The drawing immediately conjured up the tarot readings, and she exclaimed, "You're the man with the sword." She grabbed hold of Emma's arm and shook her trying to get her to stop crying. "Em, look at his arm. He's the man with the sword."

Emma cried harder and said, "But I thought we were supposed to look out for the man with the sword."

Savannah started to laugh and cry at the same time. "We were supposed to look out for him, meaning watch for him."

The gruff man smiled, erasing every menacing line on his face. "I'm not sure what you're talking about, but I'm Detective Graves." He glanced at his tattoo. "And I got this after I retired from the Navy." He looked from girl to girl. "So which one of you is Savannah?"

"I am," said Savannah still holding onto Emma's arm. "This is Emma, and that's Jade."

His smile grew even wider. He stuck out his hand and said, "I'm very happy to meet you. I'm a friend of your Aunt Helen's."

Savannah's eyes grew wide as she shook his hand. "You're her friend?" He nodded. Her brow furrowed with confusion. "I don't understand. If you're her friend, then why have you been following us? Emma saw you looking in her car at the motel. Then we all saw you pulled over on the shoulder near the mine." She looked perplexed and then her eyes grew wide. "The cigarette butts. You were at our motel last night, weren't you?" It was more of an accusation than a question.

Emma cranked her head around and stared at her. "You didn't tell us you saw him there."

Savannah grew angry. "He was peeking through our window last night."

Detective Graves held up his hands. "Now hold on a minute. I wasn't looking through your window. I was standing guard, making sure you girls were safe."

"But why not just come up and introduce yourself? Why follow us? You scared us half to death," sniffled Emma. She brush away the last of the tears and added, "We thought you were a stalker."

He lowered his head slightly. "I'm sorry that I frightened you girls. I sure didn't mean to."

"So why *were* you following us?" said Savannah.

"Because your aunt called me and asked me to keep an eye on the three of you." He pulled a handkerchief and a bottle of water from his pack, doused the handkerchief and gently placed it over Jade's forehead.

"So my aunt told you we were staying at Motel 6?" said Savannah.

He nodded. "She did."

"But why?" said Savannah. "Why would she tell you to keep an eye on us?"

"She thought you might be getting into something over your head, so I told her I would check out the situation. After I saw you being followed by that guy out of the mine," he nodded toward the dead man, "I got concerned for your safety. So I called your aunt back and told her that I was going to introduce myself to you." He let out a snort and looked directly at Savannah. "Well, your aunt said in no uncertain terms that I was *not* to interfere with . . ." he looked over to where the three had been digging, "With this."

Savannah looked puzzled. "I don't understand. Why would she tell you not to help us?"

He smiled at her. "Because, according to your aunt, if I interfered, you would never believe that it was your psychic abilities that helped you solve this case."

Savannah's eyes widened. "She told you about me?"

He nodded his head. "Yes. She said you were just like her, maybe even more gifted. And she assured me that if my team and I were patient, you would eventually lead us to Katie's body."

"Wait a minute. So you know about my aunt's psychic abilities?"

"Oh, yes. We've worked together on dozens of cases. She's been very instrumental in helping the authorities solve the majority of them."

Savannah's head was whirling. "She never told me about that."

Even though Emma's tears had stopped she was still sniffling. She looked at Savannah and said, "I wonder why she didn't tell you she was working with the police."

Detective Graves dug out two more bottles of water from his daypack, crack open the caps and handed them to the two girls. "She said that if she had told you she's worked with the police it would have influenced your decisions and, most likely, caused you to rely on her to help solve this case." He looked again at the pile of car debris and added, "I guess your Aunt Helen was right. You did it without her help." He stood up. "So, is this where Katie McCall is buried?"

Savannah nodded her head and got to her feet. She stood next to the detective and said, "I'm pretty sure that if we keep digging, we'll find her Corvette, and I believe that we'll find her body inside it." She looked at her raw hands. "But I don't think I can dig anymore."

He patted her on the shoulder and said, "It's all right. You don't have to." He pulled out a walkie-talkie that had been clipped to the back of his belt and pushed the talk button. "This is Detective Graves. I need my team at the bottom of the canyon near

Flowery Peak trail." He glanced at Jade who was still passed out and added, "And I need a medevac chopper ASAP."

"Right away, Detective," came the response crackling over the radio.

He clipped the radio back to his belt and sat down next to Jade. "As soon as the chopper gets here, we'll load her up and have them take her to Carson Tahoe Hospital." He looked at Savannah and Emma. "You two are welcome to go with her if you'd like."

"If it's all right with you, Detective Graves, I'd like to stay," said Savannah. If the detective's team was coming out here to dig Katie up, she wanted to be here when they did.

Detective Graves smiled. "I suspected as much, especially if you're anything like your aunt."

Savannah looked at Emma. "But you can go with Jade if you want."

Emma still cradled Jade's head in her lap and nodded. "I think I will. You okay if I go?"

"Absolutely. You stay with Jade, and I'll come to the hospital after we leave here. Just let me know how she's doing, okay?" She pulled her cell phone from her pocket. "Darn, I don't have any service down here."

Detective Graves pulled a satellite phone from his pack and handed it to her. "Don't worry, we can connect you with anyone you want to talk to."

Savannah knew exactly whom she wanted to call.

Chapter 52

After only one ring, a familiar voice said, "Hello?"

A smile streaked across Savannah's face, and she said, "Hey."

"Vannah? Is that ye? Are ye okay?"

Her smile deepened, and she blushed knowing that all eyes and ears were on her. "Yes, Brady, it's me. And I'm fine." She turned her back so the others couldn't hear her. "How are you?"

"Aye, much better now. I don't know why, but I've been so worried about ye. Ye sure ye'r okay?" He paused. "Whose phone are ye callin' from? I dunna recognize the number."

"Actually, it's a satellite phone. Detective Graves loaned it to me. He said that I could-"

"Hold on a minute. Are ye in some kind of trouble?"

Savannah laughed. "No, not at all."

"Thank goodness. I thought I might have te come te Nevada and bail ye out of jail."

"No, nothing like that. So guess what?" Savannah could barely contain her excitement.

"What?"

"We found her."

"Ye found the missing girl?" Brady's enthusiasm mirrored hers.

"Yes. Well, almost. We've uncovered parts of her car and some of her clothing. It's just going to take a lot more digging to get her out of there. But yeah, we found Katie."

"Vannah, I'm so proud of ye. I knew ye could do it. So when are ye-"

The whirling sound of chopper blades fast approaching caused Savannah to interrupt him. "Hey, Brady, I've got to go, but I'll call you tonight from the hospital."

"Hospital?"

"Yeah, I forgot to tell you that Jade broke her leg. It's pretty bad, too. Gotta go. Talk to you later." She hung up, trotted over to Detective Graves, handed him the satellite phone and then squatted down next to Jade.

"Hey," Savannah said quietly when she saw her friend's eyes open. "You're awake." She could tell that Jade was in a lot of pain. Her face had paled and the swelling on her leg had tripled.

"Hey," said Jade weakly. "How's Mr. Sexy Pants?" She shifted slightly and groaned. Just the slightest movement caused Jade's eyes to well up with pain-filled tears, and she sucked in her breath.

Savannah fought back her own tears. Seeing her friend in such pain caused her to blurt out, "I'm so sorry for getting you mixed up in this. If it weren't for me you wouldn't be here."

Jade flashed her a feeble smile. "You're right. If it weren't for you I wouldn't be here. And I never would have been able to watch you do what no one else has been able to do. You never gave up." She reached over and draped a weak hand over Savannah's. "You're my new hero."

"And you're mine," said Savannah through tears. "That was pretty brave what you did back there. Brave and stupid." She tilted her head. "Why did you put yourself in danger, throwing yourself over us like that? You could have gotten shot."

Jade squeezed her hand. "Because that's what best friends do."

By now the chopper was overhead. A stretcher with two men seated on it was being lowered to where the group sat. When it got within two feet of the ground the two paramedics hopped down, waved up to the chopper, and then guided the stretcher to the ground.

The first paramedic shook Detective Graves' hand and yelled over the deafening noise, "Will you help stabilize the stretcher while we pick her up? The slope's a little too steep right here."

"Sure." Graves stood downhill of the stretcher, then braced it with his thigh to help keep it level. When he made eye contact with Jade, she looked back at him with frightened eyes. "Don't you worry, Jade. They're going to take good care of you. And Emma is going with you."

Her eyes migrated over to Emma who smiled down at her and said loudly, "You're finally going to get that helicopter ride you've always wanted."

Jade chuckled then groaned. "Don't make me laugh. It hurts too much."

The paramedics carefully picked up Jade and loaded her onto the stretcher. They covered her up with a bright yellow solar blanket and strapped her in. The first paramedic clipped himself to the stabilizer bar above her and then signaled for the chopper to haul them up. Before they lifted into the air, Savannah grabbed the paramedic's arm and said, "Please take good care of her."

The two began to lift up into the air. Within minutes, Jade was loaded onto the chopper and the stretcher was sent back down again. When it got two feet from the ground, the remaining paramedic jumped on and said to Emma, "C'mon. I'm going to take you up."

Emma sat down next to him. He strapped her in and then wrapped his massive arm around her. "Hang on tight," he said with a smile.

Emma arched her eyebrows, flashed Savannah a mischievous grin and then snuggled into the cute paramedic's side as the stretcher lifted up to the helicopter.

"You sure you don't want to go with them?" said Detective Graves.

Savannah pulled her gaze from the helicopter, glanced at the detective and then stared down at the excavated area. "Not a chance."

Minutes after the helicopter had flown away, Detective Graves' walkie-talkie began to crackle. "We've got a chopper and a crew on the way. Unfortunately, it's too dangerous to get any digging equipment in there so the team's going to have to do it the old fashion way — by hand with picks and shovels. Over."

"Ten four. We'll be waiting."

Detective Graves clipped his walkie-talkie to his belt and turned to Savannah. "Looks like we have some time before the team gets here. Maybe you can fill me in on some of the details."

"Sure."

Savannah told him briefly about meeting with the McCalls, Mrs. Dolan, Dr. Wells and Benjamin Burke. "Dr. Wells said he found something on Marty's computer, but he didn't say what, only that it was quote *disturbing*."

"And what about Burke? Do you know if he was able to find out anything?"

Savannah shook her head. "I doubt it. He probably hasn't had enough time yet. We only told him about my dream this morning."

Detective Graves pulled his wallet from his back pocket, retrieved a business card and handed it to Savannah. "If you get any new information, please call me."

Savannah nodded, programmed the number into her phone and then tucked the card in her back pocket.

After a few moments, Savannah walked over and sat back down next to the pieces of fiberglass. And with each minute that passed the more anxious she became. Detective Graves seemed to be talking to her but she couldn't hear him.

All she could hear was Katie's voice in her ear saying, *I'm here, Savannah. Find me.*

She scooted over to the hole and started pulling more rocks out.

"Savannah, the crew will be here in a few minutes. You don't have to do that anymore. Just relax."

Savannah ignored the detective's advice and continued to pull rocks from the hole, making the concave area larger and larger. And with each rock she pulled out, the faster she dug. Soon she vanished from sight inside the hole, yanking at anything she could wrap her hands around. "I'm coming, Katie," she whispered. "Just hang on."

On hands and knees she wedged scraped fingers in between rocks, wiggling the boulders until they came free in her bloody hands. And with renewed strength she tossed them up and out of the hole.

To her surprise, Detective Graves stood at the top of the hole and stared down at her, making no attempt to help. She looked up and a moment later smiled at him, knowing that he had done this same thing with her aunt so many times before. That seemed to fuel her even more, and she dug and dug until that little voice in her head said, *I'm here!*

She pulled one final rock from its place and reached an arm into the dead space. Her fingers touched something slight, the size and dimension of a stick, causing an electric current to travel up her spine and into her very soul. And she knew right then that it was Katie's hand reaching up to her.

With tears pooling in her eyes, she looked back up at Detective Graves and said, "I found her!"

Chapter 53

Savannah sat in the hospital waiting room flipping through a magazine while Emma went to the cafeteria and fetched them more coffee. After a few moments she slapped it shut, tossed it on the end table next to her, and picked up the next one on the stack. The process for it was the same.

When Emma returned, Savannah said to her, "Did the doctors give you any indication how much longer Jade would be in surgery?"

Emma handed her a coffee, plopped down next to her and shook her head. "No."

"Did they say how she was doing?"

"Nope."

"Well, what *did* they tell you?"

Savannah's tone caused Emma's eyebrows to arch. "I told you. All they said was that they were going to have to put pins in her leg and that she probably wouldn't be able to walk for at least four months, maybe longer."

"They didn't tell you anything else?" Savannah drummed her fingers on the side of the disposable coffee cup.

"Vannah, you know as much about it as I do." Emma reached across Savannah's lap and grabbed a magazine with her free hand. "They'll come out and talk to us when they have more information. Until then there isn't much else we can do but wait and pray that it all goes well." She closed the magazine, dropped it on her lap and draped a hand over Savannah's arm. Savannah glanced at her then lowered her eyes. As if interpreting her friend's reaction, Emma quietly said, "It's not your fault, Vannah."

"Of course it is. Dominic tried to warn me, but I wouldn't listen." She looked back up at Emma. "Remember his reading? He even said that Jade would not be going to college this coming semester. And he was right. She won't be going to school because of me."

"She'll probably only miss one semester."

"Even so . . ."

Right then, a doctor walked up to them, pulled off his surgical cap and said, "Your friend is out of surgery and resting comfortably in recovery." The girls visibly relaxed. "The operation went well. It was a pretty severe break so we had to use pins and put in a temporary plate to help the bone fuse back together."

"Will she have to keep the plate forever?" asked Emma.

The doctor shook his head. "No. Once the break begins to heal it can be removed, but that won't be for several months."

Savannah said, "Can we go see her?"

The doctor shook his head. "Not tonight. We have her on some pretty heavy-duty painkillers."

"Then when can we see her?" asked Savannah.

"Not until tomorrow. She needs a good night's rest."

"But can't we at least-"

"Okay. Thank you, doctor," said Emma, interrupting her.

He nodded, turned to walk away and then stopped. He faced them again and said, "I've already spoken to her parents to let them know that she is out of surgery. They said they would catch the first flight out in the morning. You girls should go get some rest." He turned back around and hurried toward a set of double doors.

Jade's parents!

Savannah's face paled and she turned to Emma. "They're going to be so mad at us."

"What are we going to tell them?" Emma clutched her disposable coffee cup so tightly that the lid popped off.

"We have no choice but to tell them the truth," Savannah groaned, "about *everything*!"

Emma gasped, "Oh, Vannah. They're going to kill us."

Savannah stood up, tossed her half empty coffee cup in a nearby trashcan and said, "C'mon, let's go get some sleep. We're going to need to be sharp when we talk to her parents."

"You mean when they interrogate us."

~~~~~~~~~~~~~~~~~~~~~~~~~~~

The next morning the two girls walked up the hospital hall toward Jade's room on the third floor. Savannah carried a bouquet of brightly colored Gerber daisies mixed with yellow daffodils, while Emma clutched a plush stuffed teddy bear in one hand and a helium "Get Well Soon" balloon in the other.

"So I forgot to tell you that Benjamin Burke called me when you were in the shower this morning," said Emma.

They scooted around two nurses loitering by a nurse's station and Savannah said, "So what did he have to say? Did he find out anything?"

"He said he was able to dig up some pretty interesting information about the prostitute, but that he wanted to speak with us in person."

"So what did you tell him?"

"I told him that we were going to spend some time with our friend in the hospital and that we could meet up afterwards. But I didn't give him a set time." She looked at Savannah. "Have you talked to Dr. Wells?"

"Crap. I completely forgot about him. I'll call him when we get to Jade's room. With everything that's been going on, I didn't even think about what he might have uncovered on Marty's computer."

"What about the McCalls? Have you contacted them yet?"

Savannah shook her head. "Detective Graves asked me not to until they were able to extract Katie's body and take the remains to the morgue."

"I can't imagine how they're going to react when you tell them you found their daughter. Then maybe Mr. McCall will apologize for the way he treated you."

Savannah's lips slid into a slight smile. "I don't need an apology, or even a 'thank you'. I'm just happy to bring some closure to them so that they can finally move on."

"But we still don't know why it happened," said Emma.

"Yeah, I know." Savannah sighed. "There are still so many unanswered questions. She looked at the numbers on the wall beside each door as they walked by and said, "I think Jade's room is just up there."

When they got to her room, they quietly tiptoed through the doorway thinking that she might still be asleep. Immediately, they stopped with their mouths gaping open.

The room was packed with people.

When Savannah realized who all of the visitors were, she began to stammered, "Why . . . How . . . When . . ."

"Yes, Vannah?" said her mother standing near the foot of Jade's bed with her arms crossed over her chest and shooting imaginary lasers at her daughter. Mrs. Swift glanced sideways over at her husband who stood shoulder to shoulder mirroring her.

"Something you girls want to tell us?" said Pastor Swift.

"I-I-"

"Mom? Dad?" said Emma staring at her parents who stood on the left side of the bed directly across from Jade's parents.

"Speak up, you two. We're listening," said Mrs. Swift.

"Oh, Vivian, for crying in a bucket, leave them alone." Two arms scissored in between Mr. and Mrs. Swift, prying the two apart, and out stepped Aunt Helen from behind them. "Let them at least come in and say hi to Jade before you start interrogating them." She walked over, wrapped protective arms around the two girls and escorted them to Jade's side.

A traction bar held Jade's leg elevated at a forty-five degree angle. Two metal halos encircling her lower leg were attached to eight metal screws protruding out of her skin, giving her a Frankenstein appearance. When she saw the girls she tried to sit up but her apparatus kept her immobile.

"Hey," Jade said weakly, "You guys made it."

Savannah handed the flowers to Emma, leaned down and kissed Jade on the forehead. "How you doing, Jadie. You feeling okay?"

Emma put all of the goodies in one hand and rubbed Jade's arm with the other. "Hey, girl. You hanging in there?"

Jade smiled slightly and cleared her throat. "Can't really do much but hang here." She looked back at Savannah. "Did you find her?"

Savannah nodded. "We did." She glanced at her parents then back at Jade. "They're going to finish digging her out today. Detective Graves will call me just as soon as they're done."

"I'm really proud of you, Vannah." She shifted and winced when she tried to move.

"Easy, Jade," said her father. "We should all probably go and let you get some rest." He flashed Savannah and Emma a look that said, *no argument.*

"Um, yeah, Jade. We should go. We have to meet up with Benjamin Burke," said Emma glancing at Savannah. "But we'll be back this afternoon."

"What did Burke say?" Jade's voice was beginning to fade and her eyelids seemed to be getting heavy, making it difficult for her to keep them open. "Did he find out anything?"

"Okay guys, that's enough," said Jade's father. "Time to go." He bent down and kissed his daughter's forehead. "Get some rest, sweetheart."

As the crew began to shuffle out of the room, Jade opened her eyes part way and murmured, "Hey, Vannah, guess what."

Savannah turned back. "What, sweetie?"

"The jeep was my graduation present." She closed her eyes, but the smile remained on her face as she fell fast asleep.

Chapter 54

Once outside Jade's room, the gang erupted with questions, comments and accusations. Both Emma and Savannah began backing down the hall while the parents verbally pummeled them.

"Hang on, everyone," said Savannah raising her hands in the air. "Can we please take this outside?"

"Listen here, young lady . . ." Savannah's dad shook his finger at her.

Aunt Helen put her hand on Mr. Swift's arm. "Carl, let her speak."

When there was silence and all eyes were on her, Savannah said, "We'll tell you everything you want to know, but can we please do it somewhere else?"

Jade's parents looked at each other then back at Savannah and Emma. "We want to know how Jade got hurt," said her mother.

"Maybe we can go get something to eat and talk about it," said Savannah. "We know this great little restaurant right across the parking lot from our motel. It's called Grandma Hattie's, and it has the best-"

Bzzzz! Bzzzz! Bzzzz!

Savannah pulled her vibrating phone from her pocket and glanced at the name associated with the caller. "Hold on a minute. I've got to answer this." She held the phone up to her ear. "Hello, Detective Graves." She grew quiet for a moment and then said, "Sure, we can meet you there. We'll call them to see if they can join us. Say, in an hour? Okay, sounds good. We'll leave right from the hospital." She hung up and looked at the group. "Detective Graves would like us to meet him down at the Reno police department. We can talk about everything then. But I need to make a phone call first." She turned to Emma. "I need to call Dr. Wells. Will you call Mr. Burke and see if he can meet us there?"

"Who's Mr. Burke?" asked Emma's mother, ringing her hands. Though Emma's parents stood next to each other, an emotional wall and an impending divorce separated them. Emma walked over and put an arm around her mother. "Mom, he's an amazing author who I know you're going to love, once you meet him."

After the phone calls were placed, the group caravanned to Reno. Aunt Helen's suggestion that Savannah ride with her was met with a resounding "No!" from Savannah's parents. It was decided that Emma and her mom would ride with Jade's parents while Mr. Reed would ride with Savannah and her parents. Savannah was grateful for the extra person in the car. It guaranteed a lecture-free ride.

Forty minutes later, the cars pulled into the Reno Police Department parking lot. They all got out of the cars, and as one group, they walked into the building.

"Hi, we're here to see Detective Graves," Savannah told the receptionist.

"Sure, let me see if he's available."

Before she could place the call, the detective came from around the corner. He smiled when he saw Savannah, held out his hand toward the group and said, "I'm Detective Graves. Thank you for meeting me here."

Savannah's father was the first one to shake his hand. He made the introductions, ending with, "And this is my sister-in-law, Helen Alliette."

Detective Graves flashed Aunt Helen a quick wink that went unnoticed by everyone except Savannah. "It's a pleasure to meet you all. Will you please follow me? I have a conference room ready." Ushering the group down the hall, he stopped in front of a set of double doors on his left, opened one of them and gestured to the oval, conference table. "Please have a seat. Can I get any of you coffee?" When everyone raised a hand he said, "Be back in a few minutes." Then he closed the door behind him.

Though no one spoke out loud the internal conversations bouncing from person to person were deafening. Each glance contained a mixture of curiosity, hope, confusion, and condemnation. Though she didn't want to, Savannah couldn't help but hear them all.

Ten minutes later Detective Graves returned followed by Dr. Wells, Benjamin Burke, the McCalls, the Dolans, and finally his secretary with a pushcart filled with coffee cups, condiments, a box of pastries, and three carafes of coffee.

"Mrs. McCall! Mrs. Dolan!" Savannah jumped up and gave them both a hug.

Mrs. McCall's eyes glistened and were rimmed in red. She looked like she had been crying for quite some time. She took hold of Savannah's hands in hers and said quietly, "You found her, didn't you?" It was more of a statement than a question.

Before Savannah could answer, Detective Graves said, "I'm sure you all have a lot of questions, and we will get to all of them, I promise. But first I'd like to tell you everything that I know about this case. Then perhaps Dr. Well and Mr. Burke can fill in any blanks."

With Emma on her left, Savannah pointed to the empty chair on her right and motioned for Mrs. McCall to sit next to her. And when she did, Savannah grabbed her hand and held it under the table, offering her this small gesture of support. Mrs. McCall tilted her head in thanks and then directed her attention to Detective Graves.

The detective stood at the front of the room next to a large white marker board attached to the wall. He held some eight by ten photographs in his hand. As he spoke he attached the first one to a metal strip at the top of the board with magnets. It was a headshot of a young woman with light brown hair that feathered around soft Bambi eyes.

"This is Kaitlyn McCall, Mr. and Mrs. McCall's daughter. She went missing in May 2009. The department has spent the last three years looking for her, but we were never able to uncover any clues regarding her disappearance, that is, until now." He glanced at Savannah with a look that could have been one of admiration. But just as quickly, it turned professional.

"While hiking in the canyon near Flowery Peak, Savannah, Emma, and Jade stumbled upon her missing car. Upon further investigation, Kaitlyn's body was discovered buried inside the car." He slipped another photo underneath the magnet right next to Katie's picture and said, "We believe she was murdered by this man, Louis, aka 'Lou' Evans. Based on our findings, we believe that Mr. Evans pushed Kaitlyn's car over the cliff near one of the Comstock mines off of Six Mile Canyon. What we don't know is why."

Tears tumbled down Mrs. McCall's cheeks. Savannah squeezed her hand tightly as they both stared at the picture of the man from the white pickup truck. The picture must have been lifted from his driver's license, because in this one, the man was clearly alive.

Dr. Wells raised his hand and said, "I might be able to shed a little light on that." He pulled a file folder from his briefcase, scooted out from the table and walked over to the white board. "With the help of Savannah, I was able to recover some pertinent information from Marty Dolan's computer." While he talked,

Detective Graves slipped a photograph of Marty under the next magnet. "Marty and I met while he was in college. He was one of my students. After he graduated he began working for the Reno Gazette.

"Back in May of 2009, Marty called me one night, told me he was working on a big story and asked if I could run a few test for him. My assistant ended up running the tests, so I actually never saw the results until yesterday."

He pulled a graph from the folder and stuck it under the magnet right next to Marty's picture. The top of the page read, "Parts Per Million". The graph had different colored rectangular bars varying in length across the page. Underneath each bar was a different two-letter initial. Numbers, rising up in increments of a thousand, lined the left side of the page.

Mr. Swift leaned forward in his seat, as if to get a better view, and said, "What is that?"

"According to Marty's notes, while hiking on the Flowery Peak Trail, he found a trickle of water seeping out of the mountain near one of the Comstock mines. It had an iridescent sheen to it and smelled like a combination of licorice and rancid garlic. So he took a sample of it, and a soil sample."

"That's the same thing we smelled," said Emma.

Dr. Wells pointed to the graph. "These are the results of those tests." His finger drew an imaginary line along the bottom of the graph. "These initials represent the chemicals found in those samples. We have arsenic, cyanide, selenium, thallium, and carbon tetrachloride.

"The markers on the left hand side of the graph represents parts per million. The standard and acceptable rate for these compounds, set by the EPA, is anywhere from zero to less than one tenth of one percent parts per million." He looked at his audience. "According to these results, Marty's samples were all over ten thousand times higher than what the government deems as safe."

"What does that mean?" said Emma's father.

Dr. Wells adjusted his glasses. "What it means is that the water flowing from Flowery Mountain Range which flows into the Carson River and eventually ends up in every home and business in Reno, Carson City, Lake Tahoe, and all of the surrounding areas, is massively polluted."

"But what about the area's filtration system?" said Jade's father. "Wouldn't that have been able to filter out the pollutants?"

Dr. Wells grimaced. "Partially. Unfortunately, though, it's not just in the water. Based on Marty's sample, those same chemicals are in the soil, as well. Which means that every crop, every fruit and vegetable grown here has absorbed those toxins. And we've been consuming them, whether directly or indirectly through livestock.

He looked back at the graph. "I fear we are on the precipice of seeing an unprecedented amount of cases involving toxic poisoning, just like what happened to the folks in Little Lyon a few years back, only on a much larger scale."

"But how did it get that way?" asked Jade's dad.

"And where did it come from?" added Jade's mother.

Dr. Wells pulled out an eight by ten photo and stuck it under the magnet next to the graph. "Marty had taken this up at one of the mines a few nights before he died. It's a little grainy, but you can see several fifty-gallon drums lined up behind some sort of delivery truck." He glanced around the room. "Based on all of the evidence that Marty provided, I believe that for years the Comstock Mining Company has been storing chemical waste down their dry mines."

"But why?" asked Emma. "Why would they do that?"

"I'm not sure why," he said looking back at the graph.

The room fell silent for several moments.

Boss man.

Savannah sucked in slightly.

"What is it, Vannah?" asked Aunt Helen.

Boss man.

Savannah frowned. "I don't know. Something about that video Marty shot is bugging me."

"Now I'm gonna have to tell the boss man. He ain't gonna be too happy about it neither."

She heard the words from the video replay in her mind and a thought struck her. "What if the orders came from higher up, like a boss?"

Detective Graves shook his head. "According to Comstock records, Lou Evans *was* the boss of the entire mining operation."

"No, I mean higher," said Savannah. "Someone even higher up than him." She thought for a moment and then looked over at Emma. "Do you remember when we were at the library doing some research? You found a website called NevadaAppeal."

"Yes, I remember," said Emma. "There was an article that said the dry mines had been purchased on behalf of Harrison Taylor, CEO of their holding company, the Geneva Corporation, and that any plans would remain private until he decided to make them public."

Savannah looked back at the detective. "What if Harrison Taylor was the one who ordered the Comstock Mining Company to get rid of those barrels?"

"But why would he do that?" said Emma. "That doesn't make any sense at all. Mr. Taylor is a philanthropist. He started his non-profit organization, EarthFirst, as a way to help clean up the planet, not pollute it."

Detective Graves leaned back against the wall and crossed his arms over his chest. "I'm sorry Savannah, but I have to agree with Emma on this one. Mr. Taylor owns so much land here, why would he want to pollute his own back yard?"

Benjamin Burke, who had been silent this entire time, slid his chair back, grabbed his briefcase off of the floor next to him and stood up. "I think I might be able to answer that."

Chapter 55

All eyes were on the author as he walked to the front of the room, set his briefcase on the table and opened it. He pulled out a stack of eight by ten photographs and set them face up on the table.

He glanced around the room at the small group and said, "For those of you who don't know me, my name is Benjamin Burke, and I am a local historian. I am also one of the world's leading authorities on the Comstock Lode. I thought I knew all there was to know about the subject," he gestured toward Emma and smiled, "until I talked to this young lady. She brought me some new information that, I believe, will help us all understand why Harrison Taylor did what he did. That is, if he is, in fact, responsible for the toxic poisoning here in Nevada. But in order for me to do that, I'm going to have to take you back to the very beginning."

He picked up the first photo off of the stack and attached it to the white board. It showed a large group of people standing around a wooden coffin covered in roses. The headline read,

"Mourners Lament the Sudden Death of Cripple Creek's Renowned Madam, Pearl De Vere."

"When Emma told me about the possibility of Henry Comstock having an illegitimate child with a local prostitute, I immediately began going back through all of my data. I already knew that Virginia City had several brothels due to the amount of miners coming into the area and gaining wealth. But my focus was only on the madams. I neglected to find out what happened to the prostitutes who were forced to leave the area."

He picked up the next photo and attached it to the board. It was of a vintage painting of a madam lounging on a gilded fainting couch. The woman in the painting wore a salmon colored chiffon gown, covered in sequins and seed pearls. Her hair was done up in a loose swirl on top of her head, secured by a diamond and gold tiara. "This is Pearl De Vere, the most famous Madam of Cripple Creek, Colorado."

Savannah gasped when she saw the colored photograph. The slight build, the red hair—though the person in the picture was older than the prostitute in her dreams, she was certain they were one and the same.

Burke stepped to the side of the photograph and said, "Pearl De Vere started out in Denver as a prostitute under the name of Isabel O'Tally. She made quite a sizeable fortune servicing the wealthy gentlemen of the area and soon became a madam.

"When Denver ran into its first financial slowdown, Ms. O'Tally changed her name to Pearl De Vere, moved to Cripple Creek along with four of her 'girls' and opened up a brothel. Because of Colorado's gold rush and her generous clientele, Pearl quickly became wealthy. But she spent it as fast as she made it."

He attached the next picture to the white board. It was a photograph of an old black and white newspaper clipping. It showed a room packed with gentlemen wearing suits and women dressed in elegant but revealing gowns. The title read, "Pearl De Vere, At It Again."

Burke looked at his small but captive audience. "Pearl De Vere was known for her lavish parties. And it was no different the night she died. She had cases of French champagne and Russian caviar brought in for this occasion and even hired two orchestras from Denver to entertain her guests.

"As the night progressed, Pearl began to feel woozy. She excused herself and retired to one of the bedrooms. Hours later, one of her girls checked on her only to find that she was barely breathing. A doctor was summoned, but by the time he arrived she had already passed away."

Savannah sniffed and quickly pushed back a tear that threatened to fall. Logically, she knew that this young mother from her dreams had long been dead, but it still shot a pain of loss through her heart hearing Mr. Burke talk about it.

Burke pointed to the photo of the funeral. "Pearl De Vere was buried in her sequin gown and laid to rest in a lavender casket smothered in hundreds of red and white roses.

"She died penniless. And if it weren't for some anonymous wealthy benefactor, she would not have had this lavish funeral. Nor would it have ended up on the front page of this newspaper."

He moved closer to the white board. "What I want to draw your attention to is this young man right here." He pointed to the image of a solemn looking adult male standing near the front of the casket holding a rose. He looked to be in his late twenties. "We now know that this was her son, *Harry* O'Tally."

Savannah and Emma glanced at each other, excitement beginning to bubble in both of them. Savannah's dream was starting to solidify.

Mr. Burke continued. "I wanted to make sure that it wasn't just coincidence that Pearl's name was originally Isabel and that this young man's name was Harry. So I contacted the Denver Historical Society and, luckily, I was able to find their medical records. Apparently, not long after they moved to Denver, Harry, who was only a few weeks old at the time, became extremely sick and was rushed to the hospital. The doctors thought that he had come down with a case of cholera. But instead, it ended up being a severe bout of colic due to an allergic reaction to his mother's breast milk.

"According to those records, Isabel O'Tally, who was nineteen years old at the time, gave birth to Harry right here in Virginia City."

"But what does any of this have to do with Harrison Taylor disposing toxic waste?" said Mr. Swift.

"I'm getting to that. Just bear with me."

Burke attached the next photo—that of another newspaper clipping dated August 26, 1907. The headline read, "J.P. Morgan Opens His Newest New York Office." A distinguished looking older gentleman wearing a top hat, a suit and tie, and sporting a long white beard stood next to a brick building. Behind him stood a group of men.

Burke tapped the image of the bearded man in the top hat with his finger. "This is JP Morgan. He was the most important and profitable investment banker in the United States during the early 1900's. To keep up with the surge in business, Morgan opened several offices around the Eastern states, this being one of them."

Burke pointed to the group of men standing behind him. One of them had a circle drawn around his face. "I'd like to draw your attention to this man right here. Through face detection algorithms I was able to determine that this man was, in fact, Harry O'Tally."

Emma leaned over and whispered into Savannah's ear, "Facial recognition software. So that was the trick he must have had up his sleeve."

Burke continued. "After his mother's death, Harry left Cripple Creek and moved back to Virginia City. At some point, he moved to New York City where he began working in the investment banking industry with JP Morgan. But according to JP Morgan's employee records, no one by the name of Harry O'Tally ever worked for them. And yet, here he is." He pointed to the man's image again and said, "So if this isn't Harry O'Tally, then who is he?" He paused dramatically.

"According to their salary records, the man in this picture is named . . . *Harrison Taylor*.

Chapter 56

"Wait a minute," said Savannah. "You're saying that Harry O'Tally changed his name to Harrison Taylor?"

Burke nodded. "That's exactly what I am saying." He tapped the image with his finger. "This man is the great grandfather of your Harrison Taylor, which means that your Harrison Taylor is the great, great grandson of Henry Comstock."

"Say that's true," said Jade's father, "it still doesn't explain why he would bring toxic waste here."

"Well, I believe it does," said Mr. Burke. He turned to Emma. "Do you remember the chapter in my book regarding illegitimate children and their right to inherit?"

Emma's eyes lit up. "Of course I do. Originally, according to Nevada state law, illegitimate children could not inherit property. But when Nevada became a community property state that all changed. If a wife died first, all the community property went to the husband. But if the husband died first, the wife could only claim half of their property, and the husband could bequeath the other half to whomever he pleased."

Burke nodded. "That's right, *whomever he pleased*. And that's exactly what Henry Comstock intended to do." He clipped a black and white photo of a land deed up on the white board. "It's well documented that Peter O'Riley and Patrick McLaughlin ended up giving a portion of the land they were mining back to Henry Comstock after he asserted that it belonged to him. The history books suggest that he sold all of it." He pointed to the deed. "This document contradicts that. It shows that this portion of the property remained in Henry Comstock's possession until the day he died. And I believe it was his intent to bequeath it to his illegitimate son, Harry."

"What makes you think that?" said Mr. Reed.

Burke walked back and forth in front of the white board. "Henry Comstock died penniless—except for this piece of property. Now, as far as anyone knew, Henry Comstock never had any children. So, there would have been no reason for him to hold on to this property, not when he could have sold it and made a substantial bundle. The only reason to hold on to property is to pass it down to one's heirs. And in this case, we now know that it would have gone to Harry O'Tally."

"So you're saying that Harry O'Tally was the rightful heir to Henry Comstock's land?" said Savannah.

"Well, half of it, anyway," said Burke. "The other half would have gone to his wife and would have either been sold or passed down to her heirs."

"Do you know if he had any children with his wife?" said Detective Graves.

Burke looked over at him and shook his head. "Not that I'm aware of." He glanced over at Emma. "But who knows what I'll find if I keep digging."

That made Emma grin.

Mr. McCall shoved his chair back, stood up, and slammed his fist on the table making everyone jump. "What does any of this have to do with the death of my daughter?" Spittle flung from his mouth. "If Harrison Taylor had anything to do with my daughter's death than I want him to pay."

Detective Graves stepped forward with his palms out, as if to quiet him, and calmly said, "Yes, Mr. McCall, so do I. But as much as I would love to, I can't arrest him based on this information. As compelling as these stories are, there's nothing to substantiate Mr. Burke's claims. A few pictures and a couple of newspaper articles won't give me what I need to arrest him."

"So what do you need?" said Mr. McCall, his arms crossed tightly over his chest.

"Well," said Detective Graves, "the smoking gun, if you will. I would need irrefutable proof that Harrison Taylor willingly and knowingly ordered the murder of your daughter."

The room grew quiet for several moments. No one moved until Mr. McCall acquiesced and took his seat. He put his arm around his wife and pulled her close as she quietly sobbed into his chest.

"Well, can't you look at Taylor's financial records or something?" said Savannah. "Maybe you could uncover some evidence there."

Detective Graves shook his head. "Even if we could get a warrant to search his books, that still wouldn't prove that he was responsible for Katie's death or for storing toxic waste down in his mines."

Savannah lowered her head on to the table and groaned.

"But what if it could?" said Aunt Helen with a glint in her eyes.

All eyes turned to her, and Detective Graves said, "What do you mean, Helen?"

Helen looked at her niece. "Vannah, do you still have the item I gave you?"

Savannah stared at Aunt Helen. She knew that her aunt was referring to the box with the tarot cards in them. She glanced down at her purse then back up at her aunt.

"If you have them with you, now might be the time to use them," said her aunt.

Mrs. Swift's glare bounced from her daughter to her sister, and her eyes narrowed. "What are you talking about, Helen?"

"She knows what I'm talking about, don't you Vannah?" Aunt Helen continued to stare until Savannah slowly nodded her head. "They might help you find that smoking gun Detective Graves is looking for."

Savannah swallowed hard. She couldn't believe that her aunt had just put her in this terrible position. She was asking her to do a reading in front of everyone including her parents. "I-I . . ."

"Now is not the time to shy away from your gifts, Vannah. You have an opportunity here," said Aunt Helen without breaking eye contact.

"Helen, don't," warned Savannah's mother.

"Stay out of it, Viv," replied Aunt Helen still looking at Savannah. "You had your chance a long time ago. Now it's her turn."

Mrs. Swift glared at Savannah and slowly shook her head. "Don't do it, Vannah. You'll regret it."

"What the heck is going on here?" ordered Mr. Swift.

Aunt Helen looked over at her sister and said matter-of-factly, "Do you want to tell him, or shall I?"

"I will never forgive you for this, Helen," hissed Mrs. Swift.

"I know. But right now putting an end to these poor people's suffering and bringing whoever killed their daughter to justice is more important than your forgiveness." Aunt Helen focused on Savannah once more. "This is your chance, sweetheart. What are you going to do?"

"Will someone please tell me what's going on?" said Mr. Swift abruptly.

Savannah sat as still as a statue, staring into her aunt's eyes. *What should I do?*

After what seemed like an eternity, she leaned down, grabbed her purse and set it on the table.

As she opened it and pulled out the ornate box, Emma leaned over and whispered, "Are you sure about this?"

"Nope, not at all," said Savannah.

In spite of her uncertainty, she opened the box, pulled out the tarot cards and set them on the table in front of several pairs of astonished eyes.

Chapter 57

As Savannah began to lay out the cards face down in the shape of a pyramid, her father yelled, "Savannah! What the *hell* are you doing? Drop those things right now. I forbid you to use them. They're Satan's tools."

"No they're not," said Savannah calmly. "They're God's tools. Satan didn't help me when I used them to find Katie's body. And he didn't help me when I used them to save Carrie's brother and his girlfriend from dying in a fatal car accident. But God sure did." She looked at her father whose red face had suddenly paled. "And God's going to help us again, right here, right now, so that we can solve this mystery once and for all." Her hand hovered over the first card. "All I have to do is turn these cards over, and God will do the rest."

Pastor Swift fell back into his chair as though an invisible arrow had pierced his heart. He opened his mouth to speak, but no words came out.

Aunt Helen draped a hand over his forearm and said quietly, "It'll be fine, Carl, you'll see."

He slowly turned his head toward her, seething. "You did this. You are responsible for filling her mind with all of this garbage."

Aunt Helen tried to appeal to him. "Carl, you don't understand-"

"Oh, I understand all right. I understand that you are a terrible influence. Now I know why your sister disowned you so many years ago," he hissed. "She didn't want to subject us to your appalling fascination with the occult." He turned to his wife. "Right, honey?"

"Well, I-uh . . . She-uh . . . We-uh . . ."

His head swiveled back to Aunt Helen. "You're a disgrace to this family, Helen. And I forbid you to ever see my daughter again!"

"Forbid? Oh, get off your high horse, Carl," huffed Aunt Helen. "She's an adult, and if she doesn't want to see me anymore then that will be her decision, not yours."

"Fine," he fired back. "Then you're no longer welcome in our house. And *that* I do have control over."

"Why? You afraid I'm going to tarnish your pious home with my beliefs? Because, if so, then you're too late." She looked over at Mrs. Swift. "Right, Vivian?"

Pastor Swift looked at his wife. "What is she talking about, Viv?"

"I-uh . . . We-uh . . . She-uh . . ."

Through gritted teeth Aunt Helen said, "Let me spell it out for you, *Pastor*. If you didn't want any psychics in your home then you shouldn't have married my sister!"

Pastor Swift gasped. "Blaspheme!"

"Stop it!" said Savannah with her hands over her ears. "Please, just stop arguing. I can't concentrate." She had already turned over the first row of cards.

When the room fell silent, Savannah touched the first card. Immediately, the expected shock traveled through her fingertips, up her arm and right into her brain.

When she spasmed her father jumped up and cried, "Vannah! Are you all right?"

"I'm fine, Dad. Really." She offered him a compassionate smile knowing that what she was doing contradicted everything he had taught her and all that he, himself, had been taught. She looked back down at the cards and her mind focused on the image of a vast field full of yellow pentacles. They reminded her of blooming sunflowers. A man leaning on a rake seemed to be admiring them from a distance.

She looked at Detective Graves and said, "For some reason, EarthFirst keeps popping into my head. I think what the cards are trying to show me is that instead of focusing on Harrison Taylor, we need to look at the companies who have donated to that organization."

Detective Graves said, "Okay. Is there any company, in particular, we should focus on?"

Savannah turned over the next row of cards. Her mind seemed to latch onto a knight lying on his back with swords aiming down at his head. A full suit of armor protected his face and his identity. "I think it might be an individual who will have the information you need. But I can't tell you who it is because his face is covered up."

Aunt Helen, who sat across from her, leaned in over the table as if to get a better look at the cards. "Vannah, I know this card. And I know that it means whomever this represents wants to help, but they're too frightened to. Look at how the swords are threatening him. He's covering his face and identity so that he doesn't get hurt." She looked up at her niece. "But you can find out who is under that armor."

"I can? How do I do that?"

"You lift it up with your mind."

Mr. Swift rolled his eyes. "Oh, come on. Lift it up with her mind? This is ludicrous." He looked at Detective Graves. "It's preposterous that you would even entertain this, let alone encourage it. As far as I'm concern, you've just lost all credibility in my eyes." He looked over at his wife. "This is ridiculous, and I'm not going to be a part of it anymore. C'mon, we're going." He stood up and snapped his finger at Savannah. "You too, young lady. Let's go."

"No, Dad," she said, "I'm staying here." She blew out a conflicted breath. She didn't want to upset him, but it was time for her to grow up and take a stand. "I know this is hard for you to understand, but I've discovered so much about myself in the last couple of weeks.

"You've always taught me to be proud of who I am and to not back down from a challenge. Well, Dad, I can't walk away from this, because this *is* who I am." She paused. "I'm a psychic."

Without looking at her, Mr. Swift quietly sat down, turned his head and stared at the photographs still attached to the white board.

"Dad, say something." When he didn't respond, Savannah sighed and closed her eyes. She began to focus on the tarot card. In her mind, she tried to lift the armor from the man's face, but it wouldn't move. She looked over at her aunt. "It's not working."

"Keep trying," her aunt encouraged. "Now is not the time to give up."

Savannah nodded and turned over the next row of cards. Her eyes focused on another knight holding a sword as if preparing for battle. Only this time, the face piece was lifted. An image slowly began to form in her mind, and when it solidified she frowned.

"This can't be right," she said.

"What do you see," asked Aunt Helen.

"I-I know this person." She shook her head. "It can't be right."

"Who do you see?" said Emma.

Savannah looked at her friend and said, "Congressman Seavers."

Emma started to laugh. "You're joking, right?"

Savannah slowly shook her head. "That's whose face I see." She looked at her aunt. "But that can't be right, can it? I mean, we know him. We went to a party at his house last Friday night. We go to school with his daughter. He lives in our little Podunk town. Why would he be involved with Harrison Taylor? It doesn't make any sense whatsoever."

Aunt Helen looked at her. "Don't discount anything, Vannah." She looked up at Detective Graves.

"I'll look into it," he said then turned his attention to Savannah. "What else do you see?"

She turned over the next row of cards and her mind focused on the seven of cups. Each cup seemed to be filled to the brim with people, animals, jewelry, and other items. She sucked in her breath and said, "It isn't just one or two companies involved with this thing. There are lots, hundreds even. And it looks like, somehow, they're all benefiting in a big way from contributing to EarthFirst."

She turned over the final card at the top of the pyramid and studied it for a moment. It was of a boy and a girl looking at each other. They had the same color hair and similar attributes. She looked over at Benjamin Burke and said, "This one is for you." She paused and took a deep breath. "I think Henry Comstock had another child—a daughter."

Chapter 58

Savannah stood with Mrs. McCall in the parking lot outside the police department, while Mr. McCall remained in the lobby talking on his phone. The parents congregated next to their cars, their voices elevating occasionally. Emma, Mr. Burke and Dr. Wells stood near the doors of the precinct, chatting with Detective Graves and Aunt Helen.

Each group seemed to be lost in their own conversations.

A few minutes later, Mr. McCall exited the police station and walked over to his wife. He nodded once and said, "Dental records confirmed it. It's Katie." When she started to cry, he pulled her in and hugged her. "At least we know for sure now. It's better this way."

After a few moments, Mrs. McCall pulled away from her husband's embrace and looked up at him. "Did you make the arrangements?" When he nodded, she turned to Savannah, tears still spilling down her cheeks, and took hold of the girl's hands. "I am forever grateful to you for all that you did to find our daughter." She glanced over at her husband and said, "I know I speak for both Harland and myself when I say we would be honored if you would stay and attend our daughter's funeral."

"When is it?"

Harland cleared his throat. "The day after tomorrow, five o'clock in the evening, at Grace church. It's not too far from here, just off of Highway 80." He lowered his head slightly as if embarrassed. "It would mean a great deal—to both of us—if you could make it."

Savannah smiled up at him, "I would like that. Thank you." She glanced over to where the parents stood. "I'm not sure what my parents' plans are, but I'm pretty confident Emma wouldn't mind staying an extra day." She glanced over at her friend, noticing that she seemed to have the author cornered in a one-sided conversation and added, "Although, I can't say the same for Mr. Burke."

"Well, if you can make it, we'd love to see you both there." He reached his hand out, and Savannah shook it.

As the McCalls drove out of the parking lot Savannah waved good-bye to them. She continued watching the car until someone placed a gentle hand on her shoulder.

"Vannah," came her father's voice, causing her to turn around. His face held a look of resolution, and he said quietly, "Do you mind if we talk?"

"I don't want to fight with you, Dad."

"Neither do I. But you have to understand that this is very difficult for me."

"I know. It is for me, too. Believe me, this psychic thing isn't something I chose. It chose me. Just like it chose Aunt Helen," she paused, "and Mom."

Mr. Swift slowly nodded his head. "I know. Your mother told me." He brushed a hand across his brow as if to wipe away his worry lines. "You know this whole psychic thing goes against everything that I believe. So I can't condone it."

"But Dad-"

He held up his hand. "Just let me finish. I can't condone it. But I won't stand in your way if you want to pursue this path." He offered her a tired smile. "You're my daughter, and I love you. But more importantly, I trust you, and I trust your judgment. So if you say that this is what you need to be doing, then all I can do is pray for your safety and wellbeing, and send you off with my blessings." His eyes were rimmed with tears.

"Oh, Dad, I love you so much." She flung her arms around his neck, and they hugged.

~~~~~~~~~~~~~~~~

The evening of the funeral, Savannah and Emma walked up the steps to the church, followed by a long line of mourners. Savannah wondered how many of them were friends of the family and how many of them were here because they had seen Katie's picture in this morning's Reno Gazette. A photograph of the partially uncovered mangled Corvette and the headline, "Missing Girl's Body Found", had been plastered across the front page, along with follow-up stories about her and Marty on pages two and three.

As they walked into the church, Savannah whispered, "It's packed in here, but I want to go pay my respects first before we sit down."

Emma nodded in agreement.

The two girls reverently walked up the aisle to the front of the church where a table draped in a white tablecloth held a portrait of Katie, an ornate urn, and an arch of lit candles. Freestanding bouquets of pink and white roses with white calla lilies surrounded the table.

Savannah lightly touched the picture frame and whispered, "Thank you for everything, Katie. Thank you for believing in me, and thank you for pushing me to find you. I never would have done it if you hadn't been so persistent.

"The amazing thing is, in searching for you I found myself, and I can never thank you enough for that." She kissed two fingers and placed them on the urn. "I will never forget you, Katie McCall."

After Emma paid her respects, the girls turned and began to walk back down the aisle.

The McCalls sat in the front row by themselves, and when the girls walked by, Mr. McCall reached out a hand and said, "Please, come sit with us."

"We would love to. Thank you," whispered Savannah.

The McCalls stood up allowing the girls to pass by them. And when they all sat down, Mrs. McCall pulled an envelope from her purse and handed it to Savannah.

"What's this?"

"Just open it," whispered Mrs. McCall.

Savannah opened the envelope and pulled out a thank you card. When she opened the card, a check fell into her lap. Her eyes grew wide. "Five thousand dollars? I can't possibly accept this." She tried to give it to Mrs. McCall, but the woman gently pushed it back toward her.

"Yes you can, and you will. You brought our daughter back to us. So you deserve the reward money."

"But I didn't do it for the money."

Mrs. McCall smiled kindly. "We know you didn't. But what you gave us is worth so much more than five thousand dollars. So please, take it. Use it for college or a car, whatever you want."

Savannah swallowed the lump in her throat. She tucked the check and card into her purse and said, "Well, thank you. I promise to spend it wisely."

There was silence between them for several moments until Mrs. McCall leaned back over to Savannah and whispered, "I have a big favor to ask of you."

"Anything. Whatever you need," whispered Savannah.

"Would you mind saying a few words about how you found Katie?"

That caught Savannah off guard. "Well, I . . . Geez, I don't-"

"Please. I know Katie would want you to. And it would mean a great deal to us."

"But I'm not comfortable talking about, you know. Especially in a church."

Mrs. McCall smiled. "Who knows, maybe by sharing your story you might end up helping someone else."

Savannah scrunched her brow. "I don't know that I can do it."

Mrs. McCall patted her leg and said, "Well, just think about it."

A few minutes later the pastor walked up to the pulpit and began giving the eulogy. When he was finished he looked across the congregation and asked, "Would anyone else like to say a few words about Katie?"

In the silence, Savannah heard a tiny voice whisper in her ear. *Please share my story.*

She looked over at the McCalls, who looked back at her expectantly, and her face flushed. Finally, she whispered, "Okay."

Savannah stood up and walked to the front of the church, faced the congregation and said, "Hello, My name is Savannah Swift, and I'm the one who found Katie." She took a deep breath and let it out. "Katie was my friend. Though we never met in life, I knew her well." She glanced over at the photograph on the table. Katie's eyes seemed to come alive and dance in the candlelight causing Savannah to blink in astonishment.

Thank you, whispered Katie's voice.

Savannah looked back at the congregation, and when she saw her father and all of the parents standing along the back wall she smiled. But it wasn't until her father smiled back at her and offered her a nod that she said to the congregation, "So, let me tell you how I found Katie. It all started with a dream . . ."

Chapter 59

Two Months Later . . .

"Mom! Dad! Get in here. It's on the national news." Savannah snuggled up closer to Brady on the couch. "C'mon Em, scooch in here so that Mom and Dad can sit there."

"Put it on pause," yelled her dad from the kitchen, his voice nearly being drowned out by laughter. "We'll be there in a second."

Emma scooted in next to her friend, turned her head to the left and said over her shoulder, "You doing okay back there, Jade? You need anything? You want me to move you closer to the TV?"

"No, I got it."

Jade struggled to maneuver her wheelchair from behind the couch. "Ouch!" she cried when she bumped her elevated leg on the corner of the La-Z-Boy's armrest.

Emma jumped up. "Let me do that for you."

Jade grimaced. "No. I've got to learn to drive this hunk of metal on my own. I can't exactly call you up at college and have you come home just to move me around, now, can I." She backed up slightly and carefully rolled the wheelchair next to the recliner. "I'm getting the hang of it. It's just taking me longer than I thought it would."

From behind them they heard more laughter and then a screech from Emma's mother followed by giggling. "Stop that right now." More giggling. "I mean it, mister."

Mrs. Reed entered the living room, her face bursting with an ear-to-ear grin. "Where shall we sit?"

"How about the loooove seat," came a voice from behind her.

"Oh, you're terrible," giggled Mrs. Reed. And then she squealed when Benjamin Burke pulled her by the hand into the love seat causing her to fall partially into his lap.

"I see *that's* going pretty well," whispered Savannah into Emma's ear.

"It's crazy. They're like two love struck teenagers," she whispered back while watching the two cavort on the small couch.

"It's good to see her happy," said Savannah snuggling closer to Brady.

"Aye, lass, tryin' te get into my lap are ye?" Brady laughed.

Savannah punched him lightly in the arm and chuckled. "You wish."

"No fighting, you two." Mr. Swift set a kitchen chair down beside the couch and motioned to Jade's parents. "Why don't you two sit there next to Emma, and I'll sit here in the chair. That way I can keep an eye on these two." He tossed Savannah and Brady a fake glare then called over his shoulder, "C'mon, honey, we're waiting for you."

"Coming." A few seconds later Mrs. Swift entered the living room carrying three buckets of popcorn, followed by Kyle who had his own bucket. He flopped down on the floor in front of the TV and grabbed a handful of kernels.

"Kyle, don't even think about it," warned Mrs. Swift before he could toss them into the air. She set one of the buckets on the coffee table in front of the couch, handed the other one to

Benjamin and carried the third one over to the La-Z-Boy. "Did we miss anything?"

"No. We waited for you," said Savannah.

"Are Dominic and Leslie coming over?" asked her mother as she sat down in the recliner.

"No. He said he had a reading to do, but that they would see us in church on Sunday. He said he was really looking forward to it."

"Well, so are we," she replied with a genuine smile.

When everyone was ready, Savannah pushed the button on the remote and a female news announcer sitting behind a desk came to life. A still shot of a tall slender gentleman with a full head of salt and pepper hair appeared on the screen to her right.

The announcer looked into the camera and said, "Earlier this week, Nebraska Congressman, John Seavers, gave his testimony in the case of the State of Nevada versus Harrison Taylor."

The screen changed to a still shot of Congressman Seavers seated in the witness stand. "Seavers testified that several months ago he discovered toxic chemicals being stored in a local warehouse owned by Harrison Taylor. When asked why he didn't go to the authorities with this information, Seavers replied that to do so would have put him and his family at risk."

The screen switched to a video clip of a somber looking Seavers still on the witness stand. "I didn't go to the police because Harrison Taylor threatened to hurt my family if I did. He said, 'People who mess with me tend to wish they hadn't. And if you think this is an idle threat, just ask Katie McCall and Marty Dolan.'"

The scene cut back to the news announcer. "We now take you live to Reno, Nevada with details on the verdict."

A blonde reporter ran a quick hand across her curls and looked into the camera. "I'm standing outside the Reno courthouse where Harrison Taylor, CEO of the Geneva Corporation, has just received sentencing for the criminal charges brought against him by the State of Nevada."

She turned toward the two men standing side-by-side at the top of the steps, and the camera followed. "A spokesperson from the Justice Department's Environmental and Natural Resources Division, as well as, one from the Reno Police Department are about to speak."

Emma pointed at the screen and said, "Hey look, there's your Aunt Helen standing next to Detective Graves. What's she doing there?"

"They're working on another case together," said Savannah.

The spokesperson for the Justice department leaned into a cluster of microphones and said, "Harrison Taylor pleaded guilty to federal charges brought against him for criminal violations of the Resource Conservation & Recover Act and the Clean Water Act.

"Taylor admitted that for the past five years he has been illegally disposing hazardous waste in Nevada.

"Authorities removed over one thousand, fifty-gallon drums of toxic waste from his abandoned mines, most of which had been sealed improperly and were leaking unknown chemicals into the soil.

"Has Taylor been sentenced?" yelled out a reporter.

"As per his plea deal, Taylor has agreed to pay 1.8 billion dollars in restitution, cleanup costs and legal fees. He has also been ordered to repay the State of Nevada an undisclosed amount for the class action lawsuit that was filed against the state back in May of 2008 by the families of Little Lyon.

"Today it was determined by the courts that Taylor, not the State of Nevada, was solely responsible for those tragedies."

When reporters began shouting more questions, the spokesperson held up his hands, quieting the crowd once more. "I'd like to introduce Detective Graves of the Reno Police Department who has further information on the other cases against Harrison Taylor."

Detective Graves stepped up to the microphones and said, "In addition to the environmental law violations, Mr. Taylor also pleaded guilty to two counts of conspiracy to commit murder, with a potential third charge, pending further investigation.

"Taylor admitted to ordering the deaths of Kaitlyn McCall, who went missing three years ago, and her boyfriend, Martin Dolan."

"Will he be incarcerated for those murders?" asked another reporter.

Detective Graves nodded. "Yes, he will. Harrison Taylor has been sentenced to two consecutive lifetimes with no chance of parole."

When the newscast was over, Emma said, "Well, good. I'm glad Taylor finally got what he deserved."

Jade grabbed a hand full of popcorn and tossed a few kernels in her mouth. "I still can't believe all of those manufacturing plants from our little town could be involved in such a huge scandal. It just doesn't make any sense."

"Actually, it does," said Jade's father. "Some of the largest fertilizer manufacturers in the country are located right here in Scottsbluff. And combined, I'm sure they produce a lot of toxic waste."

"And Scottsbluff was just a small part of what was going on nationally," added Mr. Swift. "Hundreds of manufacturing companies across the country were doing the same thing— handing off their toxic waste to Taylor so they wouldn't exceed the EPA limits. And in exchange, they donated millions of dollars to EarthFirst."

"I guess paying Taylor was cheaper than paying a hefty government fine," said Jade's father. He shook his head. "What a racket."

Mrs. Reed snuggled in closer to Burke. "But none of this explain why Taylor did it. What was his motive? Why would he dump all of that toxic garbage on his own land?"

When Benjamin's phone buzzed, he pulled it out of his pocket and glanced at the screen.

Mrs. Reed craned her neck and said, "Who's that?"

With a sly smile on his face, he turned the phone so she couldn't see the screen, typed out a text and hit send. "You'll see."

When the doorbell rang fifteen minutes later, Savannah jumped up and said, "I'll get it."

She opened the door and glanced at the taxi as it pulled away from the curb, and then she scrunched her brow at the stranger standing in front of her.

A few seconds later when recognition set in, her jaw dropped open, and she said, "No. It can't be."

Chapter 60

Savannah's eyes widened and she said, "Dolly? Is that really you?"

Dolly, dressed in a classy gray pantsuit with her nest of red hair now dyed back to its natural chestnut color and cut into a sleek pageboy, flashed her the same over-the-glasses looked. "Sure is. Can I come in?" Her looks may have changed, but the gravel in her voice hadn't.

"Of course." As soon as they walked into the living room, Savannah said, "Look who's here."

"Dolly!" exclaimed Emma jumping up from the couch and giving the woman a hug.

Dolly returned the gesture. "Hey, bookworm. How are you?"

"I'm good. What are you doing here?"

She nodded her head toward Benjamin. "He asked me to come. Called me yesterday and asked if I wouldn't mind makin' a quick trip up here." She smiled. "Course I said 'sure.' Wanted to see how you girls were doin'."

Benjamin walked over to her, hugged her and said, "Did you bring them?"

"Sure did," she said patting her Louis Vuitton briefcase.

"Bring what?" said Savannah.

Benjamin grinned. "The smoking gun."

"Smoking gun?" questioned Savannah with a furrowed brow. "I don't get it."

"Harrison Taylor's motive for doing what he did," said Benjamin. "Let's all sit down, and we'll explain."

As soon as Dolly sat down in the extra chair that Mr. Swift had brought from the kitchen, Benjamin began to share his findings.

"Based on the reading you did at the police station, I immediately started searching for information on Mrs. Comstock. I knew that she was from Salt Lake City. So I suspected that after she left Henry she went back there.

"Through the Utah Census, I found out that Mrs. Comstock did, indeed, give birth to a girl in August of 1870—two months before Henry died."

Dolly pulled a document out of her briefcase. "When Benjamin first showed up to the motel, I thought he might have come to ask me out on a date on account of his divorce and all. But then he said he had some information about my ancestors. When he told me what he found, I just couldn't believe it." She set the piece of paper on the coffee table. "This here is a copy of Delores Comstock's birth certificate, Henry Comstock's daughter. Turns out, she was my great, great grandmother."

Everyone in the room gasped, and Savannah said, "Seriously? You're related to Henry Comstock?"

Dolly nodded. "It appears I am."

"Which brings us to the reason why Harrison Taylor did what he did," said Benjamin. "You remember me telling you about Henry Comstock's land? Well, when he died half of it went to Mrs. Comstock, who was still his wife at the time. But because Henry never actually bequeathed the other half prior to his death, it went into probate."

Dolly pulled two documents from her briefcase and handed them to Benjamin. He set them on the table next to the birth certificate and said, "I went to the state library to search their compiled list of court cases dating back to the late 1800's to early 1900's, and I found these: Harry O'Tally versus the State of Nevada, and Harry O'Tally versus Delores Comstock.

"According to these documents, in 1899 Harry moved back to Virginia City and tried to sue the State of Nevada for his share of the land. Because he couldn't prove that he was Henry's heir, the entire parcel was awarded to Delores. So he tried to sue her but lost that case, as well." He leaned back in his chair. "I think that's why he ended up changing his name and moving to New York City."

Dolly pulled another piece of paper from her briefcase and set it on the coffee table next to the birth certificate and court documents. "This here is a copy of the deed to the land belonging to my great, great grandmother. And you'll never guess where it's located—right smack dab in the middle of downtown Dayton. Right underneath the Comstock Mining Company's headquarters." She laughed and said, "I'm rich, stinkin' rich."

"And she's about to get a whole lot richer," said Benjamin.

"Why is that?" said Savannah.

Dolly looked at her over her glasses. "Because, the Comstock Mining Company built their entire operation on land that wasn't theirs. So now, they've been ordered to pay me back rent since they opened in 1902."

Benjamin laughed and shook his head. "All that money and she still insists on working at Motel 6."

"I like it there," said Dolly. "Who knows, I might even end up buying the place." She reached, once more, into her briefcase and pulled out the last document.

Benjamin took it from her and said, "And finally, we have the smoking gun." It was a photocopy of a hand written letter dated 1907. "Harry O'Tally wrote this to his son which was found in

Harrison Taylor's possession when the police got a warrant to search his home."

He read the letter out loud:

My Dearest Son, Harrison.

The law has robbed you of your family's land. It has stripped you of your roots, your rights and your inheritance. This battle began with me, but it will continue with you. And when the time comes, your children and your children's children will carry this burden upon their backs until the day that we, the rightful heirs to Henry Comstock's fortune can, once more, stake claim to that which is justly ours.

This is your charge, Harrison—to avenge your family.

The Good Book says 'an eye for an eye.' So what I ask of you is not my will, but Thy will. We must vow to the Almighty that we will continue this fight until the day He summons us home.

Your father,

Harrison

Benjamin looked into their stunned faces. "Harrison Taylor did what he did because he truly believed that what he was doing was God's will. An eye for an eye—it's what he'd been taught his entire life."

Savannah shook her head. "It's hard to believe that he would go to such lengths and do all that damage just to avenge his family."

"Blood and beliefs," said Benjamin. "The ties that bind us run oh, so deep. Don't you agree?"

Savannah was about to answer when her phone rang. She pulled it from her pocket and smiled when she recognized the caller. She held it up to her ear and said, "Hey, Aunt Helen. We saw you on TV. You looked great. How's it going with you and Detective Graves?"

"Well, that's why I'm calling. You know that case I told you we're working on? We sure could use your help solving it. You interested?"

Savannah glanced briefly around the room at all the pairs of inquisitive eyes staring back at her. But her gaze rested on the ornate box displayed front and center on the fireplace mantle. Knowing what lay nestled inside it, wrapped in that faded swatch of russet colored fabric, caused her to grin wildly and say, "Heck yeah!"

Epilogue

Four years later . . .

Savannah sat on the love seat in her studio apartment sipping a cup of tea and skimming over her philosophy notes. She glanced up at the clock on the wall above her dinette set and murmured, "It's time."

She got up, walked over to the kitchen cabinet and pulled a light blue tablecloth from one of the drawers. She covered the small table with it and then walked over to the bookcase and grabbed the ornate box off of the middle shelf, along with a candle and an amethyst crystal.

She set the candle and the crystal in the middle of the table and set the box on the edge, opened it and pulled out the tarot cards, still wrapped in their russet colored cloth.

A quiet *tap, tap, tap* on her door caused her to say, "Be there in a second."

She put the empty box back on the shelf and hurried over to the door.

When she opened it, a young girl with dark brown hair that hung down to her shoulders stood gawking at her, eyes wide and round as silver dollars.

"A-are you Savannah? Savannah Swift?" She clutched her purse strap with both hands.

"I am. Please come in." She opened the door wider.

"Thank you. My name is-"

Savannah interrupted her. "Your name is not important." She gestured to the table and said, "Please take a seat."

"I . . . But . . . Okay." Flustered, the young woman walked over to the table and accidently bumped into it causing a card to fall from the deck and land on the floor by her feet. "I'm so sorry," she said bending to pick it up.

"Leave it." Savannah bent down, picked it up, and stared at the image on the front of it. "Interesting," she murmured. "Quite interesting." She looked up at her guest and smiled kindly. "The reading starts the minute you get here."

Savannah slid into the chair and when the woman sat down opposite her, Savannah handed her the deck and said, "Here, shuffle."

As the young woman began to shuffle the cards, she said, "So, I was hoping you could tell me why I keep having these-"

Savannah held up her hand, silencing her. "Don't say anything else. I don't want to know anything about you because I don't want to be influenced." She looked at her guest. "If I ask you a question, just answer either yes or no, nothing more. Do you understand?"

The young woman nodded. "Yes."

"Good. Then let's begin."

Savannah took the deck of cards from the young woman and laid them out face down in the shape of a pyramid. She rubbed her hands together and said, "So let's see if we can figure out what's going on with you."

Her hand hovered over the bottom row of cards for a moment, the excitement of what she might discover already beginning to build inside of her.

She closed her eyes, took a deep breath, then she turned them over.

The End

ABOUT THE AUTHOR

Kathryn Dionne lives in Southern California with her husband, Jeff, and their Shar Pei, Bodie.

From an early age, Kathryn's love of treasure hunting sparked an interest in archaeology. As an amateur archaeologist she has been fortunate enough to uncover some very unique artifacts in different parts of the globe.

Kathryn also manages their five-acre property and their grove of Italian olive trees. Her husband has lovingly named their business, Saint Kathryn's Olive Oil.

In her spare time, she makes cookie jars and throws pottery in her studio. She also creates mosaics from discarded objects and sells them under the category of Found Art.

In addition to **Six Mile Canyon, Pleasure Point**, and **Cathedral Rock,** Kathryn has also written a trilogy called, **The Eleventh Hour**. It is a supernatural thriller that takes place in Israel. She has also co-written a historical fiction with author Abby L. Vandiver called, **At the End of the Line** under their pen name, Kathryn Longino. The story takes place in the 1950's during one of the most tumultuous times in American history. Kathryn's children's book, **Derek the Fireless Dragon,** is a collection of humorous and thought-provoking poetry.

Currently, Kathryn is working on, **Puck's Fairy Glen,** the fourth book in the Savannah Swift Psychic Mystery series.

If you enjoyed it, please consider telling your friends or posting a short review. Word of mouth is an author's best advertising and is much appreciated.

To learn more about Kathryn, please visit her at http://www.kathryndionne.com

Books by Kathryn Dionne

The Eleventh Hour: The Enlightened Ones
The Eleventh Hour: Day of Atonement
The Eleventh Hour: Resurrection
At the End of the Line
Derek the Fireless Dragon
Six Mile Canyon
Pleasure Point
Cathedral Rock
Murder at the Holiday Bazaar
Murder in Marrakech
Murder in Rhyme